ALL THE LIVES
WE NEVER LIVED

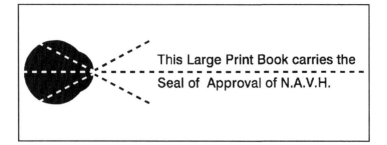

ALL THE LIVES WE NEVER LIVED

ANURADHA ROY

KENNEBEC LARGE PRINT
A part of Gale, a Cengage Company

Farmington Hills, Mich • San Francisco • New York • Waterville, Maine
Meriden, Conn • Mason, Ohio • Chicago

LIBRARY OF CONGRESS CIP DATA ON FILE.
CATALOGUING IN PUBLICATION FOR THIS BOOK
IS AVAILABLE FROM THE LIBRARY OF CONGRESS

ISBN-13: 978-1-4328-6317-3 (softcover)

Published in 2019 by arrangement with Atria, an imprint of Simon & Schuster, Inc.

Printed in the United States of America
1 2 3 4 5 6 7 23 22 21 20 19

For my mother
Sheela Roy

and for
Sheila Dhar
(1929–2001)

"This is a book of memory, and memory has its own story to tell."

— TOBIAS WOLFF, *THIS BOY'S LIFE*

"Tagore is enthralled. . . . Many things seem to be preserved in Bali that have been lost in India."

— WALTER SPIES, 21 SEPTEMBER 1927

1

In my childhood, I was known as the boy whose mother had run off with an Englishman. The man was in fact German, but in small-town India in those days, all white foreigners were largely thought of as British. This unconcern for accuracy annoyed my scholarly father even in circumstances as dire as losing his wife to another man.

The day my mother left was like any other. It was a monsoon morning. I was nine and at St. Joseph's School, which was not far from our house, only a fifteen-minute cycle ride away. My bicycle was still a little too tall for me. I wore my uniform: white shirt, blue shorts, and shoes that were shiny black in the morning and powdery brown by midday. My hair lay flat to an even, straight line that came down to just above my eyebrows. In the mornings it was a wet cap plastered to my head. My mother used to cut my hair, seating me on a stool in the inner courtyard next to the kitchen, and through the half hour of the haircut the only words spoken were variations on "How much longer?" and "Don't move."

Every morning I rang my bicycle's tinny bell until my mother emerged, nighttime sari rumpled, hair and face fuzzy with sleep. She came and drooped against one of the verandah's white pillars as if she might fall asleep again, standing. She was a late riser, summer or winter. She lingered in bed for as long as she could in a tight embrace with her pillow. Banno Didi, my ayah, woke me up and got me ready for school, and in turn I woke my mother. She said I was her alarm clock.

My mother didn't care how she looked, yet she was always striking, dressed up or smeared with color across her forehead. When she painted sitting outside in the sun she wore a wide-brimmed straw hat with a red ribbon into which she stuck flowers, paintbrushes, feathers, whatever caught her eye. None of my friends had mothers who wore a hat or climbed trees or hitched up their saris and rode a bicycle. Mine did. The first day when she was teaching herself to balance the bicycle, she went on and on, tottering, falling, sucking the blood off her grazes, getting back on again. Screaming with laughter, showing all her teeth like a wolf, my father said. She rode the bicycle into a line of flowerpots along the front verandah, her long hair came loose, her eyes sparkled, her sari was torn at the knee. But she sprang up and went back to the bike.

I don't remember anything different about my mother in the hours before she ran off with the Englishman who was actually a German. Bulbous slate-gray clouds sat in wait that morning, low enough to touch. When my mother came out to see me off to school, she glanced up at the sky and shut her eyes with a squeal as she was showered by drops of water.

"Last night's rain is still raining," she said.

The big trees that shaded the house gleamed and when the wind shook their branches they set off showers from their wet leaves.

"The clouds are so dark, it'll be a beautiful day. It'll pour and pour and when the sun comes out there will be a rainbow right from here to the railway station." She wiped her face with a corner of her sari. "You'd better hurry, you mustn't get wet. Are you carrying an extra shirt in your bag? You are not to sit in class soaked to the skin, you'll get fever." I was about to go when she said, "Wait, leave that bicycle, come here." She hugged me tight for a long minute, kissed me on the top of my head and then on my forehead. I wriggled to break free, I was not used to sticky displays of affection from her, it made me awkward and self-conscious. But her touch sent a current of joy through me and I cycled away hoping she saw how fast I was going through the puddles, churning up slush.

"Remember what I said!" she cried out. "Don't be late."

"I'll be back in time," I shouted. "I'll cycle fast."

I ran high fevers when I was little, waking with my body on fire, aware that my head was tipped back over a bucket and someone was pouring mug after mug of cold water over it. If the convulsions came, I could recall nothing other than a great exhaustion afterwards, when my skin turned damp and my mother's voice near my ears said, "Will he get well? Will he get well?" My grandfather said, "Breathe deep," and put his stethoscope against my chest. He brought his cotton-white head closer and shone a torch into my mouth. "Aaah?" he murmured. After that he made up bitter potions that he put into corked bottles marked with lines. The room was quiet. Shadows floated across it throughout the day and all I could hear was my mother rustling in and out, anxious whispers, the *thup* of a bottle being put back on a shelf, the splash of water going into a glass. And I slipped into darkness again.

My pet name was Myshkin, and unlike boyhood names which fade into distant memory along with the people who used them, this one stuck. My grandfather gave me that name because of my convulsions — like the epileptic prince in a book by Dostoevsky, Prince Myshkin in *The Idiot,* Dada told me.

"I'm not an idiot," I said.

"When you read *The Idiot* you'll want to be one," he said. "Innocents are what make humankind human."

My fevers and fits made relatives pity me and ladle out advice that infuriated my mother. Once I was going up the stairs to the roof, and a visiting uncle from Karachi tapped my legs with a ruler and said to my father, "See how the knee flinches? That's a sure sign of bone disease — no surprise the boy is so puny. I know a man. I'll give you his address. He sends medicines all over India."

This uncle had a know-it-all air that my mother detested. Whatever the subject, be it

13

botany or architecture, he spoke with perfect authority. It was never simply a pillar, it had to be Doric or Corinthian, and if he walked past the big church at the corner of Bell Metal Road, he would point out the *flying buttresses* and then shake his head when I studied the sky to see what was flying. My mother asked him how he knew my bones were weak and he said, "Simple. I was a whisper away from a medical degree. The course was too dull for me."

He turned from her to me. "Tell me, what's heavier — a kilo of iron or a kilo of wool?"

I felt myself growing tense, I was sure it was a trick question, but before I could stop to think it through, I had blurted out, "Iron."

"Think again," he said, with a smirk. "Think again, my boy. One kilo of a heavy substance is the same weight as one kilo of a light substance." He tapped my head with his ruler and said, "Can't be weak everywhere, eh? If the body's weak, the mind must be made stronger!" I must focus on developing my mind by learning chess, he said. "Alekhine, Tarrasch, Capablanca! Great minds in ailing bodies, all of them."

I did not know who these chess masters were, nor if they had ailing bodies. I could only nod and search for an escape route, but my mother made sure this uncle never came to stay again. "Myshkin has chicken pox; Banno's son has measles; the *khansama* seems to have cholera. One can't be too careful," she would write back if there was a letter from him announcing a visit. She made sure the excuse was a long-winded, contagious illness and if anyone pointed out that a string of infectious diseases with a doctor in the family was hardly believable, she would say the more patently false the excuse, the more obvious the truth.

As I grew older, the fevers and convulsions came less often. It was not epilepsy, it turned out. For a few weeks, then months, and then a whole year, there were none. After the second calm year my grandfather stopped pushing thermometers into my mouth at the slightest hint of fatigue in me and relatives no longer suggested quacks who had cured a second cousin twice removed with magic potions to be swallowed on the night of a new moon. After the third year, the fits became a story from my past, although they are in my present: the illness permanently ruined my eyesight. From when I was six I had to have glasses that grew thicker every year. Without my glasses the world became a painting of the kind my mother copied at times: dabs of color against other dabs of color adding up to a sense of a lake with a boat or water lilies in a pond.

Sometimes I take my glasses off to see differently from other people. Colors and words swim into each other, meanings change on the page. In the distance, everything becomes a pastel blur. There is a kind of restfulness in not seeing well that the clear-sighted will never know.

Close to sixty years and maybe half as many pairs of glasses have gone by since then. It is 1992. Things around my house have turned squalid enough to make me take my glasses off more often so that the rubbish heap outside my gate turns into a mass of bright colors and the billboard beyond is a hazy blue-and-yellow rectangle that might have been the bungalow which stood there before blind-eyed apartments replaced it.

What has not changed is the anticipation with which I wait for the postman. The other day I was rewarded, a package arrived. A padded airmail envelope, bulky, and the postmark tells me it has been on its way for three weeks, all the way from Vancouver, Canada. I have put it on the chest of drawers. Every day I bring it down, feel its

16

weight, pick up the knife I will use to slit the envelope open, and then I put it back where it was. The package has something to do with my mother, I know, and I hesitate to open it. What if it contains nothing of consequence?

What if it does?

The morning after it came, I woke to the sound of my dogs howling in unison, who knows at what, and I was overtaken at that instant with the single thought that it was imperative for me to make a will. There are things I want people to remember, and these I must write down. Things I want people to forget that I must burn. A few saplings I still need to plant even if I don't live to see them grow to trees. I need to see that the dogs are provided for, that Ila has enough on which to survive. She is widowed, she lives in the main house with her daughter and grandchild. Her daughter's husband is in the merchant navy and is gone half the year. She depends on me.

It is irrational, this certainty that my time is over when I am only in my mid-sixties, but I have felt the earth wobbling on its ungainly axis for a few years now. I could put away my thoughts of gloom and doom and open the parcel, but I decide not to. For the moment there it sits, pulsing with

17

the energy every unopened letter in the world has.

But why not open it? What, after all, will it contain that I don't know? Am I deferring pleasure or am I afraid of what I might find?

I might find a photograph or drawing of my mother in it — I might not. There was a time in my life long ago — I was thirteen and had just started smoking — when I thought that if I had a picture of her in front of me, I would press the glowing end of a cigarette into the circles of her eyes, as I did into those rubbery gray ticks I found lurking in my dog's coat. I would blind her. I would kill the spell cast by her absent presence.

Immediately horrified at myself, I would shoot at a bottle with my old airgun or slash a sickle through the long grass at the back of the garden to rid myself of the nausea that came from thinking such thoughts.

For me, making a will should not be as momentous an event as it might for richer, more successful men who have wealth and estates to worry about. I have few possessions. I still live in the house where I was born — not the same building, but the old outbuilding in its grounds. I have never left it except for a few years when I went to New

Delhi for my first job, which was to work with an Englishman named Alick Percy-Lancaster who was responsible after independence came for laying out the city's public gardens, planting the trees that would line its avenues, managing the government plant nurseries. I was twenty when I went and could have made a life there, but I did not stay long. I needed Muntazir, the sense of hills nearby. When Mr. Percy-Lancaster decided in 1956 to go and live in Rhodesia, I came back home. I got an appointment with the district magistrate and told him our town deserved more than a mere municipal department that watered the parks and planted bougainvillea; a horticultural division was required, for the whole district. The work involved ecology, city planning, botany, water management: it was a science that needed someone qualified. I brought with me drawings and city plans that showed how our town could be transformed into a green oasis of tree-filled beauty, how its outlying areas could be turned into watersheds. By the end, I was exhausted by my own loquaciousness.

The district magistrate was a man in his first posting, not much older than I was then, and eager to make a difference. To my surprise, my persuasion worked and a new department was created. For quite a few years I was its sole member. Superintendent of Horticulture. I had nobody to superintend, and no office, only a desk in one corner of the municipal corporation, but every morning I presided over meetings with half a dozen gardeners, typed up minutes nobody would read, and then walked around the town for the rest of the day making notes, telling myself changing landscapes was slow business.

My horticultural work took me to tea gardens in Assam and orchards in Himachal; once I was a consultant at a butterfly park; another time an ecological advisor at a national park, but I always came back to my own job, glorified gardener in a small town. Where other people have fixed deposits and money and houses to bequeath their descendants, I point to avenues of trees and say, "I am leaving you those." I show them the line of *Ceiba speciosa* in front of the courthouse that turns brilliant pink every year. On the roads where I planted alternate white and purple *Bauhinia,* the orchid-like flowers cover the pitted pavements of the grim little suburbs, transforming them for weeks. Parties of bulbuls and parakeets arrive to feed on the blossoms; stout matrons beg little boys to climb the trees and pluck the buds for them to cook. Now that I am thought of as a crank, I have no compunction charging at the women with my walking stick aloft.

"Leave those buds alone. Let the flowers bloom!"

They break away from the tree, grumbling curses, "Old crackpot, chews up your head for nothing." They call me a grouch, a humorless pain in the arse.

I don't mind. This is what I am leaving the world, I think to myself in grandiose moments such as these, when I sit with paper and pen before me, only the words *I, Myshkin Chand Rozario* written down. I am leaving the world trees that cover the town with shade, fruits, flowers. I am old enough to have watched saplings I planted grow into trees forty feet high.

I thought of the amaltas and gulmohur along Begum Akhtar Marg, a road near the station. I pulled every possible string and wrote off letters to editors and governors to ensure the road had that name. A woman who had given the world passion and music all her troubled life — and they only name roads after politicians. Afterwards, I planted *Delonix regia* and *Cassia fistula* down the length of her avenue — something to reflect the romance and intensity of the singer —

21

and now it is a fireworks display of red and gold through the summer.

I can remember cycling furiously down Begum Akhtar Marg when it was nothing but a barren, baking earthen path on the way from school to the railway station. It was the summer of 1942, and I had to get to the station before a train left because rumor had made its way to our school that it was a train with a cargo never seen before. When I reached the platform it was olive and khaki with soldiers and there was a small crowd staring at the train, a long one with barred windows and policemen standing guard at every door. Heat hummed around the train. I touched one of the coaches and my hand felt as if it had been burnt. A policeman grinned, asked if I wanted to climb in and go to jail too.

Through the windows I could see men who appeared too dazed to do more than look outside with dead eyes. The train had only men. White men. They leaned their heads against the window bars, some of them asleep, others awake but stupefied, tired zoo animals crammed into cages too small for them. Their faces were dirty and drawn, their greasy hair was plastered to their skulls with sweat, flies sat on them but they did nothing about it. In the gloom of the compartments, further inside, there appeared to be more men just like the ones at the windows. Legs and arms dangled limply from the upper bunks, bodies slumped against other sleeping bodies.

We had never seen white people so abject. We were accustomed to Indians being skeletal and diseased but white men were born never to resemble them.

I walked along the platform and then back again as the train waited. Trains with foreign prisoners of war normally went through Muntazir without stopping, and some people said the halt that afternoon had been made for the train to stock up on drinking water and food; some said a few prisoners had died of the heat and their decaying bodies were being offloaded because of the stench.

Muntazir's train line terminated at the start of the Himalayan foothills twenty or so miles further ahead, and from there the men would be transported to nearby Dehradun to be imprisoned for the rest of the war. Italian prisoners of war were being sent mainly to Rajasthan, Poles to Jamnagar, and Germans to Dehradun — or so the newspapers said. The camp at Dehradun was the largest and now had prisoners from several countries, thousands of them, sent there from long distances away, even from Africa and the Mediterranean. My grandfather said the world had been replicated in miniature at that camp.

As the train blew a few impatient whistles and set off in a cloud of smoke, one of the men pressed his face against a window. His head was shaven bald and tiny insects buzzed around the many sores on his scalp. I could see a band of gray skin through his open shirt front. The man smiled straight at me. After a second's hesitation, I started to run alongside the train and pulled out a few boiled sweets I had in my pocket. I passed them to the man through the window. Nobody stopped me, a schoolboy chasing a train. I ran alongside it until the shade of the platform's tin roof ended, the platform turned to grassy dirt, and I was out under the impassive white-hot sky, my head reeling from the change of light, my sun-blinded eyes swimming with dots of bright color.

What had I hoped to find at the station? I did not know then that the answers to a hundred urgent questions in my head were stored in one man lying in a heatstroke stupor in the coach fourth from the front on that train which was going further and further away from me with every exhalation of soot.

By the time my eyes adjusted to the light, all I could see was the guard's van in which a soldier stood facing the retreating station, green flag in one hand, jug of water in the other. He tilted his head back and poured the water all over himself, soaking his shirt and his face.

I have long had a habit of noting down the interesting plants and trees that I spot, whether in my daily rounds of this town or when I traveled out, especially during my plant-gathering treks with two friends from my undergraduate class. I find now that my brisk scientific jottings and the drawings that accompany them can bring back particular walks in mountains and marshland, long nights in flimsy tents, the leopard we once saw perched stone-still on a tree branch, observing us with an expressionless menace that turned our bones to water, the river that almost swept me away as I bent too close to examine a weed, and the cliff on which I lost my footing trying to reach a saxifrage on a rock just out of reach. A botanical journal. A route map of my wanderings. On some days it appears as if all my time on earth has gone like a blurred, inconsequential scene rushing past a moving window, and at such times my jottings slow me down, return me to places, give those places names and meaning. A note about the differences between *Datura suaveolens* (angel's trumpet, innocuous) and *Datura stramonium* (thorn apple, poisonous) brings back the whole scene — snatches of our argument that night about the differences between the two plants, how we cooked rice in our saucepan, then smoked and talked of things one talks of only when one is young and sitting around a fire miles away from home, sheathed in darkness, no sound but rustles in the trees, no smell but the dizzying scent of the datura and our harsh, unfiltered cigarettes. I am of a temperament that needs the written word. For anything to have meaning, it has to be set down, it must live on paper before it is fully alive in my head. It has to be a series of words in sequence in order to reveal a meaning and pattern.

I have put aside my unmade will.

The package is before me, still sealed, the image of a god with powers I cannot fathom. Before I make preparations for a tidy ending to my life, it appears necessary to write down whatever strikes me as significant about the beginning.

When I began to put down the words that follow, trying to make my growing-up years coherent to myself, I found I had only a hazy notion of the time or the weather on the particular day I was writing about, or the words that were spoken, or the sequence of events. Yet many things I want to forget remain painfully vivid. Images pass through my mind like flashes of light enveloped by darkness. At first I tried to be diligent. I got in touch with my two trekking mates from college, I asked Dinu questions: Do you remember this? Don't you remember that? His recollections so often differed from mine that our conversations ended in arguments. I returned to the places of my childhood to check — was there really a cave by the river or a Gothic mansion at the corner of Hafizabagh where my grandfather took me once? We had seen two horses grazing on the front lawns and inside the cavernous house were four-poster beds, enameled washbasins, jardinières, and a ballroom with a sprung floor where the wild-eyed Nawab of Hafizabagh had appeared in a grimy cotton vest and lungi and begged my grandfather to sell everything in the house for him because he had no money.

At the riverbank I found a power plant, its four monstrous chimneys throwing out smoke that drained the sky of color. The mansion in Hafizabagh was still there, although half of it had become a pile of fallen masonry and what stood was blackened by time, wind, rain.

In telling the story of any life, and certainly when telling our own, we cannot pretend we are narrating everything just as it happened. Our memories come to us as images, feelings, glimpses, sometimes fleshed out, sometimes in outline. Time solidifies as well as dissolves. We have no precise recollection of how long things took: a few days, weeks, a month? Chunks of time are a blank, while others grow to be momentous in retrospect. I believe this is true for most people. Over the years, when friends contradicted me over details, my uncertain hold over my memories began to make me think I would no longer recognize myself in old photographs, the person in those black-and-white images was somebody else. Think too hard and you might think yourself into lunacy.

In one of his poems Rabindranath Tagore says:

I cannot remember my mother
But when in the early autumn morning

The fragrance of the shiuli floats in the air
The scent of the morning prayers in the
temple comes to me as a scent of my
   mother.

The poet lost his mother when he was fourteen; I was only nine the year my mother left. How can it be, then, that she is as close to me as my own reflection in the mirror? Present in every detail and yet imprisoned in a different element, unreachable. Entire conversations come back to me, incidents, arguments, the way she would line her eyes with *kajal,* the fresh flowers in her hair, the circle of red kumkum on her forehead which was invariably smudged by mid-afternoon. How she recited rhymes to make me memorize them, how her skin was the color of beaten gold and her eyes slanted, how those slanted eyes had an impish gleam. I am certain I truly remember these things and have not built impressions up from stories and photographs.

Yet the older I grow, the less certain I am of certainty.

One of my mother's contemporaries — of whom I will have more to say later — wrote a book in which she recalled events from forty-two years before. I can make no more than a clumsy translation of how she describes the machinery of time in the working of memory.

"As I went down the stairs my body was trembling . . ." she writes, and then interrupts herself to ask:

Did it happen that very day? I can't be sure. I kept no journal, I am writing neither from a diary nor from memory. I cannot tell if I am writing these events as they happened, one by one. But what appeared then as if they happened one by one — now they have neither beginning nor end. Now these days are simultaneously in my present — oh, I cannot explain. Why is it hard to explain? After all, Arjuna saw all of the universe, past and present, in Sri Krishna's opened mouth. I too see things in that way. You have to believe me. These are not memories, these are my present. At every moment I am getting closer to the year 1930. I can feel the year 1930 on my skin.

It is the year 1937 that I feel on my skin.

2

The biggest adventure in my mother's life took place just months before she married my father, and many of their quarrels ended with my father saying, "The trouble with you, Gayatri, is that all you want to do is live off your memories. Past glory." He stated this in the mild tone he adopted while arguing — first with her, later with me — as if he were the sole repository of sanity and reason in a set of people deranged by illogical passions. My father believed feelings had to be kept on a tight leash. Or else they were likely to run away with you. If my mother appeared annoyed, he said, "You gain nothing when you lose your temper."

The joyous adventure my mother fell back upon when daily life defeated her was a boat ride. The way she told it, it was 1927, she was on the brink of turning seventeen, and she was with her father, Agni Sen, in a boat on a lake in Bali. They sailed towards a raft moored in the middle of the lake and when they came closer they could see that there was a man on the raft, lying on his back, face hidden by a flat straw hat of the kind farmers wore in that country. The man pushed away his hat and stood up when he heard the splash of their oars. Standing, he was a tall, angular figure with golden hair thrown back by the wind. He could have been the figurehead on the prow of a ship. He wore a white shirt that was open down the front and his sleeves were rolled up to his elbows. His trousers were sand-colored. The man began to laugh when he saw them. "The whole way from India — and you know where I hide out in Bali!" He held a long, sun-browned hand out towards Gayatri and said, "Come on, come aboard now that you are here."

The man was a German artist and musician called Walter Spies and over the next few weeks, he took Gayatri, her father, and their friends to dance performances, to concerts, to beaches, to painting schools. She sat beside him, every nerve alight with excitement, as he narrated to her the stories behind the dances they were watching. Rama and Sita. Hanuman and Ravana — mythological figures she knew from home. Different here, yet familiar. How strange that most of the people around her thought the whole of the Ramayana had taken place in Java and had no connection with India at all! Gayatri was wonderstruck that the myths and legends she had grown up with should exist in this altered form so far away. It was precisely this that her father wanted to show her when he took her traveling around the East Indies.

In the early part of the twentieth century, this was not the usual thing — today it can scarcely be comprehended how unusual. It was not as if Indians never traveled abroad, but it was almost unknown for a father, however wealthy, to spend his money on nurturing his daughter's gifts. Daughters were meant to have talents: those that would work as bait to catch a husband. But Agni Sen stood at an odd angle to things around him, he could tell the difference between talents and gifts, and he had seen a spark inside his daughter that could light up whole cities if tended. He got tutors for Gayatri to learn languages and painting, as well as dance and classical music, all this in an age when women sang and danced to entertain rich men and were derided for it. He took her to musical salons and to see artists at work. To historical monuments in Delhi, then further away.

At one of these, when Gayatri was sitting on a boulder, sketching a dome and doorway, a flight of gray pigeons erupted from a window, the only things living in that ruined palace from the eleventh century. It prompted in her father the usual thoughts about evanescence, decay, the rise and fall of empires, but he also told Gayatri that if she stretched her mind back to the terracotta figurines found in the Indus Valley, to murals glowing jewel-like in rock caves, stupas buried under earth and stone temples under water, then forward to these tombs and palaces that were now ruins where banyan sprouted in the cracks, she would see that the power and tyranny and cruelties of those civilizations did not survive, the rulers fell and their courtiers lay in parallel lines of narrow marble caskets next to their king, their cats and wives too, but the beauty that had been created remained. The filigree in the windows, the calligraphy on stone, the perfection of the dome she was struggling to draw. The creators of those things, the masons, sculptors, painters, who had no role to play in the great games of power, whose minds were thought inferior, whose opinions were of no consequence, whose wealth counted for nothing: their work remained after all else had vanished.

When the world was in turmoil and devastation appeared inevitable, art was not an indulgence but a refuge, its fragments remained after a cycle had run its course from creation through to destruction and begun again. Power crumbles, people die, but beauty defeats time, he declared in the way middle-aged men have of imparting wisdom to the young.

Gayatri listened, and all along her pencil traveled in rapid lines over her open sketchbook. The dome began to take shape, then the arch below it. A pigeon took flight in three quick strokes. They went on from Agra to the necropolis of Fatehpur Sikri, then to Jaipur. She rode an elephant, clung to a camel's undulating back as it walked, gagged at its smell. She drew the camel.

When she was older Agni Sen took Gayatri further, to Santiniketan, to breathe the air Rabindranath Tagore and his students breathed. On that trip, a friend who knew the poet well told him Rabindranath was planning a journey to Java the next year. The knowledge settled in Agni Sen's mind, germinated, and he became consumed by an idea that would not let go: why not travel there with Gayatri, and on the same ship as the poet? What better chance would she have to meet Rabindranath, to speak to him and learn from him, than by their confinement on a ship? Who knew to what it might lead for Gayatri? The poet was to travel with a group of friends, including Dhiren, who had mentioned the plan to Agni Sen. Letters flew back and forth, tickets on trains and berths on ships and steamers were booked, passports were requisitioned, and at the end of much complicated planning, Gayatri's father, emptied and triumphant, announced the trip to his daughter and to his family. He would take Gayatri to the Borobudur, to Angkor Wat, to the temples of Bali. He would show her there was a shared cultural universe in Asia which had not been swallowed up by colonization.

The crossing to Java and Bali began on July 12, 1927, on a ship from Madras which would sail to Singapore. Gayatri and her father were to travel on the same ship as the poet and his friends, and then after the days together on the ship and a week in Singapore, they would go on to Malaya and Cambodia on their own, coming to Bali in time to meet Tagore's party after their travels elsewhere. Was it not too ambitious, given Agni Sen's age and his heart condition? Gayatri's mother had fretted. What a dangerous, fanciful, expensive plan! She was brushed aside.

They stood at the rail as Rabindranath came on board, exhausted by his three-day train journey from Calcutta to Madras. He came with friends, learned and eminent men who formed a protective ring to save him from the harassment of adulation. Agni Sen had to content himself with the briefest of introductions, while Gayatri saw him only from a distance — nobody was allowed to come close. This was not what Agni Sen had expected. He was hurt by Dhiren's possessive zeal, and retreated behind a book.

They found out later that the poet, who had expected three days of contemplative solitude gazing at the landscape of India as it passed before his train window, had managed nothing of the sort. At Kharagpur, the first stop after Calcutta, a group of schoolboys clambered into his compartment and thrust a motley collection of notebooks at him: school exercise books, sheaves of paper stitched together at home. They wanted autographs, and one of them begged Rabindranath to dash off a new poem before the train started moving again. As they went southward, they stopped every hour or so and at each station the platforms were crammed with people who had heard he was on the train. At one of these, an old man climbed on, joined his hands in a namaste, began what sounded like a speech in Telugu, finished it, bowed deeply, and left. At another a man came out of the crowds to the poet's window, bearing a brass tray with a lemon, incense, flowers. He lit the incense and trailed the smoke over Rabindranath, then without a word melted back into the crowds. One supplicant begged, pleaded, then harangued Rabindranath to stop overnight for a dip in the Godavari river, which he insisted was holier than the Ganga. At Kakinada, a professor of English who had lived for a time in Calcutta came in to speak to the poet in halting Bengali, gave up because he had forgotten the lines he had rehearsed, but — desperate to wish the great man an appropriately literary Godspeed — began thundering "Half a league, half a league onward!" At Rajahmundry, two hundred students came to tell him they had got the date wrong and had been waiting at the station since the day before. The poet sat on his berth, tired and gray, pushed against the window, hidden by a mass of heaving bodies shouting *"Rabindranath ki Jai!"* and *"Vande Mataram!"* People came in during nighttime halts to shine lanterns in his sleeping face.

If he had thought he would find peace on a ship in the middle of the sea, Rabindranath was mistaken. An American padre and his wife kept edging towards him if he so much as approached the deck, even as he turned away each time, casting pleading glances for rescue in the direction of his friends. At last, with no way out, he allowed them time. Once seated, they tried to prove to him that Christianity had much in common with Hinduism.

"I have grave doubts about that," Rabindranath said.

"Why, we too have God the Father!" they said.

"But you see, we also have God the Mother, God the Son, God the Friend, God the Lover. We even have God the Sweetheart," said Suniti Chatterji, one of the poet's companions, with a mischievous gleam in his eyes. The padre, realizing the improbability of an illustrious conversion, left the old man alone after that and he sat in his deck chair listening to the sea, reading, and sometimes lying back with his eyes closed, as if infinitely tired.

Gayatri edged towards him, retreated. She wanted to ask him if she could go to Santiniketan to learn painting from Nandalal Bose. Santiniketan was all she had dreamed of since her visit, what she craved was to be under its open sky in the company of other students, with pots of paint and bundles of brushes, grinding her own pigments as she had heard they did there. She had discovered that one of the friends with Rabindranath was the vice principal of Santiniketan's art school. It was as if all had been divinely ordained: she would tell the poet about her visit, how she had longed to join the school then and not been able to. He would tell the vice principal to admit her to the school instantly.

Dreaming in this way as she leaned over the deck's railings, no land in sight, only blue water, the conviction glowed within her like a secret flame: this voyage would lead her to her future. To her only possible life.

Yet she did not speak to the poet. She would not add to his sense of being besieged.

For a day or two she kept her distance on the deck, never coming close to where he sat, nor going so far that he would not notice her. Her calculated reserve worked: one day he called out to her. She ran to the empty chair next to him before he could change his mind. He had a presence that illuminated the deck like the glow from a second sun, she was stricken speechless, she sat straight-backed and tense, waiting to be spoken to. He said nothing. As far as their eyes could see were dancing waves and blueness paled by sunlight, above them lacy white clouds in a clear sky. All of a sudden, he asked her if she had noticed that when the ship cut a path through the foam and waves it sighed constantly. Did that never-ending sigh not sound as though the waters of the ocean were washing the earth with tears of grief?

She did not know what made her so rude, but she burst out laughing. "I'm not sad, I'm not thinking of tears. The water is blue and beautiful, I want to paint it." Then she clapped her hand to her mouth, aghast at having contradicted him. Would he be too offended to speak to her again? But it must have been precisely her spontaneous refusal to be worshipful, so refreshing after the fatigue of being relentlessly adored, that made him seek out her company. He asked her to come and sit by him on the deck every day. She told him about her dance lessons and her painting in such garrulous detail it made her abject with shame to think of later, but if he found it vain or absurd he did not let it show. It was he who told her father about the German man they were to find on the raft. This artist, Walter Spies, knew more than anyone else about

41

the dance and arts of that part of the world, Rabindranath said. He had been told that Spies would be his guide on his travels there. Gayatri too must meet him.

"One day you will go to Bali and Java, Myshkin," my mother would say when ending these stories. "I'm going to take you. We'll make the same voyage. We will find Walter again, and he'll show us a thousand things." She told me about her journey so many times, adding a new detail, leaving out an old one, remembering and forgetting, that I knew it backwards. When she started off on her stories, what I listened to was the hum of her voice. It was a clear voice, as if it had been washed in a mountain stream, and she could do things with it that nobody else did. It turned into a low growl when she told stories with lions in them, it became rich and melodious when she sang, it rose and fell like a high-pitched songbird's when she tried enticing me to finish my glass of milk, it reached the corners of rooms when she whispered.

The journey to Bali would be Gayatri's last with her father. He collapsed on his way to work days after their return. She never said much about the weeks that followed, and I imagine it is because she had never before known such grief. She had for all her life been her father's adored child and he had made her everything her mother was not: accomplished, educated, aware of her gifts. Following some perverse logic, her mother blamed her for his death. If Gayatri had not been so headstrong about traveling the world, her indulgent father would not have dreamed up that misguided trip. All those journeys — more than two months away from home! Train journeys, sea voyages, car rides, and strange food. Didn't those people in Java even eat an animal that lived off ants?

In the photographs my mother had of her childhood, it is just her and her father. It did not strike me as odd when I saw the pictures as a child, but when I was older this intrigued me more and more. Why were none of her brothers in those pictures? Did Agni Sen never take his sons anywhere? Where was his wife during these travels?

I saw my grandmother just twice, once as a toddler and once when I was six or seven. Of the first time I have no recollection; of the second, I remember gagging at the smell in her room of something putrid mixed with something chemical. Her skin was like stale dough and she complained in a shrill voice the entire time we sat with her: she was not fed properly, the daughters-in-law were witches, her own daughter was no better. My mother, grim-faced, kept asking me to go and play outside, but my grandmother ordered me to remain in the room. When we got up to leave, my grandmother reached inside her blouse and drew out a crumpled rupee note that she pressed into my hand. It was still warm from being stored against her old skin, it felt as if I was touching her. I dropped it on the floor and ran out, right down the corridor, down the stairs, and out of the main door into the road, and only then did I let out my breath and draw in a gulp of air greasy with the smell of hot oil from a nearby samosa shop. My mother reached me a minute later and took my hand and pulled me away from the road. "Happy?" she said. "You wanted to come to Delhi, didn't you?"

Gayatri was so much younger than her five brothers that she was only ten when the last of them married. The tumult and festivity of that wedding, the mounds of flowers, the *shehnai* players perched high up on a platform above an ornate gateway, these became her most vivid memories. At the wedding she had stood enthralled before the red and gold bride, crying, "I want to be married! I want to be a bride!" She could not have guessed the irony of that childish wish.

Gayatri's tutors for dance and music were dismissed as soon as her father died. It was decided by the family that she must be married off without delay; a young, fatherless daughter was too much of a responsibility for her brothers. What happened next was represented by my father as a romance, and he loved retelling it, each time with new flourishes. My mother listened poker-faced, doodling with her fingers on her sari. My father told us how the word about finding a match for her went around. Names of possible grooms were suggested by relatives — not many, because word had also got around that my mother was *taze,* sharp-tongued, over-clever; besides, the girl danced and took singing lessons. And who knew what she had been up to during her travels? What on earth did a young girl need to cross the oceans for? It was all a little too much. At this point my father stopped his narration to glance at her and say, "I was never scared off by brains and spirit. What is a woman without brains?"

My father was a regular visitor to my mother's house before they were married. Whenever he went to Delhi he looked up his old college professor, Agni Sen. He had encountered my mother over the years: first as a young girl, then as a teenager, and as soon as he heard his old teacher had died, he turned up at their door unannounced — to offer his condolences, he would say. It happened to be an opportune moment; Gayatri was being paraded before a possible groom's family. The groom and his relatives sat in a row in the drawing room being served tea by my mother so that they could examine her as well as her drawing-room manners up close. Soon enough they would ask her to sing a song or show them how long her hair was. My father said he could tell even from a distance, as he waited, that Gayatri was about to fling the tea-tray to the floor. After a few minutes he saw her stumble out of the room and run up the stairs two at a time, to another part of the house. This strengthened the resolve he had come with: he would rescue her. At this point my mother stopped her doodling and sat up shaking her head. "That is not how it was! That is not *at all* how it was!"

"Isn't it true you left the room in a huff? That you spilled hot tea on the groom's clothes? Did they come back with an offer? No? Q.E.D.!" My father was fond of ending arguments with a Q.E.D., which he wrote in the air with his forefinger.

My mother was a Bengali Hindu from Delhi, my father was a part-Anglo-Indian from north India. In Muntazir, my father's family was considered by Hindus to be a godless bunch of Christians, while to Christians they were a heathen gaggle of Hindus. But my father had contempt for categories such as caste and religion, he maintained that all humans were born equal in the eyes of nature. God he did not believe in. He had been an atheist since he was a boy. The only god he followed was the Nation, and this was what he told Gayatri's family, who had not seen in him a possible groom.

Why then did they agree that my father fitted the bill? Were they afraid my mother would smash all their tea sets on future suitors? Was he the only one on offer for a fatherless girl with no dowry who sang and danced and had done things in foreign lands that one could not speculate about in the presence of children? Was my mother asked her opinion about this startling new prospect? I do not know. Probably not. So anxious were they to be rid of her that they were willing to put up with the scandal of a daughter marrying an outsider. The troubling difference was in my parents' ages: she was seventeen, he thirty-three. But she would catch up with him, they said to each other, differences of age became more insignificant with every passing year. Besides, motherhood was bound to temper her wild spirits. They were married in September, within a month of Agni Sen's death.

My father repeated his notions of motherhood and maturity when he forgot about what he called my jug ears. He ended, "Painting, singing, dancing, these are wonderful things. Everyone needs hobbies. But there are hobbies and then there are serious matters. Try and read something other than novels — I've given you so many books and . . . what about that history of India? Have you read the first chapter even? Think of Myshkin."

"Myshkin? Myshkin! What has he to do with this?"

"He looks to you as an example. Now, what sort of example are you setting, dancing like that in the garden? With Ram Saran and Banno sniggering behind a bush. Dignity, Gay, our most precious possession."

"I would have thought imagination or happiness, not dignity. And that was just once. Five years ago. Myshkin was too little to learn anything."

"He's older now."

"And I have not been dancing in the garden. I haven't been dancing anywhere.

I've stopped everything. I don't sing. I don't dance. I hardly ever paint. What more do you want?"

"I don't want you to stop any of it, I just beg you to be less . . . what shall I say . . . impulsive."

"Im. Pul. Sive." My mother said the word as if she were trying it on for size.

"Have you any idea how tolerant I am? I despair sometimes. Everyone admires me as a progressive man. Allows his wife every freedom, they say in my staffroom, lets her do anything she pleases. And yet the other day . . ."

"So my freedom is something you store in a locked iron safe? To dole out when you see fit?" When my mother flared up like this, the clock stopped ticking, the dog hid under the bed.

"All I ask is that you don't speak to me this way," my father said. "As if we're in a fish market — and in our son's hearing. What will he learn? I despair."

My father's bewilderment was genuine. They were like two people stranded on an island together with no common language. An incident concerning a paint box comes back to me. My mother once ordered paints and brushes from a shop in Calcutta, which in turn ordered the goods for her from

England. After a long, impatient wait, the paints arrived in a brown paper package tied with twine. The plump new tubes of cobalt blue, viridian green, and her favorite, burnt umber, lay newly exposed to the world in a bed of torn paper. My mother admired the perfection of those tubes for several days, picking them up, putting them back into her box of paints, before she could bring herself to twist open one of the lids and squeeze out the first slug of color.

Then one day my father took those paints with him to his college and put them away — I cannot remember why, perhaps to teach her the difference between hobbies and higher matters. He brought them back after a week, left them on the dining table, and walked into the bathroom as if he had done nothing that could be construed as a violation. My mother saw her paint box, dropped what she was doing, and picking it up stalked outside and flung it into a corner of the back garden. The precious tubes and squirrel-hair brushes were strewn far into the undergrowth. "They're gone for good. Happy?" she shouted at the bathroom's closed door.

My father made me crawl on my knees in the wildflowers and brambles and spiky grass that day, sweat pouring from my body, to search out every last paintbrush and tube. He followed my mother to the kitchen, the storeroom, even to the terrace when she went to hang her saris to dry, and kept repeating, "It was just a joke, Gay, can't you see that?" Some weeks later he came back from work bearing as a peace offering an unattainable, lavish art book.

A fragile contentment held us together for several days after that. My mother sang as she worked and my father read out nuggets from the newspaper. He declared he would not allow her to go to Delhi that summer because the house was too still and dull without her. I longed for our lives to be this way forever.

Although the quarter of an hour in my grandmother's sickroom in Delhi had revolted me, I was happy enough through the rest of that trip. My father had dropped us off and gone back to Muntazir after a day, not pausing in his strictures until his tonga had turned the lane's corner: "Don't wander about on your own. Don't swim in the river, it's much deeper than it seems. Don't let your cousins take you to a cinema house, you're still too young."

My mother's childhood home was so big I could not finish exploring it in the week we were there. I found myself in courtyards that opened out into more courtyards, a tank filled with lotus in the corner of a patch of green, verandahs from which dark staircases vanished upwards, who knew where, room after room along narrow corridors, terraces at different levels. Each set of rooms contained one of my uncles and his family and each one looked and felt different. If one had a long Belgian mirror that swung on its stand, another had songbirds in a cage. The food for the whole family was made in a mud-plastered kitchen where fires blazed and cooks stirred giant pots with ladles as long as brooms. At mealtimes we sat on the floor, bell-metal plates and bowls before us, children at one end, grown-ups down the other side. At the head of the row sat my mother's oldest brother, a weedy, ash-haired little man. He had a voice like a saw on wood and when it rasped around the room everyone stopped eating to pay respectful attention.

I developed a doglike adoration for the son of the third uncle, who was a few years older. He took me under his wing, an eager and worshipful protégé. He would say, "Come on, let's go and have some fun," and thump my shoulder in a way that made me swell with pride. He was lanky and tall and had a smile that turned his eyes into slits. Everyone called him Tobu. As soon as my father left, having delivered his warnings against all life's pleasures, Tobu took me to the Yamuna, which flowed quite near the house, and told me to strip down to my underpants. Dark green watermelons as big as footballs grew on the sandy bank of the river. He slashed a stem with a knife and rolled the melon towards me. "Hold that to your chest," he instructed me, "and I'll teach you to swim." After that he tore his own clothes off, jumped into the brown water. I stood on the bank inching backwards, away from Tobu, the river, the melon. "Get in. I'll take care of you," he shouted towards me. "Come. I won't let you drown." That was how I learned to swim — holding a melon to stay afloat, Tobu's arms steadying me, his voice in my ears. "Move your legs, move your legs, idiot!"

One of those days, Tobu and I, along with some of the other children in the house, went to the Olympus Circus with my mother and my youngest uncle. The circus was taking place in a multicolored cloth tent pungent with the smell of animal hide. We had seats in the front row because my mother had bought the tickets and she was never one to be sensible when she could be extravagant. I entered the tent clutching To-bu's hand, afraid and wanting to leave, to go right back home where I was safe, but I could not confess it for fear of ridicule. My mother would have been the first to mock me. Tears and fears never got anyone the Victoria Cross, she would say. If I cried, she would turn away saying, "Come on, Mysh-kin, we are made of stern stuff, you and I. Have you ever seen me cry?"

The first few acts of the circus came and went: Mr. Doso on his one-wheel bicycle, the wire dances of Miss Olga and Miss Zulla, the tigers who sauntered into the ring with Captain Gavin, who held up a board saying R.B. TIGERS as he introduced himself. A tusker elephant and an African lion were next. Then came an Indian lion in a harness by which he drew a rickety cart. He was egged on by a scrawny boy in a dhoti who tapped the lion with a switch and stuck his tongue out when we laughed. Three girls, Juanita, Pepita, and Senorita, made up the trapeze trio. The middle one, Pepita, smiled at me each time her swing came towards the front. She had plaits that were flung out by the air as she swung high above. After the third or fourth time, she leaped off the bar, turned a few times in the air, and landed on her feet right in front of us. She gave me a wink.

Then came the act we had been waiting for. The magician, Ivan the Terrible, who appeared to the sound of trumpets, wearing the same scarlet cloak and golden silk trousers he wore on the Olympus Circus hoardings. It was as if he had walked down from the billboards into real life by a sleight of hand. He worked through the tricks I was to become familiar with over the years: He showed us an empty pot and then began pouring water from it, more water than could be held by a whole bucket. He pulled birds from hats. Blindfolded, he opened a cupboard with a key and read out a letter someone from the audience had put into its drawer. He freed himself from chains in which he had been trussed and padlocked. And then all at once he fixed his gaze on my mother and said, "Come. I need a volunteer. If you are brave enough, madam, come up here." He stepped back theatrically and waited. "Our show cannot go on without you."

My mother was sitting with me on one side of her and a small nephew on the other. From down the line, my youngest uncle craned his neck towards her and said, "Gayatri, you are not to go. Stay where you are. What sort of absurd demand is this?"

Her brother's words were a cast-iron guarantee that she would do the opposite. Propriety, sobriety, obedience: these were the very things she had made it her life's mission to annihilate. The magician had his eyes on her, mocking, challenging. So had her brother. The choice was clear. She got up, settled the gray sequined stole she was wearing over her dark blue sari, walked into the ring, and climbed onto the platform in the middle. There was a tooting of trumpets and a rolling of drums. Silence in the tent, as if all the people in it were holding their breath wondering what the magician would do to my mother. I had heard they cut people into two with swords or locked them in a box and sliced them into pieces. My hands went cold with fear. My knees were knocking. I felt Tobu give me a friendly slap on my head and whisper, "Nothing's going to happen."

The magician held out a black sheet embroidered with silver stars. He shook it ostentatiously and bowed at my mother from the waist saying, "See for yourself, madam, this is empty. There is no monster hiding in it. The circus lion is not inside it, the dogs are not inside it, there is no snake or alligator. Am I right?"

My mother smiled. The magician said,

"Your children are in the first row. There. What is that little boy's name? Is that your son? The one with the spectacles? Give him to me for a week, I'll spirit his bad eyes away and give him good ones. He is scared — what will this wicked magician do to my mother? he is thinking. Tell him. There is nothing in the cloth."

My mother repeated his words. "There is nothing in the cloth."

"I will even tell you, madam, that it is a clean cloth. It is a laundry-washed cloth. It smells of flowers. I can see you are from a noble family, madam, and I thank you for gracing my show. I would never use an old unwashed cloth for you. Not many ladies from noble families would appear in public this way." At this another roll of drums and trumpets sounded and a red-nosed clown leaped up from nowhere, startling us all, screaming, "No, no, no!! Noblewomen would not do this! The circus is for jokers and clowns! It's for trained asses and donkeys." The clown tumbled about, whinnying like a horse. The magician waved his stick at the clown and said, "Disappear! Out, you foul-smelling lump of stupidity." The clown left, yelping.

At this point I saw that my mother was becoming irritable. A look I knew so well —

57

the one that preceded an explosion or a snapped-out, curt sentence. "I don't have all day," she would have said, if someone else were putting her through this. "Perhaps you do."

With much fanfare the magician asked my mother to sit on a low stool beneath a cross made of four poles. He showed us the black cloth again with a flourish, and then draped the poles with it so that she was no longer visible. All I could see now was a tent-like shape made by the cloth. Ivan the Terrible's eyes gleamed. Insects bumbled around the hot gaslights. The lights made the man's skin shine with sweat. You could see the pomade stiff on his henna-red mustache. When he spoke, a shower of silvery spittle flew from his mouth.

The magician cried, "Where has the good lady gone? Has she gone to Persia? Or has she settled down in Ashkabad? Is she in Peshawar or Rawalpindi? Because . . ." and here came another drumroll as he swept away the starry black cloth to reveal an empty space. My mother was no longer where she had been sitting a few seconds before.

The lunch we had eaten — kababs and korma and roti from an eating shop by a mosque — rose in my throat as if it would pour out of me in a gushing heap. I cannot remember how she came back or when we went home. I remember that I screamed and cried and tried to run into the ring when I saw the empty space where she should have been, and that Tobu had to clamp a palm on my face and hiss at me, saying, "It's just a trick, she'll be back."

She never did tell me what the trick was when she came back. In the next many weeks, every time I asked her to explain where she had gone and how she had returned, she smiled mysteriously and said, "There are some things in life you never find out, Myshkin. Sometimes things happen that nobody understands." At first I was too angry to ask her anything. I pummeled and kicked her and yelled, "Go away! Stay with the magician. I'll tell Papa." She scolded me all the way back from the magic show. "Myshkin, you ruin everything. To shout like that. When will you grow up? Really, one cannot do anything anymore without a huge fuss. As if the sky's broken and fallen down."

When in Delhi with her family, she spoke a mix of Bengali and Hindi and English and I could not always follow what she was saying, but I could tell she was furious and I was the cause of it. I suppressed my sobs and began to kick a stone. My rule was that it must not roll away into a pothole or gutter, the same one had to be kicked all the way back to the house. I was not allowed to change stones if I lost this one. My toes hurt through my shoes, but still I kicked.

"And why wouldn't he scream?" her brother said, planting himself in her way to make her stop walking on. "Can't you understand what that kind of thing can do to a child?"

"Come, Myshkin," my mother said, sidestepping him. "Stop that, you'll stub your toe and ruin those shoes. I think it's time to go home. Never a good idea to be in my loving parental home for long."

Did I really think my mother had died when the magician made her disappear? That she was gone forever, in a puff of magic smoke? Did I know of death then? Maybe I did. I was given to fits of melancholy as a child, and when I was perhaps only five or six years old and lying in the center of my parents' bed in the middle of the evening, apparently asleep but actually quite awake, surrounded by people chatting and laughing, I would be in tears, agonized by the thought that my mother, my father, my grandfather, and Dinu were all going to die someday, leaving me alone. How the concept had entered my head I do not know, but ever since then I have wondered when it is that a child becomes aware of death. Is it at some precise moment? Does the idea enter our consciousness along with life itself, at the time of conception? Do we learn about it from watching ants and grasshoppers die? Or from losing someone close?

When my mother went away that monsoon day of 1937, I wondered for some time whether she had died while I was in school and I was not being told. But fairy tales were not for my father, who believed in honesty and accuracy. I think he told us she had gone away for a short trip because he truly believed that. It is the only thing that accounts for his impassive adherence to routine in the weeks that followed. He went for his walk at dawn, came back and drank his glass of hot water with honey and lemon, was ready as usual by eight, and cycled off in his year-long uniform of khadi kurta-pajama. He clipped up the pajamas to be able to pedal without muddying them and went to his college, where he lectured on ancient civilizations, the Mughal Empire, historic battles, and then went to the Society for Indian Patriots for two hours. He came back by six for his cup of Darjeeling with three drops of milk. After that he read, listened to music on his gramophone, and over dinner quizzed me about school and suffered my grandfather's stories of patients at his clinic.

From time to time one of his students would come over to discuss a thesis or an essay, but the biggest change after my mother went away was that we had fewer visitors, to stay or to come for a meal. Now I know it must have been because everyone was scandalized by her flight and tackled the disgrace to the family by pretending we no longer existed, but at the time I thought it was because my mother was not there to plan out sufficiently exciting food. Instead, Banno Didi now came every morning to my grandfather and stood before him, sighing with weary fatalism.

"What will be cooked today?"

"Whatever will not kill us."

Banno Didi was given to theatrical self-pity and considered herself much put upon, but she was domineering and monumental. She walked away, muttering loud enough for everyone to hear, "Not a word of help and if the food is not to their taste? Who will be blamed? Who but Banno. Poor Banno, who cares about her?"

She had begun working for our family

long before my mother's time, as a cleaner and washerwoman, and over the years had acquired authority and consequence, turning herself into a housekeeper and ayah. She ordered around everyone else who worked in the house in a hectoring voice that carried all the way to the cowsheds. She had leathery old skin, she colored her hair orange with henna, and chewed zarda-paan so that her cheeks bulged with its juice and lines of blood-colored spittle trickled down either side of her mouth. My grandfather, who enjoyed filling my head with what he termed useful ideas, had told me the best time to say something to her was when her mouth was so full that she could not open it to reply. I tried always to follow his advice.

3

My grandfather was born in Dehradun and inherited from his father a furniture shop called Rozario & Sons. My great-grandfather, a businessman called Rai Chand, had married an Anglo-Indian woman, Lucille, and because he believed her surname, Rozario, would be thought more exalted than his own in a country ruled by the British, it was what Rai Chand called his shop. Why he chose a Portuguese-sounding name rather than a straightfor-wardly British one was a source of enduring puzzlement to my grandfather. "If we were called Woodburn or Carlyle or Wright," Dada would say in a wistful tone, "we'd still have been timber magnates."

At first it was only the shop that was known as Rozario, but by degrees the name took over the family. My grandfather's unlikely name, Bhavani Chand Rozario, was shortened by his close friends to Batty Rozario; to me, he was Dada, and everyone else called him Dr. Rozario. My father, however, was Nek Chand. He had discarded the "Rozario" because it reeked of being colonized. Being a progressive man (he said), he would leave the final decision about my name to me, but urged me to follow in his patriotic footsteps and registered me in school as Abhay Chand. Abhay: Fearless. He had not picked a deity's name as other people did. It was also short, easy to remember. But for some reason not even my teachers called me anything but Myshkin Rozario.

That our surname confused people about our religion did not matter because nobody in our house appeared to know for sure what we were. There was no shrine with Hindu gods, as at Dinu's house, nor a crucifix flanked by assorted angels and saints as at Lisa McNally's. My mother did not fast for the welfare of her family, nor did I ever see her pray. One of the few things she and my father appeared to agree on was their lack of faith in any kind of higher power. If things went wrong they blamed themselves and if anything good happened, they thanked their luck. As for Rai Chand, the only religion in his life, my grandfather said, was the making of money. If converting to Christianity or Jainism or Islam had improved his prospects, Rai Chand would have seen no reason not to do so.

My great-grandfather made his fortune in timber. At the time of the great war of 1857, when upper India became a slaughterhouse, his parents were both killed. Rai Chand escaped Sikandra in a bullock cart, hidden under hay. He was fifteen. I often asked Dada to repeat the story of the escape and marveled at the fact that Rai Chand was only a few years older than me then, all alone in the world, parentless, on the run — how I envied him. I thought of him as scrawny and bespectacled, as I was, but in my heart I knew he must have been different, he must have been like Dinu: the kind of boy who could run fast, swear hard, tell quick lies, bring down mangoes with a catapult. After each retelling of the story I wandered the garden with a lump of jaggery and some dry roti tucked into a waistband I fashioned for myself out of an old rag. That was all the food Rai Chand had taken with him when he escaped — so Dada said. I skulked behind bushes and lurked by the cattle shed where our two cows Lalli and Peeli chewed the cud and offloaded great gobs of dung. Despite the stink and the insistent flies I sheltered resolutely in the cowshed behind piles of old gunny bags, fighting off imagined British soldiers.

That day in 1857, Dada said, Rai Chand's bullock cart went only as far as the next village. After that he walked, hitched rides, starved, and begged his way northward, and by stages went beyond Dehradun into Garhwal, then higher still, ending up on a Himalayan mountainside close to the source of the Ganges, in a place of fierce streams and precipices, where rain turned to ice and snow in winter and the steep sides of the mountains were covered by deodar trees. At night leopards sawed, antelopes honked, jackals howled. But these sounds of lurking savagery were less terrifying than mobs with bloodred eyes, and here, in Harsil, Rai Chand stumbled upon the remote outpost of an Englishman called Frederick Wilson who had made his way there several years before. Rai Chand joined Wilson's wild band of hard-drinking loggers and hunters, living by hunting, fur and musk exports, and taxidermy, and by acting as guides to British mountain travelers. It was here that Rai Chand married Lucille, whom he met on one of the expeditions he assisted Wilson in guiding across the high passes.

When the British started building the railways and needed wood for sleepers, Wilson turned to logging. Deodars taller than hills had lived undisturbed across dense, secretive forests all around him. They took centuries to grow to their two hundred feet and the timber was oily, immune to time and termite, virtually imperishable. He felled them in their thousands and floated the logs downriver to Haridwar. In time, he became a local potentate who minted his own coins. Some said he was more powerful than the Raja of Garhwal.

One of Dada's stories was of how once he found himself at night by the ruins of a rope bridge said to have been built by Wilson on the Jad Ganga river. Full moon, the leaves on the trees shining like mercury, not a soul around. Only the soft whooshing of the wind. The silence was broken by the clopping of hooves, coming closer and closer — at this stage I always buried my face in Dada's bony, tobacco-smelling chest and his smiling voice whispered above me, "And do you know who it was, my little Myshkin? The ghost of a white man, all in white, on a white horse with white hooves. The ghost of Frederick Wilson searching for his bridge across the river. Then I heard the far-off tinkle of anklets and I was so frightened I ran for my life."

I tried to visualize Dada running, but it

was not easy. I had never seen him so much as hurry. He was satisfied that the world would wait for him — to finish a sentence, to spoon up the last mouthful from his plate, to get dressed and leave the house, to climb into a carriage. I have mulled over what set Dada apart, what made people deferential to him, and it was this. He was never in a hurry because he knew, even if subconsciously, that everyone wanted to hear what he was going to say, or see what he was going to do. Nothing rattled Dada. Once when a large red-bottomed monkey invaded our dining room at lunchtime, leaped onto the table, and sat peeling oranges one by one, Dada was the only one who remained in his place, fixing the monkey with an amused gaze, saying, "Sir, are the oranges to your taste? Perhaps you would prefer apples?"

It was profitable to be Wilson's friend and Rai Chand was for several years a kind of manager, recruiting loggers from Kangra and sawyers from Punjab, supervising the timber depot in Haridwar. The pickings were good and when his fortune became substantial he started a carpentry workshop. After some years he had shops in Dehradun, Karachi, and Muntazir, as well as in Nainital, where he built a summer home.

Rozario & Sons was known all over the hill stations of Kumaon and Garhwal as furniture makers to the sahibs.

The success did not last. Both Rai Chand and Lucille died of cholera within a week of each other when my grandfather was sixteen. He and his several siblings did the rest of their growing up in the homes of Lucille's relatives. Despite these upheavals, Dada had salvaged some remnants of the Rai Chand days, which were displayed in his bedroom. One corner had a tiger skin draped over a settee. Its head was upright, resting on its chin and its eyes of amber followed you around. The taxidermist had left its mouth permanently open, its long, yellow fangs ready for combat. The paws drooped down the settee's side. A moth-eaten, ever-watchful Monal pheasant said to have been snared and stuffed by Frederick Wilson himself presided over another corner of the room and by the doorway to Dada's dressing room was a sola hat perched on an ancient rifle. When I was little, it was a ritual for me to tiptoe in on Sunday afternoons and for him to exclaim, "There you are, my man! Not a minute to lose! Time to bag that tiger!" He would clamp the hat on my head and his pipe in his mouth. He would balance the rifle on his shoulder and we would prowl around his room circling the tiger-draped settee. He kept some whisky hidden in his wardrobe to sip in peace, away from my father's abstemious eyes, and he would take it out on those afternoons. "Some Dutch courage, Myshkin," he would declare, "before we go hunting for that fiendish man-eater. It's going to be a long, hard day in the Burmese rain forest. Here, you have one too." He would hand me an empty glass and I would knock back the imagined whisky.

I do not know whether losing his father early in life is what made Dada a physician instead of a furniture seller or if it was merely that he had not inherited his father's head for commerce. None of his brothers had either, although one of them held on to the vestiges of the business in Karachi and lived a life of genteel decay on money borrowed from my grandfather. There was still a big barn of a shop in our town, the only substantial part of his father's possessions that my grandfather formally inherited, with the words *Rozario & Sons, Since 1857* embossed in green and gold on a wooden signboard that went all the way across the front above the door. A small sign below it, barely bigger than a child's slate, announced *Dr. Bhavani Chand Rozario, General Physi-*

cian, plain white on black. His nameplate was not crowded with a string of acronyms, as with other doctors, and few outsiders knew the genealogy of my grandfather's medical degree, which started in India and ended in England, where he was when my grandmother fell ill. He was not able to come back in time to save her life. It was local lore that his wife's death so devastated Dr. Rozario that he swore he would never leave to find money or fame in a big city, he would be the doctor for the people in his own medically ill-equipped town.

My grandfather presided over his junk-store clinic with as much assurance as a white-coated surgeon in a shiny hospital. His consulting room was in a sectioned-off part of the old shop. All kinds of things still turned up there, from chipped tea sets and chairs to crystal wineglasses, which people brought in to be sold off secondhand. If a table or tea set caught anyone's eye, Dada sold it and gave the owners the money. If not, until they were claimed again, they remained as furniture in his clinic.

It was here that Walter Spies appeared one day in 1937.

I first met Walter Spies on a summer afternoon, one of those dull, interminable parts of the day when the house felt as if it were struck by a spell, everyone dazed with the heat. Blinds striped the front verandah with swaying lines of light and dark. The fans whirred, the blinds rustled, the sawdust-covered ice block that was delivered every other day melted into an expanding puddle. This was all that happened in the house every summer afternoon.

Rozario & Sons stood at one corner of the arcade below Miss Lisa McNally's Home Away from Home, a series of rooms she let on long and short leases. To reach our house you had to walk all the way down the arcade past Prince Ideal Barber, Minerva Laundry, Peshawar Fruits, Books & Books, and Ishikawa, Dental Surgeon. The dental clinic had been closed from before I was born because (so I had been told) one morning, after he had already practiced in Muntazir for two decades, Dr. Ishikawa had woken up unable to speak any language but Japanese. His clinic still had a signboard across it showing fleshy pink lips stretched over two rows of white teeth, but he was sighted only rarely, tottering off to the market where he bought things using sign language or to the post office to retrieve money orders from Yokohama.

Round the corner from his clinic, past a

patch of wilderness that surrounded the tomb of a Muslim pir, was our house, a single-storied building in a line of four plain whitewashed bungalows with verandahs along the front. It was even then hidden by big trees. Today it is the only one left; Dinu's was the last to go. Tall buildings now crowd our house on every side but the house itself is much as I remember from my childhood. Dim, cool stillness, high ceilings, long mirrors, heavy furniture. The smell of old books, furniture polish, and attar of musk. The dining room clock's deep gong. The land around it was too unruly to be called a garden, but then as now, it had trees, grass, bushes — a stretch of mystery where chameleons went from orange to green as they turned themselves into leaves. Next door on one side was Dinu and on the other, two more houses which did not interest us. The road in front of our house sloped gently downward to the river that ran at right angles to it, and that afternoon in May, I was sitting on the riverbank with Dinu, fishing.

We sat with our lines in the water in the shade of the trees that bent over the river where it curved round a corner. It had been almost an hour and we had caught nothing; perhaps the fish had come to recognize our footfalls and were no longer fooled by the worms we so diligently dug out of the earth and threaded onto our hooks. Across the water, with a red flag on its conical roof, was a small stone temple. It was from here that the man emerged. He stood on the opposite bank for a while, shading his eyes with his hands and looking in our direction.

"It's an Englishman," said Dinu.

We had seen Englishmen before. Big men surrounded by clusters of salaaming Indian flunkeys whose job it was to shoo away other Indians. An Englishman appearing on our riverbank was as unlikely as a penguin or a giraffe.

Dinu did not take his eyes off the man as he spoke again.

"He's naked."

The foreigner was bare-bodied. He wore shorts and nothing else, not even slippers or shoes. Even as we argued over whether he qualified as naked or not, the man flipped into the water and began to swim towards us with strong, scythe-like strokes. The river was not very wide and we had swum in it too, but never across, always along the banks. We waited, immobilized with fear and excitement as he came closer. When he emerged to take a breath we saw his face — pale hair and a grimacing mouth.

He hauled himself onto the bank right next to us, and like a ship he was bigger once he was out of the water. I had to tilt my head back to see his face, plastered with strands of wet hair. I remember being powerfully struck, even as a child, by his beauty — or perhaps it was just his unfamiliar coloring and the strangeness of the way he spoke. His eyebrows were a dark shade of gold and his forehead sloped high above a straight, rather long nose.

He said, "You boys have not stolen my clothes, yes?"

Dinu and I scrambled to our feet, our fishing rods entangled, standing at attention as we were used to doing at school when teachers quizzed us. "We have not taken anything, sir," Dinu said. "On my honor, sir." He was a few years older than me, a little bigger than me, his limbs had grown longer all of a sudden and he was like a bamboo in danger of toppling over. His loose, too-big shorts flapped above his scarred knees. The Englishman smiled. His eyes shone with amusement. "I'm not sir, I am Vaaltor," he said. He bent to retrieve his clothes from behind a bush and discarded his wet shorts, his back to us. I had never seen the naked buttocks of a grown man before, the most extreme instance of nudity in my house being the rare sight of my father or grandfather with bath towels round their waists. Dinu's eyes bulged with alarm, but the man chatted as if it were normal for him to be stark naked with two strange boys as onlookers. His English sounded different from the English we heard in school. Sometimes he stopped to search for words and said things in what sounded like a different language, and we had to half-guess what he was telling us. He was an artist, he said, he had been painting on the riverbank and had gone across to see the temple. He had arrived in search of a long-lost friend and planned to be in our town for maybe a fortnight, maybe longer. Did we come to the river often? Did we live nearby? He straightened, and by now fully clothed and shod, he hoisted a canvas bag onto his shoulder. Ah, Rozario's, he said, he had seen it of course from his room at Miss McNally's guesthouse. Wasn't it an antique shop? Whatever it was, it looked interesting, perhaps he would go there. "Why not today? Take me there with you, boys, please? Maybe he has a folding table for me."

Which was why I took Walter Spies to my grandfather's on a hot afternoon in 1937: to find a folding table in a doctor's clinic.

When I was a boy, Muntazir had a sense of village about it, a settlement from the Middle Ages that progress had pulled by its ears into the present day, where buildings poked their way out between orchards of lychee, mango, and custard apple, interruptions in a landscape with more trees than houses. When spring came, our town went scarlet with the explosion of huge fleshy flowers on the bare branches of hundreds of silk cotton trees and in winter the fields turned into sheets of gold as the mustard bloomed. At other times it was dark green with sugarcane or russet with wheat. In the far distance, on clear days, were the blue-green humps of the Himalayan foothills. I notice these colors when I turn the pages of my mother's old drawing books now. I can see how the landscape had imprinted itself on her mind.

The road to the mountains passed through our town, and our northbound railway line went on to terminate where the flat land turned into hills. Our railway station had vaulted roofs, tall windows, lofty pillars, and crenellated walls: a grand Gothic building even though only three or four passenger trains wheezed into it every day. All the others steamed past, billowing great clouds of black smoke, as if too weighty for pause in a town so slight.

One of our favorite occupations, Dinu's and mine, was to run to the railway line near our house at dusk and watch the fast trains flash by in their sudden storms of light and sound. We waited for the days when a train passed slow enough for us to see the people inside. If I asked my grandfather why such few trains stopped at our station he would explain in a sorrowful tone that in Urdu the meaning of the word *muntazir* was to wait for with anxious impatience. The destiny of our station was to live in the hope of trains stopping, but it was doomed to disappointment.

The nawabs who once ruled our town had been deposed by the British, and many of the things in Rozario & Sons came from their decaying mansions, which were being sold off object by object. My grandfather's clinic, not far from our house, was in the twilit region between the British-built cantonment and the old city of the nawabs.

Walter Spies paused to examine the signboards outside the clinic and tapped the smaller one, *Dr. Bhavani Rozario,* with a puzzled air. He peered into the mullioned

79

windows. My grandfather was often away on house calls, but today I could see him inside, talking to someone. I pushed open the heavy glass door, feeling important for having brought him a visitor — a foreign visitor. Dada was busy showing the workings of a cuckoo clock to a round-faced man with a bottle brush for a mustache, who glared at the clock as if daring the cuckoo to come out. They were speaking a mix of Hindustani and English and Dada was saying, "It won't strike four any faster if we wait for it — in fact, I do believe clocks slow down when you do that."

"What do you mean? Does this clock run slow?"

"No, that is not what I meant. It runs correctly to the minute — why, I time all my work by the cuckoo's calls now. In fact, I don't know what I will do when you take this clock away. What I meant was that as watched kettles boil slower . . ."

"Watched clocks don't strike the hour." Walter Spies completed Dada's statement. He picked up the clock and turned it round to look at the back.

The prospective clock-buyer's mouth fell open, his round cheeks wobbled in alarm at a foreigner so casually close. *"Hari Om,"* he exclaimed, and then in a defiant tone, *"Jai Hind."*

Continuing in Hindi, the man said to my grandfather, "As you know, I refuse to have anything to do with the British as long as we remain their slaves. It is abhorrent to me that they breathe the same air that I do. I will be their friend once they treat me and my countrymen as their equals, not one moment before." He tapped his cane on the floor perhaps to test if it was still strong enough to receive his weight, then rose from his chair. "I'll come back later . . . maybe." He slid past Walter Spies, and after a burst of blinding sunlight when he pushed open the door, the clinic sank back into its usual penumbral gloom.

There was an awkward pause. My ever-calm grandfather appeared disconcerted by the brusque departure. I did not make matters easier, asking in a shrill voice, "Why did he say he hates the British for breathing the same air? Is there any other kind of air?"

"I am not British, I am from Germany. We have these clocks there," Walter Spies said. "In my childhood home we have one. I see the cuckoo as a child, I think it is a real bird and I grow fond of it — and then my mother finds pieces of bread near the clock. I gave it food every day. Every single day."

He put the clock down and his eyes roamed the clinic. The place could have been the overcrowded sitting room of a haphazard collector. The cuckoo clock was one of five that hung there, chiming out of time with each other when the hour approached. There were mysterious bottles and globes, music boxes and hookahs, books, peg tables, mismatched chairs left for sale. It was these chairs that Dada's prospective patients occupied as they waited to be called into the inner sanctum, which was sectioned off with a wooden partition and a swing door.

On the other side of this door was the usual paraphernalia of consulting rooms, including charts depicting the human anatomy in grisly detail. One jar on a high shelf fascinated me. It was filled with a clear liquid in which floated a hand with two limp extra fingers, fingernails and all, dangling from the thumb. Whose was the handless body from which it had been severed? It was the bottled essence of everything I feared and loathed yet could not keep away from. I was sure it would escape the jar someday and come for me.

Walter Spies peered at the jar with a bemused smile, ambled further inside, turning back once, saying, "May I?" and carrying on without waiting for a reply. When you found the inside door, you saw that the clinic opened out quite unexpectedly into an inner courtyard. A staircase led down into it from Lisa McNally's and she hung all the guesthouse's laundry in lines across the yard.

"Ah! That is where the staircase goes. I was wondering."

"I've begged Lisa not to hang those sheets . . ." Dada said. "Come this way, let me show you . . ." He tried to draw Walter Spies away from the squalor of the back. He had plucked up courage once and told Lisa that the sheets lowered the tone, but she had said wet sheets won no wars, and the declaration flummoxed my grandfather enough to silence him.

If Walter Spies noticed what a shambles the courtyard was, he gave no sign of it. Once he had finished his tour, he came back in and settled into one of the *For Sale* chairs as if he intended staying for a long time. It was only after two cups of tea and half an hour of conversation that he told Dada it was neither accident nor tourism that had brought him to our town.

"I come hunting," he said, "for one Gayatri Sen. I have met her and her father in Bali. She is like a friend of mine. I went to her house in Delhi and I was told that her father is long deceased and she is married here in this town? I have an address, even. Here — this notebook of mine — somewhere here. Ah, yes. Number Three, Pontoon Road. Is that close? Perhaps you know her?"

A scene from my mother's childhood comes back to me. It is so vivid after her many retellings I can see it before my eyes. She is thirteen or fourteen, running along a red-earthed pathway through a forest in Bengal. Above her is a canopy of chhatim trees in full bloom, and, though the flowers are hardly worth a second glance, their scent makes her head spin. Around her everything is vast and wild, and the sky is a brilliant blue cut into jagged edges by leaves. Her father's voice sounds dimly in her ears, "Gayatri, the birds! There!" She looks up at egrets floating away like white paper that the wind has torn from the books of children in the nearby school. Her arms are outstretched as if she is flying and she wheels round and round till she is dizzy. She runs without pause or direction, is brought to a halt when she reaches the school. She can hear music. A song. It is a new school Rabindranath has started, a serene ashram where she can see girls and boys her own age or younger singing in Bengali, a language she knows but does not read well enough despite a tutor. The song stops her in her tracks. The blood rushes to her head, she has to hold a tree trunk for support. The egret-streaked sky, the leaves and flowers. The song feels both sweet and painful, a sensation she has never felt in all her years, and she turns to her father and cries, "I want to stay here! Let me be with them here!" Even as she says this she feels in her heart the weight of the hundred things that tie them to their life in Delhi. Her mother never stops ailing and will not get up from her bed. Her father needs her at home to be his little friend, which is what he always calls her.

"One day, I'll live far away," she says to me at the end of the story, solemn hand on heart as I gape at her. Her nostrils are flared, her eyes focus intensely on me, her thick straight eyebrows are joined together in a frown. She is scratching her head with the wooden end of a paintbrush and her hair stands up in an untidy clump as she pushes the brush. "I'll take you with me, Myshkin. We'll wander the world, have lots of adventures. We'll join a circus and live in a tent. Not a circus like the one with the magician. A good one. With baby elephants."

"Let's go today!" I cry out. I am seven, I cannot imagine waking up and not curling up against her, warm and sleepy. My stomach churns. "Are you going away? Will you really, really take me?" When she doesn't reply, I say, "Will you take Lisa Aunty?" Lisa McNally is her best friend, they see each other every day, at least once. My mother cannot possibly leave her or me behind, and if she tells me she won't go without Lisa it means I am going too.

My mother laughs one of her inscrutable laughs and says, "Whatever you do, don't stop dreaming." She presses both my ears back, perhaps one day they will stick out less, her eyes say. She springs up from the sofa we have been sitting in and shakes out her sari. When she dresses up to go out she is always in something sparkly and pretty and wears earrings that match; at home she doesn't bother, she wears old, soft cottons stained with turmeric, darned blouses in faded colors. But she has a sweet-smelling strand of flowers around her bun every day. The gardener picks white jasmine from the bushes at the edge of the courtyard and makes a string for her each evening after watering the plants. Or she wears one or two red champas. When I am sitting close enough to her, I have the droopy scent of plucked flowers in my nose. She tweaks my ears and says, "Time to get dinner started. And have they filled the water or not? Go, see where Banno Didi is." She jangles the keys to her cupboard as if it's just another day. As if one day after another will follow this one in exactly the same way.

Some nights, my mother sings the song from that day in Santiniketan. She only sings it when she and I are alone on the roof and (she tells me) if the sky is like a pincushion of stars so that she can count at least two thousand and twenty-two of them. It is our song, mine and hers, she says, and if ever I feel sad or afraid, I must sing it. When I was littler she would scoop me up in her arms and whirl me in a circle as she sang, now she wafts around the shadowy rooftop with her arms outstretched, a bird in flight. In seconds, she forgets I am with her.

Skyful of sun and stars,
This universe exploding with life,
And in the midst of this: I!
I have found a space.
In wonderment it is born —
That is why it is born — my song.

87

In the infinity of time
Spins the earth.

With the ebb and flow of tides
Sways the world.
In my veins, in my bloodstream,
I feel a throb.
In wonderment it is born —
That is why it is born — my song.

I've opened my ears,
I've opened my eyes,
I've poured out my soul
Upon the bosom of the earth.
I've searched out the unknown
Within the familiar.
In wonderment it is born —
That is why my song is born,
Under a sky full of sun and stars.

As I write this, I pause, I put my pen down.
It is a broad-nibbed Sheaffer that has drunk
up many bottles of ink and blackened my
fingers. I think back to that afternoon in
Rozario & Sons and wonder if that was the
moment when everything changed. If Walter Spies had not thought up his improb-
able plan to search out a girl he had met
more than a decade earlier, would my father
and mother have remained together, fitted

uneasily within one domestic box, their edges rubbing against each other until worn down and smoothened over the years? That is how it appears to be with most married people I come across. Or was my parents' destruction inevitable, a matter of time?

I bend down to pet the two dogs at my feet. They grunt in their sleep and shift and make it clear they do not like being disturbed. They have no compunctions, on the other hand, about waking me, and I wonder again how they have trained me to love them all the more for the innocence with which they harass me for their every need. At night they are in my bed, heads on my pillow, sometimes pawing me, sometimes whimpering aloud. I stroke them back to sleep. I need nobody else. I am contented and complete with my animals in a way I never have been with human beings. People think of my solitude as an eccentricity or a symptom of failure, as if I am closer to animals and trees because human beings betrayed me or because I found nobody to love. It is hard to explain to them that the shade of a tree I planted years ago or the feverish intensity of a dog fruitlessly chasing a butterfly provides what no human companionship can.

It may be because I had animals and trees

in my life from the start. There were our cows, of course, but my friend from the very beginning, and sometimes my only friend, was a dog, Rikki. It was my grandfather who found her — or she found him — he had many one-sided discussions with her about this in the years afterwards. One cold December when I was three, there was a puppy on the street outside the clinic, playing alone, chasing bits of paper and her own stump of a tail. Sometime later this fawn-colored scrap slipped into the warm clinic. My grandfather picked it up and took it outside to the courtyard — could he leave it there? He consulted Lisa McNally, hoping she would offer to keep an eye on it, but Lisa said she would not look at it, no dogs she had told herself after her own died. Lisa was only a little older than my mother, but old enough in those days for people to write her off as a lifelong spinster who ought to be grateful for any companion, even a dog. "Oh, that Lisa," her relatives sighed. "So funny where her high horse took her, it's left her on the shelf." Lisa said she loved her shelf. Only decorative objects lived on shelves.

Lisa's obduracy in the matter of shelves and puppies settled it. Dada brought the puppy home and said we would call her

Rikki after Kipling's mongoose. I have had other dogs, but none have been as distraught as her at partings or as boisterous with joy when reunited. It was as if the fear of being left again on a pavement was her ruling emotion. Or maybe the truth is that all dogs understand from their infancy that when you have found your friend, you need to spend every moment of your lives together. Why part?

The thought of persistent human companionship is abhorrent to me. I have never married. The words of Gabriel Oak to Bathsheba, although meant romantically, struck me as a threat: "And at home by the fire, whenever you look up there I shall be — and whenever I look up, there will be you." There was a woman forty years ago who wanted me to be there each time she looked up. Kadambari. She was not alone, a man does not have to do very much to be coveted. Once I was taller than my father, and the jug ears that my mother used to press back had miraculously flattened, and I had acquired a degree and a job in Delhi, I became conscious that when I came home for holidays, girls were merrier around me and their parents kept inviting me home and praising me for taking after my grandfather. "Ah, old Dr. Rozario, such intellect and wit, such a handsome profile," they said. "If only he had lived twenty years more! But you are his mirror image, Myshkin, that is a consolation." I knew this was not in the least true but I was just too unthinking at that time to understand what they were after.

Last night, probably because of all this dredging up of memories, I woke from a dream in which I was with Kadambari, the heavy, dark scent of her in me again. She would come to my rooms in Delhi at night, when her parents thought she was safely in bed. She would enter, lock the door, throw off her sari, pop the buttons on her blouse, clamber out of her petticoat, and stand by the door in the lamplit room, stripped and triumphant, to let me look at her before we had said a word to each other. She insisted on the oil lamp. No electric lights.

When I woke from my dream yesterday, I closed my eyes again, to preserve for a few moments her glowing face contorted as if in pain, her hair disheveled. "Don't stop. Go on forever," she breathed in my dream.

I switched on the light.

4

It must have been soon after Mr. Spies's first visit to the clinic that he came to our house. I have no recollection of what my mother said or did when she saw him again after a lifetime — maybe I was not there when they met again. What I do remember is the woman he used to come with to our house and how she walked around the garden dipping her head to smell a flower, darting with an excited shriek towards a peacock strutting on a nearby wall, then plucking a green mango off a low branch. I regarded all the mangoes as my personal property to distribute as I thought fit, and Golak and I protected them from monkeys with our catapults through long, hot afternoons. What right had anyone to pluck them without asking permission? At first I was afraid to protest — she was British after all — but I could not contain my indignation and said, "That mango is too small, it was not to be plucked. Anyway, you can't eat it, it's sour and hard."

The woman was as thin as a pencil. A curtain of jet-black hair was plastered against her face. She wore long black clothes that flapped around. A magician or a witch. Her dress was loose and long enough to hide anything. A wand. A broomstick.

She stopped her wandering and turned to fix her gaze on me. "Do you know the things I eat? I eat raw eggs with a spoonful of sugar. I eat beans from tins and grapes off vines. I eat little boys baked in the oven. With extra salt." I stepped back. "I loathe children usually," she said. "But you — I like the look of you. Come along. Show me around."

She did not smile as she spoke, and returned to her strolling as if expecting me to follow as a matter of course. When I didn't she stopped again and held her hand out, saying, "Come on, what are you wait-ing for?" Her fingers were covered with rings and she had beads around her neck, long strings of them. "See? Seven rings. All silver. And they clack if I do this. Do you want to see?" I had trouble understanding all she said, her English sounded different from the kind I was used to. But I had not missed the part where she said she ate boys and I kept my distance.

"Beryl," Mr. Spies turned and called out to her. "Please behave. Don't steal their fruit, don't scare the child. Here, come meet your guide to Indian dance. This is the lady I told you about, she found me on that raft in the lake."

Beryl de Zoete stopped talking to me and turned her gaze to my mother, then sprang towards her. She towered over her — they both did. She put her hands out and in an earnest voice said, "Delighted . . . finally! I need to watch a *thousand* dances. Kathak, Bharatanatyam, all. *Understand* them. I need someone who speaks the language and tells me what is going on. I am all at sea. Will you help me?"

Beryl de Zoete had learned dance from Émile Jaques-Dalcroze in Hellerau, Dresden, she said, who taught a form called eurythmics. It was one of life's coincidences, she said, that long after the dance academy had ceased to be, Walter Spies went to live there in the artists' colony it turned into. In her early days, until an inheritance made it possible for her to stop working, Beryl taught dance. She was said to be a remote figure, strange in her clothes and manner; but everyone admitted she could instill a sense of rhythm even in those who had no musical sense.

Beryl was British but spoke three or four other languages as fluently as English and I have a vague memory that she carried around a book which went back to front. It may have been in Persian, which too she tried to learn. My grandfather found out soon enough that she had a degree from Oxford and traveled the world writing on dance. She told him she had experimented with marriage and failed, then lived most of her life with a translator from Chinese who was blind in one eye and twelve years younger than her.

"He does not speak at all, but since I talk enough for both of us, it works wonderfully," she said.

Arthur Waley was his name and I came across it not long ago on a book he had edited, of Beryl de Zoete's essays. Names from a vanished time. Names from when my universe was real and dreamlike in equal measure. Until I saw that book, I was not sure I had considered Beryl to be a real person. In the private mythology of my childhood, I had her down as someone who was a person by day but changed into an old crone by night who really did eat humans. I did not know then that in fact she saved lives, rescuing Jewish dancers in Germany from being put to death by the Nazis, spiriting them away to Britain, enlisting the help of every friend she had.

Not long after their first meeting, Beryl de Zoete must have decided that Gayatri Rozario — young, beautiful, gifted, tortured, stifled — was an obvious subject for rescue. Some days later, or maybe weeks later, by which time she was a regular visitor to our house, she narrated the story of a man-woman she had met on her travels in the Libyan desert, at the oasis of Siwa.

I can still hear the story today as Beryl told it one evening, her musical voice spreading over the garden. They think nobody else is home. Beryl sways on the swing that hangs from one of our trees, my mother sits on a stone bench nearby. I am back from playing, and as I flit through the shadows at the back of the garden on my way into the house, I stop at the sound of that voice. My mother has eyes only for Beryl, so intense is her attention she does not see me though I tiptoe closer until I am not far from them. She has her elbows on her knees and her chin in her palms. Her sari has slipped down her chest, but my father is not there to chide her for immodesty and she does not set it right.

"On the way back through the oasis, we knocked at the door of a young woman called Aisha, famous in Siwa for her singing and dancing and defiance of convention, and to whom I had an introduction. But she was out. That a woman would live alone in Siwa is as shocking as it would be in England for her to live with ten husbands. Her story is this. She was formerly the wife or mistress of an English captain, very well known out there, who used to keep a little hotel in Siwa. After his desertion Aisha could no longer bear to return to the absolutely cloistered life of a woman in Siwa, so she had the originality to become a man, just as in modified form certain strong-minded English women did at the end of the last century, not wearing stays, cutting their hair short, going about freely and heartily returning the dislike which men felt for them. Aisha's case was much harder and she solved it in a different way and less respectably than our New Women. But she is like them in having cut off her hair and she wears the long white shirt or jibbah, which the poorest Siwan men wear. She supports herself by machining and by selling bangles, rings, and baskets and her room by night is a kind of low-class salon where she entertains men by drumming and singing."

I had thought Siva was a Hindu god, but it appeared that the name had other lives elsewhere. Is this why the story has never left me? Or because it became clear later what a powerful impression the story had made on my mother?

The year they came into our lives, Beryl de Zoete and Walter Spies had already completed a book on Balinese dance. Documenting India's dance was their next plan. Walter Spies had first met my mother at a time when she was a young girl learning Indian classical dance. He half-remembered the things she had spoken of, her dreams of joining a troupe like Leila Roy's or Uday Shankar's, dancing in ballets at Santiniketan. Dance was changing in India, she had told him. They were shedding the coy gestures, the biting of lips, the batting of eyelashes, and turning to athleticism and music instead. She would dance in one of those troupes — this she had declared with the conviction of the young, who have no reason to believe life usually turns out different from everything they planned. Walter Spies could not have known that dance and the passionate Indian girl he had met were to be separated forever.

My mother had a pair of heavy anklets from the days when she was trained in Delhi by her tutor. She would take them out of their box sometimes, shake them to hear their *jhan-jhan* sound, then put them back again. I had never seen her dance but once, when she waltzed in Lisa McNally's drawing room to Strauss on the gramophone. The room was crammed with peg tables and knitted cats and miniature Big Bens that went tumbling and flying as she and Lisa whirled around. They went on until the music stopped and then they collapsed in a heap of crimson and turquoise silk on the sofa.

No other house down the road, no other friend of our family's, no other boy in school — nobody else we knew had visitors from another country. And these people were not merely from elsewhere, they lived on an island, surrounded on all sides by the Indian Ocean that held thousands and thousands of islands, some still unexplored, some no more than rocky outcrops in the sea, and some that were like the world in miniature, with mountains, temples, palaces, seas, rivers, fields, villages, and cities. My mother told me you could walk around their country end to end in a few days and to go anywhere else you had to take a boat. Dinu and I began to play games which had sharks, alligators, ships. We lived off wild pigs and fish roasted over open fires. We ate imagined figs and climbed imagined trees for coconuts to drink from. We split the coconuts with the same machetes with which we killed deer for meat.

My mother went off with the visitors in a tonga one morning, soon after they first came to our house. She had found out about a Kathak dance maestro who lived and taught in the old part of Muntazir, a maze of narrow alleys from the last century crammed with old houses, mosques, markets, brothels. As she climbed into the tonga and seated herself next to Beryl de Zoete, the wizened watchman at Dinu's began to shout, "Bibiji! Tell those sahibs I have seen their country! I have crossed the black water for them. I have fought for them! I have killed for them! Tell them to give me land! Tell them I need a house! *Khabardar!*"

The watchman could hardly see or hear any longer, but he still wore the army cap that had been issued to him when he fought in the First World War and every night he marched up and down outside Dinu's gate shouting his warning to all intruders, *"Khabardar, Khabardar!"* as loudly as if he were still on a battlefield. A bullet was said to be lodged somewhere inside him still. My grandfather, woken at night by the watchman's war cries, said the man should be sent back to Ypres or to an asylum, but Dinu's father felt that retired soldiers had earned our respect, mad or sane. My mother thought so too. She waved from the back of the tonga and cried out, "I will! I will tell them, Kharak Singh! They will write to the King of England."

Had my mother sought my father's permission before she went off on her expedition with her new friends? I don't know. It must have crossed her mind that it was like poking a snake's pit of gossip and speculation. I wonder if that is precisely what made her do it. She went off on her adventure after my father had left for work and she came back home before he returned. She was unusually demure that evening, stirring one pan and then another in the kitchen, making bright, cheerful conversation at dinner. My father too had an amusing story to tell about a student who had taken to tying his Brahminical pigtail to a hook in the ceiling as the Bengali scholar Vidyasagar was said to have done, to stop himself from nodding off during late-night study sessions. All was well until I added to the chatter.

"Ma, next time you go in a tonga with Mr. Spies, take me also."

Everything went still.

I knew that stillness. I dreaded it. I put my head down and examined my feet. I swung them. The lingering vanilla-and-milk smell of the bread pudding we had eaten was making me feel sick. I wanted the clock to strike, the dog to bark, a branch to fall: any noise at all.

Dada ruffled my hair, then took my hand. "Let's go and see if the owl has come back to the roof, Myshkin," he said.

This was how my mother had always been. She was the kind of reckless person who read the weather report after her boat was already miles away from shore. I could not imagine her any other way. When I was older I understood how different she was from other women — the wives of relatives, the mothers of my friends. Dinu's mother would never have dreamed of leaving her house in a tonga with two strangers, to go to the red-light area of the old city in search of a traditional dance teacher whose work it was to train courtesans. Dinu's mother was known only as "Dinu's Mother"; nobody remembered her name anymore. She rarely came out of the house and met no men other than Dinu's relatives and my father and grandfather. Her year-round attire was a starched sari with matching gold jewelry, and an immaculate circle of red between her brows. What need had women to go tramping about the town, she asked anyone within earshot. Would some divine spirit drop in to supervise the household? It was a disgrace, it really was — and, well, anyone could see now where all of it had been leading — the way Gayatri was given to sleeping on after daybreak when the household was up, how once she bolted to Delhi leaving a child ill at home, how she chattered away with Arjun's reprobate brother Brijen whenever he went to their house. His brains had been addled by drink, but what of hers? A hundred other things too tedious to list, each of them a sign of what was bound to happen.

Dinu's father, Arjun Chacha, was more emphatic. "Have you taken leave of your senses?" he said to my father the day after my mother's tonga ride. "Study Indian dance? What is there to study, my friend? Dance was invented so that men could look at women, not for women to look at women." He slapped the bonnet of his car and laughed. "You keep an eye on that girl-wife of yours, Nek. Remember the time she was dancing about in your garden? All your servants . . ."

My father cleared his throat and raised an eyebrow, gesturing at me. "Was she?" he said, his voice very even. "Your memory for the trivial is better than mine." Whatever my father said to my mother at home, he took care never to betray the slightest hint of discord to outsiders. And in some curious way, opposition from Dinu's parents could persuade him that my mother had done nothing wrong. Why shouldn't she go where she pleased (within reason, naturally)? Women had rights too. This was what he had heard Mukti Devi say only the other day at a Society for Indian Patriots meeting when she made a fiery speech exhorting men to bring their wives out of purdah, make them join the fight for independence.

My father gripped my hand firmly as he spoke, I had the sense he was warning me to keep my mouth shut. Usually he wore slippers, but that day, despite the heat, he had new black leather shoes on. They seemed oddly large on his feet and his pajama legs flapped a few inches above them, his skinny, white-socked ankles a stick-bridge between the two. As if that were not strange enough, he had put on one of those cloth caps that looked like an upturned boat. I tried to tug my hand out of his. He did not let go.

Dinu's father stroked his car some more, changed the subject. "It's a new model. Dodge. One of these days I'll take you for a ride, drop you off at your college before I go to court. You won't believe how smooth it is, like being on a barge."

"I'm a walking man, you know that. If we were meant to move faster our stomachs would have had petrol tanks."

Dinu's father shook his head in exasperation, puffing his cheeks and letting out a breath with a *fooof*. "You know, Nek, we have been friends since we were boys and still I don't understand you. You have to give up your airy-fairy philosophies someday. Time you discovered the pleasures of life."

Arjun Chacha had a round paunch, plump cheeks, and flared nostrils below which his mustache bristled black and lush. His eyes were tiny and ever alert. A barber came to his house every morning to shine and comb his hair, shave him, trim his mustache and the hair in his nostrils. He sprinkled himself with Old Spice before he went to the courts and you could always tell when he had walked past because of the fragrant cloud in his wake. Nobody could accuse him of not enjoying money, Arjun Chacha said with a smile, one needed to know how to make money, and also how to spend it.

"Every night I stand at my open window before I sleep and I gaze out into the dark — the summer wind is blowing, the trees are dusty and half-dead, but I know at dawn the plants will be watered, the driver will wash the car, the cows will be milked, the mangoes are ripening, I have five cases sub judice, ten clients to see, advocates to interview, solicitors to hire, the cloth mill in Kanpur to manage, and fields of wheat and sugarcane. All this goes through my head and I marvel — this is my kingdom, this springs from me and rests on me."

"How true, how true," my father mumbled, trying to get away. He was supposed to take me for an eye checkup. I was happy to be delayed. Eye tests were worse than school examinations. At school I had a slim chance of passing. At the eye test, never.

Dinu's father, however, had not quite finished. He was in full flow now, the advocate whose eloquence and anglicized accent were legendary as far away as the Allahabad High Court.

"It's not mere improvements to a house, Nek. I think of the thirty-five people in my charge and my chest bursts with pride." He thumped his large torso. "A lazy rake of an alcoholic brother who has a love affair going in every alleyway. A writer! A household name! But do you think he earns a single paisa he doesn't drink away? Then there is my aged mother, my aunts, staff. The lot. I think of the cooks, the maids, the driver — I can hear a hum of peace, like the engine of a good car, from the back quarters. Would anyone else take responsibility for a senile old watchman as I do? Would anyone else have provided for Munshiji? That imbecilic clerk's a remnant from my father's days! Once they are under my care, they know I won't let them down. But they have *rules.* Every dog, cat, cow, every human, needs clear-cut rules."

He made a meaty fist of his hand and held it out. "The iron is there, Nek, under the silk and velvet. What families need — what this country needs — is a benign dictatorship. That's all there is to it. People say, throw out the British, they are tyrants. I say, keep them. There'll be anarchy without them. Once I give an order, it is written in stone, my friend, carved in granite. Gayatri's a lively girl. But the company she keeps! When will you take charge of your own ship?"

I sensed my father bristling now, about to say something scathing, but he was forestalled by the crash of shattering glass. The sound came from inside the house and what followed was silence for a few seconds and then a rising crescendo of women's voices. We could hear Dinu howling, "It just happened! It was an accident!" Arjun Chacha jerked his head towards his house. "That idiot with his cricket ball . . . Dinu, Dinu! If he doesn't get a caning today . . ."

Arjun Chacha considered himself generous, wise, and above all just. His three sons had the best cricket bats, bicycles, the latest air guns, and the most money to spend, but Dinu lived in mortal fear of him and every now and then, especially if he was caught breaking a rule, he was summoned for an audience with his father.

He would trudge up to the office room to be interrogated: "So, young man, which class are you in now? Are you the head boy? Why not? Tell me, what is the capital of China? Who is the prime minister of Britain? Straighten up, boy, square chin, square chin." The questions came as a rapid-fire bark, with barely enough time for Dinu to mumble answers, and all along his father would do something else as well, such as write notes in the margin of a document or ask his clerk if the next day's work had been typed up.

Dinu was older than me, at school he was my protector. When the boys in senior school got after me, he took them on, punching, kicking, and if the bullies were taller, he charged them in the belly with lowered head, uncaring of the consequences. But at home he was as watchful as a hunted animal. I think he knew even then that he would never measure up. He would always be too gangly, too clumsy, too awkward, and neither his chin nor his cover drive would ever be square enough.

My father was not like Dinu's, he never summoned me or interrogated me. Even so, I was wary of him. My mother knew this and if I was being difficult, all she had to say was "Wait till your father comes home, wait till he hears what you've been up to." My father's personality was forbidding and the things that occupied the rest of us were too frivolous for him.

For example, one evening my grandfather, mother, and I were sitting together and talking of nothing in particular, when my father arrived and announced in grave tones that the police had raided the college that day. "Three students in the lockup. Third-degree questioning, no doubt. They've done nothing seditious." He slumped with his head in his hands as though he were Atlas and the weight of the world had doubled. "All this anxiety and anger — is this what student life should be about? It should be about learning, discoveries. You aren't bothered now, but in a few years, Myshkin will be one of them."

He sighed. "We are fugitives in our own land."

All conversation had to come to a halt, nobody could escape the feeling of guilt with which my father could swamp a room. It was bad form to discuss anything but politics when our countrymen and -women were going to jail for us. I did not understand it except for the part where revolutionaries threw bombs and started armies to fight the British. This I wanted to do as well, but my father was of the view that the nonviolent methods of Gandhi were both more moral and more effective. That is what Mukti Devi argued as well, and he was utterly persuaded. "You must come and listen to her," he urged us. "The air around her is charged with the spirit of sacrifice and service. You sit in her presence for a couple of hours and come away feeling cleansed."

Mukti Devi was the head of Muntazir Seva Ghar, which was also called the Society for Indian Patriots. She had been born with a different name but had changed it to Mukti, which meant freedom. By this time, she had already done two jail terms and lost her hearing in one ear after a blow from a police baton, because of which she had a way of tilting her head to one side when spoken to. Before I met her, I thought of her as a comic figure, forever chanting and spinning cotton. Then one day my father insisted I come to a meeting. Despite my protests, he made me wear a white, hand-spun kurta, and when I reached the meeting, I saw why: everyone wore white there. The courtyard at the Society was a restless sea of white as people sat, rose, changed places. Mukti Devi had not yet arrived, and while people waited for her, they drank tea, cracked open peanuts, and gossiped in loud voices. She entered through a side door and a hush of expectancy fell over the crowd. I saw she had a wide, open smile much like Mahatma Gandhi's. As she walked towards the front, she kept up a constant stream of questions to people she recognized there. "So, Mushtaq, I see your wife is feeding you well. Sunita, is it possible you are still so beautiful? Ramu, there you are, the secret police himself! Tell the Inspector I'm missing his hotel!" She shook with laughter and the plainclothes policeman hung his head.

Mukti Devi's skin was the color of boiled potato, with green veins threading her arms. Constant fasting had made her so thin that her shoulders were hunched and her clavicles were like rods you could have hung hooks from, yet she did not appear to be suffering. If anything, she seemed to find the world vastly entertaining, and sat cross-legged on her cotton mattress regarding her audience like a tiny, amused deity. She spotted me squashed between two or three bulky men in the second row and called me and made me sit beside her, saying, "Isn't that much better? Always a good thing to face people than have them behind you." As the speeches by visiting speakers went on and on and I began dozing off, she bent towards me and whispered, "Do you know what I think of British rule? I think the best thing about Lord Clive is that he's no longer alive. There's a good deal to be said for being dead." And then, without a second's pause, she interrupted a ponderous man's views on the provincial elections with a sharp comment that made everyone clap. When she started her speech and I saw how the people in the hall listened to her with the kind of stillness that came from suspending everything, even breath, I understood in some obscure, childish fashion how extraordinary was her charisma.

My mother and grandfather never went to listen to her, nor could my father persuade them to adopt her austerities. A mocking smile curled around Dada's lips whenever my father talked of the benefits of asceticism and spartan diets or the need for wealthy Indians to go and live in a slum for a week. My father did few of these things, nor had he ever been arrested. He complained about the difficulties of fighting for freedom while working for the very government he wanted to overthrow. But how else was he to earn a living and support his family? If only he were single! He would have lived on nothing and devoted himself to the cause.

Dada never commented on the ironies of my father's way of fighting for freedom, but once, only once, he referred to my father as a *dabbler.* Not knowing better, I asked my father what it meant.

"A dabbler?" my father said. "Your grandfather said I am a dabbler? Is that so?"

Dada hemmed and hawed. "Myshkin overhears things he doesn't understand and then says things he does not know the meaning of. I called him a babbler, he misheard me."

My father went on with his dabbling. He

114

woke before sunrise and went for a walk to the river along with other members of the Society. Mukti Devi would set off with a few followers from her own neighborhood, some distance away. They held little brass cymbals which they knocked softly one against the other as they passed, singing hymns and patriotic songs. From lane to lane they went in the dark heat before the birds had woken. A quiet stream of people would trickle out from doorways along the route, until it became a little procession led by Mukti Devi. The chimes grew louder and lingered by our gate as they waited for my father to join them. After that they went down past Dinu's towards the river, and the sounds of bells and songs softened by degrees until they were gone. They walked along the riverbank until they came out at Hafizabagh at the other end and there they sat for an hour in the grounds of the Nawab's mansion, his two horses cropping the grass nearby. They sang hymns and listened to Mukti Devi's discourses. Afterwards, my father came back and drank a glass of lukewarm lemon water sweetened with honey while I got ready for school.

My mother did not join him on these walks. She lay in her cot on the terrace, sheets rumpled, sari bunched up at her knees by her tousled, heat-oppressed sleep under the open sky now alive with birdcalls and Brijen Chacha's dawntime singing. She woke once he had finished his morning ragas and I had rung my bicycle bell before leaving for school. She clung to every last shred of sleep until the shrill jangling of my bell could no longer be ignored.

5

Beryl de Zoete and Walter Spies had taken
several weeks to reach Muntazir from Bali,
and although they had planned to stay for a
fortnight, then move on to other parts of
the country, Beryl said she did not feel as if
they had even *begun* to do all the things
they wanted to do. This was how it had been
all the way, she said, this was why it had
taken them so long to come. They had
thought they would not pause in Java, but it
was enchanting and in Batavia they were
dizzy with studying beautiful sculpture, buying things, seeing friends from the time Walter had lived there as head of the Sultan's
western orchestra. On the ship to Singapore
they made friends who insisted they stay for
a few days before going on to Madras. The
process was repeated in places big and small
throughout the journey. "Why not pause for
an eternity where there is reason to pause?
Why stay an extra minute when there is

117

reason to leave?" she said, and I know my mother listened to her carefully because I found the words written down within quotation marks in her notebook.

Walter Spies was restless to leave the town and find natural landscapes and rural people. He felt at odds in cities, he said, they made him yearn for wilderness and simpler ways of living. Soon enough, he found a village nearby where he retreated to paint and ended up staying three nights in a mud hut with farmers. How he managed to communicate with them nobody knew, but he came back green-eyed from the grass of the fields, one canvas half-finished, ready to go back the very next week.

There was something about the two men he met in the village, he said, that appealed to his deepest sympathies. They were sitting outside their hut on a rope cot and were about to start eating but when they saw him, lost and tired, they invited him to perch on their cot as well and pushed towards him a plate with a hot, thick roti on which a fat blob of white butter was in the process of melting. He was hungry after his long walk and he ate all of it without a thought. He realized later, when he understood how poor the family was, that someone in the house — probably a woman —

had gone without food that afternoon on his account. They said nothing, they offered him two more rotis and pickle and raw onions that night, as well as space to sleep in their courtyard. He was overwhelmed by their kindness. He left them all the money he had in his pocket, but money was not the reason they had done it, he was certain. They reminded him of the villagers in Bali, he said, understated and soft-spoken to such a degree that outsiders mistook their modesty for ignorance and thought of them as incoherent peasants. Nothing could be further from the truth. They were cultivated, civilized, gentle people. Their sense of art and music was supreme.

"I have never heard their music," Dada said.

Walter Spies jumped up from his seat and ran an excited hand through his hair. He waved his pipe about. "It is sublime! I heard the royal gamelan at Yogyakarta when I first went to Java — it played softly at first, in drops, and then came the deep convulsive strokes of the gong, so deep they almost make you anxious. And the agitated drumming in between. Sometimes all the music simply dissipated and then it came back — drop for drop — from somewhere. It made me passionate with joy! I wanted to do nothing else but listen to that music, learn everything about it."

"And did you?" Dada said.

"I had to earn money. I had no job then, I had just landed off a cargo ship. You can imagine how I felt after that, bashing out the fox-trot on the piano for mounds of Dutch flesh to heave to. That is what I was doing then, to earn a living."

"Well, I have nothing against the fox-trot," Dada said. "I have fox-trotted and even waltzed in my day. Lisa McNally will confirm that."

"Ah come, Dr. Rozario." Walter Spies laughed. "Is that the best you can do? I am searching for Indian music. Find it for me."

Ultimately, Walter Spies's first experience of Indian music happened quite by chance. One night Dada and he and I — I don't recall anyone else with us — went out to a small *dargah* on a hilltop just outside Muntazir, with a view of the city. We took food with us, a hurricane lantern, and a couple of rugs, planning to spend the night in the open. The sky was clear but for one spreading cloud which hid the moon. The edges of the black cloud glowed silver and bright rays cut the black sky into pale strips. As the moon swam westward, one edge appeared for an instant, then sank behind the cloud again. And then we spotted movement far below. We could not tell what it was.

Time passed, the movement ceased, hidden from view until it revealed itself again: a wavering line of fireflies. It came closer, and we saw it was a stream of women and girls, holding candles that lit up their faces. The girl at the head of the procession might have been one of those angels from my mother's art books, ethereal, calm, remote, and exquisite. They were singing a slow, melancholic tune in soft voices joined together. The chorus rose and fell, rose again. When it died away altogether, the girl at the head of the procession lifted her head and sang alone in a pure, high voice that seemed to reach the cloud and the moon hidden behind it. It was more melodious chant than song. A *marsiya,* Dada whispered, a Muslim mourning chant, a dirge-like song usually sung at Muharram. What were they mourning? I did not know, but I had never heard anything like it before. Neither had Mr. Spies.

They passed without seeing us, and went towards the *dargah.* For a while we could hear them still, but more muted, and then the voices faded, the candles grew fainter. As if a spell had been broken, the huge full moon slid out from behind the cloud. It was so close you could see the speckles in it.

Mr. Spies sat looking down from the hill at the few lights that twinkled at that hour in the far-off town — our town. "Have you ever been on a ship, Myshkin?" he said in a faraway voice. "When it became unbearable for me to live in Germany, I decided to leave and go to Java. But how to go to Java? I needed a ship and so I signed on as a ship hand. I was twenty-eight — the oldest on board. Good for nothing! I pretended to know only Russian so they would put down my stupidity to language trouble. They gave me very light duties. One duty was to keep watch in the crow's nest. What's a crow's nest? You climb a ladder to a very small, swaying basket on a ship's pole and from there you observe the sea around you, if anything is coming at you . . . I sang songs, and the water around me was black. Water, white froth, stars. Nothing but sky and water and stars! And I thought, this is what I want life to be! I don't want to be wasting time with art when I can live. *This* is life! To be right in the middle of life, living each minute intensely. Hearing those girls sing tonight. I've never heard anything so moving from a human voice. On this hilltop. Nothing above us but the moon and sky. Nothing around us but silence and dry heat and wind in the grass. This is the center of everything."

He took a harmonica out of his pocket, put it to his mouth, and began to play. The sound filled the air as if there was an orchestra on our hilltop. As he played, he moved in time to the music and his bare feet tapped the ground. The melody he was playing seemed to leap and dive in the night air.

Mr. Spies put the instrument away. "A song by Schubert. 'The Trout.' Do you know it, Dr. Rozario? It's better on a piano. Or violin." For a time he was still, gazing at the lights below us. He was with us, but he was not with us. Then he took off his shirt, bundled it into a pillow, and flung himself onto the grass. He ruffled my hair and said with a quick grin, "I'm happier than a pig in mud! Happiness somehow just comes to me." He shut his eyes, still with a smile on his face.

Flat on the ground, his stomach had caved in and his ribs stood out like the frame of a boat. His face too was sharper now: angles and hollows. Eyes shut, he was defenseless, a man to whom anything could be done. He was something that had washed up after a long journey. Driftwood. A shipwreck. A message in a bottle that I could not decipher.

Soon after that night in the open, Mr. Spies decided he had to understand Indian classical music with some seriousness. He made my mother persuade Brijen Chacha to get him entry to private music soirées and to the homes of old masters so he could listen to them practicing. He started sarod lessons with a young man called Afzal Khan who was himself still a student. Afzal was slim and graceful, long-fingered, long-haired. He lined his eyes with kohl, wore gold studs in his ears, and always smelled of cloves. Mr. Spies found him so fascinating he would take him into his room at the guesthouse and photograph him for entire afternoons. Several times, he kept him back at night to photograph him at first light, which was best for portraits, he said.

One unforgettable, candlelit evening at Lisa's, after Mr. Spies had told him of the shadow theater of Bali, Afzal made a friend of his play notes on the sarod while he created an arabesque of delicate shadows on a wall using just his hands: now a bird, now a flower, two deer. In the end, Walter Spies knelt on his knees and gave each of Afzal's hands a theatrical kiss, first one, then the other.

The sound of twanging strings added to the general cacophony at Lisa McNally's guesthouse, where Beryl was trying to dance the Kathak. She did not enjoy it. "It is dull, dull, dull! Like flamenco without the eroticism! And in two weeks I'll have feet as flat as an ironing board!" A traveling salesman who was in Lisa's third room at that time complained of the noise of drumming feet, and the teacher did not take to her. In private he told my mother he had never taught a stork to dance and certainly not in an Anglo-Indian guesthouse. He was a widely respected teacher and if she wanted to learn, she would have to come to his house, where he taught his other disciples.

Our lives appeared to have found a new pattern that now included the visitors. The seismic movements that followed after my mother's first expedition to the old city with them had arrested any further attempts of the kind. Things settled into a routine. Beryl even found an old British acquaintance in the cantonment, an officer who had a piano he let Mr. Spies use. Maybe uneasy, fractious adjustments were being made at home, but I was not aware of all that. I did not feel the heat of the summer, I lived in my make-believe world with Dinu, the weather was different there. We took turns to be the Nazis that Mr. Spies had fled from or we stood in the crow's nests of ships, sighting pirates to shoot down. Sometimes we became soldiers on the revolutionary side in Spain, living off olives and wine and killing every priest in sight. I yearned to be in a real war where I could hide in jungles, shoot. I could not see that battle had already begun in Muntazir, both at home and outside.

My sense of how long the visitors had been around is hazy, and the sequence and details of most events I have been describing may be more conjecture and reconstruction than the kind of truth given as evidence in law courts. But one evening, clear in every aspect, will never leave me. Now when I think back to it, I know that was the day when the ground shifted, and a crack appeared in the earth that would turn into an abyss.

The evening plays in my head scene by scene like a film watched too many times. My father comes home, he finds Walter Spies settled in a cane chair, drawing our banyan tree, and Beryl de Zoete giving a demonstration of eurythmics in another part of the garden. Lisa is there too, in a red dress with a flared skirt, which she is holding with dainty fingertips as she tries following Beryl's steps. "Let your body flow, let it move with the earth, feel the joy," Beryl says, "and let go of your skirt!" She says the dance form is based on the principle that music's emotion must be expressed through the whole body, it should come from intense feeling. To us it appears to involve a lot of energetic waving around of hands and legs in apparently contradictory rhythms. Perhaps it looks less good to viewers than it feels to the dancer. Nevertheless, my mother whistles and cries, "Lisa, you are born to it!"

Brijen Chacha, lounging on the grass with his legs stretched out, says, *"Wah, wah!"* in the ardent manner of a visitor to a soirée of Urdu music. He has his bottle of rum with him even at that hour, and a steel glass from which he sips between his cries of appreciation. A grasshopper appears from nowhere and begins a tentative exploration of his kurta; he notices nothing but the women dancing until my mother leans forward and uses a leaf to brush the insect off his back.

My father has two students with him, earnest boys in black-framed glasses, piles of books in their arms. They gape at the dancers. Banno Didi, Ram Saran, Golak, having abandoned their work, are watching from the steps that separate the back garden from the front. For a better view, and at enough distance for our shouts of laughter to be inaudible to the grown-ups, I am standing with Dinu, Mantu, Raju, and Lambu-Chikara on the wall between Dinu's house and mine.

His students surely expected their teacher's house to be a hushed temple for books and scholarship, my father later says, and it would be all over his college the next day that Professor Nek Chand held dancing classes in his garden of a kind never before seen in Muntazir, while his wife sat there with strange men whistling at an Anglo woman in a dress. My father does not find this funny. Lose face and you lose authority; lose authority when you are a teacher and you have lost everything.

"Authority. Respect. Discipline. When has anything new ever been done by obedient little slaves? Your college sounds like a prison cell."

"Discipline does not signify slavery, Gayatri. Everything has to have method. Anarchy does not lead anywhere."

I am in the shadows outside their bedroom door and I can see my mother sitting at the dressing table tearing hairpins out of her bun one by one. On her dressing table is an overripe mango I had left there that morning and she stabs it with each uprooted hairpin until the mango turns into a messy porcupine. She throws out the yellowing strand of jasmine from her hair and shakes her head in exasperation. "I am going to take a pair of scissors and chop all this off and throw away the pins."

"What has that to do with anything?"

"Do you know there are women flying planes now? And you lecture me about authority and respect for just sitting in the garden with some friends!"

"Friends? Since when are these your friends? You did not know them a few weeks ago and now they are your friends? Is that because they are foreigners? Aren't Indians good enough for you?"

"That is ridiculous, and you know that. It is narrow-minded of you," my mother says. "Besides, Brijen was there too, and he is not a foreigner as far as I know. Neither is Lisa."

"Brijen makes the whole thing more disreputable, not less. The amount he drinks I wonder how he ever gets his books written. And I — narrow-minded! How many times have I begged you to come to the meetings with me and listen to Mukti Devi? Open your eyes to something new. Meet people who think beyond trivial selfish needs. Our country is in turmoil, our people are fighting for freedom, and you think only of yourself."

"What good will the great nation's freedom do for me? Tell me that! Will it make me free? Will I be able to choose how to live? Could I go off and be alone in a village as Walter has been doing? Could I be there and paint as well? Or walk down the street and sing a song? Could I spend a night out under the stars away from the town as your father did the other day? Even Myshkin is freer than I am! Don't talk to me about freedom."

"There's a time for everything, Gay. Now is not the time to think of your needs alone," my father says with a sigh. He is quiet for a while. When he speaks again it is in slow, patient tones, as if explaining to an especially dim student. "This is your fundamental problem. Your notion of freedom is superficial, you can't tell the difference between personal and national freedoms. What we have on our hands is a monumental battle. We are fighting to free a whole nation from foreign oppression. Men and women are sacrificing everything. They are setting their own desires aside for this. One day, after the British are thrown out, centuries of oppression will be gone and we'll all be free. The untouchables. The poor. We will wake to a new dawn in which the very air will be different. And you? You can only think of hairstyles and singing songs."

My mother turns from the dressing-table mirror to my father, her eyes blazing. "Do you know what I would do if I were free at this minute? I would leave this house. I would go away and never come back. I would go to Santiniketan and fall at Rabi Babu's feet. I would beg him for sanctuary. I would paint. I would be able to look at the sky without feeling it's a glass jar under which I'm trapped. The air would certainly be different there."

My mother flings the pin-stabbed, oozing mango into a corner of the room. She throws herself on the bed, puts her head into her hands, and starts to sob with rage. Her shoulders shake, her hair covers her face like a shawl. My father watches the yellow mess of mango-pulp trickling down the wall vomit-like, then turns back to her. He puts a cautious hand out towards her shoulder and places it there. She shakes it off.

"Listen, Gay, you are making it sound as if you are in jail," he says in pleading tones. "I don't want you to feel that way. I want you to be happy. I want you to be as happy

131

as when I first saw you. With your father . . . those days when I used to come to see him? But really to see you, you know I loved you from the start. You always waited by the door and let me in. You led me up the stairs into his study. You brought up a tray of tea. I brought you a book of Renaissance paintings. You still have it, the one with the Botticelli angels you love so much. Don't tell me I don't care for your feelings. I can't have you feeling caged, of course not. I know you had hobbies, I want you to have them. Everyone needs hobbies. Especially women, who are so bound up in the home."

My mother's sobs become louder and more uncontrollable. She is mumbling words incoherent with tears.

"I wish we didn't fight this way . . . everyone can hear us, I am sure. Can you imagine the effect on Myshkin? Don't cry, Gay, please stop. Think of him."

"Myshkin. Myshkin." My mother's voice is choked. "As though nothing else matters. As though every other part of the world stopped after Myshkin came into it." For the next few minutes the only thing audible is my mother trying savagely to stifle the spilling over of her desperation. She is scornful of tears, but today the dam she has built up inside herself has broken. My father sits beside her, wordless. Finally, he gets up from the bed.

"If that is how you feel about your own child, there is little point in continuing this conversation." He picks up a book from the side table. "Have you ever thought of my feelings? That I might have some too? That maybe you are not the only person in this house who feels imprisoned?"

My father comes towards the door and I inch into the darker part of the passageway. I stand by their bedroom for a long while after he is gone. My mother's sobs are muted now, at times nothing is audible. The moments of silence grow in length until I think it safe enough to peer into the room. I see that my mother is lying flat on her stomach, her face in a pillow buried in a dark tangle of hair, her outstretched hands clenched as if she is fighting.

The story goes about Picasso that he had an unusually accurate visual memory and when he looked at things, his gaze was deep, still, intense, as if his eyes were taking a photograph and printing it onto his brain. If he wanted to paint a new interpretation of an old picture, he would spend hours studying it at the museum, day after day, then paint from recollection. I do not know how his way of working affected the men and women who sat for him. When he was to make a portrait of Gertrude Stein he observed her for almost a year, seating her and standing before her, but he did not draw or paint a line. When he did paint her, it was from memory.

I am no Picasso. I am not an artist. Nor can I add and subtract very well as men who know how to survive do. This must account in part for my affinity with plants and is the reason why I turned my love for them into my life's work. Plants don't ask you to shape a sentence or solve an equation, they ask only that you are regularly, consistently, caring and watchful. I was. And as I observed trees and plants, I started to draw them. This was long after my mother had gone. I am a good draftsman, I have stacks of sketchbooks covered with leaves, buds, flowers, trees. I had watched how Mr. Spies drew the banyan tree at our house, concentrating on each leaf and hanging root as if every separate millimeter had to be imprinted on his mind. That tree is still in the garden, almost double its girth, and I have lost count of the number of times I have tried to draw it in his style. I watched him draw insects and flowers and dogs too. I do not have his ability to transcend mere precision, but I did imbibe from him the attention to detail I witnessed early in my life.

Mr. Percy-Lancaster was impressed by my botanical drawings, and if I was trying to describe a plant I had seen, he would always say, "Stop the talk, my boy, draw it for me." I know I can still bring back almost every line of a plant I might have seen two days or a week ago. Even though I no longer had the plant to hand, I swiftly produced an impression of it, enough for him to be able to identify it, and sometimes to compliment the drawing as "observant," or even "beautiful." Once he used the word *exquisite* and suggested I frame some of my drawings. For days after he pronounced his words of praise, they lit me up with a satisfied glow, for he was hard to please.

The reason for my digression is this: I was unsure at the start of writing down these memories what I might be able to remember. I find that as I dwell more and more intensely in the time I am describing, it is as if incidents from my childhood are playing out before my eyes again. I am not sure I want to go on. I have been waking up at night confused about where I am, and my nightmares and dreams bring up things from long ago in unrecognizable forms. There is nothing unrecognizable about my parents' terrible argument that night, though; it is as if it happened yesterday, and my mother's cry is branded on my mind.

Myshkin. Myshkin. As though nothing else matters. As though every other part of the world stopped after Myshkin came into it.

My arrival had stifled my mother, it shrank her world, it tormented her. That was how she felt about me. It had struck like a punch in the stomach then, and it has been years since I allowed myself to dwell on it. But I had to. I am writing about it.

Every now and then I wonder why I am doing this: to revisit, recall, write all of it down, who is it for? Are we our deeds, or are we the record we leave behind? Neither, maybe. I have read somewhere that someone asked Rabindranath Tagore, towards the end of his life, to write his autobiography. The poet wanted to know why. Was it because the world wanted to know about his romantic entanglements? Did prurience demand life stories? He was not going to do it. He had lived through phases so painful he could not bear to revisit them.

It is not easy for me to revisit pain either, nor is it with the idea of telling other people about my life that I am writing this. I have no descendants with questions for me, neither am I a famous man who excites curiosity. Maybe it is just a way of buying time: I have still not opened the envelope from Lisa McNally's relatives in Vancouver. It is weeks old now, locked away so that I don't see it too often and wonder what is in it. Why don't I just open it? What am I afraid of?

I am afraid of fresh pain.

Just as our feet shape new shoes for themselves so that in time they stop hurting, I have shaped my past for myself. It fits me well enough now, I can live in it. It is a shell into which I can retreat without fear of injury. I do not want to change it for a new version of the past.

As I write this, however, I also find it surprising how much I am able to revisit with perfect equanimity. Happiness, even. It wasn't so bad, not really, I said to my dogs when we went for a walk this morning. So much fishing, so much cricket. My grandfather's long-ago antics with his tiger skin and sola hat. My explorations on the big black bicycle.

See, I say to the dogs, that's where the road to the river used to go when it had not been blocked off. The river? Well, the power plant has taken over the banks so we don't want to go there anyway, but let's walk back towards the house that used to be Dinu's.

That is a five-story fortress now, where strangers live, and the low wall between the two houses that Dinu and I vaulted over a dozen times each day is ten feet high and ends in barbed wire, so we will walk past it towards my house. The only things that have not changed on Pontoon Road are the pir's tomb and my own run-down bungalow and its overgrown garden. Even the name Pontoon Road, which reminded me of a long-dismantled bridge of boats that used to straddle the river, has been changed. It does not matter to me what it is called now, in my mind it is the same.

The dogs race in through the gate, I shut it after them. The banyan tree Mr. Spies liked to draw has a full-blown bird fight on, feathers and leaves flying. And here's the stone bench where my mother sat when Beryl told her the story of Aisha cutting off her hair and turning into a man. (The swing that hung from the tree next to the bench is long gone.) Looking at the bench is easy. I can even go and sit on it and nothing happens to me. I pat a spot next to myself and both the dogs climb on, then try to push each other off. They are always tumbling around in amiable combat. The absurdity of their antics and the innocent violence of their play makes me forget everything else for a while.

Beyond us is the neem tree and then the patch at the back where I plant vegetables. I have a great ally. A gardener who used to work with me at the government nursery. He was young then, but is a middle-aged chap now, Gopal, and comes to the house once or twice a week on a creaking bicycle, with his *khurpi* tucked into his waistband. He smells of fresh manure and smoke. We have our routines, he and I. Now, in spring-time, the two of us will walk around the vegetable patch and work out where to plant the bottle gourd and yam and ladies' finger — they are the only things that grow in my garden in summer and the trick is to find them spots under trees so that they have some shade. There is very little water to give the plants. I know I sound like Mr. Percy-Lancaster when I tick off Gopal for leaving the hose-pipe on yet again.

I stayed in touch with Mr. Percy-Lancaster for years after I came back to Muntazir and even now, when I run into a horticultural problem for which there seems no solution, I think him up and talk to him, I ask him what I should do. I imagine his reply, all his possible replies, and it moves me towards something like an answer to my problem. I have had long years of practice speaking to absent people, those who left too early, our conversation unfinished. There are days when, in retrospect, my questions seem foolish, and I feel I should never have asked them. At such times I am reminded of Mr. Percy-Lancaster's habit of coming up with Chinese proverbs. He produced them like rabbits out of a hat, he had one for every occasion. "Better to stay silent and be thought a fool than to open mouth and remove all doubt" was one with which he shut me up when I asked him something particularly foolish, and though I forget what the provocation was now, the horse sense of the proverb remained and has worked well for me, making me cherish the value of reticence, recognize the maddening ability that words seem to have to slip your grasp and say what you never intended, or to fall far short of saying what you so badly wanted them to.

One of Mr. Percy-Lancaster's frequent complaints was that the gardeners did not know the difference between light and heavy watering. "They'll leave the hose on till the bed is entirely flooded, and the next lawn and the road beyond." Managing the greenery of the city of Delhi was his passion and anything that stood in his way incensed him. It could be parakeets ruining baby corncobs or jackals digging up flower beds. It could be gardeners sowing things awry and disregarding instructions in spite of years of training. Despite all the frustration, though, there was nothing other than gardening that he wanted to do.

Once, when I told him I was thinking of finding a more lucrative occupation and getting married (there was that time in my life too), he had his Chinese proverb ready: "If you wish to be happy for an hour, drink wine; if you wish to be happy for three days, get married. If you wish to be happy for eight days, kill your pig and eat it; but if you wish to be happy forever, become a gardener."

"The horticultural department," he told me, "is unable, for lack of facilities, to assist in getting you wine, wife, or pig, but we can help you become a gardener."

6

Walter Spies came to see my grandfather much more often than his friends did, almost every day when he was not out in the villages. He came back from his rural outings laden with crude little string instruments, terra-cotta cups, clay animals, bamboo flutes he tried without success to play. He brought them to Dada and their heads together, one blond, one white, bent over some broken-down bit of clay, became an everyday sight at the clinic. Afterwards they would sit wreathed in the smoke from their two pipes, drinking cups of the sweet, thick tea that Jagat, my grandfather's man Friday, made in the lulls between patients. Mr. Spies told Dada he felt at peace in the clinic, and considered it an eccentric shop where one could find anything: good health, tea, knowledge, or an antique chaise longue. Once he found crackly old piles of sheet music someone had left, and these kept him occupied for days. If Mr. Spies had to wait while Dada examined patients, he was content to sketch people waiting their turn outside the folding doors or to scribble notes into a book he carried with him.

They were strange drawings, Dada told my mother. "You'd be puzzled, Gayatri, how oddly childish they are, and yet they are not childish at all."

"I've seen his drawings, they are very good," my mother said.

"It's what they call modern art," my father said. "Maybe he can't draw."

"He is no amateur. I'd say it's likely we are in the presence of genius — no, really, don't make a face, how many of us are able to know a genius when we meet one? We can't because we are ordinary."

"Genius! That is like saying Brijen is a real writer. He is not. He's a hack. This Spies seems ordinary enough to me," my father said.

"Not at all, Nek. I think we haven't been able to . . . to grasp his brilliance."

"Brilliance!"

"Yes, that is what I said. The man is neither boastful nor dismissive nor temperamental so you take him for ordinary. Actually, I'm sure I've never met anyone so unpretentious before who calls himself an artist," Dada said. "Beryl tells me Walter had the best teachers in Europe. She says he worships a painter called Rousseau and has learned from some very famous artists called . . . what did she say now? Otto Dix and . . . ?"

"Clay," I said, "Paul Clay."

"Yes, of course, Paul Klee. Myshkin, what would I do without you?" Dada said, patting me on a shoulder. "Gayatri, please tell Banno the potatoes need more butter."

"I think she feeds all our butter to her children," my mother said. "I can't make sense of where it's going if not into the potatoes. We made a great big tub of butter the other day — Myshkin and Dinu helped to churn it, didn't you? And now it's half-empty."

"What's all this fuss about butter? Mukti Devi eats just two meals a day — daal-roti and boiled vegetables, sometimes a bit of milk at dawn after her prayers. A little goes a long way when you understand that you eat to live, not live to eat. That is what Gandhiji says you should do. Control your appetites, all appetites. I wish I were strong-minded enough."

"Worse than a Bengali widow's food," my mother murmured.

"A Bengali widow's diet is a good one.

144

Wholesome and plain. The food on this table? It could feed a poor family for two days. In a country where half the population gets nothing to eat. Try to learn from others. We can't be born knowing everything. At least have an open mind, Gayatri."

"Open mind?" my mother whispered. "Where is your open mind when it comes to paintings?" With my father, her voice was usually low and controlled, in contrast to his declamatory tones. Yet he never failed to hear things that appeared to contradict him.

"I like paintings where I can tell what I'm looking at," he said. "I understand abstractions when they are in words. But why should a picture on your wall need explaining? Shouldn't pictures be beautiful? What else should they be? Would you like flowers to turn into frogs in real life?"

"Walter was imprisoned in a camp in Russia during the war — because he was German — and he discovered new things. Cubism, futurism, expressionism, he calls them. He found beauty and meaning in lines and squares and circles," Dada explained, helping himself to more fish. "And after that he discovered the work of this Rousseau, he says, and it changed him forever."

"I don't blame him, if he was imprisoned. Lined up and encircled," my father said, with a sarcastic smile.

"Come, come, Nek, don't be prejudiced. That's not what a scholar should be," Dada said. "Especially a teacher of history." Dada had a rueful way of shaking his head that made you feel you had disappointed him. He had a hooked nose, a forehead that swept up from it into thick silver hair and bright, appraising eyes that made people feel they were in the presence of someone they needed to impress but might not manage to. Maybe my father had felt this way all his life.

"I have a very open mind, I read all kinds of literature . . ." my father began.

"How can you condemn pictures you have never seen?" my mother said, putting another piece of fried fish on my plate. "They may be good in a different way. Myshkin, eat that, please, don't just push it around. Literature has nothing to do with it, people who understand words often cannot understand other things."

"I'm not condemning anything," my father burst out. "I was just joking."

"You make these opinions sound like jokes, but that's not what they are," my mother said.

"A man can have an opinion, can't he, even if he isn't an artist? That Englishwoman in black is ridiculous, she springs about on the verandah at the guesthouse and calls it dance. Why don't you tell Lisa to put a stop to it? I come across people gawping from the pavement. Do they even know what dance is, in the West? All they have is ballet and all ballet is swans pirouetting on toes. Think of the number of dance forms we have! It'll take them a lifetime to write their dance book. Shakeel was saying the other day that this German artist struck him as a fraud. And Shakeel's been to Europe and seen all the art there is to see."

It was my father's habit to quote either Mukti Devi or his advocate friend Shakeel as the final word on everything under the sun. Shakeel was widely read, my father liked to say, he was a true scholar, a man who could turn his mind to anything.

Shakeel Uncle held his head at an angle and had one eyeball that did not move — Dinu said it was made from the bottom of a soda bottle. Each time he came, he fixed his good eye on me while the soda-bottle one aimed opaquely at something else, and he ordered me to name the Mughal emperors in the correct sequence.

"Why stop at Aurangzeb?" he demanded when I faltered. "What happened between him and Bahadur Shah? Is not all of our present misery contained in those years? Well, young Master Rozario, any thoughts?" He would wave a peeling, gray-skinned forefinger at me before sinking into a chair to slurp tea and discuss politics with my father.

My mother's dislike of him bordered on loathing and the mention of his name ignited one of her sudden, scorching tempers now. She put a spoon down with a clang into the serving dish. My grandfather shifted uneasily in his chair and made as if to get up. "Some people have no time for what doesn't match their view of the world," my mother said. "They think they know all there is to know and nobody can bring them anything new. They squeeze the joy out of life, dry it up, and chop it into a set of pellets they call rules. What is a good picture, what is a good book, what is the food you should eat — they know it all."

When she realized her voice was raised and her words were coming out in a torrent, my mother stopped and pushed the dishes on the table around, passing the fish to Dada and the butter to me although neither of us had asked for anything. I kept my eyes on my plate and chewed the cold fried fish. I did not know then that Dada felt as much at a loss as I did when my parents fought this way at the dining table. Were we to carry on eating as if they were not fighting? Should we speak up too, take sides? My head was a muddle at such times. I wished the meal would end, I kept stealing glances at the long wall clock whose uncompromising arrows jerked no faster than usual to nine o'clock, the hour I was allowed to leave the table. A giant spider was exploring the green curtains that covered one side of the dining room. It might have been the Englishwoman in the black tunic stepping long-legged on grass. In a lame aside Dada said, "Today a patient told me he was losing his sense of smell. What could be done? What did it mean? He can't taste food anymore because he can't smell."

For some time nobody could think of anything to say. Sounds outside the room amplified. Someone squabbling in the kitchen; the fan whirring, the frog croaking in the garden as it always did at this time of night. The high-pitched whine of Dada's breath that made him cough and replenish his stock of air. At last Banno Didi came in with a golden dome of a pudding shivering on its platter. Ribbons of syrup trickled down its sides and it stood in a pool of shining caramel. When Banno Didi set it down on the table all of us just looked at it for a while.

"Now, that is what I call art," my father said. "Someday there will be art you can eat. First you observe it and make deep, learned notes on it for an essay, then you eat it and write more notes."

My father could sometimes produce the most mischievous of smiles and when it came, however brief its effect, it was miraculous. My mother remained unmoved, but Dada heaved a sigh of relief and said, "Now, won't that be delicious, eh, Myshkin?" The pudding, which had seemed enormous when it was brought in, began to shrink fast. A small last piece remained that everyone pretended not to notice until my father took his spoon to it. He held the spoonful of pudding poised over his plate for a second, after which he tipped it onto my mother's. My mother gave him a polite, tight smile. She picked up the piece with her spoon. We waited for her to eat it. "Myshkin should have that," my mother said. "He remembered the artist's name."

My father sat in silence as I ate the last spoonful. Once dinner was cleared away, my mother retreated to their bedroom. She had a terrible headache, she said.

We slept on the roof in summer, my

parents and I. Dada said the night air no longer suited him and kept to his bedroom, however stifling the heat. Our rooftop cots had bamboo posts to hang mosquito nets from and once I was inside, it was a room of my own under the open sky with my parents a little distance away. That night my father sent me up, saying he would follow soon. I lay in the dark with my head covered so that the ghosts in the trees would not see me. I could hear Brijen Uncle on the roof next door, singing a slow, meandering thumri. He usually sat on their roof drinking till late into the night and occasionally his voice stopped as he took a sip, then it came back again. The mad rooster which crowed only at night interrupted the singing, but Brijen Chacha went on with his mysterious, melodious song as if oblivous. I was starting to fall asleep when I heard footsteps on the stairs. I threw the sheet off my head and cried, "Where were you? I was scared."

"What's there to be scared of?" my father said in a tired voice. "You sleep here every night, has anything ever happened?" He had a jug in his hand. He made me get up from the bed and sprinkled water over the mattress to cool it down. He did not sprinkle any on the other bed where he and my mother slept. Instead of getting into their bed, he lifted the mosquito net on mine. "Is there room for me?" he said.

We lay on the cool, damp sheet inside our mosquito net, looking up at the night sky through its sieve. My father waved a breeze over us with a palm-leaf fan, letting it fall every now and then when his arm tired. Brijen Chacha started on another meditative song in a voice that now sounded somewhat drowsy.

"Tell me again about how I was born."

"You've heard it so many times, Myshkin, be quiet and listen to Brijen. He is singing well today."

"No. Again."

"One summer morning your Dada was in the garden and a very, very old man in a faded blue kurta opened our gate and entered. How old? Maybe a hundred years old. He had no teeth. His head was shriveled up like an ancient lemon. His shoulders were bent. Dada thought he was tired so he asked the old man, would you like a glass of water? Some *sharbat*? The old man said he needed to catch a train all the way to Kanpur to meet his daughter, but he had lost his money. Someone had stolen it from his bag, now what was he to do? He had nobody in Muntazir, no home, no relatives, no friends. Dada got up and went inside, brought his wallet out, and gave the old man enough money for his train and more, enough to eat on the way and to find his daughter."

"Was it stupid of Dada to trust a stranger or was it kind?"

"You tell me, Myshkin."

"Dada was kind. It is wiser to be stupid and kind than to be clever and cold. The old man told him, you have been kind to a stranger so I will be kind to you. I am actually a wizard and I grant you two wishes."

"And what was the wish your grandfather made?"

"You tell me."

"Your grandfather's first wish was that he should have a grandson just like you. So you were born. His second wish was that all of us, Dada, you, your mother, and I, would live here happily ever after with many dogs, lots of food, and flowers in the garden. And he made a third wish I never told you about before. That this grandson should go to sleep early at night."

The next afternoon, Beryl de Zoete arrived carrying a bag with her dresses. She handed it to my mother saying, "If you would be such an angel and have your woman launder

153

them. Miss McNally's washing is . . . well, the kindest thing one can say is that the clothes in her washtub cry out for soap, but soap rarely answers their call." Beryl de Zoete had often asked these things of my mother in the weeks they had been there. She begged for music, ink, dressmakers, shopping tips, notebooks, washed clothes, boiled drinking water, Flit spray, books to read. This infuriated my father.

My mother took the laundry bag from her with a tired smile. Beryl de Zoete narrowed her eyes and said, "It's not that time of month, is it? You're like an owl blundering in daylight." My mother turned away and Beryl pursued her. "It's pointless for me to go to those dances just with Walter. Neither of us understands anything. What will I do? I am not at all good at being learned. Everything I speak of I have seen with my own eyes and felt with my heart. You help me to see and feel. Can't you come with us?"

My mother's head drooped. "I . . . actually, there is so much to do at home. And I haven't been feeling very well."

Why had my mother got it all wrong? I could not understand how she had forgotten all the things my father had told her just the other night. I said, "My father has said she must not leave the house and go running about the city with foreigners."

"Shhh, Myshkin. Be quiet!"

"My father says all of you are welcome to come home when the rest of us are here . . ." At this point a rap on my head stopped me saying anything more.

"Haven't I told you a hundred times not to talk out of turn? When older people are talking?"

"In Bali, something always happens to revive your spirits when something has happened to crush them. Here too. It will be the same," Beryl de Zoete said, paying no attention to my mother's exchange with me. "Whatever feels insurmountable today — we will glide through it tomorrow, we will pirouette and twirl through it." She took her purple scarf off her neck and draped it over my mother's shoulders. "Now, that suits you much better than that drab brown you're wearing today, don't you think? Brings color to those lovely golden cheeks. You have enchanting eyes, child, go and wash them, put a smile and some red lipstick on. Think of tomorrow — which is always, but always, a new day. That's such a comfort."

My mother's face lit up, as if she had had an idea. "Wait, Beryl," she said, "sit and read something. I won't take a minute." She put the scarf aside on a chair, tucked the end of her sari into her waist, and gathered her hair into a tight bun as she ran to the kitchen and summoned Golak. Together they fried the whole pile of samosas she had filled with stuffing through the day. They were meant to be for our teatime, and I knew my father was looking forward to them, but she handed the warm, aromatic package to Beryl. "For you and Walter," she said. "To say sorry for no longer being able to help you with your dance work."

My father came home from work and I heard him say, "Only toast? I thought you were making samosas." He pushed the toast around on his plate. He had a long, gentle face and now it suddenly became longer. His dominant feature was large, dark eyes which seemed to concentrate a private universe of anguish and passion in them. One of his colleagues told me much later — with some envy even though he was by then past retirement — that most girl students at the college were in love with my father when he was their teacher and thought of him as impossibly handsome, unbearably tragic, and in need of succor.

My mother remained unmoved.

"I thought you had lost your taste for fried

food," she said. "I thought Mukti Devi had told you gluttony was a sin greater than pride or dishonesty?"

My father dipped his chewy, cold toast into his tea to soften it. A part of it plopped into the teacup.

7

Whatever the crises in my parents' lives —
their contrary sense of wrongdoing and
right-thinking, their clashing views of necessities and indulgences, freedom and captiv-
ity — the first crisis in my personal moral
universe came that summer from an entirely
unexpected quarter.

Those days, mealtimes apart, neither Dinu
nor I were much seen inside our homes. We
fished or played, mainly with Banno Didi's
sons Raju and Mantu and Dinu's driver's
son, Lambu, who was a few years older than
us. His face was already volcanic with
pimples. He resembled nothing so much as
a coconut tree: his long, thin, somewhat
stooped frame had the same narrow girth
from hip to shoulders and culminated in a
giant bush of hair that stood on end no matter what. We used to dance a jig around him,
singing out a nonsensical rhyme making fun
of his height that began, *"Lambu chikara,*

Doh anne may barah." He would join in with gusto even though the jingle was in no way complimentary to him. But he was wiry and strong and we relied on his narrow shoulders to reach tree branches or shelves too high for us.

Lambu was our bridge to the adult world. He taught us to smoke, he knew which of the garden weeds was marijuana, and it was from him that we acquired a rudimentary acquaintance with sex and the body parts relevant to it. This happened one evening when Lambu was making a pile of rotis in a shed outside the kitchens of Dinu's house. He beckoned us with a dough-encrusted finger. "Want to see something? Keep it to yourselves."

The shed was lit by an oil lamp. Beyond the reach of the lamp were dark shadows in which bales of hay, alive with mice, were piled one on top of the other. Nobody from Dinu's family ever came here.

We squatted beside Lambu as he patted his mound of dough into a round, shaped it some more, then bisected it carefully with the tip of his little finger. "See?" he said.

"Of course," Dinu said. "It's easy." Dinu never liked to confess ignorance, he was happier bluffing when he was out of his depth. All I could see was a big lump of dough. I said so.

"Buttocks, you ass," Lambu said, following it up with more sculptures of the same kind. He accompanied his artwork with a lecture on the sexual possibilities of every body part he was molding out of the dough. We were spellbound.

The next day, Dinu put his knowledge to use by drawing dirty pictures on the walls of our school toilets. I never found out how the pictures were traced back to the artist, but it was followed by a summons to Dinu from his father. Dinu went to his office room, where Arjun Chacha locked the door and kept it locked for a long time. I was not told what transpired inside. All that Dinu would say afterwards was that he would break the neck of the person who had tattled to his father about Lambu's role in the saga because his father had come to the conclusion that Lambu was a bad influence on Dinu, and needed to be sent away. He had sacked the driver and ordered him to clear out of the servants' quarters with his family by the evening. When the driver groveled and wept, Arjun Chacha consented to give him work at the family cloth mill in Kanpur on condition that when he left Muntazir, he would take his misbegotten son with him.

I know now that a move to a cloth mill then was practically a prison sentence for a man used to living in the countryside. The machinery at those mills was old and badly maintained and the men worked long shifts month after month under asbestos and tin in broiling heat until their bodies collapsed or a machine killed them. Lambu's father knew what was ahead.

The night the driver was condemned to the cloth mill, we were woken by guttural cries, high-pitched wails, men's voices, women's voices, a child crying, things falling. From our roof we saw Banno Didi, Golak, and Ram Saran hurrying to Dinu's, lanterns in hand. We could see people come and go into the compound behind Dinu's house, crowd around, disperse. Then a few heart-rending screams and silence for a moment, after which the noise started all over again, even louder now.

In the morning, from Banno Didi, who told it with much relish, we came to know that Arjun Chacha's driver, blind drunk and crazed with rage at losing his job, had beaten up Lambu. Who told him to make friends with Sahib's son? Didn't he know servants needed to keep a distance?

Lambu, taller and stronger than his father, had hit back. His mother had tried pulling her husband and son apart. Others jumped into the fray. And then the driver charged at his son with a grinding stone and bludgeoned him with it. Blow after blow. Nobody could stop him. The stone smashed one side of Lambu's face, shattered his rib cage, and broke an arm. Lambu was in hospital now, in a coma. One side of his face was like jelly.

"If he'd had a cleaver he'd have chopped the boy to pieces," Banno Didi said with relish. Golak could produce no response macabre enough to match this and said, "Why, I have a cousin who once sliced his thumb clean off with a knife." Banno Didi snorted with the contempt this pathetic accident called for.

That day, I did not seek out Dinu. I spent it lurking in the broken-down old carriage in a corner of our garden and when everyone had eaten lunch and the usual afternoon lull had taken over, I ran down to the river. I lay flat on the riverbank, arms outstretched, ears to the scorched ground. The grass was yellow, the reeds on its bank were burnt brown, the river had receded, baring several yards of dark, fissured earth. The sun hung in a haze of dust and the water was too dazzling to look at for long. If I opened my eyes, I saw the shadows of black kites wheeling overhead like omens, so I shut them and pressed my ears closer to the ground. Maybe I was crying, although now, hardened by Ivan the Terrible of Olympus Circus and my mother's view of tears, I did not often give in to them. I started to feel the grass scratchy against my nose, hear the buzz of insects. I heard a voice next to me, very soft, saying, "What is it you are listening to?"

It was Walter Spies. He had swum across from the other side as he did almost every day, and now he spread his towel and lay on the grass beside me, still wet and smelling of river water. "Is it the earth you are listening to?" He pressed his ear to the ground as well.

"Can you hear the sound of the earth?" I said.

Walter Spies's face was next to mine, and his eyes were shut as he concentrated. "I can. A sound like thunder, everlastingly, yes," he said. He pressed my head down with his hand, gently. "Listen! The mighty being is awake."

"What mighty being?"

Walter Spies burst out laughing. He ruffled my hair. "It is from a poem. An English poem Beryl likes a lot and she recites it every time the sun sets nicely. I think the

163

poet means God. But how can we ever know what poets mean?"

We turned and lay on our backs. It was hazier still, the kites were gone, the light was yellow and murky, a storm was coming. The wind was gathering somewhere, you could sense it.

Before I knew what I was saying, I had said it. "Lambu will die. It was my fault." While Dinu was sitting in detention at school for drawing those pictures the way Lambu had shown us, it was I who had run home bursting with knowledge that nobody else had, needing to tell someone. The minute Dinu's older brother asked me a few questions about why Dinu was late, I had blurted out Lambu's role in his disgrace. Dinu's brother had told Arjun Chacha and he had sent away the driver and now Lambu might die.

"But it was the boy's father who hit him," Mr. Spies said. "Not you. If you had not said anything someone else might have. Such things, they are never hidden for long."

Tears did fill my eyes now and water ran down my nose. I tried not to sniff or sob. I did not lift my head.

I heard the rustle of paper and the familiar sounds of a pipe being tapped, a match struck. I could smell tobacco smoke. I thought of how Beryl de Zoete hated tobacco smoke. Then I thought of Lambu, and how I might never see him again even if he lived, and misery clutched at my throat again.

"I was very sad this morning," I heard Mr. Spies say. "I was thinking of someone I was close to. My cousin, Conrad. Kosya I used to call him. He came to Bali because of me. His work was to take care of my animals — I have many, you know."

"How many?" I did not raise my head.

"Oh, monkeys, birds. Frogs. Many animals. I always thought nature was the best thing, jungle the best place of all. That is what I told Kosya. We walked in the jungles and swam in the sea. It was joy. One day someone told him that in the Balinese astrological calendar, something they use to tell the future — it said Kosya would be eaten by Kala Rau. What is Kala Rau? A big fish. What is the future? Who knows the future? I laughed my head off, told him to just go and swim and not be stupid. Some weeks later, the water was cloudy so nobody wanted to swim, but Conrad stripped off his clothes and raced in. He fooled around, he screamed and shouted, he made faces. So much that when he really did scream for help, we paid no attention. I worship nature.

But terrible things happen in nature all the time. His right leg was bitten off by a shark. We took him to hospital, he didn't live. For a long time I was tormented. I was in great grief. I thought, Bali is saying go back, you will be destroyed here. You have done something wrong. You did not warn Kosya about the sharks."

Mr. Spies put a hand on my shoulder and said, "But that was not it. Bali was not telling me anything."

His eyes were very blue in the afternoon light. His gaze had the intensity of a magnifying glass trained on paper to burn it with refracted sunlight. "The calendar was nothing," he said. "The shark did what nature told it to do. Some combination of forces larger than Kosya or me or the shark had driven him to his death. It was a tragedy. A tragedy is too big for you to see it coming or stop it. If we could see ahead and know the future there might be no tragedies."

I told nobody else about my conversation on the riverbank with Mr. Spies. I do not know why I had broken my habit of reserve to speak to him, almost a stranger, but it was as if the world had contracted for some moments to the riverbank that day, he and I sitting on it, and in that contracted world I was safe, I could say anything and be comforted. For years afterwards, I would speak to an imaginary Mr. Spies if I was troubled, as if he were really there, a friend I could trust. In some intangible way, what he said that afternoon diluted the intensity of my horror at what had happened to Lambu, though for many weeks after that, when I was alone in my cot in the darkness, all I could see if I shut my eyes was his face, as misshapen as melted wax, resting in a nest of flowers on the bier which the servants were to carry on their shoulders to the cremation ground. The head kept lolling to the right, whatever Lambu's mother, broken with weeping, did to keep it still in the center.

8

Yesterday, I paused in my writing and drew up a calendar. I had to use reasoning rather than memory to do this. As far as I can be sure about months and weeks during that summer of 1937, Walter Spies and Beryl de Zoete came in early May — they had been there awhile when Lambu was killed, sometime in late May or early June. Our summer holidays must have started soon after — the next thing I remember is the few weeks when we went as usual to the Kumaon hills for the holidays. I used to count the days till the journey, the excitement of it building up in me as I crossed out squares on the calendar. After the train dropped you off at the railhead, you had to go on horseback the rest of the way, halting at night in wayside villages. Almost our whole household traveled with us on mules: pots and pans, stoves, bedding, lanterns, blankets. Golak and Rikki. Nothing more thrilling happened all year.

We would troop into the courtyard of the cottage my grandfather rented each summer and go from room to room, then out into the garden, exclaiming over the baby peaches on trees or a new bird's nest. From the windows you could see the snow peaks, and far below in the valley squares of yellow and green fields quilted around white village huts. In the mountains I did not need to be shaken awake in the morning, my eyes opened to the sun pouring through the skylight.

My mother had a feverish lightheartedness about her through the holidays. Maybe this was because my father only came up to the hills for a week, or ten days at most. "It's the best time for research and real work. Summer," he wrote to us. "Peace at home, to read and write as long as I please. Library empty at the college." He spent his days working alone, meeting Shakeel in the evenings, going on his early morning walks. "I can concentrate wholly and entirely on ancient India through the morning and on philosophical works in the evenings. I have made a notebook in which, each day, I write down an important thought that has crossed my mind. Yesterday my thought was this: that every thinking man needs solitude and freedom if he is to realize his full mental potential. In the days of old, ascetics went away to meditate. We can no longer do so now, we have jobs, we have families. But could the Buddha have been the Buddha if he had stayed home? What a laughable thought. I will bring up the notebook and read out my list of thoughts to you all when I come. I am impatient to be there. How contradictory feelings are! We want to be hermits one day and family men the next."

Neither my father nor his notebook of virtuous thoughts had arrived when Walter Spies and Beryl de Zoete appeared one day. I do not know if Dada had invited them or if they had hatched the plan with my mother. All I recall is that one afternoon there was a great deal of noise just as we were sitting down to lunch and they were there, followed by an extravagant caravan of mules laden with bottles of whisky and gin for Dada, and boxes of food for us. Our days became festive. Golak would go off to buy provisions and come back followed by a woman with a basket on her head in which chickens squawked anxiously under a net, their heads poking out between bottle gourd and brinjal. My mother went off with the visitors to distant hillsides, painting and sketching, far beyond the need for food or

170

drink. When the three of them came back laden with pinecones and stories of the animals they had sighted, my mother refused to tell me why she would not take me with her.

"I can't take you everywhere. Besides, your grandfather needs company" was all she would say, locking me into sulks that I could not free myself from for half a day. Her joy had a wild edge that made me wary of her, as if she had turned into a stranger: eyes sparkling, hair loose, she gathered armloads of wildflowers and flitted around the house turning every spare jar or bottle into a vase. The slightest thing would charge her with excitement. "Come and see," she would cry out. "A giant moth on this windowsill!"

We lost track of days of the week. Every morning began with the luxurious promise of a whole day and evening and night of enjoyment. But my father was to arrive quite soon and Mr. Spies and Beryl had already been with us for a week. They were thinking of departure. It was left unsaid, but it was understood that they would leave before my father came.

Dada said, "What's the hurry? Don't you know what the sage said?"

Beryl and Dada spent hours together in

the wood-bound verandah that skirted the cottage. Here they read day-old newspapers and wrote letters and at some hour that was mysteriously settled by unspoken mutual consent, they began sipping gin with drops of juice from the yellow and green lemons that hung like paper lanterns from a tree in a corner of the garden.

Beryl looked up from her paper. "What did your sage say?"

"Oh, I don't really remember. I'm quite sure it was something on the lines of 'Why go when you have just arrived, O weary traveler!' We are to harvest our apricots today. Wouldn't you like to stir the jam?"

On the eighth evening, after apricot tart had been eaten and Mr. Spies had played "Ode to Joy" on his harmonica, and Beryl had objected yet again to everyone smoking indoors, she said, "Well, tomorrow we must really ask for the horses and be off. The mountains will not come to us, we must go to them, Walter. Almora is next. Mightn't it be possible to persuade Gay to come with us?"

On the tenth afternoon, they were still there when there was a telegram from my father: *Mukti Devi arrested. Cannot come as planned.*

"What could have happened?" Dada said.

"Should we pack up and return? I hope Nek does not end up in jail with her."

"The politicians who go to prison do rather well! They write books, make friends. They don't become any thinner."

"Gayatri!" Dada said. "Do be serious. Mukti Devi may be too frail for prison."

"Why would they put that harmless old lady in jail?" Beryl said. "My countrymen. Oh, such idiocy! What is the world doing to itself? Look at Walter's country."

"Germany is not my country," Mr. Spies said. "My country is the world." He went back to his harmonica.

"Darling, don't be frivolous and don't interrupt, please. What if there is a war? How many people can one rescue from fiends?"

Mr. Spies put his harmonica down and said, "If the world is in danger, we must still sing and dance and live. I am free in Asia. We are oceans away from all that."

"Nobody is oceans away from anything, Walter. The world is round and oceans meet," my grandfather said. "When you have lived to be as old as I am, you will understand that no place is safe from evil. Did anyone take Hitler seriously when he first said he would wipe out Jews? Fifteen years ago! I remember how in the twenties everyone was sure he would go back to Austria and tend his vegetable patch."

"I don't think of all that. What we have to think of is how to live a life, love a life, play a life, be there at the heart of life. And not go on about the earnest things, worrying ourselves to death. I think I'll learn how to play the bamboo flute. I can't get the sound of it out from my head."

"Oh, do be sensible, Walter Spies," Beryl said. "If they have Mukti in jail, they might arrest Nek next. Is it not widely known that he is her chief confidant?"

"Anxiety, anxiety! We're in danger of dying from it. We live in despair. We work in despair when we must work from delight! You wear yourself out, time sweeps by, you are tired, and then you want to get away from it all, where life can be forgotten. Even music and art become a reward for *putting up with life* — which is full of imagined fears and worries. How can I help it if life will not take me seriously?"

Mr. Spies picked me up and gave me a whirl. "Life is one long birthday. Or if it's not, we have to make it so. Let others fight. For me, I believe that people may kill each other and countries may explode but there is music in everything, beauty everywhere. We just have to find it. Mr. Tagore found it,

Gayatri has found it. Don't let them ever tell you otherwise, Myshkin Rozario."

Mr. Spies lived his philosophy, he did find music in everything. One night, there was a sharp spell of rain. The next morning, breathing in the washed air, he asked me to tell him how many sounds I had heard during the night. I came up with the sound of rain on the roof. I offered thunder. Mr. Spies listed at least half a dozen more. The sound of water gurgling in the drains. The sound of rain on tile roofs, which is different from rain on tin roofs or brick roofs. The sound of water trickling onto mud. The croaking of frogs and toads, the chirring of crickets and cicadas. The whoosh of wind in the trees. The creak of branches when the trees swayed in the wind.

Another day or two, and a letter came from my father summoning us home. Mukti Devi was in the lockup in Muntazir and things were in a state of crisis. We ought to be home to show solidarity. We could not carry on with our holidays as if nothing had happened.

And so we began our journey downhill while Beryl and Walter carried on to Almora. They would come back to Muntazir after a few days in the hills, they said, and then, by and by, it would be time for them to pack their trunks and go back home.

On our way up, every step had been an adventure; the way down was nothing but drudgery. The horses smelled of dung, Rikki got lost twice on the road to the railhead. Dada had to lie down in a wayside verandah because the heat made him feel faint. Golak had a stomach upset and kept dashing off behind bushes. Each time we had to wait for Golak or shout for Rikki, Dada sat on any rock or parapet that offered itself, drooping, as if he might never get up again. When we reached the dak bungalow where we were to break our journey the beds were infested with bugs and we woke covered with red, itchy weals.

From the moment we were in the train and it began moving, my mother leaned her head against the window bars and was lost to us. Her eyes were on the countryside rushing past, and twice I saw them shining with tears. She did not stir, she had forgotten we were there. I was hungry, Rikki was sniffing the bags for food, and Dada lay on a bunk, hollow-cheeked and hollow-eyed, his breathing shallow, his legs seizing up with cramps. He whispered, "Mix some salt and sugar into a cup of water, bring it here. Don't worry, it's a simple heatstroke." Golak and I took turns at tipping sugared water into Dada's mouth. He gasped and opened his mouth like a chick in a nest. He would drift off to sleep and so would I. I would wake to see my mother still by the window, staring sightlessly out, her hair blown back by the wind. The hours passed. She ate nothing, drank nothing, spoke not a word.

Mukti Devi was meditating on the roof of the ashram when just after three in the morning, the hour she usually woke for her prayers, the police arrived. They had barely even given her time to put her prayer beads away. The few followers who lived in the Society building with her were given no answers to their agitated questions: Where was she being taken? Was she under arrest? They could see the shadowy bulk of a police van on the still-dark street. One of the officers put a hand on Mukti Devi's shoulders to propel her towards the door and it was this gesture, more than the van or the unearthly hour, that appalled her followers. That a bully in a uniform had the power to touch their revered leader this way. What else might they not do? She was old, her health was shaky, how could she survive the impending brutality?

When she was arrested, my father said,

her courage became more apparent than ever. A woman alone, being marched off to prison by a squad of burly men, yet she showed no signs of fear. She gave her followers a set of instructions in a steady voice. She told them not to make any trouble. They were to do exactly the same as they did when she was with them: spin the loom, meditate, pray, demonstrate against British rule, but only as peacefully as the Mahatma had instructed. They were to put food out for the birds, dogs, cows, and cats who were fed daily at the Society.

The truth was that the British feared her influence. They were finding it difficult to dismiss her as a crank now that her morning sermons drew two hundred people. A few days before her arrest, she had held a meeting in the dusty patch by the river, to which more than a thousand people had come, many trudging from distant villages. She had urged her followers to make sure there were no Union Jacks flying on any Indian building by the year's end. She had meant it metaphorically, my father said, but some overcharged protesters had stormed off to the courthouse and the post office and torn down several flags and burnt them on the riverside promenade — where Indians were not allowed to walk, far less set fires. They had also placed an upturned bucket on the head of the statue of Curzon that stood at the entrance to the college where my father taught. Tear-gas shells and beatings had followed.

Given the unrest it was thought prudent to send Mukti Devi to a jail in another town where fewer people knew of her. The police took care to transport her at an out-of-the-way hour, early in the morning, yet the road from police station to railway station was jammed with people. My father was among them. Overnight, he had discarded the circumspection that had made him shelter in the shadows. He no longer appeared to care about holding on to his government job. He was at the front of the barriers that held the crowds back from the driveway down which the police van would come. He had taken me along because this was history in the making and I needed to be part of it. He held my hand in the surging crowds, only letting go for an instant when the police van appeared and we saw Mukti Devi's face behind the barred windows of the van. I half-expected her to call me to her and whisper a rhyme in my ear, but her white sari was wrapped around her head, her face was barely visible, and all she did when she saw the gathered people was bow her head and join her hands in a namaste. The van swept out of the police station and we followed on foot. Nobody shouted or shoved now. It was as subdued as a funeral. We were not allowed to enter the railway station. We saw the police van going into the station through a gate that we did not know existed.

It was just a day or two ago that we had got off our train from Kathgodam, but the bustling station we had seen then had been turned into a prison yard guarded by lines of men in khaki. I tugged at my father's hand to make him go home. But he stayed until word went around that the train had left.

"Where to? Where to?" everyone shouted.

"Lucknow," someone yelled back.

The crowd scattered as if a show had ended at the cinema.

In a few days, schools and colleges opened, my father had to return to work. He did go back, but there was a new sense of reserve in him about his college. He would work not an iota more than he had to, he said. He no longer bothered with whether my mother was reading Brijen Chacha's detective novels or wasting time painting or gallivanting with her foreign friends. If he came home and found Mr. Spies or

Beryl de Zoete there, he paused for a minute only to be civil and then kept himself out of sight until they had gone. Twice he went to Lucknow to visit Mukti Devi in jail. He came back vibrating with reverence.

"She is an inspiration to all women — this is what the liberation of women is about," he said. Emotion made his voice shake. My mother got up and left the room.

My father began to do much more at the Society. He went with groups of people to villages to teach them about irrigation, crop rotation, fertilizers. Or the others with him did, while he gave lessons to village children. After his college hours he went to teach at an evening school for the unlettered poor. A tide of nationalistic fervor was sweeping the country, he told us, because of inspirational figures like Mukti Devi. He began to lead the early morning walks — she had asked him to. The walks did not end with a daily sermon from him, but a thought for the day from anyone who had one serious enough. The everyday thought was not unpremeditated, it had to be proposed earlier and approved in advance by my father. This his brain wave, and it came from the time he had started noting his own ponderings down during the summer holidays. At breakfast, he reported what the thought had been at that day's meeting. His favorite was from the Bhagavad Gita, Chapter 2, Verse 47, which he translated from Sanskrit as: "Work for work's sake, not for yourself. Act but do not be attached to your actions. Be in the world, but not of it."

Seeing the blank look on my face, he explained that I must always do whatever I had to, such as arithmetic homework or keeping my room clean, but I must not expect any rewards for this. I ought to feel fulfilled by the doing of the task and not seek more.

"More? What more?"

"If you clean your room you must not do it thinking now my father will be happy with me and bring me sweets. In the same way, you must not do your sums thinking that you'll come first in class."

"But I never come first in class. And you never bring sweets."

"Exactly," he said, and turned back to his book.

9

Towards the end of summer, as every year, Dinu's uncle Brijen set off for the station in their Dodge, which was washed and polished with wax by Dinu's driver the day before so that its blue-black body became as shiny as beetle wings. Dinu and I stroked the long line of the bonnet and the two round headlights that turned the car into a frowning man in glasses. We caressed the case of the spare tire mounted by one of the doors, spat on the winged Dodge logo and rubbed it with our sleeves. We put our noses in through the window to smell the leather of the seats. Opening the doors was forbidden.

The next morning we woke early and sat on the wall waiting for Brijen Chacha to come back from the station. He had gone to receive a troupe of musicians.

Dada used to say Old Monk and Old Musicians were the only two things in

Brijen's life. Barely out of his nappies, he had sung his first flawless song one fine day to his wonderstruck audience of cook, coachman, and ayah, after which, at the age of nine, he had sung an entire thumri, following that at the age of eleven with a quart of rum before he fell down in a stupor. He had stopped neither singing nor drinking ever since. As if to prove my grandfather right, Brijen Chacha sat in the front row at concerts with his bottle of Old Monk beside him, drinking it down from full to empty through the evening.

We spotted the car on its way back from the station when it rounded the corner and reached the wilderness around the pir's grave. We stood on the wall for a glimpse of the chief singer, but the back seat appeared to have only a bundle of cloth in it, the end of which flew like a banner from the open window. After the car had swept into Dinu's drive and out of sight under their portico, there was a period of quiet. Then, with the clopping of horses' hooves, a tonga appeared, piled with a confusion of boxes, trunks, harmoniums, and hookahs, and the long stems of tanpuras sticking out between luggage and people. The singer's party would stay for a few days.

Every year we hung around the performers throughout the day but this time we were not allowed anywhere near the singer's quarters. We could not fathom why until we heard Arjun Chacha take Brijen Chacha aside and hiss, "A woman! A singing, dancing girl? Take her to the mango orchards! Invite your other drunk friends for the show. Not here. Not in front of our women. *Even* our mother! God! Has the liquor addled you completely?"

The quarrels between Brijen and Arjun were legendary. They were as opposed to each other as water and oil, people said. Brijen was the drop of cold water that made smoking-hot oil explode.

Almost every wealthy family of our acquaintance had a brother or uncle, usually single, more often than not the younger sibling, who laid waste any inheritance and then fell back on his family, a lifelong burden. Here the situation was different in one detail. Brijen was younger than Arjun by a decade; yet, unusually for that time, their father (who doted on his younger child) had divided his wealth in half between both sons. Knowing he was no good at managing industries and farms, Brijen had made over almost all of his money to his older brother in one grand — doubtless inebriated — gesture saying he owned nothing but music and nothing and nobody would own him but music. This was not strictly true, because he made a sort of living by writing. Somewhere between his drinking and music, he managed to concoct novels in Hindi featuring an alcoholic detective with perfect pitch and a flawless memory for melodies. These novels, with titles like *Silenced Anklets* and *Killer at the Concert,* were published serially in a magazine devoted to detective fiction, and to my highminded father's endless annoyance his students waited agog for each installment, as did my mother.

Brijen's female relatives adored him. He listened when they needed to talk, he laid down no rules, his eyes danced, his voice melted every bone in a woman's body. He only had to sit down in the inner quarters, narrate the next chapter of his book, make up a funny poem, or call for a harmonium and a bottle, and the room lit up with laughter and singing. There was a boyish carelessness about his good looks and all over Muntazir, it was said, were smitten women who waited on their verandahs praying that Brijen would walk past, that their eyes would meet. Arjun could only gnash his teeth and suffer Brijen's effortless popularity. This was how it had always been.

What set him apart from other layabouts was not only his writing, it was that his gift for music was undeniable. He was widely accepted as an authority, famous singers counted him as a friend.

Every woman who sang or danced was not a whore, it was time to understand that, Brijen said to his brother in as patient a voice as he could muster. Akhtari Bai was a renowned and dazzling singer and you had to be a special kind of philistine not to be on your knees thanking your luck she had agreed to come. So what if she had been a courtesan, so what if she had acted in movies, there was nobody who sang with such purity. It was only because she had found a kindred soul in Brijen many years ago that she had agreed to come and it was their duty to make her feel as luxuriously sheltered as a pearl in a cushion of silk.

When his reasoning failed, Brijen Chacha stalked off to our house, to my mother. We were used to him turning up at odd hours to give her magazines, examine her new paintings, read out from his stories, but this time his visit was charged with purpose. Could my mother come and tend to the singer? Arjun would let no woman from their family take care of her, but she needed someone. She had a tempestuous personality, she could go from calm to distraught in minutes, and Brijen was afraid she would be offended at being put into a guest room and left alone there with nobody to make a fuss of her. "You will understand her," he begged my mother, "you too are an artist. You paint, you sing."

Over time, I came to hear the many stories about the singer, Akhtari Bai, as she was known until she married a barrister about a decade later and came to be called Begum Akhtar. It was well known that a poet in Lucknow, who had gone mad for her beauty and her voice, had roamed the city robbed of every word other than her name, writing it on the walls in chalk, wandering dementedly until one day he was found dead in the street. It was said that the Nawab of Rampur was so infatuated by her that he wrapped her in gold, swore her smile was brighter than the sparkle of diamonds, and worshipped her every whisper. She grew tired of the gilded cage. She devised ingenious ways to infuriate him to her heart's content, then ran away, taking with her all the jewelry he had draped her with.

The day before the concert at Dinu's, Akhtari Bai turned melancholic and she dredged up old stories about false promises, broken hearts, and dark conspiracies to my mother, who spent the entire day in her room, emerging in the evening smelling of cigarette smoke and rum, oddly bright-eyed, tired and so distracted she talked of nothing else at dinner. Akhtari Bai was convinced a rival was trying to feed her herbs that would permanently ruin her voice, she could feel her voice going and the world crashing down. She had been poisoned once as a child and her sister had died of it, but she had lived and swore she knew how poison slithered through your blood to suck your veins dry. Between her spells of grief and suspicion she burst into uncontrollable, loud laughter. She laughed until her stomach ached, but she could not stop. My mother listened and sympathized and Brijen Chacha sent in bottle after bottle of rum and packs of Capstan cigarettes to her room while his brother fumed.

"Sometimes you simply have to have something. You feel something pulling you towards it. You can't fight it," my mother had said to my father once. It occurred to me much later that she was talking about herself. When was it that the thought of leaving first crossed her mind? I have so often tried to work it out. Did she start dreaming of escape soon after she met Mr. Spies and Beryl? Did it happen on the train ride down from our mountain holiday? Perhaps it was after she met the singer that it became inescapable — the sense that she too was made for a different life.

I speculate about what Akhtari Bai told her in that room over the hours they spent together, when they shared stories of lost opportunities and rash chance-taking. A young, beautiful singer living as she pleased, loving as her fancy took her, throwing tantrums, earning fame and money from her own gifts. In my mind's eye I have often seen my mother trying one of Akhtari Bai's Capstans, then her first sip of rum. When we played our hunting games, my grandfather called his sips of whisky doses of Dutch courage. I think Akhtari Bai was my mother's dose of Dutch courage. The days with the singer gave her the final push towards a decision.

The evening of the concert, gaslights buzzed with insects in the front verandah, where a spotless white cloth had been spread over a big carpet. Bolsters and cushions covered with snowy white linen had been laid there for the singer and her troupe. This was to be the stage. Everything shone in the brilliance of the new lights. The rest of the garden was in darkness but for the flickering of a hundred earthen lamps. Incense sticks had been lit to perfume the evening and drive away mosquitoes. There was an air of throbbing excitement in the people streaming in for the concert: nobody could believe that a singer of this eminence, notoriety, and allure was in our staid neighborhood.

A quarter of an hour before the concert, I saw shadowy figures scurrying around searching for Akhtari Bai, and when Brijen Chacha cross-examined one of the accompanists, the man confessed that nobody knew where the singer was; she had not been seen for the past hour or more. Brijen Chacha roared at the watchman, Kharak Singh, who had put a dented pair of binoculars to his eyes and was peering over the wall in search of the singer. "Are you watching birds with that thing? Where is she?"

On the other side of the house, you could hear the guests chatter while we fanned out as a search party. Some went to the roof, others scoured the front garden, one determined enthusiast who seemed experienced in the ways of tracking down lost maestros walked through the rooms of the house checking the beds and shaking out the curtains as if nothing could be put past singers afflicted by gloom. But there was nobody in the house, only Dinu's mother, grand-mother, and aunts, who had been warned against stepping out, huddled listlessly together. In the end it was Rikki who spotted her, and barked the way she did when she was half-afraid: soft, tentative woofs.

At first the voice only lapped at the edges of our ears. It was a quiet voice, trying itself out, cracks at its edges. There were pauses for coughs; the clearing of a hoarse throat; fresh starts. By degrees the voice gathered power until it spilled from the back of the garden to where we stood. *Who knows why your very name fills my eyes with tears today,* she sang, and the darkness around the trees brimmed over with anguish. The air was laden with the powerful scent of *Raat-ki-rani,* the night jasmine that flowered in a great big bush at the edges, beyond the tree. Akhtari Bai was sitting in front of the perfumed shrub, eyes closed, lost to the world, one hand on an ear to shut out all other sound as she sang, dupatta off her head, nosepin sparkling in the light of our lanterns.

What is it about the evening that fills my eyes with tears today?

She was in shimmering white clothes and a pearl-and-gold tikli covered one side of her forehead. We could see Beryl de Zoete sitting beside her, back very straight, eyes never leaving the singer's face. Next to them stood my mother, leaning against a tree. She wore a soft white muslin sari and no jewelry other than her usual gold earrings and a chain of twisted gold around her neck. Her hair was up in a bun that had loosened in all her running around. It was studded with crimson champa flowers. She saw us and came to me to whisper, "Quiet — tell Rikki to be quiet." But at that moment, Rikki, ever obliging, let out a shrill volley of barks.

Akhtari Bai stopped and stumbled to her feet. She put her dupatta back on her head and shook out the folds of her clothes. "Don't get up, please," Brijen implored her. "You must sing wherever you want, whenever you want. We will come and listen wherever you choose to sing." He turned and, with a dramatic change in tone, yelled ferociously at nobody in particular, "Gag that bloody cur!"

My mother stroked Rikki and said to Brijen, "Please don't lose your temper. I'll take her away."

"Stay where you are," he growled. "You are not to go anywhere."

Akhtari Bai was not smiling when she turned to him. "Why won't the dog bark? I'm no more than the village cockerel imitating a koel, the dog knows that. But this Englishwoman says she has spent one whole month here in this town and heard nothing worth listening to." Her eyes glowed in the dark. "I told Gayatri, let me show the memsahib what real music is! The scent of these flowers, this sky cut with lightning, a head crammed with memories, and suddenly this ghazal came to me and filled me. The funny thing is that for once I was singing just for two women, not a roomful of men." She broke into a merry laugh. "Women are nicer to sing to, Brijen Bhai! They are listening, not looking."

Her voice rich with the liquids she had been drinking, she took a few steps towards the front garden. She swayed. Maybe she could not see in the half-dark, and she was very likely a little drunk. She reached out for Beryl de Zoete and held her elbow as she stumbled over clods of earth and tufts of grass. There was something tender and moving about the way a woman so small and unsteady placed her trust in a stranger from another country who towered over her. Beryl's sweeping black dress was getting tangled underfoot, the feather she had stuck into a jeweled band around her head floated away, but she did not let go of the singer's hand, propelling her slowly to safety.

When she reached the front garden, Akhtari Bai turned her face to the sky. Rapid lines of lightning shot across it, disappeared, returned. A low rumble came towards us through the trees. "Who knows if this is the end of the summer or the start of the rains? Who knows if anything is the end or the beginning?" she said with a wide general smile. Her lips were dark red, her eyes thickly lined with *kajal.*

"Well, your singer appears to have recovered her spirits," my father said to Brijen Chacha. "With the help of a barrelful, no doubt."

We progressed towards the verandah, and an immense wind came, blowing out the lamps and tugging bedsheets away to the corner of the garden in unruly bundles, sending some people fleeing for cover while others turned their faces up to the sky to feel the first rain of the monsoon. The shower set free the scents stored in the dry, hot earth and Akhtari Bai took a deep breath and cried, "Now I will sing!" She let go of Beryl and ran across the garden and into the verandah calling out, "Come, come, we will all sit on the verandah. I'll sing a monsoon song." Everyone stumbled towards the verandah to find places to sit, etiquette thrown to the gusty winds.

In the middle of the shuffling and scurrying and finding of places to sit, I saw my mother. Her hair cascaded to her waist and red flowers were trapped in its strands as if she had walked through a shower of blossoms. Gold glinted at her neck and ears, her sari trailed the grass. Her face was bright in the gaslights. In that split second, I saw a man's hand reach out and place some fallen flowers into her palm and close it. I saw the hand, and the sleeve of a shirt or kurta, I could not tell which. For an instant her face shone with sweat and rain, then she disappeared into shadow.

This is the most vivid image I have of her in my head.

10

A few days after the concert, my mother told me a secret. A secret she and I alone would share, like the song she sang for me on the roof. I had to promise to say not a word to anyone, not even Rikki. She seated me on a chair and knelt before it so that her face was level with mine. When I swung my legs to bang them against the chair, she held my knees. "Don't do that, be still, I need you to listen." I stopped with an effort, although my legs started again in a minute, of their own accord.

She held my head between her hands and brought her forehead to mine. This close, her eyes were huge, her breath was warm and moist, her hair tickled my nose, and I went cross-eyed looking at her.

"I'm passing on my thoughts, can you feel them? They are very important thoughts," she said in a whisper. "Can you keep them for me?" She pinched my nose gently and said, "What a little owl you are in those glasses. Who made you choose round ones?" She pushed my ears back, flat against my head. All this unaccustomed attention — I started to feel wary. Preparations for a visit to the eye doctor?

When she told me what the secret was it didn't seem so important. The secret had two parts. The first was that she wanted me to come back from school on time the next afternoon. Not a minute late. This was vital, she said.

The second part was that she would take me on a little trip somewhere. A treat, just for me, but on condition that I got home on time and didn't breathe one word to another soul. Not even Dinu. If I told anyone at all, she would not take me.

Bulbous slate-gray clouds sat in wait the next morning, low enough to touch. When my mother came out to see me off to school, she glanced up at the sky and shut her eyes with a squeal as she was showered by drops of water.

"Last night's rain is still raining," she said.

The big trees that shaded the house gleamed and when the wind shook their branches they set off showers from their wet leaves.

"The clouds are so dark, it will be a

beautiful day. It'll pour and pour and when the sun comes out there will be a rainbow right from here to the railway station." She wiped her face with a corner of her sari. "You'd better hurry off to school, you mustn't get wet. Are you carrying an extra shirt in your bag? You are not to sit in class soaked to the skin, you'll get fever."

I was about to cycle off when she called out, "Wait, get off that bike and come here."

She hugged me tight for a long minute, kissed me on the top of my head and then on my forehead. I wriggled hard to break free, I was not used to sticky displays of affection from her, it made me awkward and self-conscious. But her touch sent a current of joy through me and I cycled away hoping she saw how fast I was going through the puddles, churning up slush.

"Remember what I said!" she cried out. "Don't be late."

"I'll be back in time," I shouted. "I'll cycle fast."

As the day progressed, my mother's secret grew bigger inside me as if I were a balloon slowly filling up with air. I could not put my mind to my work in class and had to spend the maths period out in the corridor, standing there as punishment for inattention. After our games period, one of the boys in class, Egbert Samuel, locked the gym master in the equipment room. None of the other teachers knew the gym master was locked up and he had to shout and bang the door for two hours before he was let out. The principal arrived, holding a long cane that he swished in the air. "Stand up, all of you. Which one did this?"

A silence. The inquisition. The usual long-winded punishments. The details are mundane, but all of it took so long that by the time I reached my bicycle it was ten minutes to the time my mother had told me to be home. I pushed it off its stand. Barbed wires of white light streaked through the black sky. The birds had gone to their nests, thinking it was night. Berries from a jamun tree came pelting down with the wind and I remembered Ram Saran's insistence that wind blew rain away. But he also said jamun on the trees meant the clouds were about to burst open, a storm on its way. Which of the two was right?

The rain came like curtains of broken glass. Hailstones came with it, hurtling down and bouncing off the ground as they fell. In a minute, I could no longer see to pedal and had to take shelter under a tree. A tree branch crashed to the earth, the path I was cycling on turned into a stream.

Maybe fifteen minutes passed, maybe more, but it felt as long as half a day. After a while I started again, head bent against the steady rain. Close to home, I abandoned my cycle and ran the last stretch. I entered the house soaked to the bone, yelling, "Ma! Ma!"

I ran into the first room, expecting her to be pacing there impatiently. But it was Golak who came out towards me, followed by Rikki. She leaped up at my face to lick it and flung herself onto me again and again to tell me what was clear immediately: my mother was not at home.

"Bibiji left a little while ago," Golak said. "She kept saying you were going to be here and she was to take you with her. But it got too late and she had to leave. No, she did not tell me where she was going."

In the evening, when my father returned, my mother had still not come back. My father frowned. "What? Bibiji is not at home? Where is she? She said nothing? Banno? Banno!"

"That's what I've been saying all this time. Not a word. She's gone off without telling me what to cook, how many are at dinner, what am I to do?"

My father went into his bedroom and stayed there for a long time that evening, only coming out again to the drawing room at dinnertime. His tall and spare form was somehow smaller, perhaps because of the way his shoulders drooped and his back curved. For years afterwards, Banno Didi went on about how he was like a field of wheat flattened by a storm.

When my grandfather came back from the clinic, my father called the two of us into the drawing room and seated us. The formality of it made me contract with fear. My mother had gone away on a trip, he told us, and would not come back for a while. It might be a long while. A trip, my grandfather asked in a bemused tone, where to? Whatever for? Had her mother been taken ill in Delhi?

I do not recall the details of the conversation. My heart slammed against my rib cage. My tongue felt thick and big as if it would explode if I did not use it to speak. Why hadn't I just pretended to be ill and rushed home? Was this the trip she had promised me? If it was a long trip, did it mean she would not come home for a week? Or a month? A dark, whirling storm of terror and confusion swept through me.

For some time, because of the invisible shield put around me by everyone, I kept thinking I would find my mother when I got home from school, or from the river, or from Dinu's. It was only after a few weeks, from the servants' gossip at home and the questions and comments at school, that I digested a new version of what might have happened.

My mother had run away from us. She had gone off with another man.

Mr. Spies.

Mr. Spies, who played the harmonica for us and drew pictures and talked to Rikki in German. Mr. Spies who had become Dada's closest friend. Mr. Spies and Beryl de Zoete had left with goodbyes and thank-yous to everyone, but not a word that they were taking my mother with them. They had kept it even from my grandfather.

It was a betrayal impossible to forgive. My mother knew when she left that she had poured petrol and set a match to every bridge between herself and her family. After such desertion, what forgiveness? She could never return, not even for me.

At first my father lived as he always had. He pretended — or perhaps he believed — that nothing had changed. As the days passed and my mother did not reappear my father acquired a slight hunch, as if he were trying not to be seen. Maybe he overheard some tittering from among the ranks of students and teachers — all at once he stopped going to work. He did not take to drink, nor did he start smoking. Instead he sat all day on the roof, reading. He stopped his walks in the morning, he stopped going to the Society. There were no more thoughts for the day. On some days he would not get out of bed at all and had to be pleaded with in the afternoon to eat a little. Other days he woke at dawn and sat still on the terrace, eyes shut, back ramrod straight, murmuring a *shloka* over and over again. This was extraordinary for us. Until then my father's interest in the spiritual had been that of a philosopher's — intrigued by different systems of thought but skeptical of them all.

I did not understand at the time what a catastrophic disgrace my mother's disappearance was for my father. It was not as if she had broken out of the family to go on marches for freedom which would land her gloriously martyred, in jail. Why would my father have bothered with that? He would have celebrated it as a belated vindication of the ways of thinking to which he had tried converting my mother without success all these years. Had my father ever denied my mother anything? Other women veiled their faces and served their husbands and embroidered and knitted — she had to do none of those things. My mother had the liberty to do whatever she wanted, go where she pleased, wear what she wished — within reason.

Yet, even in his darkest hour, the irony of my mother's freedom cannot have escaped my father. He always looked truth in the face however hard its glare hurt his eyes: he knew then, as I was to realize later, that each of her little liberties depended on his acquiescence. She had felt stifled and she had broken free. She had not chosen the austerity and sacrifice of the fight for a common cause, she had instead fallen as low as a woman could, she had left her child and husband for a lover. A foreigner. Poisonous whispers rustled in my father's wake wherever he went. He turned into a recluse and our home became an echo chamber.

Many years later, when I was clearing out my father's things after his death, I found a letter from my mother tucked into the back of the hidden drawer in his cedarwood desk. The paper smelled of old resin and felt as thin and brittle as a peeled-off scab. There was no date.

"I am not coming back. I am telling you this only so that you don't worry about me. Do not try to find me or stop me, please. I am twenty-six, life is running away from me. I want more! There are things in us that we cannot fight, however hard we try. I have failed you and failed my child. Forgive me if you can."

The letter was melodramatic enough, but as if something concrete were needed to emphasize the brutal enormity of what she was doing, or maybe to carry out the threat she had made a few months before, my mother had chopped off her long hair and left it with the letter in a cotton bag.

I ran my fingers through the hair in the bag. Rough, dull, repulsive, it was nothing like the perfumed silk that had brushed against my face on that last morning when she kissed me goodbye on the verandah steps.

11

Calcutta, 1930. A sixteen-year-old Bengali girl of unusual intelligence and literary gifts meets a Romanian student named Mircea Eliade. Decades later the girl, Maitreyi, writes a novel about a young Romanian scholar who came to live in her house as her father's protégé. She calls the scholar Mircea Euclid and the teenaged girl Amrita.

In the novel, it is Amrita's father who brings Mircea to their house one day and announces that his student will live with them. He orders his daughter to ready a room for the visitor, to make it comfortable and pretty. Such devotion to a student was not unusual in her father, Amrita says, nor was the generosity straightforward:

My father's students were ready to sacrifice a great deal for him, he too loved them, but it was not the love of uncomplicated people like us for one another. His kind of love has no sympathy for others. His love is for himself. For example, he loves me, he loves me a great deal — not so much for my sake as for his own. *Look, my daughter is such a peerless jewel, how beautiful she is, what wonderful poetry she writes, how fluent is her English — this is my daughter. Look, look, everyone!*

I am the apple of my father's eye. But I know that if I do a single thing against his wishes he will crush me. To him, what will make me happy is utterly irrelevant.

This is my own clumsy translation, the work of a horticulturist from a small north Indian town. Maitreyi Devi might have forgiven my ineptitude: those who have lived with a great absence, as she did, recognize this compulsion to claw at the faintest of similarities: the angle of a chin, the curve of a forehead, the flash of anger, a particular way with words, the friendship with a stranger. My mother had torn herself up and scattered her shreds in the breeze when I was nine. Ever since, I have scoured everything I read, see, hear, for traces of her.

In Maitreyi Devi's novel, Mircea is about twenty, has dark hair and high cheekbones.

At first Amrita does not notice anything special about him, but as the weeks go by she finds she is lingering at the breakfast table with him long after everyone else has left; another hour slips by at the door to her father's library. Her father passes them on his way to and from his library but says nothing; nobody stops them idling together. Amrita begins to notice things about Mircea: how his kurta is open at the neck, the triangle of pale skin revealed by his undone buttons. That his eyes seem different when he takes off his glasses.

One day, her father tells her he will teach the two of them Kalidas's classical Sanskrit poem, *Shakuntala.*

From the next day we began studying together. Who knows what people of those times thought when they saw me sitting on a mat on the floor with a foreigner, learning Sanskrit. I saw jealous astonishment in the eyes of my father's Bengali students. Older women of my mother's generation were suspicious and disapproving; those my own age regarded us with avid curiosity. My father paid no attention to any of it. The foreigner was gradually becoming a part of our family.

When I read those lines, my thoughts went back to the time Walter Spies began coming to our house. The disapproval and envy and curiosity had been identical, and evenly distributed between our neighbors and my father. My father's disapproval intensified to a kind of jealous rage as my mother grew closer to Mr. Spies. Maybe he could see that he had never, despite his lectures on patriotism and his reading lists, succeeded in animating her with the kind of passion Mr. Spies did by merely doodling an eagle or sketching a face. Did he sense the danger of a bond that shut him out? His response was to order her not to go out with the visitors and to discourage them from coming home. But forcing my mother into acceptable conduct was never going to work; he should have known that in her personal list of the seven deadly sins, obedience sat somewhere at the top and propriety followed close behind.

In Maitreyi Devi's book, the bars of the cage around Amrita are familiar. She can do nothing without her father's permission, and his tyranny, disguised as concern for her welfare, is absolute. She yearns to plunge into the river of life that she can see is flowing outside her home, but is forbidden. Once, when she ignores his strictures and joins a funeral march for a nationalist, her livid father roars at her, raging on and on until she is worn down.

Maitreyi Devi and my mother were almost contemporaries and my mother may even have met her when she went in 1926 to Santiniketan with her father to visit Rabindranath's school. They had stopped in Calcutta on the way. Agni Sen, a scholar himself, would have had reason to visit Maitreyi Devi's father, a philosopher and teacher who knew Rabindranath well. Whether she and my mother met, what they talked about, if they talked at all — I do not know. But as I read the Bengali novel, I thought that when my mother left our house with Beryl and Walter, she forced open a door that had been barred for Maitreyi Devi.

As an old man trying to understand my past, I am making myself read of others like her, I am trying to view my mother somewhat impersonally, as a rebel who might be admired by some, an artist with a vocation so intense she chose it over family and home.

As a child abandoned without explanation, I had felt nothing but rage, misery, confusion.

12

Other people tiptoed around the topic of my mother's departure, but to my grandfather it seemed to be above all a helpful marker on the calendar. "When did you get that scar?" he might say. "Was it before your mother left or after?" It was his way of stating that it was normal for life to be broken into two distinct halves, a change you made light of. Took in your stride. As if mothers left their homes and children all the time, and from Siberia to Sialkot there were boys like me who had stepped from normal life to motherless life as easily as walking through an open door into a different house. My mother had been there, and now was not, that was all. My father, on the other hand, preferred to act as if my mother had been a candle that had burnt down and away, leaving no trace, not the smallest blob of dried wax. I knew instinctively that I was not to mention her in his presence.

Around that time, Delite Cinema was running three shows daily of Boris Karloff in *The Walking Dead.* The film was about a man who is killed by his enemies, then brought back to life by a doctor who puts a mechanical heart into him. Resurrected, the man is gifted a sixth sense that makes him search out his murderers and drive each of them to a grisly end. At last, the resurrected man is shot dead, but this second time he dies in peace, avenged. Dinu could not sleep for a whole week after he saw the film, waking up whimpering, crawling into his older brother's bed for comfort, only to be kicked and told to get the hell away.

I was not allowed films, but the story proved to me that death might be reversible. The first few weeks after my mother left, when I thought she had died and nobody had told me, I lay at night talking to whoever looked after the stars beyond my mosquito net, and Rikki and me, all of us. "Let her come back, after a week, in a month, or a year. Like Boris Karloff." I added a coda to my prayer: "Let her come back exactly as she was. Not as a killer."

I had dreams in which the severed hand in the jar at my grandfather's clinic floated away and I ran after it in anguish, handless, crying for it to be restored to me. When I woke from those dreams hardly able to breathe for terror, my first act was to check if my arm was still intact, so painful and real was my sense of having lost a part of my body.

My mother did not come, but with the approach of winter the first letter from her appeared, an envelope fat with words and pictures. Although the exact month slips my mind, I know how warm her pictures felt in my cold hands. The first picture showed an expanse of water and the horseshoe of a yellow beach ahead, palm trees bending confidentially towards each other. In the foreground was a set of railings — she must have painted it on the deck of her steamer. There was another picture, this one a painted map showing a boat leaving the coast of India at Madras and making its way through white-topped waves and smiling fish to Singapore, and onward to Surabaya, Java, Bali. Like a child's drawing of land and sea. All the places were marked in the neat, tiny hand my mother used to label things with. Her normal handwriting was made of loops and flourishes and sloped away from the margins and up the page.

Yet again, my father had not gone to work and it was he who took the letter from the postman and examined the envelope. He held it towards me, his face impassive. "It's for you. Your first ever letter." The envelope contained those painted pictures and lines which began "Myshkin my darling" and went on to say how much she thought of me and of home, and how sad she was to be so far away. She asked how Dada and my father were, but did not say she was coming back. My father waited till I opened the envelope and when he saw that it contained nothing for him, he turned away and went into the house. We did not see him at tea that day, nor at dinner.

That letter altered something in my father. He said nothing, but it was the final note in a dirge that had begun to play in his head a long time ago. Over the next few days he moved his things from the bedroom he had shared with my mother to the outbuilding at the back. It had two rooms and a covered verandah, and stood at a slight distance from the main house, shaded by a tamarind tree. I had seldom seen the door to the outbuilding open. Nobody needed to go there, we had forgotten why it existed at all.

Ram Saran kicked hard to open the damp-jammed door and the choking smell of bird droppings surged from the place like poison gas. Pigeons flew out in a flurry of wings and beaks. We stepped into stacks of old newspapers glued into a block with age, limbless chairs, empty bottles, gunny bags caked with manure, amputated table legs, a warped cage made of chicken wire, rolls of frayed cow-rope, cracked lamp bases, dead fireworks. Ram Saran made a bonfire out of everything that would burn. The fire leaped and crackled and he sat on his haunches before it, warming his hands, scratching his head, and smoking until some of the fireworks, against all expectation, exploded in a bright shower of light, causing him to leap away back to his cleaning. Despite his efforts, though, the walls felt grimy, the whitewash having sickened long ago to a moldy yellow scarred with gray patches. The floor was dull red and no amount of swabbing could brighten it. The web of cracks that went across the floor remained black with dirt, impervious to soap and brush.

After the room was cleaned, my father had Ram Saran and Golak bring in his cedarwood desk and chair as well as his books. From Rozario & Sons came a narrow bed and a rigid wooden chair that had been moldering there for as long as anyone could recall. These and his bookshelves were all the furniture my father allowed. He had no rugs, no pictures, no clock, no radio. Our house had electricity, but the connection did not extend to the outbuilding. After dark it was to be lit by candles and oil lamps. Dada asked my father what he planned to do once the summer's heat came: Would he live without a fan? My father said he would see about that when the time came.

Now the house was empty all day, Dada at his clinic, my father in his outbuilding reading. In the early mornings before I left for school, when I went to the outbuilding to say goodbye, my father would be on the roof, eyes closed, murmuring his newfound Buddhist mantras. When I came back, he would be locked up in his room. I ate lunch alone, then went to find Dinu or ran down the road to my grandfather and spent the afternoon in the clinic.

My mother's first letter threw my own feelings into turmoil. I read it when I was alone, nobody there to see what I was doing. In some obscure way I think I knew I ought not to have received that letter, it was my father's by right. I was angry with my mother for many things, for not writing to my father, for going away, for not taking me with her, and yet, more than anything, I knew I wanted her back, and if I saw anything I associated with her — an empty vase that always had fresh flowers before, a white sari drying on a line — a giant fist of pain squeezed my chest hard enough to break my ribs.

I read the first letter every day. At times I hid myself in the old carriage to read it in private, and before I knew it I was back with my mother cycling, me perched on the pillion, my legs swinging away from the ground. I drifted off on a ship sailing away from India, going to her in Bali. I sat there for what felt like the whole day, dreaming until I fell asleep. I woke hungry and confused, Banno Didi and Ram Saran's voices coming closer, then fading. I longed for one of them to notice my suffering and come and get me, but they always had other things to do. When I did come out of the carriage and go into the house, Banno Didi scowled at me. "And where have you been? Not a thought about bath or food or studies, just idling."

Early in the spring, the carder came as usual to redo our mattresses. He sat outside at his twanging machine, suspended in a cloud of cotton that drifted and floated as if it were snowing in our sunny garden. My father came and sat on a stair by the carder, transfixed by the thrumming wires. He rested his chin in his hands and did not move. Gradually, flakes of cotton covered his hair in white, turning him into an old man. Wisps rested on his shoulders and lap. All day, as the carder worked, my father sat there, saying nothing, doing nothing, not taking his eyes away from them.

That evening, he said to Dada, "The carder's been coming to our house every year and I didn't know his name. Before him it was his father, he says. Do you know his name?"

"I knew the father's name, I treated him for pneumonia once, a nasty bout, as I recall," Dada said. "His name was . . . let me think. No, it slips my mind."

"Exactly," my father said. "We have no relationship with all these people who work for us. They are no more to us than cattle. In fact we know our cows' names, don't we, and our dog's. But what is Banno's youngest child's name? Myshkin?"

"He's called Dabbu," I said. "And the other two are Mantu and Raju."

"You only know them because you play with them."

"Playing together is friendship of a kind, Nek, is it not?" Dada said.

"Well, *you* didn't know their names — did you?" My father turned swiftly to Dada, who now rustled the pages of his newspaper and said, "Imagine that, Rajputana's beaten Lord Tennyson's Eleven. Do you know who Tennyson is, Myshkin?"

"Typical . . . go on about cricket and dodge anything uncomfortable," my father said. "Can we not change the subject, please? Do you know the names of Banno's children?"

"If you're determined to prove that I am unconnected with the toiling masses, Nek, yes, that may be true, though I treat them for a dozen illnesses every year. I think it's enough that I remember Banno's name — at my age." He took off his glasses and folded up the paper with a frown. "I think I'll go and see Lisa. A cup of coffee."

"Coffee? Really? Is that what you drink there?" My father raised an eyebrow and shook his head. He got up from the table. He began pacing the room, rearranging a book here, a vase there. He stopped before a painting by my mother, of the boat and river, one that she used to threaten to burn because of its childishness. He examined it as if he had never seen it before. Then he lifted it from its hook, turned its face to the wall, and with care set it on the floor. "It's got nothing to do with age," he said. "There must be another way to live. It's a question of finding it. A simpler way. A truer way."

A few days after this, he seated Dada and me in the drawing room again. We waited for news: perhaps my mother had told him she was coming back. But no. He informed us that he was embarking on a pilgrimage. He quoted Hsuan Tsang, the ancient Buddhist pilgrim who, he said, walked from China to India more than a thousand years ago in search of the Ultimate Truth and to settle the perplexities of his mind. He quoted the Buddha, who had apparently said there were only two mistakes one could make along the road to truth; not going all the way, and not starting. My father planned to follow in the footsteps of these Great Souls, going to Patna, Nalanda, Lumbini, and maybe further afield to the Bhaja caves near Poona, to Ajanta and Ellora, even Burma and Ceylon. He chanted the names of these sacred places with a kind of breathless fervor, as if he were declaiming poetry. He wanted to live as Buddhist monks did, with no money, seeking food and shelter from the charitable, meditating and learning about Buddhism along the way. He did not tell us for how long he planned to do this.

He went away one morning before I was awake. I did not hear him go. This, Dada explained later, was because he did not leave in a tonga or a car, he merely walked out of the gate with no more than a cloth bag containing a blanket, a metal bowl and tumbler, and a few clothes. He told Dada he planned to walk to the edge of our town and then down the road that led to the next village and onward to the next. He would beg for a little space on bullock carts or tongas, whatever was going in the northerly direction and where they stopped he would sleep the night in a verandah or temple or wayside teashop. He had not woken me because that might have weakened his resolve, he told me in a note he left for me along with a rupee to spend on anything I wanted. He would be back soon, he said in his note. I was not to worry.

13

Once my father went away on his journey to the center of his self, I took out my mother's letters again: a second had come, and this one was several sheets, with illustrations all over. I hid them in a book and took them with me to Dada's clinic. I made a nook for myself out of a cupboard and a rickety painted screen so that I could be shielded from waiting patients. Here, I lay on the floor and went over each word, each brushstroke.

My mother described villages, dances, medicine men, rain forests, mountains, strange flowers. "It is a storybook land," the second letter said, "one day you will come here, and you will see. There are volcanoes and springs, rivers and seas and temples cut from stone. There are foxes that can fly." She made postcard-sized paintings of her surroundings to show me what she meant. Thatched huts among circles of green fields.

The fields painted in thin, emerald-green strokes and surrounded by tall trees. In the distance a blue, flat-topped mountain. Another page was black but for an orange-and-red fire in the middle of a clearing, around which were a group of men with cloth turbans on their heads. Their faces were the same orange-red as the fire. In the area behind them were shadows of leaves and trees, through which you could glimpse the dimly glowing yellow head of a tiger. Both the letters ended, "With so much love that the sky isn't big enough for it."

I slipped them under the cupboard when Lisa McNally came in through the back door, followed by the young man she used to call Boy. Boy was carrying a tray with cake cut into wedges, a glass of hot chocolate, and two cups of tea. Lisa had made a ritual of it after my mother left. She appeared at about the same time every day and before she had said a word, a scent announced her arrival — the blend of smoke, vanilla, coffee, old books, and perhaps camphor — that her guesthouse smelled of as well. I have only to catch a whiff of any one of these things even today and I am instantly back in Lisa McNally's Home Away from Home.

Lisa seated herself opposite Dada and

after a "Hello, young fellow" to me, she sighed. "What I thought to myself today was whether Nek had gone off with . . ." And here she said something to Dada in a whisper that I could not hear. I slunk away to my corner with my cake and hot chocolate.

"Oh, do be serious, Lisa, she is a nun," Dada said. "Can't you rein in your imagination? Mukti is still in Lucknow. Nek's gone alone. On some nonsensical pilgrimage only he knows the meaning of. You come up with something of this kind every day."

"Ah, but I can't stop thinking about it, Batty!"

"You mustn't think so much, Lisa," I heard Dada say. "It's bad for the digestion. It gives you wrinkles and headaches and spoils pretty faces."

"Pretty faces puff no pastries."

"But they do bake very good cakes."

Laughter, and a moment later, the sound of a match striking, then cigarette smoke. Lisa's contented exhalation went around the room like a sigh. As their voices rose and fell, a curious thing happened to me. I could no longer hear Dada or Lisa, I was no longer in the shop, I was looking at one of my mother's paintings and there, in the one that she had drawn of the deck of a

225

boat, I saw myself sitting on a deck chair. It was not as if I imagined myself on the chair. No, I had popped out of my body, as a pea from its pod, and rolled onto that deck, that chair. I could feel wind in my hair, damp, warm air, a rocking motion in my body. My mother sat on the deck refusing food, refusing to move, seasick. I sat with her. Stars glittered in the sky as far as our eyes could see and we felt the wind touching us, moving on, rushing past. As the night grew deeper, we drifted off to sleep in our chairs, my mother and I, lulled by the sound of water. In the morning we saw other boats and ships go by, we went past islands fringed with coconut trees. The water changed from blue to green to violet to gray. Mr. Spies played a tune on his harmonica — the one he had played that night with my grandfather out in the open under a full moon, "The Trout." Rikki listened with her chin on my feet.

I don't know how long I remained on the deck of that ship. When I did move from my corner I saw that Lisa had gone, the table was clear of tray and cake and tea, and Dada was examining a patient behind the swing doors while two more waited in front of the clinic. My hot chocolate stood untouched in my corner. It had a thick, leathery layer of skin on its cold surface.

All night, all of the next day, and for the next several days, I had nothing in my ears but the notes from the harmonica. The sea breeze was in my hair when I cycled to school and back, the neem and tamarind on the roadsides turned into coconut palms, the river behind my house became the stream in Tjampuhan by which my mother sat all afternoon, drawing. If I sat by our river and focused on the temple on the other side, willing myself not to blink till I had counted to fifty-five, I could see her there, head bent over her work. As soon as I blinked she disappeared.

At odd times, especially in the first few months when I woke up and did not find my mother, or came back from school to a house without her, the emptiness was a shock, like waking from one of those dreams where you are falling from the sky — falling forever with nothing below. Only this was not a dream. My childhood nightmare — what if everyone died and I was left alone? — had taken a shape I could never have anticipated. Our overstuffed rooms echoed now. My grandfather and I sat down to dinner at the same table and we stuck to our usual places, leaving my parents' chairs where they belonged. If I banged my feet against my chair, as was my habit, it was Dada who placed a calming hand on my knee. It was he who took me to the library, waiting while I dithered over which two books, it was he who said goodbye on the verandah when I left for school. He set aside time in the mornings to go through the kitchen stores and give Banno Didi the daily shopping money as my mother had done for years. "Never too late to learn, eh, Myshkin?" he said. "Here I am, white-haired and dentured, learning how to run a kitchen. Next they'll tell me to stitch a shirt." Every Sunday he took me to the brimming street markets of the old city and we came back with laden baskets of exotic vegetables and fish nobody knew what to do with. He would then charge me with finding where, in her fat old diary, my mother had written down her recipes for Golden Lotus Stem or Banana Flowers with Coconut and I had to translate them into Hindi for Golak to follow.

I am my grandfather's age now — I mean the age he will always be for me, a grandfatherly age. I am not like him. I could not have taken such tender care of a child left adrift. I know they call me a surly old bastard. I deserve it. I rage against things beyond my control, I fulminate at the disintegration of my world. A few years ago, when the municipality decided to build a new flyover across what used to be called Atkinson Avenue, they sentenced to death forty-four neem trees along both sides of the road. I had planted them decades before, when I came back from Delhi to head the horticultural department here. It was not easy at the time to protect saplings from passing cows and goats. They needed tree guards, but bricks were too expensive after the war and iron tree guards were hard to come by — steel was in short supply. Chance sent us old bricks from a demolished house and that house, in its broken-down form, protected those saplings.

From the moment I came to know my forty-four neem trees were to be cut down, I tried everything to stop it: letters to ministers and so on. The ravings of a barking-mad fool. I went from door to door, sweating and pale, holding out a typewritten appeal for the people of the neighborhood to sign. My letter urged the government not to destroy my trees. They are fifty feet tall, I said, they give shade, their leaves chase away insects, oil is made from their fruit, the oil kills head lice, it makes skin beautiful and clear. For good measure I added a paragraph about the sacredness of neem trees — the abode of Goddess This and Goddess That, worshipped for centuries. Nothing works better in this country than ignorant religious faith or superstition.

At most houses, they banged the door in my face taking me for a robber or a detergent salesman. At one house the woman who opened the door said, "You've crossed over to the land of the crazies." But she made me sit under a fan and brought me a glass of water and signed my piece of paper. I collected thirty-eight signatures. I sent my appeal off to the Public Works Department, knowing perfectly well it would make no difference.

The day it became clear that the death of my trees was inescapable, I plucked all the roses and hibiscus in my garden. I went to each neem tree on Atkinson Avenue and placed a flower at its base. Three dusty boys started following me. "The old crock's got a screw loose," I heard them chant behind me.

I spent that night in the open, below one of my trees, watching the sky go from dirty blue to grubby orange to sickly black. In the canopy above, I saw tender young leaves, pale green against a new-washed sky. A few bulbuls hopped from branch to branch feeding on the clusters of seed pods. Their wings were black, the patch of red under each tail was bright. They perched and sang a melody every now and then. I turned and next to me was Dinu, propped on an elbow, eyes shut, shadows painting a pattern of serrated leaves on his face. Dinu had a caterpillar of hair above his lips. He was scratching a girl's name into the sandy earth with a twig. Madhuri, Madhuri, Madhuri. Who was Madhuri? I didn't know and he did not tell me. After that we both had guns in our hands and were shooting at a train.

When I went back home after my night below the trees, I saw Ila moving back and forth in her rocking chair in the front verandah, trying to look as if she were not waiting for me. She put down her book and started off the instant she saw me open the gate.

"Look at you. Dry leaves in your hair. Bird droppings on your shoulder."

"I fell asleep under a tree," I said. "I had a dream. I can't remember all of it, but Dinu was in the dream. He was fourteen, I was ten. We were lying under a tree and a bulbul was singing."

She raised an eyebrow and said, "A bulbul sang, did it? And did peacocks dance too?"

Her round face, very like her mother's, was furrowed but she got up from her chair and brought me a mug of gingery tea and toast and sat down again. She picked up the book she had been reading. For a while her face was half-hidden behind it and I knew she was reading to stay calm. Under her breath she murmured two or three lines from the poem she was reading. "The winds must come from somewhere when they blow, there must be reasons why the leaves decay." Then she fell silent. Her rocking chair creaked with each impatient push.

As explanation and apology, I said, "They are cutting down all the neem trees I planted on Atkinson Avenue. I had to be with them."

Ila went on reading — I could not tell if she had heard me — and I turned to my food. All I could see beyond a blue-and-white cover was her frown. In minutes, she snapped the book shut and picked up her latest piece of cross-stitch work with a restless, tetchy air. She stretches a particular kind of cloth on a frame and embroiders cottages covered with roses and hollyhocks, scenes from European country idylls. Then she adds lines of poetry to match. "Twilight and evening bell," "A host of golden daffodils," and so on. These are framed and hung all over the house.

Ila jabbed her needle in and out of the cloth. "You're so much trouble. All night, I've been up, wondering where you were. An old man who's disappeared. Some of them never come back. Do you know how people ridicule you? And can't you do up the buttons of your shirt? You are as ragged as an umbrella in a storm."

14

I know what ridicule is. It does not bother me.

After my mother left in the monsoon of 1937, there were whispers and hisses at school that reached me, faintly at first, like some far-off indecipherable clamor. Then my father went away as well, and the sounds came closer. I passed through the school corridors escorted by sniggers and salacious questions. I listened to nobody, I spoke to nobody. Even so, I got into fights every now and then and was badly beaten up by the older boys. One hot, bone-dry day, after a murderous encounter that left me with a broken tooth and limbless spectacles, Dinu said, "You keep your head down, you ass. Let them say what they like."

"It's all lies! They're telling lies."

"So what if it's lies?" We were cycling home and Dinu pedaled faster and wheeled an eight around me on the narrow road, then cycled ahead and yelled back towards me, "Anyway, it's not lies! Everyone knows everything." He sped ahead so I would not have a chance to reply.

Dinu used to be my protector, he would launch himself with the force of a bullet at anyone who bullied me. Yet a week or so before, when I had looked beyond the jeering crowd of older boys around me wishing he would turn up, I did see him — standing on the fringes. He had not joined in their chorus, but he was observing the scene with a grin. He turned away as soon as he felt my eyes on him. Later he said I didn't know how to take a joke, the boys meant no harm, I ought to be a good sport. I had once found him in the corridor doing a high-pitched imitation of me asking the postman if he had a letter from my mother. He avoided being seen with me in school now, as if ashamed. At home, however, he demanded I play cricket and go fishing and horse around as usual. From being my friend, this altered, ever-changeable Dinu had become another element in the hostile forces ranged against me.

The day my teeth and glasses were broken by the older boys, I had seen him in the scorched playground, I was sure of that, and though he had not been a part of the mob, he had done nothing to stop them kicking me, pummeling me to the dust, flinging my spectacles far away so that I would not be able to see to fight back.

I did not go home that afternoon, I walked into my grandfather's clinic, bloodied, my school shirt torn, my shorts dirty. I went straight through the swing doors. Dada was not in his consulting room. Why was he not at his desk when I needed him? Why was nobody ever there when I needed them? A red mist of anger made me want to destroy everything in sight. I picked up Dada's spare stethoscope from his desk and twisted it around my fist. I flung it into a corner and it lay there limp, like a dead snake.

"He's on a house call," Jagat said, picking up the stethoscope. "What's the matter with you? Got into a fight? Go and wash those cuts." He shuffled off to a cupboard in the outer room saying, "I'll find the purple medicine. It'll sting."

I opened the glass jar of sweets that Dada kept on his desk to bribe child patients. I helped myself to two boiled sweets. I put them into my mouth together and sucked on them without taking in their taste. In front of me were Dada's medical books, his tall-backed chair, a medical chart showing a man in profile with red-and-beige organs inside him. My eye fell upon the preserved hand in a glass jar. It floated in its clear liquid, as pale as wax, its extra fingers dangling like a question. Before I knew it, I had dragged Dada's chair to the shelf and picked up the jar. It was heavy. The hand moved about in it and the extra fingers moved separately, as if not quite attached to the whole. I was overcome with revulsion watching the hand touch the sides of the jar, then float away and knock against the other side. Once I had brought the jar down, I opened my school knapsack and shoved it in. The door swung behind me and I was gone, Jagat yelling, "Wait . . . the medicine!"

I cycled as swiftly as I could. The jar banged against my back each time I hit a bump on the road. What if the lid fell open? I tried not to think of the consequences. When I got to our road, I flung the bike aside at my gate and ran to Dinu's house. On its left side was the outer wing where Arjun Chacha's head clerk, Munshiji, sat. He peered through owlish glasses at sheaves of paper, picking his nose absently. Arjun Chacha was in an inner room talking to someone, I could hear his booming voice saying, "This country is going to the dogs, the Congress wants self-rule, but *who* will rule and *how*?" I took the jar out of my knapsack and before Munshiji could say a word, I had run to the inner door and flung the jar into the room with a crash so that it shattered. "Lambu sent you a gift from hell!" I shouted, then ran out of the room.

All day and all night after that I had Arjun Chacha's roar of rage in my ears and the ghastly smell from the jar in my nose. I could see nothing but a limp, rubbery hand lying on the floor in a pool of liquid. One of the two extra fingers had fallen off and lay some distance away like a dead lizard without head or tail.

After that incident, I caught Dada looking at me every now and then as if he were trying to make up his mind about something. A few days on, he said he had too much to do now and he needed as much help as he could get. Could I be of use? What he especially needed, he said, was a boy to carry his case for him on house calls, since he was getting too old to carry it, and to see that he wasn't forgetting anything on his way out, since he was too old to remember things.

When I think of these house calls now, I smile to myself even though it is all so many years ago. I see Dada at the mirror, combing his silver hair, which is standing on end because he has just shed his night kurta and put on a fresh one. Once he is dressed, down to his wallet and fob watch, he says, "Is my assistant ready?" When we reach the patient's house everyone is overcome with relief, and the whole family flocks around Dada and speaks over each other in a bid to explain the symptoms. I decide I will never be a doctor, the stomachs of the ailing are so hairy, their tongues so gray, their smell always sour, stale, anxious.

My grandfather has taken to bringing some patients home now, and he tells me to watch over them when he has to go out. These are young men with broken bones or wounds whom he patches up and cares for until they are able to slide off into the darkness or to a room in Home Away from Home to be made battle-ready again. They have injuries from police batons or bullets and cannot go to a hospital, Dada says. To him they are merely patients, but he knows the police do not share his point of view and he could be arrested for treating them and not reporting them. We are not to tell a soul, he repeats to the whole household. Talk to no one. To me he says, especially not Dinu, nor Dinu's father. There are nights when nobody can sleep because the men moan and swear in pain. I stay up memorizing the swear words.

After the house calls are done and the clinic is closed, we come back to Banno Didi clattering plates down onto the dining table. Every few days, if there are no patients at home, Dada pushes his plate away, food untouched, saying, "Let's go to Lisa's." Then the evening changes: bright lights, rose-printed curtains, Boy in and out with tureens in which chunks of soft mutton and fat potatoes float in a broth that smells of ginger and onions. There is bread and butter, then crunchy fritters that ooze syrup and bananas. There is noise from the street, noise from the guests down the corridor, the raised voices of women fighting in the shanties behind the main road. Dozens of Lisa McNally's ancestors in gowns and suits beam from the wall in approval while she plays Cole Porter records after dinner. "So deep in my heart, you're really a part of me," she sings, matching her voice to the one on the record, and winks at Dada, who tries to sing along. He goes off-key in a minute and switches to whistling.

I want the music to go on forever so we don't have to go back to our empty house where it is so quiet I can hear the owls breathing as they sleep in the corners of the verandah and I can hear my mother singing on the roof, her voice coming closer, then drifting off again. I feel her spinning me around, my head starts to swim, I want to stay awake, wait until she finds me, but everything goes into a jumble and when I open my eyes it is morning.

15

My father's first letter came to Dada from Kashi — which is what he called Benares. His hope that he would live like a monk, off whatever people gave him, did not appear to be working very well. "There are several charitable places here that give food to monks and seekers," he wrote, "but the ones I have encountered are ruled by caste. You are fed with respect if you are some variety of Brahmin, but otherwise you are treated as a beggar. At the places that will feed someone like me whose caste is indeterminate, whose religion is nonexistent, a mere beggar, in short, I have to fill my stomach with a few dry rotis and water. To be poor and of low or unknown caste in our country — I now have an inkling of what it is like. You will ask me: Why do this? I do not know. There is a storm inside me. You will say I need to return to my duties, and bring up my son. I know that and I will. In the meantime, can you send me two hundred rupees by money order to the address below? Our postal account has enough. I will remain here until the money order arrives, then make my way further north."

The postman came in the afternoons, a little after I was back from school, and I willed him to stop at our gate, counting his steps as they approached. If the letter was from my father and not my mother, I felt my spirits plummet. My mother's letters were for me, but my father's were always to Dada, with a few lines directed at me. Even when Dada read out my father's letters, I could not understand them. He put them away saying, "I'll keep them safe. One day you will want to read them."

My mother's letters took much longer to come. They were usually a month or more old by the time they arrived. They felt very foreign, with one- and two-cent stamps saying *Nederlandsch-Indië,* which made me think they were special stamps for people writing from the Netherlands to India and that Bali was in the Netherlands. Sometimes my mother put a real dead butterfly in, sometimes a leaf or dried flower. She wrote to me of a volcano you could see from Mr. Spies's house in the mountains in Iseh, she wrote of the sea mango tree with big globes of green that were both poison and medicine. She drew the sea mango as well as clove and avocado trees for me, she painted their temples and houses.

At night when I lay half-asleep, I was at the foot of Mount Agung, separated from it by a few miles of paddy fields. I could see my mother and Mr. Spies. He sat in the shade of a fern-leafed tree, a figure in gray and white, and beside him was an empty chair, a discarded bag, a green bottle. Beyond him, the mountain reared up blue and gray and green, massive and sudden at the end of the flat fields. White clouds hid it halfway up and the mountain's tip above the clouds was so high that it touched the sun, the way it did in my mother's painting.

When Mount Agung exploded, at first there was only smoke, and the air was heavy with a smell that made it hard to breathe. Then came a thick cloud of ash that climbed out from the mountain's tip as if there were a whole second mountain inside it, in flames. I could see the orange glow of fire at the top of the mountain. The heat spread from it and entered the little house in Iseh and in minutes the leaves on the plants curled up and dried to paper, the roosters stopped crowing, the cat fled into a corner. The plume of smoke grew bigger and thicker and moved westward with the wind. In a few hours the smoke stopped, the heat dwindled, the black cloud began to clear, and pale light lingered until the stars came out, far into the night.

I gazed out of the window in my room. Through the open door I could hear my grandfather mumbling in his sleep. I slid out of myself away to the sky above the village of Iseh. Iseh in Sidemen, a province of Karangasem. Karangasem in the east of Bali, I whispered. Iseh.

When one of my mother's letters came I would examine the envelope and stamps for a long time before I opened it. Once the letter was read, it would be over and I would have to start waiting again. I willed myself not to open the letter till the next day or the day after. I thought of it glowing and pulsing in a corner of the desk in my room, waiting for me as I did my classes at school, as I went fishing with Dinu, as I went on rounds with my grandfather. Something of my mother, waiting for me.

My mother's most recent letter said Mr Spies was working on a huge painting, one of twelve he had been commissioned to do, she said, and to make the paintings he had to travel all over the island in search of ruins. His monkeys went with him in his car and Mr. Spies bought bananas for them at one of the roadside markets. I could see the market as I read the letter, I could feel the air rushing past the car. One of the monkeys sat on my head and searched through my hair and when my mother happened to turn back and see that, she screamed. This made all three monkeys leap out of the moving car and scamper up to the top of a coconut tree. Mr. Spies had to stand below the tree and coax and croon for them to come down.

The monkeys went everywhere with him. Once we went to a party in Den Pasar, the capital town. Lights glittered in a ballroom, people chattered nonstop, and all of them wanted to speak to Mr. Spies. Women in long gowns, men in black-and-white suits, holding glasses with stems. One of the men was loud and self-important. "A pompous ass, that Dutch Resident," Mr. Spies said. When we reached the car at the end of the evening, he kissed the monkeys on their heads and sighed with relief. "At last some humans," he said.

On the next collecting trip, he left the monkeys at home and when he came back he found that they had torn up the newest of the twelve pictures. It was four months of work, and the picture, almost complete, was in a hundred pieces. The shreds of canvas fell through his fingers like rain. My mother knelt on the floor and picked them up, weeping over the fragments of arms, legs, eyes, trees, cows. She put a few of the pieces in her next envelope for me: the paint shone like lit gold. The shadows and light made me feel as if the bits of canvas were alive. Mr. Spies did not appear in the least annoyed, my mother wrote. He tickled the monkeys around their necks and advised them not to be disrespectful with great art in the future. Then he locked himself up to paint the same picture again from the start.

Wherever they drove, gleaming paddy fields were strewn about the slopes like shards of a mirror. People knew Mr. Spies all over the island. Even if they had not met him before, they knew who he was and as soon as his car appeared, they came out, as if to welcome a friend. He sat on their verandahs, lit a cigarette, and listened to their stories. When they stopped at the Raja of Karangasem's my mother went into the great big kitchens while Mr. Spies sat in the outer courtyard with the Raja drinking arak. My mother's new notebook filled up with fresh recipes, drawings, and notes. In the margins she drew the things she did not have a name for and later asked Mr. Spies or one of his friends what those things were called. In this way she picked up little bits of Balinese, Dutch, even German. Enough to get by.

My mother wrote of her new notebook in her letter to me and asked, "Where is my old book? I wish I had brought it with me."

My mother's notebook was where she had left it, on her dressing table. It used to be my standby for the weeks when no letters came. I have it still. It is a diary dating from the year of her first trip to Bali, 1927. She has written *Gayatri* across the front page using a brush, the strokes of the letters long and sweeping. One drawing I still linger over today is from July 1927. It shows a young girl, beatifically smiling, lying back in a meadow of flowers and grass which is framed by a sky full of stars. It is a self-portrait that needs no words to convey the feelings of the artist.

During her first sea journey, my mother kept a fitful journal. One page says in block capitals, "Rabi Babu spoke to me today. He asked me to sit beside him." As the pages progress, the words are fewer and pictures more frequent, as if she were too impatient for prose when a few lines or brushstrokes would do. For some pages my mother has turned her diary into a record of household accounts: groceries bought, wages paid. There is my schedule of medicines for convulsions and fever. Things fall out of the book: pictures clipped from magazines, tickets for *The Kid.* She had taken me for the matinee, defiantly ignoring my father's strictures on the evils of movies. When we came back from the cinema my father was pacing the verandah, cold with fury. After that, my visits to the cinema house with my mother had ended.

Between the pages in her notebook with her recipes for Kheer Scented with Oranges and Begum Farhana's Pulao my mother has stuck on photo corners and inserted a photograph of a younger version of herself with her father. Her eyes are shining, she has ropes of plaits hanging at her shoulders, her father is smiling at her, not at the camera. There are other photographs in the diary, including one of a family picnic by a lake. The lake is as flat and white as a bed and we are ranged in a row in front of it. I am between my mother and my grand-father. There is an uncle from Karachi and his wife and son, even Banno Didi, Dinu, Raju, Mantu, Lambu, and Golak. But not my father. The diary has no trace of him.

16

For my tenth birthday, knowing I coveted Dinu's air gun, my grandfather gave me one too, an imported nickel-plated Daisy. After I had practiced for several days, shooting at mangoes, Dinu came up with the plan that we would try out my new gun away from the house. Shoot at the evening train as it passed. "Moving targets, Myshkin," he said. "Hitting old tins and fruits in the garden is for babies."

Dinu now smoked, and he had a bottle of rum — pilfered from his uncle's stash — hidden away in his room. He claimed he had kissed a girl. He was so far ahead of me in the ways of the world that I deferred to him in all such matters. Accordingly, I put my pellets and gun into my bag late that afternoon, and climbed through tall grass and lantana bushes to the railway line. I was quite a lot shorter than him and had to scramble to keep up with his long-legged lope. Near the railway line, we lay on our stomachs by the cutting to wait for the evening train. We talked in whispers to each other and Dinu put a blade of grass into his mouth to chew as he had seen cowboys do in Westerns. He pushed back an imaginary hat. Not a cloud wrinkled the sky, the world was enormous, I had no parents, I had my own gun. I plucked a blade of grass to chew on as well.

Sometime before sunset, we heard a distant hooting. Dinu turned on his stomach and readied himself. He narrowed his eyes. The thought crossed my mind that it might be a passenger train and not a goods train. I sat up with a jerk. Our bullets might go through the window, they might set the train on fire. I clutched Dinu's arm to make him stop. He shook me off and aimed again.

The train hooted again and then it was upon us, so close that we felt the wind throw us back. What if my father were on it, coming home from Nepal? What if my mother was in it? The train boomed past us, Dinu pressed the trigger, I jogged his elbow, shouting in blind panic, "No, no! Don't!"

When the train had gone, the noise receded, there was not another sound to be heard. The dry grass tickled me, I wanted to sneeze, I struggled not to sneeze. I could sense that Dinu was gathering his forces to pummel me half to death, but then I heard him whistle. "My first moving target. Myshkin, I've got us a bird for dinner."

He got up from where he was and edged closer to something in the grass some distance away. The grass was moving. Then came a whimpering sound, followed by a moan and then a man's voice crying, "My leg! They've killed me! Help! They've killed me!"

Dinu turned and fled. I did not think or pause, but scrambled to my feet and pelted after him. He bounded over rocks and humps of earth, I struggled to stay close. I caught up with him and clutched his arm. "Who did you hit? What happened?"

Dinu shook off my arm. "Don't do that, you donkey."

"But what if he is dead? We should go and check."

He stopped walking abruptly and turned towards me. His face was very close to mine, his mouth smelled of smoke, he had two red pimples on his cheek, crusted with white. "And if he's dead, what's the good of checking? Not a word about this to anyone, understand? Who told you to blab about Lambu to my brother? You've got dung between your ears. You grabbed my elbow.

You spoilt my aim. The man's got hurt, he'll go to your grandpa. That's all."

For days after, I stiffened at the sight of any man with a limp. I put my air gun away. Every now and then I asked Dada with elaborate casualness about his patients, hoping he would tell me he had treated a man with a pellet in his leg. Dada raised an eyebrow after a day or two of my questions. "So, Myshkin," he said. "Do you want to be a doctor after all? Shall we lance a few abscesses together?"

Dinu and I did not talk about what had happened, as if mentioning it would bring forth batteries of wounded men on the warpath from behind the bushes. I did not see him for almost a week except in passing at school, where I avoided him, and although I could not have articulated it then, I think I knew we had begun the slow process of breaking away from each other.

Yet the sheer length of childhood friendship can keep it sputtering along despite every kind of failure. There is safety in the familiar. It is to Dinu that I turn when I have to verify details about my past and our effort to recall one thing takes us to another and in this way with one incident, then a second and a third, there is before us a series of signposts leading back to the ordinary happiness of days unclouded by adult differences. It was Dinu who reminded me about the forbidden films he took me to see on the sly, the booklets with pictures of film stars that we hoarded till they became greasy with handling. How we sat on the floor right in front of the screen and wolf-whistled through the final kiss. I had all but forgotten about our fascination for Fearless Nadia, the heat in our bodies at her length of bare thigh, and our determination to seek her out, whip and all, and free her of her clothing.

17

My father came back on a muggy day several months after he had left. Sometime before his arrival, he had sent a telegram saying only, *Arriving Soon. Clean Rooms.* Unsure which rooms he meant, Ram Saran spent a week spring-cleaning both the outbuilding and my parents' old bedroom. He chased out lizards petrified high on the walls, put brooms through the glassy webs of spiders, dusted, mopped, polished, then put everything back as it had been and locked up.

The entire household came out when my father appeared at the door and shouted, "Anybody there?" I sprang out of the broken-down carriage in the back garden where I had been saving people from an exploding volcano with Sampih, a boy my mother often wrote about. Rikki bounded towards the gate, her tail a blur of joy. Dada was at the clinic, but Golak, Ram Saran,

and Banno Didi and two of her children —
all hurried out on hearing the sound of his
voice.

I had already reached the front garden and
seen what they had not. My father was not
alone. There was a woman with him.

"Myshkin, come here, I am back." My
father held his arms out in a way he never
used to. He looked awkward, like a picture-
book scarecrow in a field with a carrot smile
on his face.

The woman was holding a toddler. She
kept rocking her whole body and crooning
to it in a language I did not understand.
The toddler whimpered, then wailed, sounding like the cats that fought at night in a
corner of our garden. I stayed where I was.
I could not bring myself to go towards my
father, it felt as if my feet had grown roots
and would never move again.

"Myshkin?" he called again. "Come, let
me see . . . you're taller."

He advanced towards me and I stepped
back, as shy as if he were a stranger. He put
his head next to mine and an arm around
me for a clumsy embrace. We were both stiff
as tree branches. The bag on his shoulder
fell to the ground when he bent towards
me. I pulled away. He was gaunt, his hair
was growing back from being shaven, he

had a straggly beard, he smelled of old sweat. He did not feel like my father at all.

Noticing the gaping faces of Banno Didi and the others, he said, "This is Lipi, my wife. And her daughter, Ilavati. We will call her Ila, now she is my daughter too." Before he could say anything more, Ram Saran began to shuffle off and then broke into a run saying something too incoherent for us to understand.

Dada came back from the clinic at a pace much slower than Ram Saran's and found my father going through the house, remarking on this and that, the woman and her baby in the outbuilding. I stood at the edge of the kitchen courtyard, able neither to go any closer to the outbuilding nor to stop staring at it. Lipi came out now and then to the outbuilding verandah casting around for help. Banno Didi muttered, "If that woman thinks she can order me to bring her hot water and all the rest, she's wrong."

Dada disappeared with my father into his own bedroom, the door closed behind them. The woman came to the verandah again and spotted me across the courtyard. She called me — not by my name, but with a gesture — and I walked slowly towards her. In the slant of her eyes she resembled my mother, in other ways not at all. Where my mother had been slender and small-built, this woman was stocky. She was not pretty, like my mother, nor anything as stylish. She wore a coarse white-and-brown sari which flapped over her ankles, and her head was partly covered with it. Her nose was pierced with a dull gold stud. A few bangles and a twisted red thread around her neck. The parting of her tightly tied hair was filled with red sindoor. As I approached she said in Hindi, "Do you know, for me this is like being in a new school. Will you help me? Tell me where the bathroom is. And the kitchen."

My father summoned the barber and sat outside with a towel round his neck, having his beard shaven. He turned to me, his face covered with foam, and said, "Go to the clinic, Dada needs you there. He says you go on house calls together. That is good. It is valuable to know how people suffer."

My grandfather did have a house call to make and we sat through the tonga ride without speaking. I fixed my eyes on the horse's ears. They were white, though the rest of the horse was dark brown. The tonga-*walla* yelled at passersby to move out of the way and clanged his bell against the wooden sides of the carriage.

Dada cleared his throat and said over the

clopping of hooves, "It will take time, but one day you might be glad of little Ila's company. A sister."

"She's not my sister."

"A friend, then. You will grow up together."

After Dada and I were back at the clinic, Lisa McNally and Boy appeared with tea and hot chocolate even though it was not yet teatime. There were also three pieces of gingerbread cake. News of my father's second wife had reached Lisa and as soon as she came in, she said, "Batty, Batty, Batty! Wonders will never cease! The Buddhist has married again. Tell me all this minute, I insist."

"Ah, Lisa, she seems a pleasant person. I am sure it will be good for all of us to have another woman around the house. Too many men make a mob."

"Much younger than our Nek, I hear? Younger even than Gayatri? And what is she? A Nepali?"

Piecing together what I overheard in the clinic and what I know from my father's letters home, I have understood that from Benares my father had gone eastward, to Calcutta, where he remained for a month or so, and after that further north, towards the Himalaya. His destination was the Bud-

259

dhist monasteries of Sikkim, but by this time he had run through much of the money my grandfather had sent him, and was tired and ill. He stopped walking and took trains, but where the railhead ended he had to start walking again. He fell in with a group of other pilgrims he had met on the train. His feet were already badly blistered and the air was so cold and dry that his fingers were oozing blood through cracks in the skin. He bought a thick shawl with the last of his money which he used as a wrap during the day and as a blanket at night, but it did not keep him warm enough when sleeping outdoors.

The others walking with him were much hardier: they were accustomed to the cold and the altitude. They moved faster. They became small, distant figures on the next hill even as my father was wheezing his way up the first. He stopped at a tea stall somewhere on the banks of a river. There was fire in his chest, he could not breathe, his head hurt so terribly he felt his skull cracking. He had passed gorges, waterfalls, peaks incandescent in sunlight, monasteries — all the sights for which he had waited his entire life — yet he was aware of nothing but the pain in his chest. His rib cage had turned into red-hot iron hoops against which his lungs pushed for air. At the tea stall the man offered him a corner for the night and lit a fire. He gave my father an extra blanket as well as tea and steaming barley gruel for which he would not take money. For the first time in days, my father was warm, but still his breath rattled in his chest and he had to doze all night sitting up because he coughed without pause the moment he lay down.

When he woke he found himself surrounded by a large Indian family, originally from the Kumaon, they said. Sunauli, at the Nepal border. My father told them of Rai Chand, of Rozario & Sons' shop in Nainital in the old days. After that they would not listen to a word of refusal from him: he was almost family. In fact they did believe one of their relatives had worked for Rai Chand! They did not live too far away, they said, they insisted they would take him with them. It was at their house, weak and asthmatic, that my father encountered the woman who was to become his second wife.

"A hill woman? A village girl?" Lisa McNally said, as softly as she could, but still not softly enough.

"Maybe, maybe not — she has only just arrived, Lisa. How would I know? She speaks Hindi, and seems educated. No

English, though."

"Did they fall in love? Really one never knew Nek had it in him to be romantic after Gayatri. He was so devoted to her — well, he certainly was when he went all the way to Delhi to propose marriage. Remember how surprised you were? Nek Chand the Ascetic who had loved his teacher's daughter without a word for years! And now he has done it again."

"I am not sure your romantic fantasies are correct, Lisa. From what Nek told me, he felt . . . what did he say? An infinite sense of gratitude. Also compassion. Compassion is a good thing. I'm proud of my son. And he said rage. He felt rage at her situation."

Lisa snorted. "Stop being sarcastic. Compassion's good for kittens, Batty R, it doesn't make for happy marriages. Now you'll ask me how would I know, having never entered into holy matrimony? But I do know, Batty, a girl knows these things. And with a child! Whose child?" She leaned forward, avid.

"Lipi was the youngest son's widow. Bad luck, they thought her — a woman whose husband dies young. She has that little girl — if it had been a son, the family might have treated her better. She tended to Nek, brought him his food and so on. He saw her all day around the house, slaving. It occurred to him that this was what the Buddha had intended all along."

"I thought the Buddha had abandoned his wife. For his Search."

"I have to get acquainted with my son all over again, Lisa. I don't understand so many of the things he says, all these books he reads. Living meditation, he calls it. What do Christians call it? They must call it something, they have a name for most things. He is not just following Buddhism, he says he is living it."

"You don't marry to serve God, Batty."

The day after his return, my father came to me with a decision: I was to call his new wife Maji. That was what they called mothers in Lipi's part of the world.

I made a decision too. I would never call her anything at all.

My father was charged with a new zest for life. He met old colleagues and friends he had not seen for months. Mukti Devi had been released from jail while he was on his travels and he started again his crack-of-dawn walks with her group. He went back to his job at the college. He started writing articles for newspapers. He bought three copies of the paper when the first of his articles came out — it was an essay about the beginning of his journey, when he left Muntazir and began walking to the next village with no fixed destination beyond.

"The world thought it was an unbalanced thing to do, but anyone who is truly spiritual is both mad and selfish. So many great seekers have spurned family and children, left them bereft for years on end: Was not the Buddha similarly guilty? And yet, would anyone say that it was a mistake for him to have left? How many millions over how many generations have been saved because he had the strength to sacrifice his family? My own misguided quest ended in failure of sorts: I learned at the feet of great masters, but my attention wandered. My back ached. My insect bites itched. In short I discovered I was human and pitiful and my physical needs were greater than my spiritual hunger. These are bitter things for me to confess but necessary: the first necessity in the quest for knowledge is truth."

And so on and so forth. But it did impress the editor of the paper, a pious man with nationalist inclinations who sensed that his readers were hungry for celebrations of austerity. He asked my father to do a series of essays on his travels: what adversity had taught him, what he had found out about the hamlets he had spent time in. My father came back from work, ate a small meal, hardly speaking to anyone, then disappeared into the outbuilding and soon after, the hammering on his typewriter began. If the child cried or I persisted with my gun, he complained that there was so much noise he could not hear himself think. The clack-clack-clack from his impatient fingers chopped up the birdsong at dusk and went on until the owls' tentative hoots were silenced too. He emerged only at dinner-time, his hair standing on end, his eyes blazing with thoughts and ideas he could not communicate to anyone else in the house.

I knew instinctively that it was important for my father's new wife to please me. Lipi would praise me when I had done nothing worth noticing, she would tell Ila that she must grow up and be like me. She would lay out fresh clothes on my bed before I got back from school, and after I had washed and changed I would go to the dining room and find that she was waiting for me there. One day when I saw the plate of puffed-up poori and tomato-red aloo she placed before me, I said, "It was the same thing yesterday. Banno Didi knows I don't like that."

"You ate it so happily, I thought . . ."

In a dim, unarticulated way I sensed even at that age that there was something pitiable about Lipi's efforts to fit in and make everyone happy. For the first time in my life I had a sense of my own power.

I pushed back my chair and got up. "Lisa Aunty will give me cake."

The next day, as I had anticipated, Lipi had made sure there was cake for me in the afternoon. She waited, watching me chew each mouthful, and I had to turn my face away so that I would not feel stared at.

"How is the cake?" she said. She had a low voice with a lilt. "Ram Saran got it from Landour Bakery, he said it's the one everyone in this house likes."

I kicked the chair leg and didn't answer until I had finished my mouthful. "It's all right, but Lisa Aunty's is better. She makes it herself."

I was half out of the room when I saw Lipi reach out for the rest of the cake. She took a bite, such a big bite that her mouth was stuffed to bursting. She could barely chew, she moved her swollen cheek as if she were a frog. She managed to swallow that mouthful and another. She sniffed hard as she chewed, even so, her nose dripped. I stood there staring, not able to go, nor to stop her as she ate all the pieces on the plate, then I escaped into the courtyard. There were sounds of retching interrupted by words in a language I could not understand.

I ran out of the house, down the road, past the river towards the railway line, and flung myself down in the grass by the cutting where Dinu had shot a man. I buried my head in the prickly grass. A train clattered by. I looked up, my eyes blurred with my tears. A goods train. A few yards away, an old tonga horse wandered the scrubland where it had been abandoned. Its belly had caved in, one foreleg had a red, oozing wound. It paused its grazing and turned its head to regard me with its dark-lashed eyes, as if expecting something.

My head crawled with as many thoughts as a hive full of bees. They buzzed and collided and fought with each other: my dislike of Lipi, my horror of what I had done to her, my need to run away and never see anyone at home again, my longing for my mother, my rage at her disappearance. I could make no sense of anything.

I don't know when it was that I dozed off, but I was woken by the sound of another train approaching. This one went past as slowly as a tonga. In the violet softness of dusk, the rectangles of the windows were bright yellow with light. I could see people inside, their faces striped by the bars of windows. The dining car appeared, lit up with men and women holding glasses and cups as if they were actors in a moving film. One day I would see my mother on that train: at that moment, it felt like a certainty. I would come every day at this time, now that I knew when the passenger train went that way, and eventually it would have to happen, she would be in one of the windows.

The last carriage went past. The grass rustled. There was an enormous emptiness and silence as if the world were a dark blue tent which stars were starting to puncture and I was the only human being alive in it.

18

When my father first came back with his new family, it felt as if the house was not ours any longer — we had visitors who simply would not leave. My grandfather and I were both careful, stiff, unnatural at home. He stayed away for long hours and so did I.

But the weeks passed and turned into months, and we began to get used to the strangers. Dada took to chatting with Lipi, and he seemed to like sitting with her even if they were not talking much. As soon as he came home, she would tell him the things that had happened through the day and the new pranks Ila had thought up. Dada would beam and chuckle indulgently and pick up Ila to give her a kiss. I felt an anger I could not fathom. Once, when nobody was looking, I pinched her leg hard enough to draw blood. She claims she still has the scar.

Dada came home one day at lunchtime

with a package. I sidled up to him and turned it to examine the stamps. *Nederlandsch-Indië?* He pushed my hand away and said, "Not this one." He held it out towards Lipi and said, "It has been so many months, and I realized I never gave the new bride a gift. Lisa helped me with this. I hope you will like it."

Lipi's face turned into a round caricature of disbelief. My father might have rescued her from a life of drudgery and poverty, but he was not the kind of person who bought anyone gifts. The only things he had bought her since they came back were five white khadi saris with borders in green, saffron, and white, the colors of the Congress Party's independence flag. These were what Lipi wore every day. You could never tell when she had changed because each sari was exactly like the other.

Lipi undid the packet with great care so that she would not tear the paper even though it was just brown paper from the shop tied with a red ribbon. What emerged from the wrapping was a sari of the palest lime green, with tiny silver sequins all over it. Along with it was a box. Lipi opened it and broke into a disbelieving laugh at the slim rope of gold and the two long earrings that lay on red velvet inside. She took the box and went to the hat stand that stood in the verandah. It had three mirrors, big and small, on adjacent panels, angled differently, and she looked at herself in each one holding the earrings to her ears.

But her luck had run out — at just this moment my father came back.

"What's this?"

Lipi swiftly took the earring away from her ear, startled, even a little scared. She turned to Dada for help. My father held up a corner of the sari.

"You don't wear clothes of this kind, Lipi, you don't like them," my father said. "Where did you . . . ?"

"It occurred to me that nobody had given her a wedding gift," Dada said. "A father-in-law is supposed to bless his daughter-in-law with a big gift."

"It's a nice thought, but you see, she wears only handspun saris. Didn't the two of us vow to live our lives with simplicity, purity — Lipi? All this . . ." He gestured at the necklace and the sari. "All this is not for us."

Having pronounced his verdict, he went inside. We could hear him calling for a cup of tea. He came out for a minute and added as an afterthought, "She is free to wear what she likes, of course. These choices have to come from within."

Lipi had long since put the earrings and necklace back in their box. She stood by the table, absently stroking the new sari, and then sat down beside my grandfather. He lit his pipe, and although he was usually spiritedly conversational, he gazed into the distance with faraway eyes, his pipe a tiny smoking volcano. The smell of his tobacco wafted across the verandah.

Lipi began fiddling with a bit of knitting, only pausing when two people, a man and a boy, appeared at the gate calling out, "Golak Bhai, bring out the grinding stones. Let's give them some life." They knew their way around, they came every few months to resurface the heavy, flat stones on which Golak ground spices. They went to the back of the house towards the courtyard and after a few minutes came the sound of chisel hitting stone. A rapid, irregular rat-tat-tat. They would chisel in fish, waves, flowers, until there was a delicate arabesque of indentations all over the stones for the turmeric and chili to be ground against. I ran to the courtyard to watch the patterns emerge.

In my letters to my mother, I wrote about my animals. There was another dog now, who had wandered in one day as a puppy and decided to stay. Rikki's puppies were to have been called Tikki and Tavi, but since she had none, this new dog claimed the name Tavi. I said nothing about Lipi or the child to my mother, only that my father was back from his travels now. I was afraid that if my mother came to know there was another mother in the house, she would never come back.

After I had written my letters, I put them in an envelope that I sealed firmly with glue and then marked with a melted red blob from Dada's stick of sealing wax. Nobody else saw what I wrote to my mother — my grandfather posted them from the shop and as soon as a letter had gone the wait began for her reply. Sometimes she wrote to me twice in a month, sometimes nothing came for two months at a stretch. At times our letters crossed and I imagined answers and questions dangling, sentences colliding with each other somewhere in the Indian Ocean. If the postman called out to me while I was playing with Dinu, he had a way of flinging his bat down and sitting with his hand cradling his chin and rolling his eyes while I ran inside and put the unopened letter in the hiding place I had for them.

In the evenings after school, I lay by the

river, dreaming on the grass, wishing my father had never come back. His very presence inside that locked outbuilding was oppressive, every rat-tat of his typewriter a stone he was throwing at the world. If only Mr. Spies would by some miracle become my father. Everything I wanted to be, Mr. Spies was. He explored the world, he made music, he painted, he was friends with animals, he slept in a boat on a lake. I did not care anymore that he had taken my mother away, I wished he had taken me too.

As my father rapidly turned into a censorious headmaster at home, driving Dada to stay at the clinic for ever longer hours, my misery became more acute, my anger about my mother's disappearance a monotonous, throbbing, directionless rage. In the time that had passed, my sense of her physical existence had dwindled. From being a real person, she was turning into the concentration of all that I longed for in my life and did not have. I wanted to be where she was. I wanted to do what she was doing. My life was going on elsewhere without me.

I ask Ila for her memories of this period and she has almost none, or will not share them with me. We talk easily enough about many things, but when it comes to my father, her mother, her childhood, her steadfast response is to say she was too young to remember. What of the things her mother told her about her infancy? Ila changes the subject.

I know that in her later years Lipi spoke less and less, watchful, timid, retreating into her own inner world as if she were afraid that words, once out of her mouth, would come back sharpened, to stab her. She and Ila were close right till her last illness and at times the two of them gave the impression of being a pair of brown sparrows stranded among hungry kites. They would huddle together talking in whispers, stopping abruptly if anyone else, especially my father, entered the room.

I ask Ila if she remembers a particular day in 1939 when it was she who triggered a crisis that turned out to be decisive. She claims she has not the faintest idea what I am talking about, her mother never discussed any such incident with her, she has no memory of it. I start to tell her about it and she pretends to be occupied by her reading, neither commenting nor adding anything — although she does not leave the room.

Was it summer or winter, were pigeons burbling and gulmohur blooming? The season is of no consequence. I do recall it was daytime when the door of the outbuilding burst open and my father emerged dragging Ila by one arm, her legs half off the ground. Lipi ran towards them with a cry of alarm and I heard my grandfather, his voice louder than I had ever known. "What are you doing, Nek? You'll hurt the child. Let her go."

My father let her go by simply loosening his hand. Ila fell to the ground. She gave two choked whimpers at first, followed by silence during which she gathered breath, and then let out a long series of wails. Lipi ran to her, scooped her up, and held her close, rocking and stroking her as she sobbed. My father went back into the outbuilding, came out holding his typewriter. It had his latest article trapped in the roller. The paper was sodden with milk and the typewriter too dripped milk. He slammed it down on the parapet bordering the verandah. He stalked off into the outbuilding again and began to fling things out. Books, checkbooks, papers: all soaked in milk.

"I had only left her there for a minute," Lipi said with a gasp.

Before Dada could say anything, my father had banged the door shut. Lipi looked at my grandfather as if she were scared and yet furious, her eyes ablaze. "What shall I do?" she repeated. "I had only left her there for a minute."

My father's rage could be heard all over the house for the next hour, punctuated by howls from Ila. He went back to his work only after he had moved Ila and Lipi from the outbuilding to the last unoccupied room that remained in the main house, the bedroom he once shared with my mother. That was where they would be from now on, he decreed, while he and his desk and his books would stay in the outbuilding, restored to solitude.

The day after the move, when I came home from school, I found Lipi sitting before an opened cupboard. My parents' cupboard. She had begun to empty it and there was a trunk next to her into which she had already put some of my mother's clothes. I plunged my hands into the trunk. I dragged out the saris and tried to put them back on their hangers. The cloth slipped out of my grasp. The endless length of a sari — when you release one from its folds, is there any way of taming it again? Within a few minutes I was standing in a soft nest of jade and emerald, peacock blue and burnt orange, my mother's most loved colors.

"You don't want me to take those out of the cupboard?" Lipi said with a worried frown. She put a hand on my arm. "What is it you want?"

When I made no answer, she gave a resigned sigh and picked up one fallen sari after another to return to the cupboard. In the evening, from my usual place in the shadows of the corridor, I heard my father say, "Let her part of the cupboard remain as it is. I'll empty out my old shelves so you have space."

"I have to share a cupboard filled with her things?"

"Come, come, Lipi, don't be difficult. We both have such few clothes. You only need a couple of shelves."

I did not hear Lipi reply. My father spoke again. "*Things* have no meaning. You and I know that it's our inner being that is everlasting."

I recognized the tone. He had settled the matter, he was the repository of a superior wisdom, there could be no further argument, and minutes later his typewriter began to fire away at great speed. The next week, he strode up and down the front verandah declaiming whole paragraphs from his column titled "The Immateriality of the Material," interrupting himself to say,

"Strange how mundane events in one's life can lead to moments of such illumination."

A few days later, a bullock cart came to our gate and then through the gate into the driveway. The wheels squeaked, bells tinkled, and the driver yelled, "Anyone there?" as he hit the sides of the cart with a switch to make more noise. Golak and Ram Saran appeared, and the three of them carried a new, carved cupboard into the house. It was Himalayan *tun* wood, the finest mahogany, my grandfather explained to Lipi, the most beautiful piece he had been able to find. It had slim rounded sides carved with leaves and flowers and mother-of-pearl door handles. It was newly polished, breathing out the clean smell of resin. Dada opened it and showed Lipi: there were drawers she could store things in, as well as shelves and a rod to hang clothes from. The cupboard had a small safe in which he had placed five thick gold coins. "Yours," he said. "You don't have to tell my son about them."

Once she had arranged her things, Lipi locked her cupboard and tied the keys to the end of her sari. They jangled as she walked. "Thinks she's a memsahib now," Banno Didi said scornfully, imitating Lipi's somewhat waddling walk. The cupboard fitted into the passageway outside the bedroom and many times I saw Lipi standing in front of it as if nonplussed. Her few saris and oddments and Ila's tiny frocks filled two of the many shelves. The only other thing hidden away in the cupboard was a glass jar of face cream she had bought with the personal spending money my father gave her every month. *However dark or dull may be your skin, it will be whiter and fairer with Valetta Radio Active beauty crème,* promised its label.

The rest of the cupboard was empty, as if proving my father's point that Lipi could have managed perfectly well with less space.

19

If Lipi and Ila contracted by degrees into a shell that contained only the two of them, I was no different. My shell was smaller, it had nobody in it but myself, and once I had found it, that was where I remained for all my years.

It has become my lifelong habit to live unnoticed, and even at work, though I briefly entertained notions of name and fame, as soon as I realized what these things entailed, I retreated. Were I a plant, I would be the shade-loving one that grows below a tree in the far corner of the garden where nobody spots it or plucks its flower for a vase.

I learned early that I preferred to live in hiding but I also realized that only the deluded place their faith in seclusion. Sooner or later, the rock you have chosen to shelter under is found and you are forked out. This was the process that began for us, even though we did not know it, in the summer of 1939, when it became obvious there would be a war in Europe.

At the time, the events in Germany were still too far away for us to fully comprehend. The Hitler whom Beryl de Zoete and Mr. Spies used to talk about — he was in the newspaper every day now, a sinister news item but still reassuringly distant. Britain ruled us, and if there was a war we knew we would be forced into it, but at this remove it was an abstraction. We had no relatives in the Western world, we knew no Jewish people, it was not happening to us.

The first changes were inconsequential. It was settled that Dinu would go to boarding school, a new one modeled on Eton and Harrow that had just opened in Dehradun to give Indian boys the kind of education that had been the preserve of affluent Englishmen. After a year or two in the school he was to start training as an officer in the British army at the Indian Military Academy that had opened in the same town. Until now, only white British men could become officers, but with the war almost upon them the government had realized it needed thousands more soldiers and had come to accept that it would need to recruit Indian officers to command the larger number of sepoys. Even so, only the sons of the rich or princelings were allowed to become officers. This pleased Arjun Chacha greatly and he came to our house to crow about the elevated company Dinu would henceforth keep. The days of running wild with the cook's children and neighborhood boys were over. It was time for him to assume his natural place in the world — at its pinnacle.

My father was instantly gifted a subject for his next article. If Britain goes to war with Germany, he asked, why should Indians be pushed into it? "What is it to us if the Germans rule Britain? Do the British not rule *us*?" he headlined the piece. "A million Indian soldiers fought for the British in the Great War. More than 60,000 died. Even today, an old sepoy from that war marches on the pavement outside my house in his ancient military cap, firing an imaginary rifle or groaning in remembered terror. People complain Kharak Singh disturbs the neighborhood's sleep. I declare he *ought* to disturb our sleep. When men are transported off as cattle, it ought to disturb our sleep for evermore. We must vow not to let that happen unless we are promised our freedom in return. This is 1939, not 1914."

The day the article was published, Arjun

Chacha stormed into our house brandishing the newspaper. "Why name Kharak Singh?" he demanded to know. His plump cheeks wobbled with rage. "He is *my* watchman. People are asking me why I haven't done anything for him. Do they have any idea how much I have done?"

"I was not accusing you — he has been used as an example. That is how we writers work," my father said patiently, adopting a supercilious tone which said that the common or garden species of readers need not worry their heads over the complex arguments of great scholars. He was sitting in the drawing room, still studying the paper, rereading his article with a satisfied smile on his face. "Do you know how many people have congratulated me for this today? Professor Shukla, Mukti Devi, Dr. Dwivedi — everyone. Shakeel said all his friends had read it. A brave, forthright piece, they said. It might get me arrested, but one has to tell the truth."

"Shakeel! What do you see in that wall-eyed imbecile, Nek? Ever since we were in school — Shakeel said this and Shakeel said that. I suppose it was he who told you boys will be grabbed off the streets and sent to fight the Germans."

"So they will, Arjun. Wait and see."

"War is good for economies, Nek. *You* wait and see: we'll be the country supplying all the goods they need. Boots, cloth, planes, guns. They will need them. We will make them."

"Is that all you're worried about, Arjun? Money may come, but at what cost?"

"I don't know about costs, Nek, but this I know, no son of mine will sit it out at home hiding behind books if there's a war the British are fighting."

Arjun Chacha heaved himself up from his chair and walked a few steps down the verandah, then came back to the drawing room and dropped his copy of the paper on the table. He turned on his heels, unsmiling. "I don't need that," he said.

War against Germany was declared by Britain and then India in September 1939 but Dinu was to leave for boarding school and his father planned a send-off nothing would stop, not even war. It was to be a concert.

They had not had a concert since my mother left because Brijen Chacha was no longer there to organize them. He had disappeared from home the winter of my mother's departure, after an especially violent quarrel with his brother. Some said the quarrel was about Brijen Chacha's liaison with a woman, others said it was because he had stolen money from the family safe. Everyone agreed he had killed himself in shame. Whatever the truth of the matter, he had no connection with his family now and it was left to Arjun to make the concert successful on his own. He went about it with grim determination, dividing the work into departments he noted down in separate registers titled *Travel, Accommodation, Food*. The work was distributed between Munshiji and his two older sons, as well as Lambu Chikara's father, who had been called back from the Kanpur mill now that Dinu was going away.

Arrangements were made for an evening as elaborate as a wedding. A red-and-white canopy was put up on their front lawns, the fabric of it thin and delicate. Immaculate cotton sheets and bolsters were spread over dhurries and scattered with scarlet rose petals. The singing, the practicing, the cooking, the lamps and decorations — all of that followed a well-worn course. If there was a sense of urgency and the threat of deprivations because of the war, my father said, Arjun had no sense of them.

Neither did we, my grandfather pointed out. Among the first things that had happened because of the war was that we got a refrigerator, bought secondhand by Dada from a British officer who had been called back to England. For a few days we would open its door for no reason at all and stand there feeling the cold air drift into our faces like a mountain breeze. My grandfather took to storing his kurtas in it so he could wear a chilled one each morning. When we opened it there was nothing inside but neat stacks of white clothing and two metal ice trays that delivered geometrically perfect cubes of ice.

Our refrigerator rattled, hummed, and vibrated in a corner of the dining room. I can picture myself today, standing with my ear pressed to its side. Nobody is in the room. Nobody can see me as I gently thump the sides of the refrigerator to a rhythm. If I close my eyes, the thumping sound blends with the hum of the machine, making me feel as if I am on a train. Where am I going? A different place each time. I set off to find Dinu in his new school in Dehradun and the hills I see from the train are like the ones on the way to the summer cottage Dada used to rent, and the same pine-scented wind is against my face. On a second day I am on a long, sweaty journey to Madras to reach a port and board a ship and then onward to Java and Bali, where I will swim with the boy called Sampih of whom my mother writes in her letters, and when I sleep I will have at least one monkey and two dogs in my bed with me.

I tell nobody that the refrigerator has this power to turn into a train, I don't want anyone else to know. My world has to live in silence within me or else its power vanishes.

Smarting from the unprecedented challenge of Dada having bought something as significant as a refrigator before him, Arjun Chacha acquired in quick succession: a gleaming Frigidaire, the latest model, not secondhand; a radio; a factory for making ammunition, and another for making army boots; a Model T Ford for Dinu; twenty cans of sardines. The brightly colored labels glued onto the tins of fish showed metallic sardines lying in tight, staring lines. Their flesh was salty, soft butter, we were told. To a small number of guests at the concert, Arjun Chacha planned to serve sardines on toast inside the drawing room, away from the crowds. Now that his brother was not there to complicate matters, the concert would be as he had always envisioned it: an urbane blend of useful conversation and entertainment that would at once showcase the family's wealth and create opportunities for adding to it.

Arjun Chacha's new radio had a big round dial which lit up by degrees, slowly going from dark to dim to bright, and voices came on a little later, as if people had to travel into it to speak. It was shrouded all through the day with a crocheted cover Dinu's mother had made for it and was unveiled in the evening by Arjun Chacha, who came home and sat by it with the glass of sherry he had taken to sipping before dinner. He listened with a solemn, preoccupied frown to the news from London. Sometimes visiting relatives would be allowed in, and while their comparative status could be assessed by the distance of their seats from the radio, they were all equal in being served lemon soda, not sherry. There was no question that women or children would be let into the room while the news was on — they were bound to chatter or giggle. We peered in through chinks in the curtains and saw Arjun Chacha shaking his head or wagging his finger at the radio as if it were alive and would come to understand how right he was about the events it was broadcasting.

There was a radio as well at one of the shops near Dada's clinic and I used to stop there on my way back from school because this one was always tuned to Germany. Maybe I would hear Mr. Spies's voice on it — he was German wasn't he? He might talk directly to me through the machine. I knew this was not likely. Even if Mr. Spies were on German radio, he would be speaking of art or Beethoven or the book he was writing with Beryl de Zoete. What would he say to me? Might he tell me how to come and find him and my mother? I knew this was un-likely. Two years had passed. My mother wrote to me as usual, and although she spoke of her paintings being bought and sold and said she was saving money, she no longer said she would come for me.

20

On the day of the concert at Dinu's, Lipi dressed up. She put on the lime-green sequined sari that Dada had given her. It was a year old now, but had never been worn. She pinned a strand of jasmine into her hair and wore the long earrings and necklace he had given her. Ila was in an embroidered skirt and blouse, and had a red rose in each of her pigtails.

Lipi came out into the drawing room, appearing triumphant as well as self-conscious. I saw her stealing a glance at herself in the long mirror on the far wall of the room. Her lips were painted red, while a thick dusting of talcum powder on her face had made it clownishly white. Despite that, the shimmering sari made her appear delicate and festive in a way she had never been before. She smiled at Dada and me.

My father walked in from his college, raised a brief, skeptical eyebrow at her. He went into the outbuilding without a word and emerged half an hour later, bathed and changed into a fresh kurta and churidar. Now we were all ready to go and gathered in the front verandah: I was in a white kurta too, Dada even had a rosebud in his buttonhole. He walked ahead and unlatched the gate, saying, "Come on, I can hear them tuning their instruments." He turned the corner and we heard him talk to the watchman as he walked into Dinu's house. I sped off after him and was halfway to our gate when I heard my father say to Lipi, "Where are you going?"

She stopped in her tracks. "To Dinu's . . ."

"Surely you have some sense. Ila will ruin the concert. She cries so often, Arjun will hate that. You wait at home with her. I will send word."

"Send word? About what?"

"You can come at dinnertime. Noise won't matter then . . . although really, to bring this child into company is asking for trouble. She'll probably spill something . . . well, that can't be helped." He started to walk off, then turned to Lipi again. "Wait till I send for you. You can listen to the music quite as well from here. In fact, if it were not for neighborliness, I would not go either, I have an article to finish. This is time wasted."

My father strode past me towards the gate, saying, "Come on, Myshkin, what has to be done has to be done."

Lipi did not take a step forward or back. She stood by the gate through which my father had gone, and nothing moved but her sari, which slid off her shoulder to the ground. Ila babbled her nonsense words. It was already dark and Dinu's garden was shimmering with tiny flames. One thousand nine hundred and thirty-nine *diya*s had been lit around the house and lawns to mark the year, an extravagance my father said even the nawabs would have considered flagrant. The little earthen lamps flickered in rows along the roof, in each window niche, among the trees, and even at the back where the servants' quarters were. You could smell jalebis and gulab jamuns being fried in ghee. A moment passed and a plaintive sarangi sounded its first notes, then a voice starting to sing. At that, I ran out of the gate and into Dinu's, leaving Ila and Lipi marooned on the drive.

It was during the second raga of the evening that someone shouted, "Fire, fire!" The singers kept singing, perhaps they had not heard the cries. They had reached the part of the raga where they took turns with the instrumentalists, dazzling everyone with the way they transformed the same notes. They had no eyes but for each other's cues and gestures. It was only when we rose from our bolsters, brushing off rose petals and jostling each other to move, that the singing faltered.

When we came out of the tent we saw that people were not pointing at anything nearby but across the wall — towards our house. The flames were high, reaching the top of the tamarind tree. Dinu vaulted over the wall first. A pile of things was burning in the area just beyond the outbuilding — we could see chairs and tables in the fire, clothes and books, and Lipi struggling nearby as puny Golak tried to pull her back. The sequins on her sari glinted in the firelight. There were voices shouting, "Stop her!" but the roar of the fire tore them to shreds. Shadows danced and darted as we pulled things from the flames. I can still see the scene in every detail. My grandfather is on the other side, near the broken carriage, trying to stamp out the sparks flying onto it. There is my father. He is running towards Lipi. Lipi has something in her hand — my mother's notebook. She has flung it into the fire before he can stop her. Dinu dives forward, plucks it out, and throws it to one side. Even today, the book's charred edges bring back that evening each time I turn its pages. I can see saris on fire: my mother's. Her blouses, her shawls. My father's papers and books, his clothes, his chair, his typewriter, even his pillow. My mother's framed portrait, its glass shattered. Her paintings. The one with the boat that used to hang in the kitchen corridor. My mother had said often enough she wanted to burn the lot. Now it was done.

People said later that Lipi fought those trying to pull her away from the flames with the strength of four horses. She bit Golak, she tore the skin on my father's neck with her nails. "I want to die," she repeated in a high-pitched howl. "I want to die."

Afterwards, my grandfather examined her. Her left hand was burnt, she had a fever and was delirious. But she was safe, he said. My father had managed to stop the fire from touching her sari. "If that flimsy sari had caught fire," Banno Didi said, relishing the possibility, "she'd have become a kabab in one minute. Another motherless child and one more wife — vanished!"

Lipi lay in her bed and refused to move. Her hand began to heal, her fever cooled, yet she would not leave the room. Twice I came in to find her lying face to the wall, sobbing. I crept out like a thief, not knowing what to do. She hardly ate, her chubby roundness turned to sagging skin. Dark patches spread like eclipses under her eyes. My grandfather sat with her and tried to make her talk to him, but to almost every question she had roughly the same answer:

"I don't feel like it."

"Won't you come to the garden for some fresh air?"

"I don't feel like it."

"Ila wants to play with you."

"I don't feel like it."

Dada said to my father, "Her mind and heart have gone on strike. This is beyond the reach of my medicines. Maybe a change will do her good. Take her on a holiday."

In the first week after the fire, when Lipi was incoherent and feverish, my father had taken leave from work to sit beside her all day, covering her if she seemed cold, fanning her if she appeared to sweat, giving her medicines at the intervals Dada had prescribed, forcing drops of sugary water into her mouth. She refused to eat anything. Even so, he would bring food on a plate to her bedside and coax morsels into her mouth. It was as if he was seeking forgiveness through these gestures of atonement. He gave up his early morning walks, he gave up most of his activity at the Patriotic Society, and he stopped sleeping in the outbuilding, going there only when he needed to write his articles. He read the Hindi newspaper to Lipi. He read out short stories. He bought a joke book and at the end of every joke he read out, he said in an eager voice, "Now, that's funny, Lipi, isn't it?"

But my father was performing in a play with no audience. The theater was empty, the listeners had gone, the clown was tumbling around and nobody was there to laugh. Lipi lay inert through all his readings and jokes.

Ila cried for her mother. She was brought into the room and Lipi turned over on her side and shut her eyes. Banno Didi's voice rolled around the kitchen all day. Was she an ayah as well? Who was this madwoman from a village my father had gone and saddled us with?

I have never discussed this time of our lives with Ila — what is there to say? The more intense the emotions, the stronger the wall of reticence I tend to build around it. The other day I lay awake at dawn, thinking of that dark, long-ago time as I listened to the morning sounds: the honk of trucks racing to reach the highway, an ambulance's urgent wail, silence for a while with birds clucking outside and then the distant siren of the 5:30 a.m. express that tears through Muntazir without stopping. How lonely it is, the sound of that train. It is a distillation of the sound of all the trains I used to wait for in the hope that one of them would bring my mother back. The delusions of a daydreaming eleven-year-old. I was adrift and alone then. Overnight, with her mother beyond her reach, Ila was alone too.

Had it not been for her mother's long illness, she and I might never have become close. Left to her own devices, she toddled about all day occupying herself with shiny pebbles or flowers she plucked from the garden. She examined her pebbles with intense concentration, as though her gaze might turn them into precious stones. As soon as I came back from school, she appeared on the verandah, gurgling and lisping. I went to wash, and she was there outside the bathroom. I sat down to eat and she stood by the table, tugging at my clothes. Instinctively, she stuck to my side for protection, a brother and sister brought together by the disappearance of our two mothers.

The first few days, I turned away from Ila and went off to get my air gun and fishing rod and go down to the river as usual. I lay there and lost myself in my mother's latest letters. Soon, I was by the river that flowed towards Tjampuhan. Its name was Ayung. Blue lotus grew in ponds and at the royal palace in the evening there was music and feasting. Masked dancers came and went in great flocks, wearing headdresses, trailing feathers. After the dances, I climbed down a hillside to the rushing river. My mother sat on the rocks above, watching me. The still pool where the river water collected had flat rocks all around it where I could sit. It was easy to reach the rocks, then slide into the water. Far away the stream disappeared into mist and mountains and blue-green fields of paddy. The water was gentle and cool and the river's current was barely perceptible in the pool. Before I slid into the water, I looked up for my mother, and there she was. Smiling down at me. Waiting for me.

I whiled away the days as I had ever since Dinu left for his new school, but by degrees, without noticing it myself, I started to come back home sooner and when I came back, I went to find Ila, though I did not play with her even if she hovered nearby. After some time I gave in entirely. I showed her my aquarium and my collection of butterflies. She clapped her hands and spoke her nonsense words. She chased a ball on unsteady feet with Rikki and Tavi. She rode on my shoulder.

One day I took her into the broken-down carriage with me and we squeezed into its mildewed interior together, Rikki, Tavi, she, and I. I found myself telling her, "We are in a rain forest on an island in the Indian Ocean. There are strange fruits there. You and I shared a rambutan and you spat it out because you did not like the taste. We are sitting very still in the forest, waiting for the deer to come out. Sampih is with us. You won't be scared, I will take care of you. Afterwards, we'll eat a roasted duck."

As I spoke, it came to me that I no longer believed any of it. I no longer felt any of it. It was just a story I was making up for her, I could stop the minute I wanted.

I cannot explain even now quite what used to happen to me and how real the travels in my mind were. They had sounds, smells, sensations, even though they were — I suppose — mere daydreams that I drew from my mother's letters. I floated about in a tissue-thin world of my own construction that was more real and present to me than anything else. But now my fragile cocoon had split wide open and I was out in the open daylight with no place to hide.

21

My dear Mamma,
Dinu has gone to boarding school. After that he will join the army. He says he will fly planes and shoot with real guns. Everything is very expensive here. Dada says that is because the government has printed lots of money to pay for their war with Germany. Yesterday Mantu and Raju came back very happy. They had big white tick-marks on their chests. They had to stand in a line in their underwear if they wanted to join the army. The British officer tick-marked them with chalk if he wanted them. Now they will get loads of nice things and go to nice places. They will go to the Atlantic Ocean. They will be on a ship. They will be something called a Lascar. It's super. I wish I could be a Lascar too.

They cannot take me because I am not yet seventeen. I will join later. I am very bored here. Papa takes me to his meetings sometimes. They all wear white caps and seem angry and when they leave the meeting they pat me on my head and say, "We were slaves, but you will live free. Everyone will be equal." Two of them got arrested last week so now they are in jail. Mukti Devi is in jail again also. Papa is in charge of the Society now. Dinu and Mantu and Raju are all gone away, but there is Ila. I have not told you before that Papa has a new wife. Her name is Lipi. She is my new mother. Ila is her baby and she is my sister now. I will also become a soldier soon. I will not have time to come to Bali. I don't want to go there anymore. I want to go to Europe and bomb the Germans from a plane. I hate Germans. I hate Mr. Spies also. Dinu said he is a German and we are on the British side and we have to kill Germans. All of them are Nazis. Nazis are evil. We burnt your saris and pictures and things in a big fire. Rikki and Tavi are well. I am well. I caught three fish yesterday. One fish was six inches long. I will keep it in my aquarium.

Myshkin

My outbuilding is an archive: letters, newspaper clippings, notes, plant drawings, diaries, work papers. I cannot bear to throw anything away. Ila says that I will die a slow death like the captives of old, immured in my own books and papers.

Among my papers was that not-posted letter I had written to my mother. More than fifty years after it had been written, it was still sealed. There are many words, over a lifetime, that I have wished I could spool back after unleashing them into the world and it is always too late, of course, to unsay things. I could not remember why I had not posted that particular letter, but when I read it the other day I was grateful that this particular missile had never been launched.

Through the next two years, our town began to appear embattled in a determined sort of way — as if it were only good form, now that there was a war, for trenches to be dug, windows to be painted black. On the river-bank, something mysterious was being built by the army. A bomb shelter, people said, because there were rumors that the Japanese would bomb us. In a burst of enterprise, the principal had the college dome and all its windows painted black, and the keeper of our zoo announced he was setting up a big game squad, just as the zoo in Calcutta was doing. Members of the squad would be armed with guns to shoot the larger captive animals through the bars of their cages should the Japanese bomb us. Arjun Chacha signed up for the assassination squad the day it was announced. It was accepted far beyond the borders of our town, he told anyone who would listen, that Arjun Sinha was the sharpest shooter in all of Upper India. The zoo in our town had one yellow-toothed senior tiger, its cub, a lion, two leopards, and six gray jackals who smelled as if they were long dead and putrefying. Chacha circled the tiger and lion cages at the zoo every few days to establish his rights. He searched the spotless sky for signs of Japanese planes, his ears pricked for the slightest hint of an airplane's drone that might allow him the grandeur of raising his rifle and saving the world.

One afternoon, I came back home to find my father, my grandfather, a gaggle of maids and cooks from Dinu's, even Jagat from the clinic, standing in a huddle by the verandah. In the inner courtyard at the back, on the wall by the servants' quarters, was a splatter of red where Banno Didi was banging her head again and again. Dada had followed me into the courtyard. He pulled me away, took me into the living room. Every small sound was unnaturally magnified. Sparrows chirruped in the window slats, the cows mooed in their shed, the refrigerator hummed, Dada's asthmatic breath rustled near my ears. "Let her be," he said as he stroked my hair.

Mantu was dead. The ship in which he was a pantry boy had been torpedoed close to Canada.

Images of Mantu scattered in me like a circle of marbles. I tried to cry, he was the second of my daily playmates to vanish. But Lambu Chikara's departure had been different: he had been killed by a drunk father, I had seen his body, I had been partly responsible for his death. Mantu was a soldier taken by the war. Far away. It did not seem real. In a house wearily accustomed to disappearances and re-appearances, might he not return?

But what if he were really dead? I could not shed a single tear, nor think of an adequately weighty response. Feeling it was too momentous a loss to do nothing, I walked out to the pavement and from old habit kicked a stone around, first to the pir's tomb, then the other way, towards Dinu's gate. Kharak Singh, the old watchman, the only person missing from the crowd at our house, was sitting there on his stool, dozing, unaware. "Did you hear the news, Kharak Singh?" I said in my most somber voice, tapping him on the shoulder. He stirred, gave me a smile of complicity, gestured at me to wait, and reached into his pocket. He pulled out a moldy onion. "See this head?" he said. "I sliced it off in foreign lands. I keep it safe."

A year passed. The town turned khaki with new soldiers. Vast swaths of Arjun Chacha's cane fields were taken away by the government to build an airstrip, making him bellow with a rage that carried to our house as though on a megaphone. There was talk that his cars might be requisitioned too and that the rich were being forced to pay large amounts of money into the war fund. My father observed that the war was not proving so good for the economy after all, certainly not Arjun's economy.

And then one afternoon, the newspaperman arrived to deliver a special issue. Just two pages. On the first page it said, *Japan Declares War on U.S.A. and Britain.* On the second, *Dutch East Indies Declares War on Japan.* The special issue cost only a pice where the daily paper was an anna.

"Bad news comes cheap," Dada said.

"Well, that means Gayatri is in big trouble, doesn't it? The Dutch East Indies is at war," my father said. And he gave a grim smile.

Shortly after that, as if in punishment, he was arrested — along with seven other workers of the Patriotic Society — for disturbing the peace, protesting against the war, writing seditious articles. By then, almost all the leaders of the Congress had been in jail for almost a year — Nehru, Gandhi, Asaf Ali. Twenty thousand others. Dinu's father was given to sneering that jail gave people an exalted status, turning ordinary men into heroes, and that an arrest warrant was the certificate that every freedom fighter craved. He told his friends that my father had been feeling overlooked, as if denied recognition.

The policemen waited while my father went in to Lipi. He remained for a while behind closed doors, then came out holding a cloth bag in which he had long packed his books and papers and a few clothes, knowing his arrest was inevitable. The policeman was at the verandah table, drinking tea. We were waiting beside him in a respectful row. My father said his goodbyes down the line to Ram Saran, to Golak, to me and Ila.

He stopped in front of Dada and said with a smile that twisted his face, "Well, now?

Do you still think I am a dabbler?"

My grandfather opened his mouth to reply, but my father had turned away.

We were not to know then that my father would not be released from jail for several years. Perhaps he had an inkling of it. His face, shadowed with weariness as he left, was fragile and steely at the same time, as if his mind would be kept alive by the strength of his convictions long after the deprivations of prison had killed his body. By now a great many people from the Society had gathered in our garden and stood waiting with anxious expressions, talking in murmurs, breaking out sporadically into patriotic slogans. It reminded me of the time I had seen Mukti Devi being taken away in a police jeep.

Until that afternoon, I had no notion of what my father meant to the larger world. In later years, whenever I thought of him, it was this last sight before his long prison term that came back to me. He waved to us, climbed into the police jeep, and was gone. He had never appeared more solitary.

22

When I finished writing about Mantu and about my father's arrest, I pushed my sheaf of paper away and got up from my chair. Almost immediately, I had to sit down again. My legs were lifeless from sitting still for hours and if I moved them just a fraction, they were pierced with a thousand pins and needles. Once I could walk again, I put on my sandals and left the room. My vision was blurred, I did not know where I was, in the year 1941 or in the present. I went out towards the front of the garden and saw Ila plucking jasmine from the bushes by the banyan tree. I creaked down onto the stone bench where, a lifetime ago, Beryl and my mother used to sit and talk.

"You've come out of there?" Ila said, lifting her head from the bush. "You are like your father, always stuck in that outbuilding. Writing endlessly. What are you writing?"

"Nothing," I said. "Nothing of importance. A man has to keep himself occupied."

"Go for a walk. Inspect your trees. Get some air."

Ila went back to plucking jasmine. Neatly. A forefinger and thumb pinched each delicate blossom from its stem, dropping them into a cane basket that was steadily filling up with a white, scented cloud.

"Do you remember, Ila, the day that Mantu died? I have been thinking of his brother Raju. I never saw him again."

"How would I remember all that? I was only two or three. I don't have the vaguest memory of them."

"Do you remember Ishikawa? The dentist? We called him the Toothless Dentist."

"I don't know if I remember or if you told me."

I got up from the bench. There were fewer and fewer people who could share any memories with me, either about people or about places. I decided to go for a stroll — perhaps the park at the other end of the road. I knew every tree and the trees would know me. I walked down the street in a daze, scarcely registering the new landmarks, the bright-lit signs, the shoe shop where Rozario & Sons used to be, the row of luggage stores and clothing stores and offices that have replaced the old shops in the arcade. Through some anomaly of ownership, the arcade itself still stood, in bad repair but intact. More curious was the fact that two of the signs in the upper row have survived, even though the one saying *Ishikawa Dentist* has faded so badly that only I, who know it, can still tell what it says.

At the park, I found my old gardener Gopal pottering about among the hibiscus bushes. He tucked his khurpi into his waistband and started walking with me. He showed me a new clump of chandni, starry with white flowers, and the bamboo at the edge of the artificial lake at the center of the park. The bamboo drooped towards the water as if trying to drown in its own reflection.

By now a straggly group of his colleagues had joined us. I knew some of them — their fathers had worked as gardeners in my day and the sons had inherited their jobs. Gopal's monologue turned into animated chatter about the developments in the park, about the new head of the horticultural department who wanted them to plant flowers in color schemes that would reflect the Indian flag. Gopal shot a jet of spittle into a corner to show what he thought of that. The light deepened to dusk and we stopped again by the lake, watching shadows and reflections change color on the shining water. I heard a noisy set of screeches and tilted my head up. A bright green flight of parakeets against the half-dark sky, heading for home.

My legs had been almost too heavy to move when walking to the park, but now I felt as if I could walk for miles more. Gopal had shown me the saplings of laburnum and silk-cotton along the park walls. A new generation of trees was growing. The winds must come from somewhere when they blow, there must be reasons why the leaves decay, Ila had said. When was that? The night I had spent out in the open under the neem trees? It seemed a lifetime ago.

That evening, I ate with Ila and listened to all her news, then took the dogs for a stroll. Late at night, when I was sure nobody would intrude or interrupt, I took out the packet that Lisa's children had sent me. I found a sharp knife and slit its sides. I wrestled with the tape that held the thick packet together. At last it opened. Inside was another layer of packaging. Much older. Across the paper, in Lisa's handwriting: "To be given to Myshkin Rozario upon my death. (Swear you will do this, or my soul will haunt you forever.)"

I smiled at that. So like Lisa to threaten from beyond the grave. I opened the second envelope. I took a breath and then put my hand into it, to take out the bundles of papers I could see inside. One of the pages was stiffer than the rest. A portrait of my mother.

Her face is unfamiliar because her hair is short. A red flower is tucked behind her ear and the jade brooch I know from long ago is holding her sari to her shoulder. Her smile is the same. There is a scrawl in her handwriting on the back. "Here I am, Lisa! I painted this! Isn't it better than a boring photograph?"

The other papers in the envelope are letters arranged by date and clipped together. All in my mother's familiar handwriting: impatient, long-looped. With arrows going upwards, downwards, and sideways into the margins to continue thoughts she had left behind and needed to return to, lines cut out and scribbled over, dashes and abbreviations, dozens of underlined words on each page when she wanted to be forceful. Little doodles and diagrams where words failed her. Every millimeter of each page covered so as to make the most of the

313

money she was going to spend on the stamps.

23

10th July 1937
(from the train)

My dearest Lis,

Half the way down to Madras, the heat still & stifling, the shaking monstrous. The air coming in through the window was fire. There was no rain. WS worries about my misery at leaving home, B says What's Done is Done. You need to be tough, she says, you need to pull yourself up by your bootstraps. Maybe they're rather alarmed at the thought of having me on their hands, like a suitcase someone's left you in charge of. It's one thing finding a joyous friendship out of the blue, another to have the friend land on you forever — not what B & WS had bargained for, I am sure, when they came on their little trip to India. The other Indians in the stations & on the train seem scandalized/disgusted. You'll say I'm dreaming up things. But I heard one man say to a woman (loudly so that I would hear & in Hindustani so that only I would understand) <u>Some women are so shameless they don't mind selling themselves to white men</u>. They weren't the only ones — mutterings & sneers in the train all around me. W asks me, What did they say? What did they say? But I don't tell him. It makes me cringe. I want him to think well of us — whatever "us" is meant to be.

At one of the stations was a food stall with a board saying Adarsh Hotel. A man was ladling out the most delicious-smelling daal pakoras & steaming-hot tea. By this time two Englishmen were in our compartment — faces very sweaty, noses puffing with each word, big stomachs straining at the buttons, but polite to me, madam, madam after every sentence. Railway guards on holiday, they said. When you go to that stall would you bring us some food too, ma'am, they said. They said the food from there is delicious, but the Adarsh Hotel man won't serve foreigners. So I went there feeling v. useful & got enough for everyone & we had a picnic inside

the train. Then we trundled off again &
in the evening, we were over the Godavari river & it was raining so I held my
face to the window & the spray cooled
it. Cool breezes at last through the
window & for as far as the eye can see,
brown wide water & green earth. I
remembered from long ago Rabi Babu
talking about this part of the journey &
it came back to me after all these years
— that time when I did this journey with
my father. Rabi Babu had said about this
very stretch that its beauty moved him
so powerfully he knew he wants to be
reborn in this country every time.

That thought made me wretchedly
miserable about leaving home — as if all
of life is lost somehow — all that I had
dreamed on the deck of that ship when I
was with the poet & my father — I had
thought I would learn painting at Santiniketan, I'd have a life that would be
different from the suffocation I saw
around me at home — <u>stupid, stupid</u>.
Ignorant. I've destroyed everything. I
can never go back now, the doors are
shut forever & I don't know if this
destruction will lead to anything good.
It is as if a giant black mouth of a
volcano is before me & I am about to

fall into it, no idea what's at the bottom.

In the train I was struck by a violent fit of crying & one of my ghastly headaches. My eyes throbbed enough to pop out of my head for the pain. Fear & misery to think of little Myshkin all alone. What must he be doing at this exact time of day? I should write to him, but I can't bear to. Not yet. Once I am calmer. He must not know . . . will I ever be calmer? I lay with my back to WS & B, wept till my heart broke. Two nights running I had a horrible dream, such a fearful dream. It kept coming back to me even when I woke, of a fetus that was like Myshkin as a baby. Bloodied & dead, swollen eyes shut. Oh Lis. I couldn't remember anything else about the dream, but I woke feeling terribly sick. How pleased my mother will be — she always thought the worst of me. This'll exceed all her expectations. She will think I've betrayed my husband for another man & run away. Didn't care for my child. What's more evil than a woman who does not love her child?

Myshkin was meant to be here with me. How he'd have loved sitting by the window. I keep thinking of those times he got fever when he was tiny and I spent nights bathing his little head over a bucket of water. Now I sit by the train window, looking out, out, out. Even when it is dark. I haven't much conversation. I listen to the others — Beryl: Say something; Beryl: Eat something. WS: Life is a painting & you've just applied the first strokes of the new brush. Still I can find nothing to say, I am afraid I will start crying if I speak. So I keep scanning the scene outside. I feel as dead as a stone for the grief & for the hideous sense of having made a mistake. Then in the next hour my thoughts change & I know I needed to leave or I might have gone mad. Actually mad — babbling, screaming mad. I cannot tell you how frightened I was the days it was almost unfightable — my sense that I was falling over an edge. Some nights, every part of my body was covered with misery inside out, like pond scum. I slept on the roof yet it felt as if I was in a room where, one by one, every window that led to air and sky was being slammed shut until I was all alone in a black cell. Once — only once — I ransacked my father-in-law's medicine chest for pills to end the misery. But maybe he knew — wise old owl — I found only cough syrups & suchlike.

I wouldn't have managed to board the train if not for you. If you had not given me the money — all your savings, isn't it, Lis? I know it must be. One of the worst things with NC was the way he made me feel guilty about every expense. The household money counted out at the start of every week & the little extra given magnanimously to me for any foolish little thing I might want to buy, a hairclip or face cream, a bauble, a tube of paint. I was surprised the other day when I counted how much I had saved over the past ten years — by not buying hairclips! All hidden safely in your house. Yet another thing to thank you for. I am going to earn now & the first thing I will do is return your money to you. You might say no & call it a gift but I need to start this new life with no debts, even to you, Lis, however generously you give things away — money, your shawl, dresses (will I ever wear them? I haven't worn a frock since I was a child, only saris!) — with no thought of getting anything back, only wanting me to be on my way, with M or without. If you had not pushed me into that coach, if you had not convinced me this was my only chance, I'd never have found the will. Life is full of regrets & thoughts going back & forth — mine are like a ping-pong ball, off goes a thought & back it comes before I know it, exactly the same. I am in pain — terrible pain that hurts my body as well as soul — these sickening headaches & stomach-aches that feel as if my gut has turned into a rope knotted up & can't be un-done. I cannot keep down a morsel.

B says it is all in my mind. She reads me Arthur Waley's Chinese poems to calm me down & I think that makes it worse. One more lost Chinese child from the 4th century bc weeping for his home & I will fling myself into the sea when I reach it, I promise. Her intensity scares me — a little. One morning I woke up & she was sitting quietly at the foot of my bunk, watching me. Just watching. When I opened my eyes, she pressed my ankle & said, "There. See, how it gets easier. You're smiling." She calls me her sunbird. Small, bright, flit-ting. Drink up all the nectar, she says, life doesn't come twice.

I feel out of my element. They will go back to their lives. And I?

Oh, I can't write any more, Lis. I'll

come back later.

All my love, Gay

(still from the train, 11th–12th)

Dearest Lis,

I am trying to chat, smile, to make things less annoying for W & B. I sketch on the train. It jogs a lot & the lines move around, but I still do it: faces of people, stations where we stop. Trees & hillocks. The folds of the valley in Chambal. Keeps my mind off things. Makes my hands move easier on the paper. It feels so long since I could draw & not be called to my duties. You are lucky not to be married, Lis, how often I have envied your freedom! The feeling of being trapped — trapped forever — I honestly thought I would know nothing but misery for my entire existence. There is a time after which the doors close & then where do you go? Nowhere.

When WS turned up out of the blue again, I thought for a fanciful moment that my father had sent him as my guardian angel. All the things that my heart & mind & soul were starved for ever since my father died — it is not just finding people who understand me, my sense of <u>myself</u> has been restored to me. As if all of life's possibilities had been locked away behind a door which has opened again. Is it arrogant of me to be certain I have something that other people don't have? At home there was a desert inside me, winds howling, scorching away every blade of green. I could not paint anything that satisfied me. Everything I do, every single thing, is meaningless when I am not able to do my own work well enough to please <u>myself</u>. It has been <u>so long</u> since every part of my mind was set alight with new ideas — oh this sounds vain, doesn't it? Don't you live in Muntazir too? Don't you make happiness for yourself? But it is not the house or the town or the country, it is more tangled up than that. If you knew everything — what would you have done if you knew it all?

But you do know the agony of misunderstandings and petty quarrels my life has always been ever since I was married, you know how your life is different from mine. You are yourself, you answer to nobody. Though you had to fight for that, didn't you? Or else your Aunty Joyce & Aunty Cathy would have had you roasting chicken for a brood of children by now, wearing a checked apron all day instead of a pretty red dress & high heels & matching nails!

NC is not a bad man in his own way, I can see that. I can see how principled & strong he is, just one encounter with Arjun & you know what a good man NC is. People respect him because he lives by rules that come from long thinking & much reading & he is not easy on himself. He is not easy on anyone else either. Not a minute's rest! Always the striving to be meaningful. It's such a bore! Before you know it you're listening to a lecture & he thinks he knows best of course & you are no more than a foolish deluded woman if you don't agree with him & his Mukti. One day I was listening to him — talk, talk, talk — and I could hear nothing, could only see how his spittle comes out of his mouth when he talks & how he sucks it back in with a "sss," & I closed my eyes & thought of someone else so that I would not run that very day. He humiliated me every chance he had. He wanted his friends to laugh at me & condescend. He ridiculed the books I read & the paintings I made. And I thought I'd never, ever hear the end of the time I danced in the garden

— when I was only eighteen — if just to not hear about that again, it's worth running away!

Or maybe there is something wrong with me — home, husband & children are the world for women, they say. Why weren't they enough for me? That woman was always up to no good, Dinu's mother will declare in her theatrical way. Gayatri Flighty Rozario. Was her husband beating her up? Did he make her swab the floors and wash the clothes? Did he drink, did he have a lover? Did she have to tend to his aching legs every night?

NC did none of these things. Q.E.D.

There was a bird trapped inside me beating its wings. I had to tear my chest open & let it free. It makes me bleed, it hurts beyond words. There are so many things I cannot say <u>still</u>, even to <u>you</u>.

I thought I had found the best solution, I would run away with my son. It was not to be. Why was he late the one day I begged him to be on time? I still don't know. Is he all right? I'll be back for Myshkin within a year, I've sworn. Please, dearest Lis, keep an eye on him, give him treats & cakes, all the things his father thinks of as spoiling a child.

Inspect his ears now & then to see they are not grimy: he hates them being cleaned. And he lets nobody else cut his nails but me. Will you cut them for him — to think of those grimy little nails growing longer & longer! He will agree if you dangle a treat afterwards.

Sometimes people are separated for a while. It can't be helped, but it's only for a time & if I didn't know this to be true I could not remain away from Myshkin another day. I refuse to be miserable, I won't be sick again or have headaches, this is adventure, not abandonment. I want to <u>eat life</u>, grab everything new & taste it. WS was gazing out of the window yesterday — we were passing a stand of coconut trees, some villages, a child near the train tracks waved at us — & he said it was like a fairy tale — all of life, the world — & he would never work for the future, only live in the here & now. I know exactly what he means. B says WS is gruff & cutting & brutal to people he doesn't like — tells them uncomfortable truths to drive them away. She told me of a violinist he was particularly sarcastic about — a puny, well-meaning youth — yet WS complained that the man incessantly took photographs & somehow managed to "insinuate" himself into each one. And in just the same way, he said, when they were playing the Kreutzer Sonata together, the man "struck poses" on the violin that obscured "the view of Beethoven." I'm not sure exactly what he meant, but WS can be cruelly scathing.

Still, he appears to like both Beryl & me & so far we are a harmonious group. We talk about dance and painting and travels. We make up stories about the passengers who come & go. We don't fight & argue for every little thing. It feels new — to talk this way. I feel as if my brain is waking up again. I'll work at last. Properly. In a new way, really work so that I am painting with concentration & intensity. The springs are rusty, the thoughts & images don't come, they circle around, but I can't reach them, they float away. I will make them stand still.

With much love,
Gay

July 14th 1937

Lis, dearest,

Madras is unbearable, the sweat drops off our eyelashes & foreheads. This letter paper is damp with sweat, the blurs in the ink you see are made by sweat. If you can imagine the heat having a damp stink, that's how it is here. If I had not been able to reach you through that trunk call today and found out the news, I'd have given this up & come back home. (What home? Where?) Poor Myshkin, how he must have fretted at being late that day — he is such a fretter! I could not have told him why I needed him to come back on time, I was sure he'd let it out. I am so very relieved that you've reassured him & he knows all will be well.

We sail to Ceylon in a week or ten days after B has seen some Bharatnatyam. There is a new dancer here called Kanta Devi whom she is fascinated by. I think she is half in love. Is that possible? Why not? Kanta Devi is so athletic & tall & striking, she could be a man. Beryl never takes her eyes off her when they are in the same room. It's quite funny.

Yesterday we went for a walk on the

Marina. It is a beautiful promenade on the beach. A storm was building up & the waves were already high. I was frightened to think of being in the sea in a ship, lurching about on such waves. I was sad & longing for Myshkin, longing for home, longing even for Banno & Dinu & Brijen — in some strange way, I am missing the very place where I felt a prisoner. At times I feel such an outsider with W & B, Lis, I wonder if I made a mistake. I know I'll be an outsider for good now wherever I am. When that thought came to me yesterday it made me go still for a moment. As if everything had stopped around me & I had too.

WS spoke to me for a long, gentle time as we walked. He told me how he had to live alone in the Urals after he was imprisoned by the Russians when they were at war with the Germans. The rest of his family had already left their home in Russia & gone back to Germany, he happened to be the one in the wrong place at the wrong time — at just 22. But he had his dog with him & had somehow got himself a piano in the wilds of Russia — typical of WS! After all, he even managed to find a piano in Muntazir, of all places. He made friends with the nomads, he learned their language & went off to the mountains with their herds of goats. He says he felt a slowing down, a settling into the rhythms of the seasons that has never left him since. The future is always elusive he told me, you have to be a chameleon & adapt to your present & live it as if it were a celebration. Can you imagine, he read books & learned enough Arabic & Persian in the wilds of the Urals to translate Arabian Nights? He said he had wanted to learn Hindi & Sanskrit also, but was released too soon, in merely three years. Beryl said she would arrange to send W back to Russia to finish his education when the next war broke out — WS was sure to be in the wrong place again & be imprisoned again.

WS told us how it had been when he set off for unknown Java. He did not feel at home in Germany after coming back from Russia. He was surrounded by Germans who hung on to Hitler's every word. Can one exist in that way? Once you have been out of Germany, he said, you notice how terrible it is to live there, what a terrible country it is & what ghastly people inhabit it, so dry & without feeling. How unhappy it must be to feel an alien in your own country, I thought. He was afraid he would become like them, he said — to come by a sense of belonging there, he would have had to surrender his whole being, somehow have to sell himself, he said. He could not do that, so even when it meant leaving his friends, family, he preferred to go away & try to find himself a new home.

And Lis, I felt he was so right. (Not that I am saying NC was Hitler! Oh no.) There are times I have been afraid I will lose all that is myself. I felt myself turning into the person NC wanted me to be, just for a few moments' peace, how easy to please people. How easy not to cause unpleasantness. My mother always said, Whatever you do, Gayatri, don't cause any unpleasantness. As though pleasantness is life's single goal.

It makes me laugh to think of your face when you read this. Fat chance, you will say & blow a big puff of your smoke into my face. Oh, I wish we were talking together in your living room, instead of me writing pages & pages in the half-dark inside a mosquito net in this airless heat.

All of the things WS told me as we walked past the boiling sea, tasting salt with every breath — they made me feel calmer somehow. A vendor came with peanuts & we bought some. We drank cold soda from those thick bottles with marble stoppers. In the end I felt stronger. I felt as if these big changes in life are like waves that take time to build up, starting miles out at sea & we only see them at the end when they come crashing onto the sand. We can't see where they began, or where they will end, we can't see what caused them to build up in the first place.

Please write to me: you know the address! Please make sure I have a <u>stack</u> of letters waiting! Give me all the news, about yourself, Myshkin, Arjun, Brijen: everyone. So that I feel I am with you all. Half of me is there still, I am a torn-up fragment.

I will write again from the ship, I know it is possible to send letters from ports, I remember my father spending all his time on board ships to Java & Bali writing letters. This trip brings back the one with him so clearly. It seemed short at that time — I was excited & young, didn't want the journey to end. I had never expected the ship from Madras to Singapore to be so massive. This time I am prepared! Five hundred or more people, French, Vietnamese, Tamilians, Mauritians, all to live on that ship together for so many days. I remember they had four cooks for just the Indian travelers and believe it or not, one of the cooks slaughtered and skinned a goat on the deck a few feet away from the other cooks grinding spices on huge stones and peeling mountains of onion and garlic while the French soldiers stood around asking for snacks.

My father pointed out that the lack of a common language did not stop man from finding a common humanity, the natural urge is to live harmoniously, he said. And Suniti Babu, who was with us, said the happy camaraderie on the S.S. *Amboise* filled him with a special kind of self-loathing about the cannibalistic hatreds at home.

The days had gone by blissfully . . . the ten days from Singapore to Batavia passed as if in a few minutes. And then two days more to Surabaya & another two to Buleleng. How very, very long we traveled & not a moment's misery. Uncomplicated joy. My father was like that, he made everything wonderful: interesting, meaningful, amusing. If only he had been alive! Everything broke into pieces the day he died.

But I have promised: I will stop all sad & useless thoughts as soon as I see them crossing the door & coming into my head. Out, I will say to the thought. When we reach Ceylon, I'll use a passport for the first time since I had one ten years ago. What strings Beryl pulled to use that old dead document to get me a new one double-quick — I shall never know. My passport doesn't mention a husband at all, it says I am an ayah! Beryl's used to smuggling people out of countries, she told me airily — she has spirited away so many Jewish dancers from Germany. I am another of her missions of mercy, I suppose.

  With much love, yours ever, Gay.

July 20th 1937

My dear Lis,

I will post this letter & soon we will leave again — for Singapore. What an explorer I feel. B plans to stay on here for several weeks & wishes me to stay with her to watch some kind of Ceylonese dance she is interested in, but I want to go on & reach Bali. I find dance doesn't interest me so much anymore, I want movement myself, I don't want to sit and watch someone else move! How to carry on ahead with W without being disloyal to Beryl? She can be commanding & sharp-tongued, sometimes she intimidates me, though not for long. Soon she makes a silly joke & all is well again. Yesterday she went to one of her grand British open-air parties to which I was not invited & Walter didn't want to go. She came back & reported that the British garden was <u>glorified</u> by the <u>most magnificent</u> banyan tree she had ever seen, a <u>forest</u> of pillars, like a temple. The branches provided such generous shade over the tea table — <u>as well as</u> bird droppings, she said, which fell <u>mostly</u> on her. She reports all of this with such a straight face that it is only a few seconds later that you laugh at the absurdity of it. She kept brushing off imagined bird droppings from her head & shoulders & shaking out her black hair as she talked. Whenever I have my attacks of terror & sadness about leaving home, she says, "My dear Gayatri, the best things in life come by chance. And you can't tell chance what clothes to wear when it comes."

How I <u>wish</u> the old life did not have to be lost for a new one to be found!

We talked a lot, sitting on the deck of the ship. That is W talked mostly & Beryl did too, while I listened. I am so silent that B says I remind her of her Arthur. Words have to be dragged out of Arthur like wisdom teeth with dental pliers, she says. I was not this way, she knows that, but chooses to forget. My words have dried up this last week with worry & fear & who knows what else.

I'm going on & on when there are a hundred things I want to ask you, but I know some of those questions are answered in the letters you have written & sent ahead for me. Have you written, dear Lis? I am anxious to know everything although it is a great deal to ask of you when you have much to do — one does not say these things face to face because it sounds so grand & sentimental, but do you know how much I have always admired you for the way you make living alone & fending for yourself appear a constant celebration? This is why people flock to you. This is why your Home Away from Home has such an exuberant atmosphere. B & W were saying so as well: Beryl said you are full of infectious "joie de vivre" — I had to ask her what that meant & she said it meant joy of life. That is so true. She was remarking on how you dress with flamboyance (she called it), paint your fingernails just so & wear everything matching whether you are expecting visitors or not. She said you have a way of laughing without restraint till you're out of breath & have tears in your eyes. I hope those tears of laughter are the only tears you will ever know.

With much love, Gay

30th July, Surabaya.

My dearest Lis,

Almost Bali. Surabaya. We have docked at Tanjung Perak. It is a curious thing — it is as if I am back somewhere familiar, as if I was here in my last life. It was not my last life — it was only ten years ago — the moment I stepped onto the jetty a whole rag-tag-bag of memories came tumbling into my head & I was as excited as a girl, skipping around, running here & there, trying to find familiar things. B & WS very tolerant, amused, happy to see me normal again, to walk around with me to take me to places I remembered. People stop WS with big smiles — they seem to know him, he has friends everywhere & they want him to inspect new musical instruments, songbirds in cages, fish in glass bowls. The market has all kinds of shops from Chinese shoemakers to Japanese dentists. Carved wood & printed cloth & animals painted in bright colors. Stone Buddhas & other gods & goddesses. The first thing I searched out was the Armenian photographer's shop — Kurkdjian, he is called — he was still there, grayer but the same — I bought his postcards again, as I had the time before — the postcards enclosed are from there. I will send some to Myshkin too. WS managed to find a car — but of course — & we drove around from place to place. We had lunch at the Hotel Orange, where I recall the Indians had laid out a big lunch for Rabi Babu & his entourage (which by then included my father & me — on the fringes though we were). After we ate, WS dropped me off at Lokumull's, a Sindhi merchant who has a shop here — I wanted to go because I remembered that too from the last time — a huge barn of a house with four floors, where the lowest floor is the shop & the rest are rooms for his family, for his workers, for storage. Bombay prints of gods & goddesses on the walls of his puja room & a dog-eared Granth Sahib open next to a copy of the Gita in Dutch! One of his relatives insisted I go up there & pray & so I did, sitting quietly for a few minutes, letting my thoughts roam to Myshkin, to home, to you, thinking how far away I am, how everyone must think me an ogre for what I have done. Strangely, that did not make me feel unhappy in the least. Let people think what they will. I know what I am & I know what I intend to do. I have never been more certain.

Lokumull sells everything in the world, Japanese silks, mainly, but also every other pretty or ugly thing from all over — what Beryl calls "objets d'art." You would instantly find a place for one of the Japanese, Chinese, Siamese, or Burmese curios he has. Oh, I wish I could send you something. It is one among a series of shops run by Sindhis & he had looked after Rabi Babu a great deal during the day we spent in Surabaya. He recognized me from that time & asked about my "esteemed father" & shook his bald head sadly when I told him. When he heard of Rozario he was ablaze with excitement, began talking of Karachi & Rai Chand. I knew Rozario's furniture shops were famous all those years ago, of course, but never imagined I would meet someone in Java of all places, who is familiar with them. This is only because Lokumull is from Karachi & the instant he knew of the connection, he wanted me to meet all his relatives, his wife, his grandchildren — it became a regular Indian gathering with much shouting, laughing, excitement. We were served very sweet, ghee-soaked halwa & sherbet in glasses tinted yellow. In the midst of it all appeared an urbane old gentleman named Badruddin, a Punjabi Muslim with a long beard & a paunch that settled comfily on his thighs. He fitted himself into a chair & held forth on Karachi, Lahore, Quetta & so on. THOSE DAYS! It was as if my presence gave them an audience for old tales they have nobody new to share with. When we parted there were loud & warm invitations to me to come to them the minute I was tired of Bali — there are very few Indians there, just a few illiterate petty traders, I would have nothing in common with them whatsoever, they assured me. Any time I was longing for home food or new saris, anything at all, I was to remember they were only two nights away by steamer. It made me smile, both their ardour & their conviction that I would pine for home food & home company. I was struck that they didn't condemn me as a fallen woman — maybe because travel is a normal thing for them. They & their ancestors have always done it & so they do not find it unusual to encounter a woman traveling alone. They think I am here for a holiday & will go back soon. <u>Of course</u> I did not tell them the way I left home.

Before we sail for the last part of our journey, I will give this letter to be posted. My dear, dear Lis, I am going to be in Bali at last! It is the final stretch. Is it wrong & criminal that I feel nothing but excitement? My pangs of homesickness are gone. Well, gone for the moment, & why (as WS says) look beyond the moment. Everything in life happens for a reason, & good things happen out of bad. <u>Onward!!</u>

With much love, yours ever,
Gay

August 1937, Ubud

My dearest Lis!

In the water between Surabaya and Buleleng I thought for a minute — no, for many minutes! — that I would meet my Maker. (He did a bad job with me, didn't He?) We could see hills on the island of Madura from the steamer and to pass it the steamer had to go through a narrow strait — would it go through safely or would it hit the coast? It seemed far too narrow for us. We stood on the deck watching, half-afraid, half-excited, even WS taut, though with excitement not fear, I suppose. In the event, we went through safely. Ships with billowing sails went past far away, nearer us were boats from which men were throwing out nets to catch fish. So beautiful when I stopped being anxious. In the early evening the moon rose big and orange, like half a setting sun, and the water became deep orange and blue. Slowly the blue darkened to almost black and at night the ship moaned and rocked and the moon hung so low and large in the sky it was close enough to pluck and eat. A hundred colors! My face is soaked in blue and orange. And then at dawn the shadows of hills on the island in the distance and a mysterious fragrance in the air — I cannot describe it, you have to be here to know it.

At Buleleng the water was shallow and the ship dropped anchor a long way away from the shore. We had to climb down the ship by a ladder and get into a boat which carried us and our muddle of luggage, including the sarod WS has brought back with him. He walked off to hunt for a car, which was supposed to be waiting for us, to drive us to Gianyar. It costs 26 guilders to rent a car for the day — new and exciting to think in guilders and not rupees! It would take us all day to reach, he said, it was almost forty miles away, over hills & volcanoes, down on the southern side of the island. The household would be waiting for us, he said. The cook must have roasted pig and duck to celebrate.

The most wonderful thing was that WS rented a car from the same woman who supplied the cars for Rabi Babu's entourage on my last trip! I had so wanted to meet her again, and I did. She is a woman called Queen Fatima — she is such a character, she had made a great impression on me the last time — a billowy creature with a loud voice & teeth absolutely black with chewing tobacco & cigarettes. The story about her is that she had been one of the queens of southern Bali & when the Dutch came to conquer it, her husband the king & all his wives decided to kill themselves. Queen F did not want to die, so she ran away — all the way over hills & mountains, to the north. Here she changed her religion & became a Muslim. Some say it's nonsense & she was no queen, she was a concubine. Whatever it is, I like her. I remember how she was terribly friendly & bade Rabi Babu "Selamat Jalan" again & again when we were leaving. After a while, a bit tired of her effusions, he had said in his dry way, "The lady is the kind of woman who has a past that is not yet wholly past." He & his friends found her rather forward, which irked me even then & I was reminded of it when I sat with her a few hours ago — she's not forward, she's forceful. She is sure of herself & lives by her own means — runs her own taxi service & her own shop & orders her staff around & bosses over her daughters & spits her tobacco juice as far into the corner as any man — I suppose these things mark her out as forward.

I felt a great sense of freedom when I sat in her shop. Her enormous bulk poured out from every side of her chair & she grilled me via WS's translations with great inquisitiveness (somehow I didn't find it offensive) — who was I, what did I think I was doing etc. To her, I had no trouble saying I had left my husband! (There, I have written it too. For the first time.) In the end she said, "When you have to leave your family & home it is not easy & nobody does it without a thought. If you have come so far, you are here to stay."

She wasn't sentimental or profound, quite the opposite, sucking on her teeth, prying them with a pin for some bit of stuck meat while she spoke to me, but when I was leaving, she pressed a mother-of-pearl necklace & a little Buddha into my hands & said that if I needed a friend I had one & not to hesitate, etc etc. Then she said something to WS, which was possibly lewd (somehow, it felt like that from the way she smacked her lips & gargled with laughter), she slapped his shoulders & also Beryl's (B loved her too) & the "Selamat Jalan" came in the booming voice I know from years ago.

And finally — here I am! Settled in a small bamboo & stone hut in W's Tjampuhan. It is a part of his estate. It's as WS described it when he came — a series of small bamboo huts with thatch roofs, each one with a verandah & above a fast-moving river that runs down a deep gorge far, far below & in the gorge are trees so tall their tops are level with our houses.

Life is quiet & pleasant here. Every morning you find someone on the steps of the verandah — they sit & wait until WS comes out & talks to them. They smoke something that smells sweetly, of cloves. WS might chat for a while, then go back in to nap or read, come out again when he wants to be with them & they just keep sitting there. They are villagers from nearby & at times from far away & they might stay for hours — very peaceably, smoking, chewing a paan-like thing just as at home & spitting out red juice also just as they do at home, blackened-teeth from it, just as Banno's teeth were. (How my father-in-law hated her red spittle.) Some of the men come to show WS their paintings or sculpture, some just to share news.

There are two managers who run this place & a small group of foreigners too, all orbiting around WS. They gossip & squabble & there are undercurrents I can sense but not analyze — but everyone is at work or at play & somehow much gets done. A famous American anthropologist is here: Margaret Mead. Rather a stodgy, humorless person who talks in long words & once she starts a sentence you know it will be nothing short of a paragraph. I want to run when I see her approach. It's like NC launching into a discourse on the economics of colonialism — all of it used to fly straight past my ears or above my head. M. Mead dislikes Beryl & calls her a sharp-tongued witch behind her back. Beryl does not say anything offensive, but I can tell the dislike is mutual. There is an American musician called Colin McPhee & his wife, Jane Belo — she's very pretty & WS adores her.

Beryl & WS quarrel a lot these days, though it is not ill-natured fighting. He is amused by her but loses patience & she can be annoying, acts the little girl, jumps around with over-enthusiasm. He says it takes a long time for him to teach her to see & understand things. I can be of some help when they are going over their notes about India, but none at all when they discuss the dance here, which I understand only from a dim distance. I go with Beryl to watch the Balinese dances, but it has fallen away from me — my absorption in dance, the way I became charged lightning if I was watching a performance. The dazzling costumes, the formal precision, the beauty of the dancers . . . and yet after a while I find my thoughts are far away, or I am interested in drawing them rather than understanding. So I stay on the fringes while Beryl complains that WS is too lighthearted & too lazy. (What must she think of me?) She says everything takes twice the time because he does too many different things & rushes around Bali once to give a concert, the next few days to help out a film crew, or just to collect old musical instruments.

I am mesmerized by everything I see around me, but I still feel an onlooker. I feel as if I'll visit for a while and then leave — I cannot think I am here to stay, it cannot be. When will I stop feeling like Cinderella at the ball? <u>Time to go! Time to go!</u> Every now and then I think I must stand up and say my thank-yous and go back home. But where is home? My home is where Myshkin is and you are. Does that mean I will never be at home again? I cannot think of not seeing you again, of course we will. You will come here.

I am somewhat starstruck. There is an old guest book here — so many visitors to this place. I have been going through it & find dozens of names I have only read in magazines before. Charlie Chaplin even! Noël Coward (he is an English playwright) came to visit WS & left him a long poem in the book. I'll tell you a bit of it:

Oh Walter dear, Oh Walter dear,
Please don't neglect your painting . . .
Crush down dear Walter if you can
Your passion for the Gamelan
Neglect your love of birds & beasts
Go to far fewer temple feasts
Neglect your overwhelming wish
To gaze for hours at colored fish . . .

And so on. It is so true, even if funny. The one thing WS needs to do — his painting — he is lazy about. He is always short of money but still he turns down work. He tells us he'd much rather sit under a tree & watch the birds & leaves or count the ants on a window ledge than waste life at an easel. This infuriates B at times & at times she finds it amusing, depending on her mood.

I, on the other hand, am already beavering away at painting with a kind of grim determination that ruins my work in the end — it is all stilted, forced, imitative — I feel down in the dumps about it — but I so want to sell & earn enough to bring across Myshkin, quickly. I want it to happen tomorrow! Right away! I would paint houses or buses or signboards if that brought money. I feel a hideous sense of urgency — as if I have only a year or a few months in which to work & earn & bring him & then the magic gate will close. It is all nonsense, of course.

In return for my board & lodging (though it is a paltry return) I help WS with some of the things his cousin Conrad used to do — do you remember the Kosya he talked about? He helped W to transcribe music, to care for his animals & so on. I will be useless with the music. I suppose I will be like an assistant, odd-job girl, animal-minder all in one. How jealous Myshkin would be! I wonder if he will grow up & be a zookeeper as he vows — only he would set all the animals free & tigers would roam the streets of Muntazir.

WS used to have a whole menagerie in Java, but in Bali they believe animals should not be kept captive. So he gave them away to a zoo in Java — except for a few monkeys from whom he refuses to part. He shares his own cottage with the monkeys & the bathroom is full of fruit bats. It is rather unnerving when you don't expect them. I am used to lizards & cockroaches & spiders, even scorpions — but bats! I don't go in there anymore. You stay in your world, I tell the bats & monkeys when I pass them, I'll be in mine & do you no harm.

The trees & plants are so familiar — many I can recognize. Banyan, milkwood, banana, coconut, champa. There is lotus and hibiscus. There are other plants I've never seen before. It will take me time to find out about. I'll draw them. Will you see that Myshkin keeps drawing? He made some nice pictures in his schoolbook this year — he has a gift. I have thought that one of the ways is for me to keep painting little pictures & sending him those in my letters. I've been drawing them for Myshkin and sending letters to him, I wonder if he gets them. Or if his father lets him read them. I suppose NC will want him to loathe me. That would be natural.

I wonder every day about what is happening at home — at precise times — my mind runs in a loop — now Myshkin is waking, now NC is coming back from his walk, now I am going into the kitchen to set out the day's necessities, now I am sitting out in the verandah & Brijen has dashed across to try out a new piece of music, his hair standing on end because he's been clutching it, now I am thinking about painting but not doing it, now I am scooting out of the gate to visit you — oh! I wish you were round the corner here too so I could run down to you. I have not had any letters from you yet — you <u>have</u> written, haven't you? I hope they are not getting lost. I hope you are getting these letters from me.

With much love, yours

Gay

November 15th 1937

My dearest Lis

At last a little news from you. It makes me so relieved to know that things are not as bad as they might have been, but Lis, do try to write me <u>longer</u> letters — <u>more</u> news — tell me <u>everything</u> that is happening. You are not a longwinded letter-writer, I am finding out, not as long-winded as I am — but then that takes time, doesn't it? And loneliness. You have neither of those things. Your days are full & you have a hundred friends & two hundred things to do every day to keep your guesthouse running.

I have started collecting money for my passage & Myshkin's & I am painting with great determination. WS has promised he will paint a big painting by next year that he will contribute to what he calls the "Bring Home Myshkin Fund." He keeps saying he will give me money to bring him right now — but there is something stubborn in me, I need to do it on my own. I think I need a little time to settle down before Myshkin comes. There has never been a time in my life when I could set everything aside &

forget meal times & sleep times & just <u>work!</u>

In the middle of the late evening, twice, I've run out & stood breathing the dark air & the dense forest around & listening to the gamelan's gong, so deep it hums in my bones. I stand there feeling the forest enter my body, smelling the scents I don't know yet. Then the sound dies down & slowly comes back chime by chime. It makes me shiver, their music. It makes me understand how far away I am from everything I used to know. I go back in & I go to bed & wake before it is light & lie still, eyes closed. I can see what I am going to paint so clearly before me.

But certainly, no handouts, none — well, other than the board & lodging — that is somehow not as bad as taking money to bring my son across. (Will Nek let him come or will I have to kidnap him?) I am saving & saving, I spend on nothing. Once M is here, W says he will take him all over the island, "fore & aft" to show him around! Why does WS do so much for me? He's not close to me in the way he is to Jane (Colin's wife, I told you about her in an earlier letter) or to the other people here. It must be because of some memory of meeting me as a girl with my father — ten years ago — but what an age ago that seems. The world's gone through two ice ages between then & now — dinosaurs & mammoths were wiped away — a new world came.

I am painting better. I noticed WS's visitors stop before a picture I finished the other day and contemplate it for a long, long time. It is a scroll-like picture, about 5 ft long, in which all of Balinese village life is happening down the levels from top to bottom, and I've done it somewhat in the style of the local painters. It will find a buyer, WS said, sounding certain, & I was as pleased as a child getting a prize!

WS long ago started a foundation to help local artists: to teach them new ways to paint & to sell their paintings. It is called Pitamaha (after Bhishma from Mahabharata — unexpected to find these Indian traces here, I had almost forgotten them). Most artists are so selfish they don't want others to succeed & here's WS who spends his own time & energy & thought trying to make others famous. When art galleries in Berlin & Paris want his paintings to be part of Bali-art shows, he does not send any because he wants the local work to get the attention. Maybe one day he will send one of my paintings! It is thrilling to think of earning from my own work, but I'll have to work hard & sell many pictures. A guilder here is only a little bit less than a rupee, and the money from home — so much of it from your savings, Lis — will serve me for a while, but not for long.

I envy WS's gift. It is a lesson to watch him at work — when he does start working he doesn't stop, for days you don't see him at all. The other day, when he had run out of money, he locked himself up for a week & painted a picture. He says it's indecent how he can paint something with no effort at all & sell it for a heap of money. And it did — it sold for enough to buy him a car. The trouble is, though, that the minute he makes any money he spends it — either on himself or on his friends & so he is perpetually short.

It will cost a lot to bring Myshkin. Somehow, on that holiday with my father, it had felt a much shorter distance. I remember one afternoon when our ship had halted in Singapore & Dhiren Babu, Rabi Babu's friend, was lost in playing the esraj all day — from Bhairavi to Ram Kali & back to Bhairavi the esraj went with its plaintive notes & time melted away — in just the way it does when Brijen sings. (Brijen claimed that every night, when he used to sing on his terrace, it was only so that I would listen to his songs from my bed on my roof and fall asleep to them. Such a mischievous flirt. How is he?)

That trip with my father has been coming back to me with everything I see. I miss him continually these days. How he would have loved to visit me here — he would have come here with me, he would have rejoiced in the painting, the music, the travel — he was always ready for adventure, endlessly thought up new things to do. He said the way to live was to fill your mind & body with pleasurable things so that unpleasant things simply had no room in your life. Which is much as WS thinks & I suppose that is why they got along. One of my life's great regrets will always be that Myshkin never knew my father — his sense of music, his love for painting, his way with children, his faith that I was something unusual & gifted. What keeps me alive through these months of separation is that this change in my life is as much for Myshkin as for me: once he is here, he won't be stifled by worthiness anymore, new worlds will open up for him, of art, or animals, of living among people who are different, who value something other than politics.

Anyway, no room for self-pity, none! I am here. I came because I chose to, I will not mope & moan, I will work.

I must tell you: Bali is not at all unlike India & not only because of the Hindu gods here. When we came here with Rabi Babu, the Dutch were afraid he would incite the nationalistic Javanese — to follow in the footsteps of the Indian freedom fighters. They sent Dutch people with him everywhere, watching him. He might have — he saw many similarities between India & Bali. When he came here to Gianyar he said it was as if an earthquake had destroyed a great old city — India he meant — and it had sunk beneath the ground. In its place had risen up the homes & farms & people of later years, but in many places the past had come back to the top & the two, cobbled together, make up the culture of Bali.

On that journey with my father, I was

too young to understand such complicated things — or maybe not too young — after all, it made such an impression on me that I have not forgotten it. All those years ago the place felt both familiar & quite unknown. The villages are very like those I saw in Bengal when I went with my father — the land is green & blue as gemstones & with little houses with two-tiered roofs of thatch. Coconut palms, jackfruit, shining paddy fields, the sound of water everywhere. The stands of bamboo are as tall as big houses & sway gently all together from the base when there is a wind — a creaking sound that goes on and on until you feel drowsy.

All around are things I want to paint! There are not enough days in my life to paint all the pictures I have in my head. The painters here make exquisitely detailed scenes of village life and although I did that one long painting of the same kind, I could never paint another like that, my mind doesn't work that way. They have an elegance & artistry that is from another time. I remember Rabi Babu pointed out how the ordinary village people here are artistic about their homes, furniture, doorways.

He thought that because they have enough food they can paint & make beautiful things out of nothing. I don't agree. Is prosperity the only barrier against ugliness & squalor? The rich parts of our country are not beautiful as the most ordinary villages are here. Every courtyard is serene & enchanting, pink & blue lotus grow in still pools. Wherever you turn your gaze there is a stone frog or stone dog below a champa tree showering it with flowers. There is no sloppiness of the wretched, shabby kind we have at home. In every village there is dance & theater. Music fills the nights. Elaborate, gorgeous costumes & jewelry at the dances. Flowers in their hair, ornate headdresses. The men wear flowers in their turbans or tuck one at their ears. Many of the women are exquisitely beautiful & have a direct, unafraid gaze that I love.

Rabi Babu's friend Suniti Babu said the men & women were as if they came off the walls of Ajanta & Ellora — & he was right. (Suniti Babu was fascinated by Balinese women. He noticed their clothes, their hair, their gait, he even noticed how they had their mouths a bit open at all times so that they have an

expression of permanent wistfulness . . .
It makes me smile now — how closely
he must have been examining them, that
old Bengali scholar! Indian men! If
lechery is not their primary characteristic
I don't know what is — though not for a
moment was Suniti Babu lecherous, he
was <u>attentive</u>.)

Suniti Babu pointed out then what I
know to be true now — that Java & Bali
are magical, exotic, fairy lands to the
Europeans who come here. But for us
from India, it is not so. It is only <u>another
version of the East</u>. Suniti Babu would
keep reminding us that patterns of dress,
rituals, homes, temples were similar in a
huge swath right from the northwest
frontier of India to Bengal to the Malabar & Indochine, Java & Bali. He used
to point to examples from archaeologi-
cal finds, from statues in Indian temples.
He knew a great deal — so many languages & history — that he could see &
hear rhythms across civilizations that I
simply could not, certainly not then, at
sixteen. At that time I listened, but did
not understand too much. Now I find
myself thinking back to the things he
said, more & more.

All along the roads here are statues &

temples. I have not seen a single beggar. The children don't seem to cry & the mothers don't scream at them as we in India do. Not many women in villages of the remote south of Bali cover their chests. In the north because of the Dutch & Christianity, they have become prudish. It was astonishing for me at first to see how normal it was to be bare-breasted here — after a while it seems the most natural thing. It used to be the same in the Malabar & in Bengal long ago as well — women wore no blouses. Well, I am relieved to have been born late!

Before you ask: no, I haven't taken to their style of (un)dress!!! I still wear my normal sari & blouse & petticoat, haven't had the nerve to wear one of your beautiful dresses yet — though I do wonder where to get new saris when I need them. I could just cut up meters of cloth. Or I could take up Lokumull's offer & ask him. I exchange letters with his family occasionally & saw them once more when we went to Surabaya to fetch Beryl. As usual they started frying and cooking the instant they saw me and insisted I eat with them. Lokumull has a grumpy old relative — nobody knows how old — she sits there in the shop all day scolding the boys who work there, but she has a sweet way of nodding off to sleep in the middle of conversation, even her own, & the room goes still while everyone suppresses their laughter. She wakes after a few minutes & notices the mirth & is scornful. "Laugh, laugh while you can," she says. "The dried fruit lasts longest, the green ones fall from the tree & rot."

I don't miss Indians, nor do I seek them out, but I so miss you, Lis. And I ache for my darling Myshkin. I even miss my sharp-tongued, fault-finding old Father-in-Law . . . at this rate I might start missing Arjun and Brijen. Or Bechari Banno. All right, all right, I know you are fond of old Batty Rozario. Sometimes I think that if you were closer in age — oh, so many possible lives! I should never have been married at all. I was never meant to be owned, I needed to be free, a vagabond or a gypsy. I'd have done less damage. But they forced me & I was so young. What else would I have done? My mother owned me, she transferred me to NC & then he owned me. Life would have been so different if my father had lived longer.

It is pointless to think such thoughts. <u>Out</u>, sad thought!

And on that note, with much love,

yours as ever,

Gay

Feb. 1938

My dearest Lis,

I have had my first letters from my son! Two came together. He doesn't seem to have got a few of my letters. Maddening. But I feel grateful NC is kind about this — he lets him have my letters and answer them. How adorably he writes, with rubbed-out black bits where I can see the spelling mistakes he is trying to hide from me & all his news of Rikki & Dinu & his Dada. He asks me what time next week he should go to the station so that he can come to me: oh, that broke my heart! Will you explain to him please, so that he understands — & you mustn't crush his hopes, just make him understand that it will take a little time. You'll need to be a trapeze artist to do that.

I am working very, very hard. I am immersed in work, it thrills me & consumes everything I have — I don't want to spend a minute doing anything else but work. It is as if I have turned a corner of a winding road that seemed to have no end & I have found my way of painting, what appears true & interesting & real. When I am not working, I think of it — continually & intensely — my dreams are drenched in color — there are nights when I close my eyes & can see nothing but topaz, gold, jade, purple, the deepest red, ocher & midnight blue & they are dazzling & brilliant & ever present. The colors of the forest and water here particularly: a million blues, & thousands of greens & the fading away of leaf into vine into weed into a blue-green distance made of hill & rice field.

We travel here & there & I carry my watercolors & a camera WS has lent me, one of his old ones, so that I can use the photographs to paint from later: this was something he advised me to do, he had done it in his early days in Java, he said. Even though it cannot capture the colors it reminds one of the scene, the positions of trees and so on. He told me not to scream and scare the animals when I hear the news . . . that I am to be included in an exhibition in Batavia next month. Can you believe that? I will have to work even harder now!

Last month we went on horseback to Kintamani in a group — it is a remote place which has a volcano surrounded by bare fields of lava, black & strange, sprouting dry straw-like grass & nothing else. The top of the volcano is flat & its sides are bare. The mist that permanently obscures the top gives it a brooding mystery quite unlike other mountains. It is a bleak beauty. Through this we wandered & it was chilly at times & exhilarating. When we were tired we would settle in the shade somewhere & eat and drink. WS has created a wickerwork basket which can be attached to a saddle so that he can carry beer & whisky & gin & port with him on these travels. He takes a childlike glee in offering a choice to his friends posted in remote villages doing survey work. You should see how their mouths fall open — you would have loved it, wouldn't you? And you'd have remembered to pack lemons to slice & top the glasses with.

We had some dried roast duck, fish, boiled eggs — and a black dog with a curly tail appeared. We threw it scraps of food & it came closer, though it was wary. It was so scrawny, as if it had hardly eaten for days. As we left, it would not take its eyes off us & that was miserable, to see that wire-thin dog lost among the black rock & weeds — the edge of the lonely world. When we'd come down & reached the villages, we saw there was the dog still, following us. To cut a long story short, it has joined the household & WS has named her Indah, which means Beauty, though she is really anything but that in her present scabby, flea-bitten, miserable state. She has blisters — from not eating enough, I am told. WS aims to set all that right & the first thing that happened when Indah came home was that she was given a bath (she smelled foul) which she hated & ran from, despite the heat! And then she gobbled down fish & a great heap of rice, hardly even stopping to breathe until it was finished. She will learn to live with the monkeys and bats, WS says, with great confidence. Let us see.

W has been tramping all over Bali collecting artifacts for a museum he is curator of. I don't go on these trips, I stay back & work — how odd it is to call painting "work"! NC always insisted it was a "nice hobby" for women, painting pictures. Everything was permitted as long as it remained trivial. He should see the way I paint now! I'm covered in paint & mud (I am making things with stone & clay too), my face is smeared, my hair is glued together.

Ni Wayan Arini, a woman who does some housework for me, laughs her head off each time she sees me. She's one of the few Balinese I can talk to, even though her English is broken, she has picked it up playing around as a child with visitors to WS's home, I think. She pauses with an open mouth & mutters in her own language when she is hunting for a word — then our eyes meet & she shakes her head & grins & gives up. It pleases me no end that the people you pay to help with menial jobs are not servile here in the way our servants are — & our servants are like that because people treat them so badly. It is ingrained in us to be savage and cruel to poor people, as if they were some other life form — neither human nor animal. I have seen Arjun slap across his face the boy who cleans his car when he finds a fingerprint on the windscreen.

Anyway — I was telling you about W's collecting trips — someone else drives while W keeps his eyes open for things to collect. The car is a bit like Arjun's Dodge — but is a different one. It is called an Overland Whippet. It's anything but a whippet, more a lumbering, trundling thing that is piled high with the oddest things from carved doors and musical instruments to kitchen goods when it comes back. Beryl said the other day that it was just an excuse for boys' days out & beachcombing, this museum. They have a few others helping with descriptions of the things in Dutch & English & then off the things go to the museum — it already has many visitors.

What surprised me here was to see how completely immersed WS is in music — he hears music in everything — there are always scores coming for him in the post. He often talks about the way Brijen used to take him to listen to singers nobody knew about, old maestros tucked away in moldy old tenements — but W could not make much sense of Indian classical music he says. He jokes that like Hinduism, you probably have to be born to it.

When WS is here rather than at his other home in Iseh, I know at once because of the music that spreads over our hillside. I am sure the birds pause to listen, it is so lovely. Colin & W are at the piano together, sometimes W alone, playing something sublime I cannot remember or hum but long to listen to again. W has retuned a piano so that it sounds like the gamelan — the gamelan is not one instrument, it is the orchestra here. I can't go into long descriptions, but it is made of xylophones & drums & gongs & the sound is a very strange, rhythmic, repetitive one which is somehow mesmerizing. Have I already told you about it? Forgive me if I have!

Colin's wife Jane Belo is an anthropologist. I get the sense when I am with them — I can't put my finger on it — but I feel she & Colin don't care for each other, they don't even like each other, husband & wife. (I wonder if people felt this way when they saw me with NC. Oh dear. Was I awful? Tell me, was I?) There is much tension in the air. WS says this is because Colin is neurotic & spoilt. But he does not mind Colin's tantrums because he is dedicated about music. They play together at a Steinway piano Colin has bought, WS loves it.

Colin is also quite a cook & tries out all sorts of strange foods: hornbills, flying fox, porcupine, there is nothing he does not turn into a roast or stew. I don't always feel happy with this & find a way not to eat: I think some animals need to be left on their trees or burrows, wherever it is they live. I don't know what Jane thinks of all this, she seems distant & is silent or talks too much & the air fairly crackles with unsaid things. It can be rather uncomfortable. I creep away & make myself scarce. WS sits aside with her at such times for ages & ages & they have long conversations — they are very close & can talk of anything under the sun. When they are in different places they even write letters to each other.

W has a gift of being close & friendly with married women — they are less likely to pounce on him with a view to seduction, I suppose! Most people here know that WS is not interested in women — not in that way — as you had guessed from the start. He has male lovers openly, nobody thinks it wrong. Do you remember how he was with that young sarod teacher of his? You found it odd, you said so then. Remember what you saw once when he had left his door ajar by mistake? Your mouth went into an O of shock, your face was as red as an apple! It was so funny!

I cannot help feeling, as I write these things, that I shouldn't. You say you find it interesting, but when one doesn't know the people or the place is it possible to be interested? I am no storyteller. But I tell you all of this, Lis, so that I don't lose you. I want you to share my life & me to share yours as closely as we used to in Muntazir — or more. Sometimes it is possible to be closer in letters than in life, don't you think? There are things we can say in letters that we never would find the word for, or the courage, when we are face to face.

Give me more news in your next, dear L. Are there any interesting guests? Is Boy behaving? Did you go for any of the parties at Christmas? I hope Myshkin is not being bullied in school — you will tell me, won't you, even if the news is not good?

With much love,
Yours ever, Gay

10th April 1938

Dearest Lis,

I am astonished to hear that NC has left home & with nothing more than a cloth bundle. What on earth was he thinking? And if you hadn't told me about it, I wouldn't have known — what a silly baby Myshkin is. He did not tell me his father had gone off in search of the Truth! Has he found it, I wonder? Was it hiding under a rock or behind a tree? Well, who am I to be sarcastic? I am the wicked, evil witch who left my husband & child & home. In the old days they would have stoned me to death or buried me alive.

And that Brijen is gone too — nobody knows where he is? How can that be? How bad was his fight with Arjun, and what do you mean it was about a woman he was in love with? He is in love with a hundred women! What was special about this one that it made him get into a fight with his brother? It is a great torment to be so far away and not know anything about the people one saw every day. Will you send me more news when you have it? I am worried sick.

Things are somewhat different here. I find it rather frightening, but the others seem to think nothing much will come of it. The police have started some sort of <u>surveillance</u> on people — including WS — to prove that they are up to <u>bad</u>

things. Apparently there is a lot of pressure from Christian missionaries to arrest men who have had relations with other men & the new Governor General is very sternly Christian, married to a woman who is from a terribly over-religious American family. WS finds this amusing (as he does most things). He says Bali has always been left alone by the Christians & men having relations with men is not thought of as illegal or bad here — no amount of Christian outrage will lead to anything. (This reminds me again — how absurd it was to know from your last letter that everyone thinks I ran away with WS for love. I suppose they think I am like that girl in Calcutta who fell in love with the visiting Romanian. Love! Nobody imagines a woman might do anything other than for the love of a man, it seems to me. Well, they are wrong.)

WS says it is as if Nazi Germany is entering Bali by way of the Dutch — the same intolerance, the same self-righteousness, the same strictures. This is why he left Germany, came halfway round the world to find the freedom to live — but it's an infection that will make the whole world ill, this joyless censoriousness, this horror of anything that is not in the rule book. The nose-puffing way the powerful have of deeming what is good & what is bad — who are the Dutch to decide? The Balinese think it is quite normal for men to love men, or men to love women or women to love women — well, who knows what, as long as somebody is loved & nobody is harmed! It is another of those things that makes me realize Rabi Babu was right — he used to say that Bali felt as India must have been in ancient times. There must have been a time when love did not have moral guardians saying you may do this but not that — this is how it is in Bali now & how it was in our country hundreds of years ago. My father had said that the Bali we were then experiencing would not last. How long can an island remain an island? Baba would say in the grimmest, gloomiest tone he could muster, "Open your eyes & ears wide, see & hear everything, memorize everything. This will vanish one day. You may never come again."

But here I am. I've come back. And things are indeed changed. It is a strange & frightening thing when you feel that people you don't know — the government — is watching what you are doing inside your home, even if you are harming nobody. Jane says her servants were being questioned about what goes on in their house. WS has harmed nobody. It's very hard to have secrets here. Yet he is being watched by the police & so are we.

WS does not take it seriously, not for one minute. They sent policemen to tail him at one of the evening dances & we spotted them at once — standing about, ridiculous in pajamas & sandals & spectacles. WS was very naughty & told the dancers to kiss the policemen & flirt with them . . . after a while the policemen were thoroughly derailed & began to dance with the boys too. It was foolish of WS to do this. Where does this desire to court danger come from, I wonder? Or is he a genuine innocent blundering about in an alien world?

You will wonder where all this libertine thinking comes to <u>me</u> from, you are imagining me in orgies. How am I talking this way when I never thought of these things before? It's just that I am finding out how limited my world was. There is so much outside it. I thought romantic love, if it existed at all, happened between men & women. (On 3,

Pontoon Road, Muntazir, it did not happen even between men and women.) I have understood I was naive. Life is far more interesting than I had thought!

It must be getting hot already in Muntazir — or is the springtime there still? You must be in your cool room, drinking your icy G&T on the sly & slipping a few drinks down the stairs to my father-in-law. One day someone will call him the Drunk Doctor & it will all be your fault! Such a puzzle of a man, so very elegant, ever civilized & considerate, yet hard to know. He found a hundred ways to make me feel better in the days when I first came to Muntazir, still crushed by the death of my father & cut up about being married off in such a hurry. He could see from the start that we were not well matched, NC & I. He didn't get into battles with his son, how could he? Come between a man & his wife! Tauba, tauba!

But he found many ways to tell me he understood my misery. Gave me books, a desk to sit & work at, words of praise if I made anything at all: whether a rogan josh or a painting. I didn't find a way to repay his kindness — he has great self-sufficiency — it's hard to see what one could do to make a difference to him. You are able to — somehow you've always known how to make him smile. You have such a gift, I envy you.

Tell me all the news. Is Dinu behaving himself? I worry he will make Myshkin grow up too soon. You say he reads & re-reads my letters in the clinic. How happy that makes me, & also how terribly sad. I wonder what you are doing at this moment. I worry about you too, managing everything on your own. You have so much to do & to add to it, my father-in-law and his wounded heroes. WS laughed & laughed when I told him about how the two of you patch up revolutionaries on the sly. He says it's lucky the Dutch don't have to deal with Lisa & Batty or their East Indies empire would certainly collapse.

I am folding in a scrap of a silk scarf with this letter. I hope it reaches. It is meant to match your green silk dress.

Write to me. Soon. I need your words.

With much love

Gay

2 July 1938

Dearest Lis,

I have received both your letters — they came together. You've no idea what they mean to me — I'm parched earth waiting for rain. I pine for news. It is a miracle any letters reach across all these seas & continents, I should be grateful only a few get lost. These letters to you have become a diary for me, you know, I almost forget I am writing to you, just scribble & scribble over many days. A letter is chatter in written form, Rabi Babu told me, when he sat on the deck writing one on that old journey. He said everyone has a special notebook, it has loose leaves, and it is for writing to which nobody attaches value. It is for writing that turns up disheveled, no turban on its head or shoes on its feet. It goes where no questions are asked for coming without reason, its whole reason for arriving is to chatter aimlessly.

That's what my letters to you are. They are me running down to your guesthouse without purpose or need, just to talk. I never know when I start a letter how many days it will take me to finish it. That's wrong, isn't it, & you must find it annoying, all my rambling. Do you? Now I can see you getting up from your chair & stomping out of the room saying, "I'll come back when you get your head in place, Gay." You never had room for mawkishness.

But I am in a sad, mad, bad temper. I was not there for Myshkin's tenth birthday for the first time in his life. How I used to wait for the 30th of June every year, to see his starry eyes when I held a wrapped present towards him in the morning. Instead, this time I went to a temple to pray for him. I had not stepped inside a temple except into the courtyards for the dances. But I felt the need to do <u>something</u>, so I woke early and when I walked down the street there were women putting out leaf cups filled with flowers and incense on their doorsteps. I never pray & I felt an impostor, I looked for a place to leave my slippers, but a man standing around there gestured to say I need not be barefoot. I suppose he could see right away I didn't know the first thing about praying at a temple in Bali (or elsewhere) but he didn't stop me. I was tongue-tied & I fumbled with the offerings, but maybe God, if he or she exists, understood what

I was trying to say. My body is torn into a thousand pieces with the pain. How could I do this to him? Will I be able to live with it? At this moment it is unbearable to think of my callousness. He'll hate me forever. (No, he won't, he'll forgive me when he grows up.)

I cannot write any more today. I will try and come back.

<u>Two days later</u>: I am posting this, Lis, with nothing further added. I haven't written for so long I want to send you <u>something</u> quickly, but seem unable to write words that will even qualify as aimless chatter. On some days I feel heavy, can't make myself get up from my cot in the morning, can't muster up the appetite for work or talk. A blackness inside me that will pass — it is missing poor M's birthday that has started this fit of bottomless gloom. Tell me if you baked a cake for him and if he got a gift from his grandfather. I cannot bear to think of a little boy spending his tenth birthday with neither of his parents by his side. I have done this to him.

With all my love,

G.

Sept. 1938

Dearest Lis,

So many changes! To think NC has come back with a new wife. How will she be with Myshkin? What did you think when you met her? Is she a kind person? Will she be gentle to him? They say a loving woman heals many wounds — I just didn't have it in me, I suppose, to be a loving woman. I was always the one causing the wounds. No, I was not cut out to be a mother — strange that there are so many opposing pulls & tugs in us — it is not as though I don't miss Myshkin achingly, fiercely. I do. But it is not a constant missing. I am glad to have time to work. There I've said it! I can confess it to nobody but you. At times when he was tiny & ailing I forgot his medicines & his meal was late because I was daydreaming or doing who knew what. Then I'd spend a week eaten up with guilt, spoiling him till he was thoroughly confused. He is so easily turned into a quiet mourner who goes into a shell. Does he still hide in that broken carriage, I wonder. He's always thought that <u>nobody</u> knows he goes there.

But to marry a village woman with a

small child — madness! (Oh, but each time I write these things I want to scratch them out — who am I to criticize? When I've done what I've done? I've forever lost my right to pass judgment on anyone.) Myshkin has not told me about any of this. It's over a year since I left home. Myshkin at first sounded so impatient about coming here, & now he hardly asks. I suppose he's lost hope, or forgotten. Children tend to forget things quickly. He writes once a month or so and does not sound unhappy, which is a great blessing. It allows me to work & plan for the future. I have saved some amount already & I think that by the early part of next year, or at most the middle, I will be able to go — or perhaps send you the money and you can bring him!

My thoughts change every minute, such a mess, my head. Can it be that there is still no news of Brijen? How is it that people think he has killed himself? That is a demented notion & it makes me go wild with anxiety even to think about. He couldn't have done himself harm, he is not like that. I need news of him, please tell me anything you find out. There is no other way I have of getting news . . . one of the miseries of leaving has been not being able to write to him for news — where would I write? To his home address? There is no choice now but to tell you — I said nothing then & I don't know if I have the courage now — will you forgive me? Will you think of me in the old way when you know? But you guessed, did you not, about Brijen? You know me too well not to have had suspicions.

For so many years it was only about music & the stories he wrote & my painting, finding a sympathetic soul next door where there were none. Someone for whom music was the point of living, as painting was for me. I can't put my finger on when it changed — at least two years ago — it stole up on me. I don't know when it was that I found we had a different way of looking at each other, seeking each other out. I would feel his eyes on me and when I turned towards him, he would hold my gaze as if there was an invisible thread between our eyes, twanging with life. On the days when my head & heart felt as if they would explode from suffocation at home, it was a relief to find him, to know he was next door when I fell asleep & when I woke.

Yes, he did sing me to sleep from his roof. Sometimes whole ragas through the late night, Bageshwari & Bahar, I could not fall asleep without. I lay in bed long after everyone else (despite Banno's endless sarcasm) right till Myshkin went on & on with his cycle bell — because Brijen used to sing the Bhatiyar from his roof. He would start before the sun rose & go on through the change of light, the songs of birds, while I lay there listening.

Lis, do not think me an adulteress, it did not feel like that. I had never been in love before, it hit me like a hammer. For a long time I could make no sense of what had happened to me & there was nobody I could talk to. Not even you. What would you have said? What would any sane friend have said? I did not tell a soul, Brijen included. Nothing was ever spoken between us — it didn't have to be — and the first time he kissed me it was without a word said, as if all had been mutually, miraculously settled. Our lives had been converging over the years to this & this point alone. No time for the niceties of proposals & plans. I did not stop to think about anything — home, husband, child — who might overhear us or see us. Not one thing. The Dodge stopped beside me when I was out in the market one day. He was alone in it, and even before he had driven us off far into the fields, his hands were recklessly off the wheel and all over me. Are you <u>filled</u> with horror? Revolted? I should have been.

When I came back home I shut the bedroom door & took off all my clothes and stood before the mirror. There was a stranger in it. A woman with smoldering red embers for eyes. I felt as tender and bruised as a rain-sodden rose. I scanned my legs, my hips, my shoulders — all of me — as calmly as I might examine a stone sculpture on a wall. But with a racing heart. Why was I looking that way at myself? I feel almost ashamed now — I think I needed to know what he had seen. My body had been nothing but a <u>thing</u> for a lifetime, like a disregarded, uncared-for, unloved house I had lived in so long I hardly noticed it. To see for myself what a man had seen and desired! I don't know how long I was in front of the mirror that day. I locked myself in for many days after that, sitting before the mirror, drawing my own body. Every stroke of my pencil on the paper made me feel his touch.

I'm sorry, Lisa, to be writing all of this — do you think me crude and disgusting? I may never post this letter. But I need to tell you, who else can I tell! It was only with Brijen that I understood there is nothing well-mannered or pretty about love, it is raw and fierce, it's not poems and songs, it is torn-off clothes, snapped buttons & sweat & blood & body parts & it scorches whatever is in its way. It destroyed all that I knew.

How I managed to keep my good-wife face on after that is beyond me. I suppose I wasn't entirely successful — things grew so much worse between NC and me, do you remember, you asked me why that was so? And I began to think it was altogether too dangerous when I spent every single minute of that last summer holiday in the hills longing for Brijen — I was happy enough but it was disastrously incomplete.

And at the same time, on that holiday, I could see I was already starting to retreat from him. One afternoon when everyone was dozing in our vacation cottage, I sat watching one of those fat round clouds come down onto an opposite hill. You know how clouds in the mountains come down low and make everything misty & romantic. So it was. Then it started to fade away & the hill became visible again & with that, I felt I could see Brijen more clearly somehow — what I had been trying not to see for many months, but now I could no longer un-see. Even as I pined for him, I could tell I was tiring of him — his wit & waywardness, all that charming irresponsibility, his conviction that the world revolved around him, his ever-tousled hair & fine muslin clothes — the very things I adored & what made him who he was — I could see its self-love & I was weary of it. It was as if a chain had begun to bite into my flesh. Suddenly that was Brijen to me.

How contradictory I am, Lisa! These civil wars inside me are continuous and exhausting. One part of me fighting another with remorseless ferocity. I was still in love with him — and yet I wanted to be free of him. I did not love him, I have come to understand, I merely loved his addiction to me. I am not made for love. I want nobody. I need to be absolutely free. I am repelled by my indifference. I wish I were another kind of woman, a lovable one, not so cold and hard that I am hateful to myself. Maybe it is my <u>own</u> self-love that I saw in him and was disgusted by.

The train journey down from the hills last summer — my father-in-law ill, poor Golak scuttling about the coach trying to medicate him — I could not stir myself to help or care. Why do we come to these agonizing crossroads where each fork leads to despair? Beryl had spent days in Muntazir and then each one of those days in the hills convincing me to go away to Bali with them — a chance at another life, the one I was meant for — she would make the arrangements, she would take charge, she said. I had never been more torn in two & never so sure . . . I knew at the end of the journey that my mind was made up. Brijen sat hunched over his knees when I told him I was going away. He left the room all of a sudden — not a word said — we hardly spoke after that — of course he took it as a betrayal. He had wanted to take me to Bombay with him, start a new life — as though that would make either of us happy. He is even less capable of loving than I am, only he has more delusions about himself. In his own eyes I am sure he was a romantic hero who was rescuing me. Imagine the hero's annoyance with a heroine who does not want to be rescued!

I laugh at the wrong times. I'm dangerous & evil, I ruin things, it would have been better if I had never been born, Lis! He doesn't have my address here, even if he wanted to tell me where he is, he cannot. Will you give him my address when — if — he comes back?

Tell me you understand. I did no wrong other than in my own head. Doesn't everyone? I destroyed no families, not in the way I might have if I had stayed.

With much love
Gay

24

I have no memory of how I had reached there but all at once, it seemed to me, I was in a market in the old city surrounded on all sides by vegetables, smells, people, cars, cycles, rickshaws. I stumbled along, colliding with people, flanked by tomatoes, beans, pumpkin, brinjals, heaps of scarlet chilies, yellow bananas strung across ropes — everything that was good and plentiful and promising about life. Shopkeepers shouted their lowest prices, they cried at me to stop and consider the redness of their melons and taste the sweetness of their mangoes, but their calls grated on my ears, the colors and smells made me nauseous. I would never want food again as long as I lived. My mouth was sour and dry, my head was pounding hard enough to blur my vision.

I could not bring myself to unread my mother's letter just as she could not make herself unsee Brijen's true self. I directed a silent stream of curses at myself for reading those letters at all. Better by far to have followed my first instincts and thrown the packet unopened to the back of a cupboard. Why exhume the dead when corpses have a stench?

Once when I was six or seven, Brijen Chacha crept up behind me in a half-lit room in Dinu's house, and took my spectacles away. I could see nothing, I could only hear his drunk voice telling me he would not give them back. I went towards his shadowy form, reaching out for my glasses, and he retreated into the darkness, laughing, then emerged again asking me why I did not come and get the glasses before he broke them. The whole episode probably lasted a few seconds, and I know now it was only a prank, but that sensation of blind terror, as if I were drowning, did not leave for a long time. I had an intense fear of Brijen Chacha after that, retreating if I saw him. I can see now that I had no sense of the danger he actually represented.

Would my mother have abandoned us if not for her affair with him? Was he responsible for the cataclysm in our lives?

Over the next few weeks, struggling to understand, I went back to the Bengali novel I had been reading, by my mother's contemporary Maitreyi Devi. This time, as I read of Amrita's love affair with Mircea, I found myself reading it differently. It was no longer a book about forbidden love, it was the story of a young woman very like my mother, who fell in love not only with a man but also with the idea of a different kind of life. Amrita spoke and I heard my mother's voice. Where the book said *Amrita* I read *Gayatri.* I read of Amrita's pain after her parents found out about the affair and it was as if I were a voyeur prying into the deepest recesses of my mother's mind.

Their homes were similar too. Amrita lived in a joint family home, as my mother's house in Delhi had been: dozens of terraces, courtyards, verandahs. Rooms that had been added as the need arose. A maze of a house. As in my mother's old home, there were uncles, aunts, and their families, poor relatives who had been given shelter, house-guests who stayed for months, visiting neighbors, servants. The house was like a big, watchful eye forever following Amrita with its gaze. She had to devise strategies to be with Mircea without arousing suspicion.

The narrow corridor outside Mircea's room leads to a verandah where the letterbox is. The postman puts letters into it, the let-

393

terbox is locked, and I have custody of the key. I open this letterbox two or three times a day and collect our letters. Although the post comes at set times, and I don't need to keep opening the letterbox, I cannot resist. Several times a day I go down to see if there are letters in that box. Especially in the afternoon when the house is at peace — although not asleep — nobody sleeps in the afternoon in our house, everyone reads — afternoons are when I feel like going down in search of letters. I know why I want to do this, I have the brains to know. How much can I deceive myself? Although Mircea has said I am either foolish or a liar, I know I am neither. This afternoon I am convinced I need to go down and see if there are any letters . . . I find myself downstairs, I don't know when I came. I see that Mircea has lifted his curtain and is standing at his door, saying, "So, did you find a letter?"

"No, there's nothing. I feel so sad."

"Whose letter are you waiting for?"

"A stranger's."

"And who might that be?"

"I don't know. The waiting is sweet because I don't know."

"Won't you come inside, Amrita? I have bought you Knut Hamsun's *Hunger.*"

This is the first time he has gifted me anything. I take the book from his hand. He has written my name in it and one word in French, *"Amitiés."*

I keep standing there. I don't have the courage to sit. Who knows why. He too is standing — he won't sit unless I do. I have my back to him and have opened the lid of the piano. Am I waiting for something? Will the impossible take place? Do I want it to take place? He is standing very close to me. But he has not touched me. He could put his hand on my back but he hasn't. Between us there is a bit of sky, and we are standing there — I can feel him right through my body. I can feel his touch in my mind. How is this possible? The sky is not a vacuum, it is filled with ether. I don't know what ether is but it must be the substance that brings me his touch. I can smell the scent of his breath every-where.

Then from upstairs someone calls me: Ru. Ru. Ru.

I thought of my mother. Was this how she and Brijen had devised ways to run into each other by accident? I read of Mircea caressing Amrita's foot under the dining table and wondered if my mother and Brijen had done the same even as we sat around the table oblivious. Had my mother ever felt, as Amrita did about Mircea, that she would not be able to live if they were separated?

As their feelings for each other intensified, the inevitable occurred: Amrita's father discovered his student was in love with his daughter and threw him out of the house. I read of Amrita's anguish at being separated from her lover and wondered if this was my mother's state of mind when she was on that train to Madras. I wondered too what my mother was in truth more tormented by: her separation from me or her separation from her lover?

My hair is tangled up. I have not let my mother touch it. I am constantly tetchy with her, she endures it. I gave the letter to the boy and went back to my room and lay down again. My hair all over me, my face covered with my arm, I shut my eyes and vowed, "I will not forget, I will not forget, I will not forget. After all, my father cannot control my mind . . ."

Morning comes, night comes, the world is spinning on its wheel. This hateful cycle is churning all my happiness, sorrow, grief and peace together and turning it into something else. My mother says the flames of grief rage high for three days, then slowly they die down. Mothers forget the death of their children, widows stagger back to their feet. I am wearing away daily, but I am also being renewed. Everyone knows this, either they hear of it or they read it in a book — but that kind of knowing is not knowing at all. Burning in my grief is teaching me how to understand the truth. I had thought I would cut off my hair — I couldn't — and I don't even want to anymore. One side of me says, What's the point of cutting off your hair? You'll look terrible. This is what hunger for life is. I know.

My mother sits beside me and talks of this and that. How badly my uncle has been behaving, that he is breaking away from the family home. That his wife is a bad egg. Goes to her parents and says nasty things about us. About me as well. I listen to nothing, I have my face buried in my pillow. What's the point of listening to all this? Let them do whatever they want. This whole family is alien to me now.

My mother runs her fingers through my hair, on and on, and untangles it strand by strand. She plaits my hair. She says to me softly, "Ru, sorrow is a gift too. Every sage has said so. Pray to God, it is only God who can heal your grief. God will give you peace. Man thinks of God only in times of grief, never otherwise. Those who are felled by an arrow, they fall at God's feet."

My mother turns off the light and leaves. The words of a song circle around in me, but my distraught, scattered mind can make no sense of them . . . Am I disgraced? Of course I am. Next door's Baidyanath Babu has declared, "These are the indulgences of the rich. They bring a Christian brat into the house and fall about embracing him." Baba is furious, he says we will move, find another house. We won't live in such an uncouth neighborhood. I am slandered left and right and my mind is in pieces, wrapped in a strange lassitude . . . disgrace and perfume . . . God, I fall at your feet . . . I fall at your feet . . . Something goes straight to my head and clang, clang, clang, clang . . . I toss and turn in my bed. All at once I fall off.

When I regain consciousness, I see everyone in my room, even my father. This is the first time I have seen my father since he banished Mircea. He says to Ma, "Give her a little brandy in milk."

"I'll call Shyamdas the doctor tomorrow . . ."

My uncle says a few harsh things and leaves the room. This is the first time I have seen him being rude in my father's presence. Such insolence, to speak to my father this way. Was it not Baba who brought him up? I look, there are two lights on in the room but somehow everyone is shadowed. My father too is a shadow. My father's shadow is near my bookshelf. He is hunting for books and taking them out. The first is a book of Japanese fairy tales. It is bound in bright blue cloth and the picture of a magical animal is stamped on it in gilt. Baba slowly opens the pages and tears out the page in it which is inscribed. A book Mircea gave me. Then he tears out the inscription from the book named *Hunger.* He removes my books one by one and tears out every page on which Mircea has written an inscription for me. He takes out the *Life of Goethe,* but cannot find the page with Mircea's words because it is glued by some lucky chance to the cover. This little scrap of his handwriting is now the only trace of him in my life, nothing else, not even a photograph.

With measured deliberation, Baba tears the pages into tiny shreds and throws them out of the window. If it were a different home and family, the books would have been destroyed. That is not possible in our home. A Ghengis Khan reigns over this house, but he cannot bring himself to harm books — he can burn people, not books. Books are his gods.

Amrita waited for Mircea after he was banished from her house, listening out for his footfall every day. He was still in Calcutta, he might turn up. She thinks she has seen him — there he is just at the end of the street! But no, that is not Mircea. She plots ways to find him but fails. She waits every minute for him to send her a sign that will tell her how to reach him. He does nothing. Four years pass. Her family decides: enough. She must marry. They will search out a groom for her, a respectable girl needs a suitable husband. She has wild thoughts of escape, she has promised she will wait for Mircea *in sickness and in health, till death do us part,* as she had once read, attracted by the sentiment although she did not know at the time these were Christian wedding vows. But now she agrees to marry a man of their choosing. Marriage will at least free her from her family, she will be able to leave the house, find a kind of freedom away from her father. Her mother goes about the job with great efficiency, she gets herself a notebook in which she lists possible grooms, their virtues, their parents' names, their addresses, and so on. Amrita realizes her life has turned into a joke; she might as well laugh.

A prospective groom appeared, a doctor, good government job, though his own wealth and property added up to a horse's egg. It's not that, the real problem is that his skin color is the deepest black. We Indians are certainly not color-blind. My mother says in a faltering tone, "Oh dear, isn't he *rather* too dark?" I am enjoying the absurdity of it thoroughly, I am thinking of saying, "Too white did not suit you either, did it?" I restrain myself. The doctor's old father does not want to let go of me, but the doctor does not pick me. He is on his own personal mission: he is worried about the Future of the Bengali. His own height is about five feet three or four inches, so he is searching for a bride at least five feet eight inches tall. I am a mere five foot two or three. His view is that if the groom is short, getting hold of a tall bride is a matter of necessity. If short mates with short, won't Bengal's future be in jeopardy? Since he has a good job, this groom is an attractive prospect. He can pick and choose. He goes about with a tape, measuring all the unmarried girls of his caste. I hear he never married in the end.

Ultimately a groom is found for Amrita. She agrees to marry him but has no interest in meeting him before the wedding. "Why should I meet him?" she says to her mother. "If I do meet him and say, oh no, I don't like him, I want to marry this other person — he's from a different race yet I like him. Will you let me?"

The preparations for the wedding begin, her mother's ever-intensifying anxiety escalates. The wedding is to happen within five days, before anyone manages to tell the prospective groom about Amrita's past. The groom appears perfectly calm, he agrees to go ahead without ever meeting her. He writes her a letter instead. It is in English.

Mademoiselle,
Understanding that you are going to choose a partner in life, I beg to offer myself as a candidate for the vacancy. As regards my qualifications, I am neither married nor am I a widower: I am in fact that genuine article, a bachelor. What is more I am a real, ripe bachelor, being one of long standing.

I should in fairness refer also to my disqualifications. I frankly confess that I am quite new to the job and I cannot boast of any previous experience in this line — never having had occasion before to enter into such partnership with anyone. This my want of experience is likely, I am afraid, to be regarded as a handicap and disqualification. May I point out, however, that though want of experience is likely to be regarded as a handicap and disqualification in other avenues of life, this particular line is the only one where it is desirable in every way.

For further particulars I beg you to approach your mother who studied me the other day with an amount of curiosity and interest that would have done credit even to an eminent Egyptologist examining a rare mummy.

In fine, permit me to assure you that it will be my constant endeavor to give you every satisfaction.

I have the honor to be

Mademoiselle

Your most obedient servant

17th June 1934

Although her husband-to-be sends the letter days before the wedding, Amrita's parents do not give it to her until after the two are safely married. She reads it. She smiles. If only she had seen the letter before, she thinks, she would have known what to say to the stranger who had become her husband: "You can make me laugh!"

My father made my mother smile — ironic smiles, rueful smiles, mocking smiles, bitter smiles, and smiles that came through tears — he almost never made her laugh. Brijen Chacha did. How had I never noticed this?

My thoughts went back to the time I was in a hospital in the eastern hills twenty years ago, strung up to a saline drip, when the voice from the next bed said, "You have her eyes." It was during my months at the tea garden when I got a virulent malaria and was brought into the hospital. I thought the bed next to mine had a man I vaguely recognized, but I put it down to my feverish delirium. Surely it was not Brijen Chacha, it could not be, he had battled his brother over a love affair and left the house in a storm when I was only about ten. He had never been seen since and everyone said his broken heart had made him end his life. Sliced to pieces on the railway's tracks, a few people said, while others spoke authoritatively of a noose made from a lover's sari.

When the malarial haze left me and I woke up properly, I realized it was one of those coincidences that only happen in real life: without a doubt it was Brijen Chacha, who had not been seen since 1938. Gray hair, shaggy gray eyebrows, but despite his illness he had the old menacing glint in his eyes that said he was up for anything and the crooked smile that invited you to join in his escapades as in the past when he lived next door, his only appointments assignations and his only preoccupation the next soirée. At the hospital a different young woman would appear with home-cooked food for him every day. I noticed a pattern — there were three of them, taking turns, each one more solicitous than the other, stroking his forehead, settling his blankets and pillows, feeding him with a spoon as if he were too weak to eat on his own. One of them slipped him a hip flask for a quick swig. She was his favorite, I could tell.

"Assistants on our film unit. We are here to shoot, I like to come along sometimes and see," Brijen Chacha explained from his stack of pillows with a contented smile. "I still write — but screenplays now, not novels. And I compose music you know, for movies. Like jingles to sell soap, but you should see how people lap it up and go on and on about how I use classical music in silly songs. They haven't a notion what real music is or what real writing is. No wonder I have a burst ulcer."

Over the next few days we lay in our adjacent beds, I fighting off the remnants of my malaria, still struck by bone-rattling shivering fits now and then, and he recovering from ulcer surgery. For long periods we slept, our waking hours tied to the schedules of doctors and nurses. I was never given to talking much but Brijen Chacha, always garrulous, would periodically shake off his stupor during those waking hours, say something, then sink back in his pillows again.

"You have taken after your mother, I can see. A relief. You have her eyes, though behind those glasses most people wouldn't know . . . I changed my name. I wanted to vanish. People thought I was dead. How happy my beloved brother was. Every now and then I send him a nameless postcard from beyond the grave just to rattle his cage."

In his next lucid moment he said, "Your father was a real innocent. Always going on and on about doing good. He made me sing at his Mukti Devi's meeting once. I sang romantic thumris instead of patriotic songs, he didn't like that, not at all."

Then one day in bitter tones: "Everyone in that bloody dump of a town thought I was a rake who had trampled on a hundred hearts. The shattered heart was mine. Nobody knew."

A few minutes later: "Your mother and I. Both misfits. If we had different families we would never have had to leave."

And with his old manner of baiting the unwary: "I told her once, *Gayatri Rozario, you and I, we're twin souls, let's run off into the sunset together and never come back.* We were great friends, Myshkin. I would have given anything to stop her going away. Do you understand?"

I did not understand what he was driving at all those years ago in that hospital bed. He was so often incoherent or groaning and cackling and humming to himself that I could hardly decipher his ramblings. But half-remembered things are coming back to me, now bathed in an altered light. Incidents, even glances, have acquired a new meaning. His hand lingering over my mother's for a fraction of a second as she passed him something. The time I saw my mother brush a grasshopper off his back. Her relentless fretful anxiety when he went off drinking and did not come back for three days. The hand that held her palm, dropped red flowers into it, and pressed it close that night of the concert. The day I came upon him storming out of our garden, the hollows of his face the color of ash, as if his blood had turned to acid and scorched his insides.

I was overcome with anger one moment and then in the next an impersonal tenderness, even understanding, would come over me for the woman who was my mother. She was a mere twenty-six at that time, and was condemned for life to the loneliness of being out of step with everyone around her. Where something so trifling as reading detective novels rather than my father's improving tracts was treated as rebellion, she fell in love with the writer of those thrillers. The audacity of it made me smile. I wished I had known her better. Instead, all that I had now, as in my childhood, were her letters.

25

December 1938

My dearest Lis,

It is wretched & tense. They arrested one Dutchman & found a whole bunch of letters (where will my letters end up?) that prove this man is some sort of kingpin supplying boys to men. The Resident of Batavia has been sacked too for no specific reason — they can't find any evidence — and off he's gone because he was mentioned in those letters. Is that enough, I wonder. Sentenced by hearsay.

It is strange & chilling when such things happen to people you know. You say people are being arrested all over the place at home for sedition — based on gossip — well, here too. And it is not a situation people like Jane are familiar with — to be powerless, to be questioned, to be watched. To feel as if the government might do anything to you — jail you, take away your possessions. We in India have always lived this way — expecting calamity — what is the colonial government but an agent of calamity in our country, NC used to say. Europeans have never faced that anywhere & here too they are used to being comfortable, rich, free. Now some of them feel a little uncertain. As for me, like all Indians I am used to expecting the worst — this situation tortures me, but it is not new.

They haven't been able to find anything wrong in Bali so far — except a handful of cases, they say — but all over Batavia, Medan, Surabaya, Semarang, places on other islands — there they have arrested many people, well over 150. They say people are being picked up for questioning, being tortured in jail and it has to do with "Matters of State." It is too terrifying to contemplate. Once they find out how WS is working with the Balinese against the Dutch government, who knows what will happen to him?

I have a very foggy understanding of politics, dear Lis, as you know — or as

NC let everyone know — my wife has no understanding of the country's political situation <u>whatsoever</u>. QED. One of the reasons I found Brijen a comfort was the absolute cynicism and disregard with which he treated every kind of politics, how he thought all of nationalism was nothing but a way of dividing people. NC tried so hard — sending me off to Mukti Devi to improve myself — I just couldn't. Partly because it was his world & I did not want to be a part of it. Partly because I simply wasn't interested in spinning cotton when I wanted to paint.

How it tears its way in by its fingernails — I mean politics — & shreds your life to pieces.

All this time I had been thinking the problem was about men having relations with other men. But the whole thing hinges on age, we have now found out — they are doing everything they can to find proof against W to show he did awful things to <u>little boys</u>. In a way this is reassuring because everyone knows he has never touched a boy. They have found not a shred of evidence.

There are people telling him he should move back to Europe for his own safety, but he asks why. He has lived here for years & made no problems. Besides, he says, draining his last sip of whisky & banging two opening notes on the piano, "I don't want to go back! I have absolutely not an iota of desire to return to Germany or Europe. Not one atom." And then he plays Beethoven furiously & paints locked away for the next many days.

Yesterday, in the evening, I heard an impromptu concert. There is a little girl here to whom WS is teaching piano — he sits her on his lap & tells her stories & plays along — this is how the Balinese teach their children music & he follows the same method. He was teaching her a sweet, simple tune by a composer called Pachelbel. On & on they went, again & again over the same set of notes & I could hear them from my hut down the slope. I sat outside & breathing in the evening air & listening to the piano & to the birds & in the river down below two people chattering to each other in words I could not understand & out of the blue I found myself yearning for Brijen, he would have loved the music, the tranquillity. I imagined he was beside me, sitting outside as well, and my present troubles retreated with every note.

How idiotic to feel this way after I've left him — when I had the chance to be with him! It would have been so much easier to get Myshkin to Bombay than to Bali. Why didn't I take a mad chance and run off with Brijen as he kept telling me to? But that would have been the end of my work. Everything new I am learning and doing would never have happened. What a tangle.

You cannot know how grateful I am that you don't condemn me and that I can still talk to you freely. That was my biggest fear — it tortured me until I got your letter. Every line of it is warm and kind and understanding. Your heart is as big as the ocean.

With my love
Gay

February 1939

My Lis,

I haven't been able to write back — I am sorry, sorry! Things are so very bad here & I cannot put it all in words — maybe the letter will mysteriously vanish if I do. WS was arrested last month. He is in what they call remand — waiting for a trial. To the end they found it hard to get any witnesses because not one Balinese would speak against him, but they managed to scrape together what they needed through the Regent, I believe, & are teaching two or three witnesses what to say. Ni Wayan says they can't understand — what has the Tuan done wrong? She simply cannot see. Her mother, the eagle-eyed old one who hides under bushes waiting for pheasants to catch & cook, says these foreign rulers who come to other people's countries are like poison thrown into a lake, they kill all the plants and all the fish. They leave a trail of waste and destruction.

Someone told me there are big politics at work in WS's present persecution. Things to do with Japan & America — yes, that must be the real reason. You met him — you know him — can you imagine him ever harming a puppy, far less a child? Nobody who knows him believes any of it for a moment. We know he is innocent. But he can be so far removed from reality, he thought nothing would go wrong and he still thinks it is all a mistake.

WS unsquashable as usual. Dashing off long letters — although letters are censored so all of us have to watch what we say. He thinks prison is a pause for him, to think, recover, work again. He's translating folk tales to while away the time. He has been allowed a gramophone & his painting materials. The prison guards are all smitten by him — naturally. He wants ping pong balls, he says, & paint . . . he feels new paintings entering him, they will settle & ripen, he says. In jail! It should be a lesson to me. I made excuses for not being able to paint at home in Muntazir & he has no trouble making paintings in a jail cell.

M. Mead says she is going to write out a defense of WS because she thinks he is of a rare artist type by birth. She has a theory that this type of person is at once <u>more</u> as well as <u>less</u> dependent on others — they want warmth & friendship, yet need to preserve themselves — keep their solitude, their personalities intact. I am of the mind that I am this artist type too, ever since I have heard of it!!! She says the Balinese instinctively understand this way of being — of light, even physical contact that is casual & easy, without being too involving. She says WS found freedom to work & affection without demands here — that is all there is to it. It is no crime & she will prove it.

This seems to me to be correct — but will the police and the court think so? I cannot imagine Dutch judges gifted with empathy for artist types.

Everyone is trying to help WS. Beryl went back towards England last year — she is in Egypt, or somewhere in that region now, trying to get all sorts of people to rally around so he doesn't get a ghastly long sentence. Let's see what happens. Things change so fast from one day to the next now. To tell the truth, I feel my isolation terribly. I know nobody well apart from WS, not really. What if he is in jail for ages? What then? What will I do?

(Are we born selfish, Lis? Why do I think about myself at such a time?)

So often the future seems hidden just around the next loop of the road & you desperately need to be able to see around that loop, but there is no way. The future is there as it always is, it is waiting, it will come, good or bad. I don't know if I'll wonder why I ever came here, so far from everything familiar. Who will help me if things go wrong? What was I think-ing?

You will say I am turning into a bundle of anxiety. Where is the Gay who used to be gay even on a bad day? Well, I am still that girl in spite of all my heartbreaks and evil deeds! One of the reasons he enjoys having me around, says WS, is that I make him laugh. He would keep asking me to imitate lions and monkeys and birds — I've discovered a talent for doing animal calls, people's voices, I can even do WS. I know many of my worries are just that — worries. I am sure Brijen will come back after he's got over his huff. Such vanity to think he would end his life for me when he had a dozen lovers scattered over town!

There. The minute I write to you, I feel lighter & can see that my head is full of nonsense & nothing will happen.

I forgot to tell you the news: I sold FIVE paintings before W's arrest. All at once — three to WS's European friends who were visiting, and two to the Raja of Karangasem, no less. He says he will put them in his palace for a few years and then in the museum. How grand I felt for a day! And rich!

My love to you. And please kiss Myshkin for me, exactly on top of his head & twice on each cheek. And not a word to him or anyone else about these troubles.

He has enough of his own, poor child.
Gay

June 1939

Dearest Lis,

It is a relief to have your note. I read it many times and have left it where I can see it. I smell it to see if some traces of your smoke and vanilla cling to it still. I feel very alone. In a hut trying to work in lamplight while the rain falls outside. Soon there will be frogs croaking & always the river rushing & gushing. The sound feels like an echo of the turmoil inside me at times, this incessant river. When darkness falls there is a small square where the village men play the gamelan & in front of it women set up candlelit stalls selling all kinds of little things & people gather to play cards, listen to the music. I go there sometimes to sit & chat — if it can be called chatting — smiles & nods, a word or two, goodwill. (Language is a problem. I have picked up words, but too few, I am slow with words.) After some time, when the mosquitoes start to plague me — you know how I get horrible weals from mosquitoes — I leave & walk home although it is pretty there & I like the sense of people around me.

Tjampuhan is quite a distance from the main town. I have to cross the river to reach it & the way is dark & empty. I am not afraid, but I can hear my footfall, my slippers' flap-flap, & I keep turning my head back because I feel as if I can hear someone walking ten paces behind me, following. I walk fast to reach quicker. The only sound is the wayside dogs barking when they smell me. The trees are as tall as towers & densely packed. Long creepers hang loose from them. They disappear into deep, deep gorges. I feel tiny among those tall trees in the blackness. All along the way I can hear the chimes of the gamelan — sometimes repeating a wrongly played note, going over the same bit again & again.

When the gong sounds, the whole forest seems to go quiet. If there's a full moon, everything is silver & gold & I sing the song from my childhood to myself — about a sky full of stars & sun — Myshkin used to love that song, it was our song, his and mine. It sounds alien here, in a language nobody else speaks. But it's my most intimate language still, the words I mumbled when I was half-asleep were always Bengali & so were the songs I used to sing on the roof. That roof was my patch of sky to be myself under — only until the moment I heard NC's footsteps on the staircase coming up. Then my heart would plummet. Here I am at least free of waiting with dread & gloom for those footsteps on the stairs, footsteps approaching my easel & stopping behind me, not a word said, but still a shout of disapproval. Maybe I exaggerate. Maybe I misunderstood.

If I am lucky, Ni Wayan or her mother walks back with me & they take pity on my solitude & tell me to come to their house & sit on their verandah & eat something with them. They have two oil lamps and that pool of flickering light shuts off the darkness. I feel sheltered for a time there with them, listening to their quick chatter, understanding hardly a word. I am happy eating as they do, sitting on the floor, a big heap of rice on a banana leaf, using my hands as at home, not a spoon. They were taken aback the first time they saw me do this — they had found a bent aluminum spoon from somewhere & kept it beside a plate as if it were a Western table setting. When I ignored the spoon & ate with my hands, Ni Wayan's mother slapped her thigh with delight. She said something I didn't understand.

She's been very loving to me ever since. Whenever I come, she finds fruit or pieces of food to give me. Food is the only way she has of showing me she cares for me. She makes dumplings with pork, she roasts duck meat, she fries fish, she grates coconut and puts it into almost everything. I love her cooking and so I have almost stopped making food for myself. The other day she had fried something crisp & crunchy & handed it to me heaped up in a coconut shell. I ate it — all at once I was sure it must be a fried insect & started to feel almost <u>faint</u>.

Then I told myself firmly, Gayatri, what did your father teach you? When you are in a new country, you must not turn your back on anything. And what is a shrimp or prawn but a big cockroach? So I ate some more of the fried (delicious) thing & asked no questions. And I'm still alive to tell the tale, am I not? But I know I am a coward at heart. If I go to a feast and see the mounds of turtle shells near the men chopping up turtle meat, a shudder goes through me. I just cannot eat turtle, cannot steel myself enough. I know you would have felt nothing but curiosity.

I was always isolated here, neither part of WS's inner circle of Western friends nor close to the Balinese because of problems of language. Without WS in his cottage next door, it feels worse. It should not, because he had moved away to Iseh these last years & only visited here now & then — but it still felt as if he would turn up any time, and he did. To think he is in prison — a squalid prison cell, all day & all night, counting the hours, wrongly accused. Before they transferred him further away, to Surabaya jail, the gamelan players did the sweetest, bravest thing: two orchestras he had helped went to the jail compound, set up all their instruments & there, outside, they played their latest compositions for him.

When I heard this I had tears in my eyes. You have seen what a free spirit he is — the way he would vanish to those villages when he was in our town. It is as if a magnificent genius of a man was caught in a machine that chewed him up & spat him out. Beryl's words in

Madras come back to me — that they would have to have another war just so he can be sent to another prison camp to learn new languages, new ways of painting. He has written to Margaret to say it is all for the best. Everything is clear & settled inside him, new ideas are appearing, all the energy & youth is back, he says. He'll return to a new life. He sounds perfectly peaceable about his time in Hotel Wilhelmina (that is what he calls jail, after the Dutch Queen). He is to be released in August.

Take care of yourself, dear Lis, & take care of my beloved Batty father-in-law. Do please try & write more — I <u>pine</u> for news, for your voice, for the smell of home — whatever comes with your brief & infrequent little notes. Is there really a chance Brijen may be alive and well? That is such good news I am almost afraid to believe it. Will you try & send me confirmed news and maybe photographs in your next? You've been promising for ages! I may not recognize Myshkin. Maybe he'll grow a mustache soon!

Much love
Gay.

Lis, dearest,

It is frightening to think of the things my father-in-law is doing, still patching up those wounded revolutionaries with a war declared & all of the problems in India. If the British find out? And NC — his articles, his work for the wretched Mukti Devi — what if they both get arrested? Who will take charge of Myshkin then? His new, mad stepmother? I was horrified to hear how she set everything on fire — I don't mind losing my things, I was never going to see them again, but ghastly for Myshkin to witness it. Oh Lis!

The sole happy part of life at this time is to know of your man. Wonderfully exciting! Jeremy Gordon. I like the sound of his name, Lis, my girl! What's Aunt Cathy saying now, eh? How lucky he was to be quartered on you, to find you where he had expected nothing but flies and mosquitoes in a foreign country. I devoured every word about him — he sounds just right for you, the blue eyes, the big build (come, come, I know you always loved tall men), the brown hair, the singing voice. And he must be right for you because you have written me a long letter at last! I loved to read how he is teaching Indian soldiers to drive. It makes me smile, your story of how Indians are used to horses so they step on the gas when they sight a ditch. I start grinning each time I think of Jeremy saying, "Ruddy idiots think the car will sail over the ditch if you kick the damn thing." I remember Arjun making this kind of complaint long ago when they first got their Dodge. (I have never seen a man who flies into rages as Arjun does, never. No wonder Dinu lives in such terror.)

My mind is not here — I am consumed with memories of home suddenly and so long to see you in your new life! I hope you're dressing up — the dark green silk dress, the navy shoes, please — when you go out with him. I'm trying to picture the new Muntazir you describe — the droves of Tommies, the new bars & restaurants, the jazz music in Hafizabagh (can't imagine that!!!), the trenches . . . oh, my mind can't fit it in, I can't see it, but I worry. Will the war really come so far? I cannot imagine Banno's sons as sailors on some far-off British ship. Myshkin must be wide-eyed about it all. Does he know about your

Jeremy? I have not heard from him for so very long. I long to hold him and smell his baby smell — milk, soap, powder — even though that went ages ago.

I am relieved to hear that it is now confirmed Brijen is alive and has thought it fit to inform you even if not his own family. Is that because he assumes you will send the news on to me? If that is the case, and it is undying love that makes him tell you now, could he not have let you know earlier? Why take more than a year over it? I have no patience with such thoughtless self-indulgence. I am sorry to think I wasted all those sleepless nights worrying about a man so feckless and inconsiderate. It confirms me in my view that I was right to leave him, even if it felt heartless and cold at that time. I shall not waste a minute more mooning about him.

W's friends are nice enough to me, but without him, the center of gravity is shifted, nothing is the same & I am much on my own. I prefer this loneliness to the one with NC. That was isolation of the most desperate, soul-destroying kind, like being alone in a boat in the middle of the ocean and nothing but water in sight and no oars to take you to safety. This loneliness is temporary, it has to be borne till WS is back and things return to normal.

The evenings feel long, but I am so tired I fall asleep quickly. All day I work like a madwoman. I have no clock on the wall, sometimes when I come out of my hut it is evening & the music has started to chime. More & more I am making things with my hands — then I use them in my painting. Bits of terra-cotta clay I shape & fire (in a very primitive kiln) & then work into a plaster surface on which I am trying to make a fresco with clay parts molded in. I've given up watercolor, I do oils, collages. I spent hours just observing other painters here at work — and I have been learning new ways to work. I've been going to the museum, and looking at W's art books — I feel as if I am growing new eyes all over my head. Like a big fat fly!

Did I tell you one of my paintings hangs in the museum now? Would you have thought it possible? I steal in every now and then, I slow down when I reach the room where I know it is and wait and linger over the other paintings that come before and my heartbeat keeps growing faster. "Still Life with Missing Woman," it says. "By Gayatri Rozario." It makes me go funny, as if I am puffing up and dissolving in a puddle all at once. Maybe one day Myshkin will be here and see that his mother did something with her life!

These days I spin clay on a wheel to make bowls, it is magic to feel them grow under my fingers. How NC would have gawped to see me sitting legs apart at a primitive wheel alongside the wiry village men in their headbands, with their bare bodies sweating. But they don't look at women here in the way they do in our country. Here the women are free & easy & self-assured. You should see the way young Ni Wayan Arini puts white gardenias in her hair & sways off to the market in her yellow & red sarong, pausing every few minutes to exchange news with passersby. No woman can loaf & lounge on the street in our part of the world, can they? People raised their eyebrows at me merely going to visit you every day or at Brijen popping across to see me. Who knows what Dinu's mother thought we got up to? She never stepped outside her home except to visit her relatives in a car.

I wish I could do what we did in those days, just sit with you on your sofa & talk, knowing you understand. What I do long for is close friends. It was different when Beryl was here. Who can explain how I found so much in common with that learned Englishwoman years older than me? She has such plans: she told me before she left (I suppose in order to comfort me as you might a child) that she would be back in India and Bali before too long.

I wish she had stayed here some more months now. Why do we have so little time with those we come to love late in life? Although she was often acerbic, even forbidding, under all that there was warmth & a sharp mind — & a funny one. Once we were talking about different kinds of friendships & marriages & she told me she had been married once, to a man call Basil & she & he decided they would go without sex. (I blushed at how calmly she said the word. We are so prudishly brought up, I don't think I've ever said "S-E-X" in my life. I have said it now. Sex.) Well, they decided not to — because it was so coarse. They gave up drinking liquor & eating meat too. A very elevated life based on platonic love was planned. Poor deluded Beryl! She found one day that her husband had abandoned vegetables for steaks, milk for beer, & platonism for carnal love with another woman. She tried to be calm about it, she said & uncaring, but then one day left him. Good thing, she said, or she may never have made her way to Arthur. Arthur has other women, she has hinted — she knows he is with them when she is on her travels. She calls them his other continents. She hasn't told me if she & Arthur are platonic or not — I don't know if that's the thing driving him off to seek out Other Continents. She seems hurt about his other women — yet has made some arrangement with her own mind & heart about it.

Is this how we live as we grow older, Lis? Our minds & bodies changing shape to make room?

My body's changing shape all right — I am an old crone, thin as a stick & skin gone all patchy & muddy. I keep getting bouts of fever & have to have quinine — it's malaria, I've been told. Never had it at home, I suppose because of the good

Dr. Rozario's precautions.

Write to me, Lis. Tell me about Jeremy. Do you call him Jem or Jimmy? How many children will you have? A whole <u>brood</u>, I hope, to be Myshkin's little cousins. I hope you will not try Beryl's experiments at platonism.

As for me . . . that part of my life is gone. It's gone forever & I feel no emptiness about it, I tell myself it is a relief. I don't mourn Brijen anymore, not even in moments of sentimental gloom. It is as if I can see my past self from far away, as alien as a woman on a film screen, and I'm observing the screen-woman's romantic oozing, nonplussed that she could be so deluded.

But I will not think of that. I will not think of love or the police or the dangers. I will not think of armies in far-off lands. All this will pass. I will not pine & worry about all of you. I will only think of you & Jeremy & wedding bells. Come here for your honeymoon! I will make you a canopy of blue lotus & a bed as big as a tennis court covered with the finest white cotton & serve you sweet oranges & whole roasted ducklings at dinner. WS will be here by then — he is out of jail, is spending some months in Java — he will play you a wedding march, we will have a temple dance & a feast, you will be dressed in gold & brocade, so beautiful that Jeremy will fall in a faint. You'll revive him with a kiss.

With much love,
Yours ever,
Gay

4th March 1940

Dearest Lis,

How are you? It is very long since a letter came from you. Is the postbox swallowing them up? When I was a child I used to think of those red pillar boxes as monsters with an open maw. A little bit of me believes that still. Where do letters go when we drop them in there, how do they ever make their way anywhere — so many trains & ships & roads before they cross the distance from Muntazir to Tjampuhan. I come back from the hut where I work in the afternoon, hot & mucky, & go straight to Ni Wayan & when she shakes her head (for she knows what I am asking without a word said) my heart sinks. But I rally & say, maybe tomorrow. My father died early but he left me this part of himself:

an undousable fire that lights me up inside & tells me things will get better, the clouds will lift. There will be a letter from you tomorrow or the day after that & maybe the day after that you will be here in flesh & blood, sitting with Jeremy, smoking your long cigarette, holding up your new silk sarong to show it to me while Myshkin goes down to our river to meet Sampih in person at last. (Did I ever tell you about Sampih? He once saved Colin from drowning — he is a fine dancer, WS's protégé.)

How often Myshkin wrote to me about Sampih when he did write. There are few letters from him now. I had felt — hoped — that this drifting apart would not happen, or I would get him here before it did. I've been a failure, not selling nearly as much as I need to — not saving enough.

Ni Wayan fusses over me now that I don't feel up to cooking, but I am not hungry. Though I long for a samosa! I woke up yesterday with the scent of Nanduram's hot samosas in my nose — it was inexplicable. I must have been dreaming of them. Did I eat them in my dream, I wonder. I do <u>hope</u> so. The only thing I feel like eating is fruit. I eat mangosteens — they are sweet and sour, and these I can still taste.

WS came back quite some time ago & spent ages cleaning his garden. He came with ferns & water lilies & many other plants & since then has been wrapped up in digging a new pond for them — it is now ready — stone bound, very simple. I had not thought the place could be improved, but this pond brings serenity, the light shines on it & changes color all day. I sit by it in the evening with a glass of tea & watch everyone come & go about their jobs. There is again a low, happy hum of normality. A cataclysm came — but it has gone & life is settled again. In another of the verandahs, the old woman — Ni Wayan's mother — is stretched out dozing and the mound of her tummy rises and falls gently. Near me one of the boys who hangs around here is polishing his kris — it is an ornamental dagger they carry. I will bring you a miniature version some day, to slit open your letters with.

Across the gorge, WS is creeping about, stalking dragonflies with a net in his hands. He is thinner but full of energy. He passionately collects these dragonflies & paints them — fragile, detailed paintings — who could have said an insect might be so elegant? He sends the pictures off to an insect specialist in Java. (A man called Gustav who came here a few times and was flatteringly taken with me, called me a great beauty etc. etc. If you saw what a haggard old stick I am! I am snorting with laughter as I write this.) WS has been running around seeing everyone on the island, there is great rejoicing that he is free & back & a general feeling that a great injustice was done to him.

All is peaceful, it is true — but I feel a shadow over us. The government is doing petty things to stop WS getting work. Why? He is unhappy about it, he complains bitterly. But everyone advises him to be quiet, keep his head down, provoke nobody & just paint. Perhaps that is how all of us have to become in this changed world. Invisible. Silent. Scurrying around in the dark under our separate rocks.

Don't you abandon me too. Myshkin's vanishing is bad enough. Write me many, many pages, <u>at least</u> twelve! Covered on <u>both</u> sides.

With much love,
Yours ever,
Gay

25th May 1940

Dearest Lis,

The news is grim. WS has been taken away to prison again — this time it was totally without warning. It is to an internment camp. This is because Germany & Holland are now at war. I do recall you telling me in a letter right at the start of the war that the British were locking away all the Germans in India. I suppose when countries are at war, our lives are not our own anymore even if the war is a million miles away.

How long will this internment be for? We don't know. Since they have scholars, planters, artists — all sorts of people among that 3000, we expect they'll check identities & set the harmless ones free to go back to their lives. After all, everything cannot be stopped, can it, just because there's a war on an entirely different continent? Germans like WS who left Germany years ago, partly out of disgust with the Nazis — what irony to imprison him. (And as for the Jews they are imprisoning here because they are German by nationality, no irony could be greater.)

The local people wonder why WS did not have the sense to change his passport years ago, since he had no intention of going back to Europe. But I suppose he had thought it wasn't important. Who does? I am lucky to be Indian — the British & Dutch are allies so I am not in an internment camp & not likely to be. I'm safe, I suppose. The German women and children are in separate camps so families are all broken up.

Pugig, who is Ni Wayan's cousin, works for the Grand Hotel in a place in Java called Lembang. He told us he was on the roadside when Dutch soldiers pulled over Bruno Treipl. Bruno T's family owns the hotel & they are local grandees. He says the soldiers made Treipl crawl on his hands & knees all the way to the prison van & that they spat at him while he was down on the road. Oh, Lis, I fear that WS will have a harder time of it now, if for no other reason than numbers — there are just too many people in those camps, people turn into things when there are too many in one place.

I am too troubled to write more. I don't know what is going to happen to me. When will we go back to normal life?

All my love,

Gay

10th October 1940

Dearest Lis,

All on my own! That is my only excuse for not writing for months, I was so busy talking to myself I forgot to talk to anyone else. Don't be angry, I am sorry! You know how it is — I hate being a moaner, yet all I was doing was moaning. (To myself, in tiny whispers, all day and all night.)

Now I have apprenticed myself to a toothless old potter called Nyoman Sugriwa and it gives me something real to write to you about. He has a face as weathered as old wood & he sits in a loincloth & spins the wheel. I sweat rivers in the heat, my sari tucked up to my knees, crouched over the wheel trying to still <u>one tiny part</u> of this wobbly, chaotic world. We need no words, he shows me things with gestures & we smile a lot & nod or shake heads.

I am trying to view this as time for myself to learn & make — am trying to emulate WS in prison. After all, I am in a beautiful prison too, am I not — no way of leaving. No money. No friends. Even Jane gone. M. Mead, whom I never liked much & would never have asked for help, left ages ago. I think — am <u>determined</u> to think — WS will be back home soon & I want to be here and take care of things so he comes back to a normal world. I know there are people who have been here longer, doing that. But still. Indah, the Kintamani dog — you remember? — she sleeps in my room now that WS is gone. The monkeys. The cockatoo. All of them need care. I can't abandon them when they are his very life to WS — who has done so much for me.

I am babbling. But I do need to take care of things, you know. The other day a Dutch woman, Mrs. Hueting, came visiting. It's nonsense to think there is any threat from the Japanese, she announced, the Allies are too many. The Japs (she calls them that) know they'll be finished if they try out any moves in the Pacific. There's no danger to the Netherland East Indies — none <u>whatsoever</u>. Her husband has told her. As though that is the conclusive word on the matter. She is a planter's wife, she said she'd come to see if WS had left any paintings she could <u>take for her drawing room</u>. I ask you! They have coffee & rubber, thousands of acres & live like kings & queens with virtual slave labor. They are brutal to the workers. She has a pudgy face & popcorn eyes & seems very pleased with herself. I disliked her intensely, I wish I had stuck a big drawing pin into her giant buttocks.

Are things at all changed at home because of the war? Are there shortages? I haven't been hearing from you. Nor from Myshkin. Maybe the post offices no longer work. Maybe our letters are sinking in the sea. I will pray this reaches you. I feel as if the world broke into a hundred pieces last year & scattered us far away from each other.

With love,
Gay

July 1941

My dearest Lis,
I have thought I will number my letters to you so that you know how many you are missing. You accuse me of not writing, but the fact is that for the last few months I have written at least every

two months. You must have missed three or four, maybe more! Letters do cost money to send, I have to be mindful of that too. Mine invariably tip over into the number of grams that takes them to the costliest level, though I try to keep them within 25 cents because I write to both you & to Myshkin . . . I sound such a miser, but am earning hardly anything now, I am down to selling what little jewelry my mother gave me & it makes me very angry to think all that effort & money & my words & thoughts are floating in the murky depths of the Indian Ocean along with sundry other wrecks. It is not fair.

I am rather crochety, have not been feeling well. Keep getting fevers, can hardly keep food down. Still am trying to work. Sugriwa is teaching me how to weave cane into pots. My fingers are cut all over, but I persist. I am tired, tired, tired. I finished one bowl yesterday, woven with cane, & Sugriwa approved, gave me a Western thumbs-up! I live in splendid isolation. People have been advising me to leave, but even speaking hypothetically, where will I go? My mother is not going to garland me with roses for coming back & NC won't let me in through the door. Where will I live? What will I do? How will I earn? Here I was earning — until WS was locked away.

I am going to stay. I will be found here one day, the mad old woman from India, surrounded by her paintings & misshapen earthen bowls. I am not going to leave, why should I? How will I take my years of work? I'm not going to just abandon it — I've done good work, Lis. When I feel doubtful I think of my painting in the museum, and the two others in the Raja's collection and all the others that people have bought. My work will come to something again once this madness is over. Or else I will be found as in those old graves of the Egyptians, buried with the things that were precious to them. If I die here, that is how they will find my body. You know, they don't cremate the dead immediately here, they wait for an auspicious day and meanwhile leave the body mummified. Maybe I'll tell them to leave me embalmed for you to find some day!

Such ghoulish thoughts.

WS is not back & nobody knows when he will come. A Dutch soldier who had once come to Tjampuhan as a guest wrote to someone to say he glimpsed WS across the barbed wire in the internment camp on his watch a few days ago. WS scrawny & thin, start of beard. Their eyes met, only briefly, then WS started rolling a cigarette, he said. A tormenting thought — W caged up like an animal behind barbed wire.

He has sent a few postcards from the camp. It is badly overcrowded, serried ranks of cots, clothes festooned on ropes overhead, not a minute's solitude. Clouds of mosquitoes. He is trying to keep up his spirits, even paint, but the last letter did sound downcast. A portrait he was painting had failed, he said, he had lost at ping pong, he has no more butter, his last Russian novel has been read through! He tried to make his misery sound funny — absurdly pathetic — but it makes me sad. I am not allowed to send anything there now. And am not allowed to visit. Nobody is.

There is another German family in Java — young parents, two infant children, and I hear the mother has died in the camp and the children are alone there. The father in a camp for men only. The Germans are putting the Jews through far worse brutality, I know —

but does one brutality even out another? Is all of human history nothing but an endless cycle of revenge carried out on the innocent? And we are caught in this ghastly machine, our lives being crushed out of us. It makes me think of the film we saw — was it at Grace or Delite — a matinee, remember, so that Nek wouldn't be annoyed? The one where a woman was being pressed to death under boulders. It has never left me — the savage glee of the people torturing her to death.

Yesterday I wasn't feeling well again — well, what is new about that, you will say. I went to Nyoman Sugriwa as usual because it was worse to be sitting alone at home doing nothing. I tried to work on the wheel, but my hand would not be steady, my body was out of tune with the clay & I ached and gritted my teeth & pounded more & more clay into balls, tearful, getting furious with myself for not being able to control one little ball of clay while Sugriwa kept saying things to me I could not understand — he was probably telling me not to waste my time & his clay & go home. Nothing in my life is in control any longer. Nothing. Finally he got up & stomped off outside.

I could see him puffing away. The scent of his clove smoke.

My eyes fell on Indah, who always follows me to Sugriwa's house. She was lying in one corner of the bamboo shed, dozing through the heat. It is so hot, so blazing hot in the afternoons, it is like being inside a volcano. You cannot imagine the sweat and discomfort, though now I am better able to bear it. (The nights are cooler, there is often a breeze.) Indah raised her head & her brown, calm eyes were on me — one long moment. Then her head fell back on the floor. She is an old dog — she was old when we found her, I've realized — & is still painfully thin despite the food. Her eyes are marbled with cataract, they see little if anything at all — I cannot tell. Her black muzzle is gray & her ribs show when she lies in that way on the floor although her coat is shiny black. At night she sleeps near my bed, but never in it — even when she accepts that she needs you, she does not woo you in the way of other dogs. You sense she has a world inside her that you'll never be able to share. Such stubborn solitude! Who knows how she lived all by herself on the rocks of the Kintamani all those years before she followed us home? What did she eat? Where did she find water?

I haven't any notion what passed between us when she placed her gaze on me for those few seconds, but from that moment the clay started spinning evenly & smoothly under my hands again. A flawless bowl slowly rose between my fingers & thumb. If only I could make you understand what happened, Lis! And how spiritual it felt. If there is the divine, it was this. I will pray to whatever force it was that steadied my hand & body that it may still the world too & reunite all of us one day. Be well, dearest Lis. If this letter reaches, or even if it doesn't, please write! Tell me about Myshkin. I will not rest till I see him again. That's a promise. I will find a way.

With much love,
Gay

13th Sept. 1941

My dear Lis,

My birthday. You would have arrived with an iced cake & being impractical, 31 candles — which we would never have got lit all together — & that would have driven NC mad. The extravagance, the childishness, the needless frivolity. Would Mukti Devi have a birthday cake, ever? Never! Tch tch, the very thought. He'd have let himself out of the back gate & not come back till he thought the coast was clear. Brijen would have sung an extra song for me and brought the creamiest kulfi from the street, tasting of salt and sugar and saffron. When I was a child, nobody did anything for my birthday, it was not important. You were the first to make it so. Every year without you, I've tried to imagine you here, have done something festive even if alone.

Well, this time I was not alone on my birthday. I had a visitor. It was very unexpected — it was a Mr. Kimura from Den Pasar, which is the next town. I had never met him, but I had heard the name — he is a Japanese diplomat or official of some sort. Anyway, I was working on WS's verandah at that time — I've taken to doing that because it overlooks the stone pond & it has a cool red cement floor on which I stand barefoot while I paint. I was actually sitting on the floor cross-legged at that time & painting designs onto a few pots, all wrapped up in my work, so I jumped in alarm when he appeared. I tried to smooth my hair

— it was such a mess & it became worse because I managed to smear it with my clayey paint.

Mr. Kimura was impeccable in a black suit, white shirt, a well-behaved & smiling Penguin with perfect English, bowing exactly as the Japanese are said to do — though I had never seen it before. He said he had heard there was a famous Indian painter here (<u>Famous?</u> I?!) in Tjampuhan & as he was passing through he wanted to see for himself. Rabindranath Tagore had once been to Japan, did I know that? He offered his deepest condolences on the Poet's recent death — oh, I had not known of his death? Then his sympathies and sadness at being the bringer of bad news. It had happened last month — perhaps the newspaper had not reached me.

After this he sat down & told me to continue, he had come all this way to see me at work, he said, I was not to stop. I sat on the floor again, as I had been sitting, but now it felt very awkward, with him watching from the broad sofa which is set against one of the walls, tapping his long fingers on the armrest. I couldn't keep my eyes on my paint nor on my pot, kept being distracted by the magenta bootlaces on his gleaming black shoes. Anyway, I tried to paint & he did not take his eyes off me & then for no reason that I could see, he went to Indah & picked her up, placed her beside him & sat again. She was restless & trying to wriggle away, but he had one hand firmly gripping her neck & one hand stroking her back.

That bony, ragged back. Lis, a shiver went down my spine, I couldn't hold my brush still. I thought he would break her neck, just squeeze so hard it would break. I told him Indah likes to be on the floor, maybe he could let her go, but he said, "She seems comfortable. Please do not worry yourself. Please continue." There was something menacing about him — I cannot pin it down to any specific thing he did — despite his polite manner. I dropped one of the raw bowls on the floor & it cracked & he said nothing. I applied myself to the remaining bowls. Tried to stick to swirls & whirls & bamboo stalks. He murmured about tenmoku & celadon glazes & straw brushes & bamboo brushes — bamboo best for painting those bamboo stalks, he kept repeating.

After this had gone on for a while, Ni

Wayan brought us some lemon barley on a tray. One of the glasses was chipped, there were no biscuits or anything to eat with it. I apologized for our slovenly service. Mr. Kimura did not seem interested in the drink anyway, but this broke the spell & to my relief, he took his hands off Indah — she slunk off <u>at once</u>. Mr K then stood up & said, "Beautiful dog, even if old. Should you be wishing to leave Bali for your country in the near future, I would be more than happy & willing to adopt her."

The way he said it, I felt a sudden chill, as though he was trying to <u>tell me something</u>. He was saying I <u>ought</u> to leave. Is that not so? Was he warning me about an imminent Japanese invasion? Everyone talks about it and nobody thinks it will happen, or if it does we think that it will not touch us here in Tjampuhan. Am I just imagining things? I wiped my hands on my cloth & got up from the floor & made some polite noises — wouldn't he please have some lemonade — lemon from our own trees etc. But he ignored all that & picked up his neatly furled umbrella from the corner & waved me away when I started to accompany him out of the verandah

& up the stairs cut into the hillside. "Please, madam. You are not fit enough to come out into the sun. You have jaundice, it is clear from your eyes," he said. If I wanted a doctor, there was one in Den Pasar he knew, not Dutch but Japanese, who knew tropical diseases well.

Ni Wayan was scornful when I told her Mr. Kimura was trying to tell us something important. What difference does it make to us if the Japanese come? We are ruled by the Dutch now. Later we'll be ruled by Japanese, she said.

No friend here. It is hard to know what to do. If only I had someone to talk to.

I've been examining my eyes & fingernails ever since he left — for yellowishness. Isn't that what jaundice is supposed to do? Make you yellow like turmeric? I feel weak sometimes, it is true, but that has been for a while, ever since the fevers started. It passes. I'm as slim & trim now as I was when I was sixteen — I can't eat too much — at last! Maybe now's the time to wear one of your dresses & feel young & pretty.

No news from WS. I miss him. I miss the sound of his piano & his mad fervor for beetles.

The Bring Home Myshkin Fund — it never took off at all. I wonder when/if I will ever see WS or Myshkin again. Is this how partings happen? No word, no preparation, it is over and you didn't even know it. Will I ever see Beryl again? She's in England now, in the middle of the war. No news from any of you either.

The newspaper comes weeks late or not at all & mostly they are in Dutch. I listen to the radio sometimes & then turn it off because the news is so grim. Better not to know. What good has it done me to know that Rabi Babu is dead? It is as if one last beautiful part of my childhood is gone. Everything feels emptier now. I would rather be the fool who lives in her imagined paradise.

I should post this letter. I started it on my birthday, but now it's more than a week later. I write it when I have energy, put it away & sleep when I'm tired. The life of a lady of leisure. Sipping lemonade spiked with the last of the gin. Once the gin goes there will be arak in plenty!

Much love to you & to my Myshkin (Will you tell him please that I am well and coming home soon?)

Gay

October 3rd 1941

Dear Lis,

I sent you a long letter only two weeks ago. This just to say — nothing to be alarmed about, but I do feel rather more unwell. Have decided to be practical & will go to Surabaya — to Lokumull's house, rest and get better — & from there back home. I am sure he will find a passage for me to Singapore, war or no war, once I am well enough to travel further. He has friends in Singapore — they will put me on a ship to Ceylon & so on & on & on until I reach you like a parcel passed from one to another.

I am taking Indah with me. I cannot bear to leave her behind, she's my only friend left here & she's old & helpless & half blind. I will eventually turn up in Madras + Kintamani dog. You will come & meet me there, won't you, so we can plot & plan my future? Bring Myshkin with you for sure, I long to see him, my eyes are starving for him.

I am running ahead of myself. I haven't even left Tjampuhan yet.

I feel all vomity. My stomach's gone — you would hate the details, I'll spare you them. I have a fever. I burn up with it, my skin goes as dry as a dead leaf & I babble nonsense when it comes. Maybe I babble in Hindi or Bengali. I do hope so — what if I'm saying scandalous things? I'm a mean old woman now, Lis, shriveled up with rage. How could it have ended this way? Just when my life was turning a curve and what lay ahead was beautiful. How could a war thousands of miles away have done this to me? I am furious about everything. If they gave me a gun, I'd kill.

They've brought me some medicine, but it smells so peculiar I don't dare. Ni Wayan has sacrificed a rooster to make me well and nailed its carcass near the entrance door by its wing. Gruesome. I tried to stop her, how could killing something make me better? She said I don't know how these things work.

I think it's typhoid, will pass. Am trying to remember what my father-in-law used to prescribe for typhoid. Can't. My head's addled. Do you remember? How will you tell me?

I am determined to be well enough to reach Madras. And I will. Once I have seen Myshkin & you again, I don't care what happens next.

Make a wish on the evening star as you

used to, Lis, that we will be together again before too long.

With much love,
Gay

26

By the time I finished reading my mother's letters, it was that hour between night and morning when the crows are about to start scraping a croak from their gray throats. My eyes were tired, my neck ached, I knew I would not be able to sleep now. I folded the letters back into their envelope and rose to make myself some tea. As always I dithered between Assam and Darjeeling, then settled on Darjeeling, the best kind, fresh and grassy, which comes from a remote estate that few people know about. The manager sends it to me now and then in gratitude for the gardens and orchards I created for him two decades ago when he bought a piece of hill near the tea estate. His ten acres included a natural spring and during the months I was there, I would sit by its side at the end of each day's work, drinking tea brewed in springwater on a wood fire that I lit on the bank. It was one of the few things that did not taste bitter at a time when my own life felt like a shirt that did not fit, it never had, it never would. But that dark interval passed as inexplicably as it had come. I returned to my work, my old town, and my outbuilding as if to an alien civilization in which I had to find my bearings again slowly, relearn the language and the rules.

My water was boiling. I took my cup from its place on the shelf. I am careful with it. It is a tall, simple cup, narrow at the base, slightly flared in the waist, and then it narrows again smoothly, like a just-opened tulip. No embellishments. Pure white porcelain, handmade, and the maker's signature is stamped on the base in Chinese characters. Ila's daughter — my niece who is a daughter to me as well — brought me this cup a few weeks ago, from one of her trips abroad. She put it down on my table along with a copy of an old book I had asked her for, saying with a gleam in her eyes, "There, Myshkin Unc, the two most exciting things a man's life could have: a cup for tea and a tatty old gardening book."

After that she had thrown her head back and laughed, running her fingers through her long hair. The stack of silver bangles on her arms rang together. "Come on, there's still time! Don't be such a fuddy-duddy! Do something new."

Like everyone else, she thinks me inconsequential. A pedant who says the names of trees in Latin. A man who chose neither pen nor sword but a trowel.

Her view of the world is not unusual. My father too was appalled by my choice of work when I first told him about it. "A horticulturist? You mean you want to be a gardener?" He had swept his newspaper off his table, his glasses along with it, he needed so badly to express his fury. "When there are a thousand things to be done? Interesting work, important work, relevant work! When you are nineteen and our country is not even a year old?" He urged me to open my eyes. Could I really not see what a gigantic project there was ahead for every young, patriotic Indian? Was I blind? Did I have no sense of the Higher Purpose? *Horticulture!* When our just-freed country had to be pulled out of poverty, hunger, violence, illiteracy — what I wanted to do was grow flowers? Perhaps the cause of his fury was a fear that I was turning out as whimsical as my misguided mother was thought to be.

If I talked about my work on visits home, he would change the subject or pointedly walk away. I told him once about my days on the outskirts of Delhi with a group of city planners, mapping out sun-hardened thorn fields that were to become resettlement areas for the millions who were homeless overnight after Partition: they could not remain in refugee shanties forever, I said, they needed places to live. Around the city was dry, rocky land that had to be swiftly transformed into dwelling areas. The houses would need to be grouped around parks and avenues, and even as the foundations were being laid we would start our work by planting several thousand trees.

My father frowned distractedly at the corner of the verandah and said, "I'm sure I left my umbrella there and now it's gone."

I soldiered on with increasing desperation, describing the scale of it — beyond imagining. The feeling of helplessness when you saw the anthills of refugee tents teeming with people who had lost their homes.

My father cut in: "Yes, there are engineers and planners. There are refugees who have lost everything. And what are *you* doing there, can you tell me? Growing dahlias?"

Through his years in jail he had acquired a new truculence and venom. Now he wanted not only to stab with his words, he also twisted the knife. On my first holiday after I started working, in a pathetic effort to impress him I had brought along the framed photograph of a letter addressed to Mr. Percy-Lancaster.

"I wish to convey my appreciation and gratitude," the letter said, "for the excellent floral arrangements and decorations that had been made at your instance at the time of Mahatma Gandhi's funeral and for the special train conveying his ashes to Allahabad. The personal interest you took in these arrangements no doubt led to their success."

The letter was dated February 1948, it was signed Jawaharlal Nehru and was addressed to Mr. Percy-Lancaster, whose chief assistant I had been for the funeral arrangements. I told my father this, hoping that a letter from the prime minister of India would make him less skeptical about the nature of my work.

In 1948, on the brink of turning twenty, I went to Delhi to start work, imagining I would discover new species, create hybrids that would be named after me. Instead, only two weeks into my new life, Mr Percy-Lancaster summoned me late one evening to give me the news: the Mahatma had been shot dead by a Hindu fanatic. What this meant for the country and for the world was for the world and the country to work out;

did I know what it meant for the office of the Superintendent of Horticulture? We had just one day to find the flowers for a funeral at least a million people would attend. An army truck was to be turned into a floral chariot to carry the Mahatma's body to the banks of the Yamuna, enough flowers were needed for air force planes to scatter petals all along the five-mile route to the river, sandalwood logs would be needed for the pyre, flowers would be needed to decorate the train that would carry the ashes to Allahabad. As I described each stage of the funeral to my father — the restless ocean of mourners, the stray dog which ambled across the road holding up the cortège, the constant fear of violence, the sickly scent of ghee and tuberoses — I saw that for all his devotion to the Mahatma, he seemed irritable.

"So the flower arrangements at my funeral will be impeccable," he said when I had finished. "How very reassuring."

Two years later, when my father died, I was in Delhi working with Mr. Percy-Lancaster to lay out the Sunder Nursery. It was to be the city's main nursery on a hundred acres of land, with a somber backdrop, the grand desolation of the Mughal emperor Humayan's tomb. After the news of my father's death came through a long-distance call on the only phone in the office, I returned the heavy black receiver to its cradle and left the room with no words of explanation even though Mr. Percy-Lancaster's eyes followed me in questioning silence. I walked for long hours among the crumbling Mughal monuments that shrouded the area. Dusk drew the trees closer. I sat against a peepal thinking that by now someone must have set a flaming torch to my father's pyre. What Hindus considered a son's sacred duty. I would not reach Muntazir in time to light the flame, I had told Ila on the phone with calm practicality. They were not to wait for me. Bodies decay swiftly in the humid heat of August.

The gardening book Ila's daughter brought for me, certainly both tatty and old, was written by the man who designed the garden for Government House in Karachi. I opened it after I sat down with my tea. A fine line of dust rested within the seams of each page, making me sneeze. Every chapter appeared to begin with a quotation from a poet called Patience Strong rhapsodizing about plants and trees. I have never been able to understand why men who wrote

books on gardens in India were so suscepti-
ble to gush. Mr. Percy-Lancaster too, despite his crusty exterior, was given to quot-
ing verses nauseating for their piety. Give
me Gopal the foulmouthed park gardener
any day.

As I turned the pages, impatiently flipping
over sections about how a part of the garden
had to be demarcated as the lady's boudoir
and another as the dining room, I came
upon a passage which made me think Mr.
Grindal had a vein of ruthlessness that
made his mush appear more sinister than
sentimental.

Where field rats are the only trouble, they
may be exterminated in a simpler way by
blowing smoke down their runs. For temporary use, all that is required is an
earthen pot and a pair of country bellows.
A hole to fit the nozzle of the bellows is
made on the side of the pot which is filled
with combustible material, green neem
leaves, and a sprinkling of sulfur powder.
The material is first ignited and, when
burning well, the pot is inverted with its
mouth over the entrance to the run. The
smoke is forced through the runs by vigor-
ous use of the bellows and either drives
out the rats in a stupefied condition, when

they are easily dealt with, or suffocates them in their burrows.

E. W. Grindal's book appeared in 1942, the year the first group of Jews were taken to a chamber in Auschwitz and sealed there for several hours until they died from fumes of poison gas that was let in through holes in the roof. In our town that year, on a spring morning, someone was smoked out as well: the toothless dentist Mr. Ishikawa was led from his rooms into the daylight. Nobody knew for sure how old he was. It was as if he had been around forever, pulling out rotting teeth, chatting with his patients in formal, halting Hindustani and English until the day he woke up with no words. After that he retreated into the shadows, emerging at dusk for essentials, then hurrying back in again.

After the bombing of Pearl Harbor a few months earlier, news came that the handful of Japanese expatriates in India, some attracted to the land of the Buddha, others running small businesses, were being rounded up, and Mr. Ishikawa shrank further into the safety of his rooms. The morning he was taken away, he appeared surprisingly straight-backed, his eyes shielded by his black-rimmed glasses, lips in a line. He wore a white bush shirt and gray trousers and had his case of dental instruments with him. There was a soldier behind him and another beside him, holding his free arm at the elbow. My grandfather came to the door of his clinic, Lisa appeared on the balcony along with Jeremy Gordon and Boy. Passersby stopped. It was still and tense, as if we were at a public execution.

For years, I, along with some other boys, would follow him chanting "Sayonara Ishikawa, Honshu, Hokkaido, Shikoku, Kyushu" in a nonsensical chorus to torment him if we ever saw him outside. But that morning, not one of us opened our mouths as the soldiers put him into a van and drove off. Later we heard he was taken to an internment camp in Bikaner, Rajasthan, where he died in the summer because he could stomach neither the food nor the heat in the canvas prison tents.

Mr. Ishikawa's internment and Mantu's death were among the few things of note that happened in our town during the war.

What was I doing during those months of the war just before the fall of Singapore to the Japanese, when my mother — unknown to me — was writing to Lisa of her extreme isolation and illness? I remember that after my father was sent to jail, I wrote to him rather than to her. Watching him being taken away by the police as his followers chanted slogans reminded me of Mukti Devi's integrity and courage and made me uncharacteristically worshipful of him for a time. Perhaps this was one of the reasons why my correspondence with my mother petered out. I cannot recall precisely how it happened but maybe I was too occupied by my present to be lost in daydreams as before. The changes around me had put a stop to my yearning to be where she was. The intensity of her absence had worn me out and then, imperceptibly, waned. There is a merciful finitude in our capacity to sustain grief. Those months when my mother felt her isolation most keenly were the very months when she slipped over the edge of my consciousness and into oblivion, soundlessly, as a pebble into the sea.

At school, every morning, assembly began with "Ourfather whoartinheaven" recited at a speed that made it all but unintelligible. This was followed by a homily from the headmaster. Usually it was about honesty, cleanliness, God, hard work, but now it ended with news of the war, every morning a different item of news — Burma's fall, then Hong Kong's, to the Japanese, read out in mellifluous, leisurely tones from the paper as a digest of the main points by our English teacher: refugees across land and across the seas were trudging into India, hundreds of thousands of them. French, Austrian, Greek. Ten thousand Poles, 450,000 from Burma. As well as from Persia, Djibouti, Aden, Somaliland.

Where was Somaliland? What, for that matter, was Djibouti? We had never heard these names before. One day, the headmaster unrolled a large world map and it was nailed onto the wall behind the podium from which he spoke at assembly. He had a box of pins with him, each pin had either a blue paper tag or a yellow one.

"Blue is for Crown victories. Yellow indicates temporary losses."

One of the boys got onto a stool and stuck pins into the places we were being told about. The English teacher announced the name of each one as the pin went in. The Andamans, he said — the only part of British India to have fallen so far. Singapore. Malaya. There were many more yellows than blues. The yellows were massed towards the east — towards us. A yellow pin pierced Burma. And then a few rapid yellows nailed an area further away, almost Australia. "Batavia, Sumatra, Bali, Borneo

— the Netherland East Indies," the English teacher said. "Dutch losses to Japan."

We were not allowed to ask questions at assembly. I could not stop the teacher. Had he just said Bali? After assembly, we were herded off to classes. Had a bomb hit my mother? Were the Japanese torturing her? The classes went on and on and it was only in the afternoon, during the lunch break, that I was able to drag the stool back from its corner to the map on the wall and examine it closer up.

A yellow flag on a tiny patch of green in the middle of a blue sea.

Bali.

The war had seemed thrilling until then, a faraway circus with interesting events bringing excitement to a town where nothing happened. The trenches being dug, the soldiers who were everywhere, a delicious sense of imminent catastrophe. One hot summer afternoon I had run to the station and seen a trainload of prisoners being transported to the Dehradun prison camp. I was jealous of Dinu, a soldier now. He had sent me a postcard from North Africa, he was in the distant worlds I could only dream about. When I saw newspaper pictures of wrecked ships and bodies floating in the ocean, it did not strike me that my mother might, at that moment, be in a ship crossing that very ocean on her way home. My mother, Mr. Spies, Beryl, Bali — they had long made the passage, in my mind, to the realm of fantasy. They had nothing to do with newspapers, weather reports, casualty lists, and timetables.

"She will not be in any danger. She is Indian, not Dutch, nor British," Dada told me when I came back from school. He tried to sound reassuring rather than worried. "The Japanese are on our side. I mean the *Indian* side."

"But isn't India a part of Britain?"

"She started out on her way home last year," said Lisa. "Was it October? Yes, just after her birthday. Can't she drop me a line?"

In her last letter, Lisa now confessed, Gayatri had said she was not well. She had not told us anything because she did not want us to worry. Since that letter, she had been waiting for news from my mother about her ship to Madras so that she could take me there to find her and bring her home. She had asked Jeremy for news now, perhaps the army would know.

But the army did not know. There was no news from my mother, not that year, nor halfway into the next.

We waited every day — for a telegram, a trunk call or letter, or for her to arrive miraculously on our doorstep. Waiting as we were at that time was like music that began softly and gathered pace until it became charged, explosive, describing an apocalypse, then died away unfinished, note by note, until you could hear not another sound.

In the middle of the next year, a telegram arrived from Dinu, who had recently been posted to Dehradun. I was fifteen, my father had been in jail more than two years, and my grandfather decided I was old enough, given the circumstances, to travel on my own. Dinu's cryptic message sounded important. "Have news. Come soon."

The evening I arrived, he took me out in his jeep and we drove uphill from the internment camp where he was posted. The air was cool, darkness would fall soon, I was out on my own for the very first time in a jeep that had no roof. I flung my head back, face to the sky. It was as if I had grown up overnight — I was free. Yesterday my grandfather had put me on the train, patting my head through the window, warning me of strangers and dangers. Today I was in an open-roofed jeep and I knew Dinu had cigarettes.

Where the road ended, we went on foot and climbed until we reached the top of a ridge. Dinu pointed downwards. "There," he said.

Far below us lay an area encircled by barbed wire and watchtowers: the internment camp. It had appeared large when I reached it, but now I could see how enormous it really was, how far its lights twinkled in the soft, new darkness. Beyond it were dense jungles that rose into the foothills of the Garhwal Himalaya, through which my great-grandfather had walked in 1857. You could see the mountains from the camp in the daytime, at night they were massed shadows.

We sat on the ridge and Dinu lit cigarettes for us both. His face had acquired angles, he was almost nineteen, he talked about North Africa, the shrapnel lodged somewhere in him. He had seen friends being blown up, limbs falling nearby, and slept with a girl in Ethiopia whose physical charms he described with careful attention to each body part. As he went over the details of his night of lust, the clock reached 10:15 and the lights in the camp went off. Searchlights came on, white, powerful beams that cut the sky in ribbons as far up as the eye could see, and we both gazed at the sky and searchlights and the dark sprawl of the camp as if we had only then realized that below us were thousands of people far away from home, no foreseeable hope of going back, soldiers, civilians, Nazis, Jews, all packed together in seven sections surrounded by double lines of barbed wire.

A few of the prisoners had spent the better part of the year collecting maps and compasses and other equipment, Dinu said. One of them, Heinrich Harrer, a famous mountaineer, had been exercising with such ferocity every day it should have warned the camp officers that he was readying himself for something, but they thought of it as masochism: he was German after all, and must relish killing whatever came to hand, even his own body. Harrer became as fit as any high-altitude mountaineer and knew every mistake he needed not to make because he had already attempted escape innumerable times. The end result was that Harrer had vanished, probably into Tibet, as had a few others. Among the prisoners who had tried running away with Harrer was a German civilian from Java, but he had fallen too ill with dysentery to carry on and had turned himself in. He was in solitary confinement at the camp.

"I searched him and his bags after he was brought back. Look." Dinu held a picture towards me and shone his torch on it. The picture was slightly creased, we had to smoothen it out. A group of people smiling at a camera. A dog being petted by a woman's hand.

My mother's hand.

My mother is not smiling, her eyes are on the dog while her chin rests on her knees, she is unfamiliar in her cropped hair. It gives her face a pointed, elfin air, as if she is a rebellious boy who has run away from school. But it is my mother, there is no doubt in my mind about that. Next to her, squinting into the sun, is Mr. Spies. All the light in the picture seems to have collected together in a funnel and poured down on the two of them. Mr. Spies's golden head is blazing and my mother's dark hair has a ring of fire around it.

The sky was vast above the mound we were sitting on, nothing but miles of black shadows around us, and there were rustling sounds in the darkness — mouse, hare, leopard — I did not care. Dinu lit a cigarette. I had forgotten I wanted another. I had not seen my mother for six years, not even in a photograph.

"It was taken four — maybe five — years ago," said Gustav, the German in solitary confinement, when Dinu took me to his cell the next day. The man seemed grubby and half-starved, he was still unwell, and twice during our conversation he had to run to the toilet. He had drunk dirty water from a stream. If not, he would have been in Tibet by now with Harrer and the rest, he grumbled.

Gustav spoke English in an accent that reminded us of Mr. Spies, and as then, we often found him hard to follow, but when Dinu and I compared notes afterwards we strung together the threads we had missed. Gustav began his story telling us he had come to India last year in December, that his ship had docked in Bombay and before he knew it, summer came, the heat was infernal, the asphalt melted, he had thought he would die. There was a storm one day and he ate a windblown mango, his first.

Dinu sensed my impatience. "Get to the point. We don't need your life history," he said.

He was an entomologist by profession, Gustav said, and his interest in insects had taken him from Java to Bali, where he met Walter Spies, who had been supplying insect specimens to scientists in Europe. He had taken the photograph with my mother and Spies on one of his visits to Bali — such memorable trips. Ah, the dances at night, the beauty of the girls, the drinks in candlelit verandahs to the sound of tinkling music! Paradise could not have been happier. Three times he went to Spies's house in Tjampuhan, and then the next time he saw Spies it was in a prison camp in Sumatra. At Sibolga, a Sumatran port. Miserable place. They tried to make the best of it, but really there was not much you could do — even Spies, who smiled through every kind of misery, was hard put to remain cheerful there. He himself was transferred from Sibolga to India in December — put on a ship and sent off to Bombay along with several hundred others. He had thought he would find Spies again, here in Dehradun, but had heard from other German prisoners that of the three prisoner ships headed for India, only two had arrived. Rumor was that the third had been bombed. Nobody was clear what had happened to the people on board the bombed ship, or who was on it.

Which ship was Mr. Spies on? He did not know. Impossible to say if he was alive or dead.

"What about my mother? What happened to her? Was she on your ship?"

"There were only men on ours. I do not know about your mother. Perhaps she is still in Bali, I would not know."

"What does he know? Nothing," I said in Hindi to Dinu. "Why did you call me all this way? For this?"

I walked out of the cell and lit a cigarette, staring at the dusty courtyard and a dismal line of gray-and-brown men shuffling from somewhere to somewhere a few yards away. I did not know what I had expected after seeing that photograph but the disappointment was acute enough for the line of men to turn into a blur.

"It's a start, Myshkin. We'll find out the rest. News will come. This is how it comes. Bit by bit. I'll keep trying."

Dinu had followed me out and put a hand on my shoulder before he went back into the cell, quickly, as if a thought had struck him. He wrote my address as well as his own in Gustav's notebook, and told him to send us news if ever he had any. The day would come when he would be out of the cell and home, who knew when, but one day, Dinu shrugged as he wrote the addresses. It was a fanciful thing to do, he knew. The war was nowhere close to ending, we did not plan anything anymore, we had forgotten about futures, we lived in the present and we hoped the present would last. He knew he was clutching at straws and said it was something to have a straw to clutch at.

"You can keep the photograph," Gustav said, turning to me. "It has your mother in it, no? You look like her. I met her a few times only, I know she was an artist. I saw one of her pictures in the museum. She was selling her pictures, she was making a name. The Indian Painter, people called her. When I saw her she had paint and mud on her face but she did not know it. She didn't care for mirrors. She was like a fire, glowing. And her voice! She could be on radio with that voice. She used to sing and mimic people. Everyone would beg her, now sing a song, now do a cockerel, now do Walter. A friend of mine bought a picture by her. Very intriguing one — unreal — how do you say it? I caught my breath seeing that picture."

Gustav got up from where he was sitting and put a thin, dirty hand out and held mine in it. "You have her eyes," he said. "You have the same way of being. Maybe you too don't like mirrors."

To think that my mother's paintings were once in a museum and I have never seen any of her real work, only the small pictures she enclosed in her long-ago letters to me.

Many times I have considered going to Bali, to find the world she inhabited, the part of it she created for herself, to see what a sea mango was, and all the other trees and animals and rivers she sent me in her letters. I have never wanted to go the simple way, like a tourist. I dream instead of making the same journey as hers, by train, ship, steamer, boat, across the Indian Ocean, passing a thousand islands, stopping every few days, pausing until I want to go on again. She had found a way to do it, she had stood on the rim of a volcano, seen the fires below, and taken the plunge. Why didn't I?

The addresses Dinu gave Gustav were to prove fortuitous. After the war ended and he returned to entomology in Germany, he found Father Unger, a man he had known a little at the internment camp. Gustav sent me a note describing what he had found out.

Father Unger was a missionary who had been put into an internment camp in Java, then transferred to the Sibolga camp in Sumatra. At that camp, he made friends with Walter Spies, struck by the way he stood out among the other prisoners. Tall. Red shirt. Lean face made leaner by the hardships of prison, and impervious to the foul conditions in the camp, immersed in painting on scraps of paper and canvas. He told Father Unger that once the war was over he would paint dragonflies and wasps, insects were his latest obsession. The translucence of dragonfly wings. Their fragility.

Father Unger remembered watching Spies walk onto the ship, the *Van Imhoff,* in which they were to come to India, with a roll of his canvases under his arm and a cigarette in his mouth, only to have them taken away from him as he started up the gangplank. Even so, Spies thought it a special piece of luck to be on that ship, he told the priest, since he would be going back to a country where he had been happy, where he had friends from before the war.

They walked up the gangplank and were packed into barbed-wire cages on the deck. Thirty men to each cage about 150 centimeters high. Spies was not far from him, but inside the cages they were no longer able to talk or even move. The ship set sail. Nobody had enough water, the sweat, heat, and stench were unbearable. There was hardly any food. Two days like this rocking in the ocean, and then at about noon on the third day a Japanese bomb fell close to the ship. It was 19th January 1942.

After some time another explosion, then a third when the ship reared up and fell back. And then silence. The hissing sound of steam. Cries of wild panic from the prisoners as the Dutch guards began abandoning ship. They took the lifeboats and were gone. They left wirecutters for the prisoners, but that was all, and in the frenzy that followed, some of the prisoners jumped off the ship and drowned while others broke into the stores and drank themselves blind.

When he was pushing his way through the prisoners to try and reach the rafts and boats left on the ship, Father Unger spotted Walter Spies. He was still sitting in a cage on the deck. The doors had been cut open and it was empty but for him and a man lying in one corner of it, ill or dead. Father Unger shouted his name but did not wait to see if Spies would come. He got into a boat. They had only a few oars; for the rest they rowed with their hands. Over the next six days, out in the ocean half-mad with thirst, some were eaten by sharks while others died of the heat. Among the few who found their way to a shore was Father Unger.

Walter Spies? He went down with the *Van Imhoff,* Gustav wrote. "I am sorry to tell you this. Also, I am afraid I still have no news of your mother, the Indian artist, but I will keep making efforts to find out."

A year after the war had ended, when my father was out of jail and Lipi had inched back to normal life and Lisa had shut her guesthouse and gone off to Canada with her husband, a letter arrived from Beryl de Zoete. It was addressed to Gayatri Rozario. Nevertheless, we opened it.

My Sunbird, I picture you radiant and beautiful, reunited with your son. I am certain in my heart that is how it is.

I have disastrous news. Walter is dead. He was in a ship full of prisoners bound for India and it sank off Sumatra. Such irony, dear Gay. To think he might have reached Dehradun — and you, and so many things he held dear — had the ship reached its destination. My only consolation is the news I have had from a friend in Siam, who met someone who knew a man who saw Walter die. He sat very peacefully and smoked his pipe as the ship went down, they said. I have no way of knowing if this is true, but it is how I would like to remember beloved Walter.

I still hope to come back to India to finish my book on dance, to watch more of Kanta Devi's splendid Bharatnatyam, to see you and talk of old times. I remember so well our journey to Bali, days of hope, fear, joy, adventure — and you in a storm of homesick tears every minute. Who knew then what deeper grief was waiting, beyond our imagining? The world threw us apart. We are no more than leaves in a storm.

Please write to me. I will wait for news from you.

With much love, Beryl

The sunbirds that so fascinated Beryl when she came here hover around the garden still, in search of nectar. I saw a pair of them one morning after rereading her letter. They went from one flower to the next: iridescent blue concentrations of whirring energy. They were so light that the hibiscus hardly swayed with their weight when they landed on the petals and dipped their long beaks into the flower's cup. I could see why Beryl had named my mother after them.

Around me were trees that had been there for more than a hundred years, born long before either me or my mother. She had a way of talking to them, complimenting them for new leaves and flowers, stroking them in passing as if they were pets. Twice I saw her standing on the roof of our house at night, eyes closed, face raised to the moon, lips moving as she murmured something inaudible. Her hair floated down her back in a black wave. At such times my mother was an amphibious creature — of earth as well as air, yet not wholly of any one element. She might have taken flight and become a night bird, or her limbs might have turned into roots and branches, her torso the trunk of a tree. Anything appeared possible.

I confess I too talk to trees I have planted, and when I walk by a river listening to the quiet sound of waterbirds and the distant thump of a washerman battering a riverside rock with clothes, it is that vision of my mother and her moon-silvered face that comes back to me. Trees, grasses, the sun, the sky, the moon, these were closer to her than humans, they were her religion — as they have become mine. My father went through his entire life oblivious of the natural world. What foolishness, what blindness, my mother must have told him. Like the man who never opened his window and lived his whole life by lamplight when the moon was outside, shining.

"I blew out the lamp," wrote Rabindranath Tagore, "with the idea of turning in to bed. No sooner had I done so, through the open windows, the moonlight burst in to the room, with a shock of surprise . . . [I]f I had gone off to bed leaving the shutters closed, and thus missed this vision, it would have stayed there all the same without any protest against the mocking lamp inside. Even if I had remained blind to it all my life — letting the lamp triumph to the end . . . even then the moon would have still been there, sweetly smiling unperturbed and unobtrusive, waiting for me as she has throughout the ages."

People think you have to travel — to the mountains, to the sea — to find what they call "natural beauty." These days, when the sky is glowing with the thousand neon lights of Muntazir's new markets and streets, the moon struggles and the stars are switched off. I can hardly see them any longer. Are they really waiting for me somewhere else? If I were a magician and the sky were the roof of my tent, I would turn off all the lights of the city to see the stars leading their own remote lives, a million years away from our blighted world.

The awareness Rabindranath Tagore had of a wider, deeper, more meaningful world that exists independent of human ephemera — I have been alive to it as my mother was, but I wonder if it is possible for those who have known nothing but crowded cities to possess this seventh sense. As a child, I would place my back against one of our trees and feel its reassuring solidity, its immobility. It was not going to move, it would never go anywhere, it was rooted to its spot. For as long as they are alive, trees remain where they are. This is one of life's few certainties. The roots of trees go deep and take many directions, we cannot foresee their subterranean spread any more than we can predict how a child will grow. Beneath the earth, trees live their secret lives, at times going deeper into the ground than up into the sky, entwined below with other trees which appear in no way connected above the ground. Had we been trees — my father, my mother, Brijen, Lisa, Dinu, my grandfather, and I — which direction, I wonder in idle moments, would our roots have taken below the earth?

I have been setting off on long, restless walks, unable to sit still after reading my mother's letters. A thousand questions crawl within my brain, as persistent and maddening as head lice, and I struggle to comprehend what actually happened in the ten years that my mother was married to a man she never loved and lived next door to the man she was in love with. Betrayal, duplicity, infidelity: these were not words I would ever associate with her, not even now, yet it is also clear that for all my life I have known only a partial version of her.

Understanding nothing of the complicated reasons for her flight, I had sometimes hated her enough as a boy to want to blind her picture with my cigarettes. I wondered if my father or grandfather had known about her hidden life but had sheltered me from the knowledge out of love — or out of shame.

If the truth had been revealed then, would I have waited quite as anxiously for news of her for years on end?

Gardeners are good at the business of waiting, they are in tune with the rhythms of the earth, which are slow. There is no anxiety in this kind of waiting, only anticipation. But to wait as we did for news of my mother, that was like blood being drained from our bodies until one day there was no more left.

Yesterday, I stopped my writing and went into the back garden. The area below the tamarind tree had overnight turned into a fresh yellow and white — tiny zephyranthus lilies stretched into the far corners. I stood there transfixed for a while and then, as if in a dream, brought paper and pen and sat down on the grass in the early morning heat of June, drawing studies of the zephyranthus one after another until the noontime sun was directly above me, burning the hair off my head.

This was the very spot, I was sure of it, where my mother had flung her box of imported paints and I had crawled into the bushes searching out each one. I could not recall if the zephyranthus was there then. It is a tiny crocus-like lily that asks for nothing, no manure, no care, it goes underground when not in bloom and emerges this way each year: overnight, hundreds of them, signaling the imminence of the monsoon.

The day after I drew the zephyranthus, I woke moments before sunrise and the first thing I did, without consciously deciding to, was that I went to the front of the house where I stood in the purple half-light, resting my back against the tree below which I used to ring my bicycle bell to wake my mother.

The impatient, shrill tones of that long-lost bell rang in my ears as I raised my face to the sky cut up by a forest of fleshy leaves. It is a *Magnolia grandiflora* more than sixty feet tall, with densely knit branches and a long, thick, smooth trunk. I got a ladder and propped it against the tree even as Ila grumbled about my sanity and held the ladder steady. I climbed high enough to reach a branch laden with ivory-colored flowers, each one as big as a bowl and scented with a fragrance that immediately brought back that last morning when the tree had showered my mother with raindrops and she made me promise to come back in time from school so that we could go on our trip together.

I placed the cut stems in a vase near the painting of my mother that had come in the envelope. I drew detailed studies of the magnolia's leaves, buds, and flowers. I painted a few of them.

Over the next weeks, my long-unused sketchbooks filled with studies of the trees and plants in the garden that I associated with my mother: the pearly carpet of parijat flowers, *Nyctanthes arbortristis,* that she loved walking on barefoot; the neem near the bench where she had sat with Beryl listening to the story of Aisha. I barely slept, I forgot meals, I drew and painted her garden as if possessed. I drew the crepe myrtle and Queen of the Night, the common oleander and hibiscus; the young mangoes on the tree in June, as raw as they had been when Beryl de Zoete and Walter Spies first came to our house.

It took me five days to finish my studies of Queen of the Night and then I turned to the garnet blossoms of the *Plumeria rubra,* the champa. I painted the long, elliptic leaves, the swollen stem tips, the fleshy branches that go from gray to green and ooze milk if bruised or cut. I blended in the ocher at the edges of the petals with the deepening incandescence of the red in the depths of the flower.

As I painted I could see a man's hand reach out and place in my mother's palm the flowers that had fallen from her hair, then close her fingers over the petals.

I went through stacks of paper and many tubes of paint, ink, and charcoal before I stopped painting as suddenly as I had begun, drained, spent, emptied of thought.

Even though it was morning and I had drunk a cup of tea, I dropped off again in my chair. My sleep was sudden and deep.

I dreamed of Indah, the dog my mother had carried with her to Surabaya. She was thin and old and she was running from one street to another, nose to the ground, searching with her blind eyes for anyone she knew. I wanted to reach her but I could not. I tried to find the house where my mother lay ill, the roads turned into oceans and I could not keep afloat, I was breathless and desperate, I was trying to swim, I was holding a watermelon, Tobu was nearby, but I kept swallowing water and he would not help. Body parts floated near me, torsos, a head, the jellified hand from the jar in my grandfather's clinic. Nearby a ship listed and fell on its side with an enormous crash.

I opened my eyes and a burst of heat and light exploded onto my face. I was glad to wake up from the dream. It has been coming to me from time to time ever since I read my mother's letters and I am always glad to wake up.

I put on my glasses, drew my sheet of paper closer, and applied myself again to my long-postponed task.

"I, Myshkin Chand Rozario, being of sound mind and body, do hereby . . ."

I put down my pen and turned away from my paper to the bustle around me of loaders, cooks, officers, engineers, mechanics, going about their business, paying me no attention. I am as good as cargo to them, the only man on board not at work. The railings of the deck were a few yards away from me: a real deck, not one I had dreamed up from pictures and letters. And this was a real ship, a cargo vessel headed for Singapore in which I had one of two cabins earmarked for passengers.

I am making the same journey as my mother, by train, ship, steamer, boat, across the Indian Ocean, past a thousand islands, stopping every few days, pausing until I want to go on. I will scour the archipelago for traces of her. Perhaps there are still some people alive who knew her and who know what became of her. I will stop at Surabaya and find Lokumull's shop, I will search for the descendants of Queen Fatima, I will go to the museums in Java and Bali and find her paintings, I will find the houses she inhabited, the rooms she worked in, the village potter who became her teacher.

I left my chair. The slate-gray iron of the deck was hot enough to scorch the soles of my shoes as I walked to the railings. Waves splashed the discolored sides of the ship, white froth churned in its wake. Had she noticed that the ship, when it cut a path through the foam and waves, sighed constantly, the great poet had asked my mother on her first journey to Bali; did that never-ending sigh not sound as though the waters of the ocean were washing the earth with tears of grief?

I could hear my mother's incredulous, impolite, teenage laugh in my ears. Grief was the last thing on the mind of a girl exulting in a new world, painting every part of it. I wanted to believe that for my mother the ocean's sigh had not changed its meaning through all her crossings.

I leaned over the railing, as far as I could. I heard a shout from somewhere on the deck: "What the hell's that old man doing?"

I crumpled my interrupted Last Will and Testament into a tight ball and tossed it high in the air, out into the sea.

ACKNOWLEDGMENTS

The point at which I knew this book was going to be written came one afternoon on a street in Ubud, Bali, when Rukun Advani and I were drooping in the heat, on the brink of giving up the search for Walter Spies's second home. And then Nyoman Gelebug drew up and opened the doors of his car.

Until then, nobody had appeared to know how to get there, and every taxi driver had refused us. As if by magic, Nyoman turned out to be a native of Sidemen, East Bali; he knew exactly how to reach the house in the remote village of Iseh, near Mount Agung. Standing in fields full of ripe red chilies in front of the house, with the calm blue volcano on the horizon, it immediately felt as if the book-in-progress had the blessings of Walter Spies.

Born German in 1895, Spies spent most of his life in Bali, where he met both Rabindranath Tagore and the renowned dancer Uday Shankar. He wanted to learn Sanskrit and come to India to research Indian dance forms, but he was drowned at forty-seven when the ship on which he was a prisoner of war was bombed and destroyed. In part, this book imagines what might have been had he made the journey to India.

Since this is a novel in which fiction and history overlap, I have relied greatly on the help of other people as well as books.

In Bali, Janet de Neefe provided many pointers, including to the splendid Agung Rai Museum to look at the paintings of Spies and his contemporaries; she also directed me to his estate in Tjampuhan, now the Tjampuhan Hotel, where his simple thatched cottage is perfectly preserved. In Djakarta, the writer Dwi Ratih Ramadhany gave me crucial help with Balinese names and Lans Brahmantyo of Afterhours Books gave me permission to reproduce material from John Stowell's magnificent biography, *Walter Spies, A Life in Art* (Jakarta: Afterhours Books, 2011). This rich, beautiful book is filled with illustrations and translations from the letters of Spies, from which are drawn many of the words he says in this novel. Rahul Sen made sure the book reached me, passed hand to hand all the way from Djakarta, via Singapore and Jaipur.

Only in one of his letters does Spies speak of Rabindranath Tagore's visit to Bali, and it is not reproduced in Stowell's book. That letter (Letter 56, dated 21 September 1927, in Hans Rhodius: *Schönheit und Reichtum des Lebens Walter Spies — Maler und Musiker auf Bali 1895–1942,* Den Haag, 1964) was obtained for me from the British Library by Professor Francesca Orsini. However, it was in German. Katharina Bielenberg translated it into English and lines from her translation now constitute one of the epigraphs. I have lost count of Katharina's many kindnesses, this is only the most recent.

I first came across Walter Spies in Cristina Jordis's dazzling travelogue, *Bali, Java in My Dreams* (translated from the French by George Bland, London: Harvill, 2002). It made me want to know more, and I turned to Colin McPhee's *A House in Bali* (London: Victor Gollancz, 1947), a poetic memoir of his life in Bali, especially its music. For a sense of Bali in the late 1920s from the Indian point of view, I have relied on two astute, learned, observant books in Bengali: Rabindranath Tagore's *"Javajatri'r Patra"* ("Letters from a Traveler to Java") in *Rabin-*

dra *Rachnabali,* vol. 19 (Calcutta: Visvabharati, 1968), and Suniti Kumar Chattopadhayay's *Rabindra-Sangame Dipamay Bharat O Shyamdesh (The Islands of the Indian Ocean and Siam with Rabindranath)* (Calcutta: Prakash Bhavan, 1940). Manishita Dass, ever-resourceful book sleuth, not only got hold of both the books for me, she then read my first draft and checked my translations.

As always, Myriam Bellehigue did a detailed reading of the first draft, and gave me a clearheaded sense of its problems.

One of the fortuitous happenings during the writing of this book was that I picked up, purely by chance, a novel by the eminent Bengali writer Maitreyi Devi. She was a relative of mine, a paternal uncle's wife; her book had always been in our house, but I had never read it. When I did, I was deeply moved, as well as struck by parallels between the protagonist of her autobiographical novel and the protagonist of my book. I began translating it, and eventually a few passages became a part of my novel. For permission to reproduce these passages from Maitreyi Devi's *Na Hanyate (It Does Not Die)*, I am indebted to Rupa Sen and Priyadarshi Sen. The translations into English are mine.

The two extracts from Tagore's writings included here were originally published in "Thoughts from Rabindranath Tagore," *English Writings,* vol. III, p. 58, edited by Sisir Kumar Das (Delhi: 1996); and "Mone Pora," from *Poems* (1922; reprint, Calcutta: Visvabharati, 2002).

The particulars of Beryl de Zoete's life would have been lost to all but scholars if not for the work of Marian Ury, whose premature death put an end to the biography she was writing. Her lively, sympathetic essay, "Some Notes Towards a Life of Beryl de Zoete" (*Journal of the Rutgers University Libraries,* vol. 48, no. 1, June 1986) provides a great deal of information. The extract about Aisha is taken from "Siwa," a lecture Beryl de Zoete gave at Dartington in March 1941. It was published in *The Thunder and the Freshness, the Collected Essays of Beryl de Zoete,* edited by Arthur Waley (London: Neville Spearman Ltd, 1963).

For events relating to the Second World War in India, I learned a great deal from the outstanding scholarship of the historians Indivar Kamtekar and Yasmin Khan. Various online archives, including those of the British Library, provided invaluable information on the war in the East Indies and India. Radhika Singha supplemented her essay "A 'Proper Passport' for the Colony: Border Crossing in British India, 1882–1920" with patient answers to my questions about colonial-era travel. For the specifics of passenger berths on merchant ships, I am grateful to Captain Soumitra Mazumdar.

Memoirs by Alan Moorehead, Rajeshwar Dayal, Santha Rama Rau, Madhur Jaffrey, and Nirad C. Chaudhuri allowed me to inhabit the 1920s, '30s, and '40s. Raghu Karnad's *Farthest Field* provided an intimate study of an Indian family caught in the war. My father-in-law, the late Ram Advani, who was born in 1920, was always available for the odd, specific questions that only someone who had actually lived through those times could answer.

Thanks also to Arundhati Gupta, Partho Datta, and Teteii for letting me pick their brains about the experiences of their families. To Elahe Hiptoola for a helping hand with Urdu. And to Piku, Soda, and Barauni Jungshun for letting me in on the daily, loopy joy of their world.

I am deeply grateful to everyone at MacLehose Press, Hachette India, and Atria Books who make publishing such a happy experience: especially Poulomi Chatterji, Paul Engles, Avanija Sundaramurthy, and

Priya Singh. To Rakesh Satyal for making the American edition possible and for seeing it through with such care, and Thomas Abraham for his affectionate, laconic calm through turbulent decades of friendship and work.

Several editorial sessions over the years took place on the most beautiful and hospitable terrace in all of France, at the home of Miska, Koukla, and my publisher and editor Christopher MacLehose. Despite ten years of working with Christopher, his ability to transform manuscripts with exasperating, anarchic brilliance is still astonishing to me — as astonishing as the fact that I have survived four books and lived to tell the tale.

My mother's descriptions of life in a many-branched joint family in Jaipur and her recollections of the 1940s have helped me construct this novel's world. Also woven into the fabric of this book — and my life — are glorious musical afternoons with the late singer and writer Sheila Dhar; I have drawn on her stories about Begum Akhtar, some of which feature in her *Raga'n' Josh* (Delhi: Permanent Black, 2005). She once informed my mother with characteristic drama that she, "the other Sheila," was my "foster mother." My mother took this gracefully in her stride, as she has done much else. This book is dedicated to both Sheelas. Finally, as at the start, Rukun.

ABOUT THE AUTHOR

Anuradha Roy is the author of *An Atlas of Impossible Longing* and *The Folded Earth,* as well as *Sleeping on Jupiter,* which won the DSC Prize for Fiction 2016 and was long-listed for the Man Booker Prize 2015. She lives in Ranikhet, India.

The employees of Thorndike Press hope you have enjoyed this Large Print book. All our Thorndike, Wheeler, and Kennebec Large Print titles are designed for easy reading, and all our books are made to last. Other Thorndike Press Large Print books are available at your library, through selected bookstores, or directly from us.

For information about titles, please call:
    (800) 223-1244

or visit our website at:
    gale.com/thorndike

To share your comments, please write:
    Publisher
    Thorndike Press
    10 Water St., Suite 310
    Waterville, ME 04901